THE IRON BIRD

THE IRON BIRD

ROBERT WOODSHAW

Unbound Digital

This edition first published in 2019

Unbound

6th Floor Mutual House, 70 Conduit Street, London W1S 2GF

www.unbound.com

ISBN (eBook): 978-1-91261-831-6
ISBN (Paperback): 978-1-91261-830-9

Image of Margaret Thatcher (adapted) courtesy of Chris Collins of the Margaret Thatcher Foundation – CC BY-SA 3.0

Somerville College coat of arms courtesy of ChevronTango – CC BY-SA 3.0

Extract from Margaret Thatcher, *The Path to Power* reprinted by permission of HarperCollins Publishers Ltd © 1995 Margaret Thatcher

Cover design by Mecob

Printed and bound in Great Britain by Clays Ltd, Elcograf S.p.A.

Super Patrons

Aldo Arditi
Gabriele Arditi
Maria Grazia Arditi
Maria Martina Arditi
Kulsum Bouzerda
David Brewerton
Melanie Cantor
Lindsay Clarke
Martha Clifford
Dawn Clode
Mike Cooper
Thomas Cumella
Cristian Gelfi
Daniele Gelfi
Sue Goss
Artis Henderson
Michelle Hoggett
Lindsay Hollinger
Jamel Labruna
Jess Labruna
Juliette Lock
John Lomax
Anna Luz
Jane Meenehan
Denise Newman
Stefano Paoli
Andrew Paskell
Caroline Pearce
Karen Raney
Emma Roberts
Sarah Shippobotham
Jenny Smith

I was asked to open a Conservative fête in Orpington and was reluctantly persuaded to have my fortune told while I was there. Some fortune-tellers have a preference for crystal balls. This one apparently preferred jewellery. I was told to take off my string of pearls so that they could be felt and rubbed as a source of supernatural inspiration. The message received was certainly optimistic: 'You will be great – great as Churchill.'

The Path To Power, Margaret Thatcher

Our revenge will be the laughter of our children.

Bobby Sands

[I]

The Undertaker's Daughter

1

Let me make one thing clear at the outset: I am a lappet-faced vulture, dear.

Of course, the species has more than one name. Indeed, I remember there used to be a specimen in another institution that insisted on being introduced as a Nubian vulture. But I'm afraid one is reluctant to regard oneself as Nubian. Goodness me, no.

Besides, there's nothing wrong with the adjective 'lappet-faced'. There is not.

Oh, I suppose the term might not conjure up quite the most attractive image, but be under no illusions: it's a compliment compared to some of the other names I've been called over the years. Dear me, some creatures can be so cruel.

You see, I have a title: I am the Rt Hon Bel-imperia Pinch. And so I should therefore be addressed as 'Mistress Pinch', or 'ma'am', but I regret to say... I regret to say that I am sometimes called the most terrible things. Forgive me if I repeat some of the more offensive examples: a cold-blooded carnivore that dines on the dead, a gimlet-eyed harpy, That Bloody Bird, a wicked witch, a milk-snatcher...

Oh, and Attila the Hen. Let's not forget that one!

Naturally, one tries to push such spiteful comments out of one's mind. One carries on. One has to; after all, there are more important things in life than being liked. Yet even so, it still hurts to be dismissed as a contemptible creature – of course it does; it hurts just the same. In fact, if I might share a little secret, sometimes it reduces me to tears.

Does that come as a surprise? The confession that I sometimes weep? Yes, I can see that it does. What was that? What was that? One is a little hard of hearing. Do speak up.

You'd been expecting a more resilient specimen? You'd assumed that I was a tough old bird?

I see. Well, I shall take that as a compliment, dear. I used to be tough. Goodness me, I used to be as tough as... Not old boots. One hesitates to compare oneself to an old pair of gardening boots. Let me choose another noun: I used to be as tough as iron. But I must admit the truth of the matter is that the onslaught of old age has rendered me rather frail.

What was that? I didn't catch the question. Don't sit there stuttering. Come on, dear, this institution belongs to the brave not the chicken-hearted. Spit it out.

How old am I?

I see it is no longer considered impolite to ask a bird her age. Next question, please. No, not you – you've had your turn. The creature sitting on that bench over there. The one scratching its flea-bitten coat. That's right. You.

What's the average lifespan of the lappet-faced vulture?

Why, what an erudite question! We seem to have a would-be ornithologist in the audience tonight. Albeit one with fleas.

The average lifespan of a lappet-faced vulture? Oh, at least 80 or 90 I should imagine. No one can be sure. But I am afraid there's no escaping the fact that this old carpetbag of feathers and bones is falling apart at the seams. Sometimes I am too tired to unfurl these tattered wings. Sometimes I forget... I forget things, dear.

No doubt I should get out more often. Indeed, I suspect I might spend too much time cooped up in this expensive cage. Not that one regrets the investment, of course. Far from it. Let me make it quite clear: one is delighted to exhibit oneself in such an elegant circle of cast-iron bars. Never mind the speckles of rust. Never mind the crumbling stucco. I remember when I was a fledgling the one thing I always wanted was a well-appointed cage. Oh, I must admit I never imagined I'd be able to afford one in such a prestigious location. Me? Take up residence in the cul-de-sac of cages behind the Small Mammal House? Goodness me, no. Neither did I imagine that an enclosure containing a crooked tree might come on the market, but it did. Why would I want to go out? I'm thrilled to roost in these desirable branches, thrilled.

Of course, it's a shame the exposed roots of this acacia have cleaved the cage floor into such brutal slabs of concrete. But at least one's droppings provide a decorative touch. Indeed, I am told the effect is reminiscent of the efforts of a certain Jackson Pollock. Whoever he might be.

I don't suppose Mr Pollock used to leave the half-eaten carcass of a rabbit on the floor of his lodgings, though, do you? I shall have to swoop out of this nest and finish that off...

What was that, dear?

This nest? Oh, I made it out of dismembered silver birch and bits and pieces of broken furniture: a leg from some old sideboard – and what's this? Why, the arm of a gilded chair... I acquired the materials and bound them together with bulrushes and mud, and then as soon as the mud had dried, I lined it with laddered stockings and other old rags. I must confess I made it as comfortable as I could so that I'd be able to sleep at night. But sleep eludes me, dear. In fact, I'm afraid most nights I just sit here and stare out at the zoological gardens. Sometimes I sit and stare until all the gas lamps strung up above the cages have guttered out. I let nothing distract me. Nothing. If a sudden squall rushes in through the bars, I hold my head perfectly still as my nest lurches up and down, so that I can continue to stare out. I stare at the rain splashing on the slats of that iron bench over there; I stare at the reflections in the puddles, alert to the slightest movement at the entrance to this cul-de-sac of cages and enclosures. But no one comes.

I am alone.

Times change, of course. It is 2010. I am told the animals have put the past behind them; I am told the zoological gardens has moved on. But it seems that even the Order of Carnivores has forgotten – or at least found it convenient to forget – that their old Commander-in-Chief is still here, propped up under these overarching bars. Still here. Not dead. Remember me?

I should like to be remembered. I should like to receive the occasional dinner guest – not a member of the Order of Herbivores, of course. I should like to receive a meat-eater. Someone to share a decomposing carcass and reminisce about old times.

What was that? What was that? The specimen sitting near the geraniums. The pangolin. If you've got something to say, then say it, dear.

You cannot imagine me entertaining a dinner guest? Vultures are supposed to be – what? Vultures are supposed to be unsociable birds.

Unsociable? Nothing could be further from the truth. Indeed, I must admit it can be most distressing, being alone. Thank goodness one still has the occasional speaking engagement on one's schedule. One appreciates the affection of an audience such as this. You see, more often than not I'm afraid one has nothing apart from one's cherished possessions for companionship. Oh, but there are some priceless treasures concealed in the branches of this nest. Let me see, what have I got here?

Oh, yes, I've got some tins of first-class protein: salmon, ham, ox tongue – that sort of thing; I've got some scraps of black-edged mourning paper; I've got a second-hand transistor radio and a bottle of sour milk. I've got some dog-eared library books: the collected poems of someone-or-other – and what's this? *On the Origin of Species by Means of Natural Selection (Complete and Unabridged)*. But that is not all. I've got a plumed helmet; I've got a bloodstained rodent fur; I've got a modest collection of earth-pig bones. Oh, and hidden in a hole sealed up with mud and a mulch-like paste made out of regurgitated rabbit fur and spittle, I've got something rather special: a string of pearls.

That's right, dear, pearls.

Of course, one seldom puts them on – not during opening hours at least. I understand the general public don't come to Old Hesper House and Zoological Gardens to see creatures draped in diamonds and pearls; I'm told it might expose me to comment. But even so, I should hate to be separated from them. Let's hope I don't have to return them to their custodian at all. I'd much rather keep them and give back – what on earth is this?

Why, it looks like a page torn out of...

Goodness me, *The Collected Pleas of Saint Francis* – I'd forgotten about that. Now, how did it begin? Don't tell me. Let me see if I can remember the first line:

Where there is sustenance... No, that's not right.

Where there is swill may we bring sustenance,
Where there is ruminant may we bring hay,
Where there is scavenger may we bring carrion,
Where there is predator may we bring prey.

How could I forget those words? Oh, this is so infuriating. I'd hoped these mementos might help me remember the past. I'm sure there must be something I can recollect...

Of course, I remember those that trespassed against me, make no mistake. Oh, didn't I mention that I've been trespassed against? Didn't I mention that I've been bitten? No, not bitten – mauled. It's hard to believe such a thing could happen, isn't it? But it did. Those ungrateful beasts I'd raised turned against me and stabbed me in the back with their sharp incisors, as if I were... Oh, what was his name, that Roman emperor? Julius something.

I shall never forgive and I shall never forget.

But I have said too much. Perhaps I should start at the beginning, dear.

I remember I said the same thing to the middle-aged man that came to see me earlier this evening. 'Let's start at the beginning,' I said. Indeed, I seem to recall I invited him to ask me a question about the morning I stood on the steps of the Dower House and summoned up the spirit of Saint Francis. The morning I became Prize Exhibit.

But he just pulled a spiral-bound notebook out of his bag and said, 'I'll come to that later, all right?'

I subjected him to a hard stare. Not the most agreeable specimen I am afraid: such an unpleasant scar across his face, such a tangled mane of hair.

'Well, where do you suggest we start, then?' I said. 'The battle to reclaim Rabbit Island? The campaign against the black-capped marmots?'

'No, I'm not interested in rabbits or marmots,' he replied. 'Other biographers have been there. I'm interested in the real beginning. Your beginning. You.'

I gazed at the nicotine stains on his fingers as he sharpened his pencil. He mentioned something about 1940.

'1940?' I said. 'Oh, but I would have been just a fledgling, dear. I doubt I'll be able to recall—'

'The Old Boathouse?'

Of course, I understood at once that he must have been alluding to the building I'd been brought up in. 'Goodness me,' I said, 'is that still standing? I thought the boathouse had been pulled down.'

'No, it's still standing. But it's just a burnt-out shell, so it is. Clumps of stinging nettles and brambles.' He put his pencil sharpener back into his bag, muttered something about not being able to picture Father's business premises. 'Impossible to imagine it before… '

'The fire.'

He told me he'd been through the zoological archives. 'Fine toothcomb,' he said. 'There are no blueprints of the building, though. No decent pictures. Just that old sepia-tinted thing in the *Official Guide*.'

'I don't remember seeing that,' I said.

He explained that the photograph is in some out-of-date edition – an illustrated article about the historic outbuildings on the estate or something. 'But the boathouse is just a smudge in the distance.'

'What a shame!'

'Thing is,' he said, turning the page of his spiral-bound notebook, 'If I'm going to conjure it up in the reader's imagination, I'll need a description. Come on, please, help me out.'

'It used to smell of SO_2,' I informed him. 'I remember that.'

'SO_2?'

'Sulphur dioxide,' I explained. 'Oh, and I remember the damp too. Goodness me, I shall never forget the moisture in that old boathouse – and of course, in damp conditions, SO_2 reacts to form H_2SO_4.'

'Spare me the scientific jargon,' he said, glancing up from his notebook.

I reminded him that some birds in these gardens have studied the sciences. But he looked incredulous, dumbfounded. Not the brightest member of the general public I'm afraid. Indeed, I must admit the thought occurred to me that perhaps I should lunge out through the bars of this cage and give him a sharp peck.

'Shall I appoint another biographer?' I said. 'Someone more suited to the position?'

'Oh, I'm sure I can rise to the challenge,' he replied. 'In damp conditions?'

I decided to give him the benefit of the doubt. 'In damp conditions sulphur dioxide reacts to form sulphuric acid, dear.'

2

OLD HESPER HOUSE AND ZOOLOGICAL GARDENS

OPEN

Monday - Saturday, 10a.m. - 4p.m.
Closed Sundays

GENERAL ADMISSION

(Prices correct at 1st September 1940)

ADULTS 2/6
CHILDREN 1/6

Visitors are advised that, DUE TO UNFORESEEN CIRCUMSTANCES, the Reptile House is closed to the general public, and several cages in the Caer Lud area of the estate have been reduced to rubble. In the Middle Gardens, both the Nocturnal House and the Majestic Flamingo Palace have also sustained significant damage. Nevertheless, these are expected to re-open in the spring. In the meantime, despite this assault on their freedom, the animals at Old Hesper House and Zoological Gardens are determined to ensure that their great institution remains

OPEN FOR BUSINESS AS USUAL

Open for business, then. But even so, it is late in the afternoon and the general public have long since retraced their steps to the gatehouse and started up their motorcars and clambered into their omnibuses and trams. True, in the great conurbation of cages surrounding Old Hesper House, a small number of stragglers still linger: an old-age pensioner is loitering near the bear pits, a short-trousered child is sprinting through an abandoned parade of bomb-damaged enclosures, his gas mask slung around his neck, his lace-up shoes undone.

Further to the north, in the suburban terraces of the Middle Gardens, a courting couple – reluctant, perhaps, to return to their disapproving parents – are still sitting in the Refreshment Rooms, staring out at the ruins of the Nocturnal House and sipping at cold cups of tea, but the remote north-eastern reaches of the estate are deserted. Indeed, there is no one loitering in the parade of sandbagged enclosures behind the Marsupial House. And so there is no one to notice the little lappet-faced thing that has just slipped out through the bars of its cage and is scuttering down the cobbled path that leads to the lake-shore.

OLD HESPER HOUSE AND ZOOLOGICAL GARDENS

The Bog-land Enclosures

THE OLD BOATHOUSE

Grade II Listed Cage, Enclosure or Other Estate Building.
Preservation order pending.

KEEP OUT

Here she is, then, just a fledgling, just a bundle of flight feathers and stubborn clumps of down – a scrap of a thing, nothing more. But despite her diminutive stature, little Bel-imperia Pinch remains steadfast and determined. She doesn't flinch from the stench of sulphur dioxide as she hops up onto the boat slip and scrabbles to gain a talonhold on its slatted boards. Neither does she stop to glance down at the thin threads of mist that are curling around her stout, chicken-like thighs.

She snatches a breath. Is that a hint of cumin she can detect beneath the smell of the geothermal gases that are spilling onto the boat slip? She shouldn't be surprised. Over the centuries, the timbers of the boathouse might have been steeped in the sulphurous mist that rises from the lake, but ever since her father took over the lease, the edifice has also smelt of exotic spices. Just like some provincial grocer's shop.

She pauses to appraise the clapboard building: the double doors hanging from their rusty hinges, the discoloured stains of an old coat of creosote – not the most impressive advertisement for her father's business, perhaps. Bel-imperia sighs. She is no stranger to the boathouse, no stranger to the lake-shore. Is she conscious that the sulphurous gas is starting to condense into droplets that cling to her undercarriage? Perhaps. But she is too accustomed to the scent of SO_2 to give them a second thought. Besides, this afternoon she has something much more important on her mind.

Of course, she is an intelligent bird – there can be no doubt about that. But even so, she sometimes finds it difficult to distract herself from a pressing concern, such as her failure to earn a scholarship to the Cloisters. Things nag at her mind. This morning, though, as she had been sitting in her cage staring out at the Marsupial House, a common rat had attempted to engage her in conversation, and one of its more sensational stories distracted her from the Cloisters problem. It still troubles her. For she is sure she can remember hearing the drone of an engine during the night – not to mention the sound of a distant explosion. Perhaps there might be some truth in the rumour that has been going around the zoological gardens, then. Perhaps some poor creature might have died.

She shakes the sulphur dioxide out of her flight feathers. She rouses. Is the prospect of a decomposing carcass upsetting? Or is that a slight spring in her step as she scuttles up the boat slip and disappears through the gap between the double doors?

Inside the building, a collection of cast-iron buckets and battered pots and pans has been set out to catch the rain that sometimes drips through the holes in the perished lead-sheet roofing, but the constant precipitation of sulphuric acid cannot be caught in a bucket. Neither can it be ignored. Sometimes a drop of H_2SO_4 lands on the second-hand cupboards and cabinets that are pressed up against the building's creosoted boards, and sizzles, as it burns through the decades of dust and the furniture polish. Sometimes it seeps into the spice drawers and ruins a consignment of cumin. Sometimes it dribbles down the wireless set. But more often than not it just gathers in puddles on the great marble-topped contraption that stands at the centre of the building, commanding pride of place.

There are no boats in the boathouse, then. Yet even so, perhaps because its slab of marble has been mounted on the undercarriage of an old slate wagon, the contraption is not dissimilar to a flat-topped barge, or the rusting hull of a ghost ship. Indeed, as little Bel-imperia Pinch peers at its couplings and chains, she cannot quite dismiss the thought that the building might be haunted, because all she can make out are subtle gradients of gloom: shifting, ghost-like shapes that seem reluctant to congregate into solid objects as her eyes adjust to the dim light.

She summons up her courage. She reminds herself that the dead might pass through the boathouse, but as long as the appropriate procedures are performed, as long as their mortal remains are bathed and anointed, their tormented souls cannot come back to haunt it. Besides, a ghost is an insubstantial thing – a disembodied spirit, nothing more. Something solid is required to produce the aroma she can detect drifting down from the marble – something that has a certain amount of muscle and mass, something that has organs that can decompose: a heart and lungs, a pancreas, a spleen…

Dare she hopscotch over the puddles of sulphuric acid and haul herself up into the air? She might be under strict instructions not to attempt her maiden flight until she has completed her first post-juvenile moult, but she is quite confident that she can make it up onto the marble. Clattering across the boathouse like a startled chicken, she attempts to alight on the—

Oh, dear. Not the most graceful touchdown. No doubt she should have lowered her landing gear a little earlier. In all fairness, though, perhaps she can be forgiven for a slight lapse of concentration; after all, she has never seen such a strange-looking animal. Dead or alive.

Strange? It's a struggle to make head or tail of the specimen. Then again, its limbs are still entangled in the ropes that are required to hoist the remains of large, cumbersome creatures up onto the marble, and it has come to rest in an unnatural position, its bulging muscles too taut, too contorted, to suggest that it had experienced a peaceful death. The strangest thing of all, though, is that the beast's hide has been burnt to such an extent that it is almost transparent, like an illustration drawn up to map the mechanics of muscle and tendon. The cause of death is clear, then. Fire. But who is the victim?

She adopts a methodical approach to the problem, makes a mental list of the anatomical features she can recognise.

Item: one pair of strapping shoulders.

Item: one barrelled chest.

Item: a clump of coarse fur – the charred remains of a short-haired coat?

But she has seen so little of the zoological gardens and the creatures it contains that she cannot name the species spread out before her.

Determined not to be defeated, she scuttles up to its head and stares into its glassy eyes. She wonders where it used to sleep at night. Did it recline on a bed of soft rush in an enclosure in Caer Lud, or curl up on the concrete floor of some provincial cage in the Middle Gardens? Did it dine on ptarmigan and grouse, or did it just subsist on grass like the great herds of gnu and plains zebra that roam the Northern Pastures? Is it Carnivore or Herbivore? One of us or one of them?

The thought of a brace of ptarmigan stirs the digestive juices in her gizzard, spurring her into action. She struts up and down alongside the creature, flapping and squawking. She stakes her claim to its carcass lest there should be some opportunistic scavenger in the area intent on robbing her of her prize. Here she is, then, caught up in the excitement of the moment. Here she is, shrieking and screaming at the black-backed jackals in her head. But just as she is about to scrabble up onto the dead thing's stomach and mount a spirited defence against a make-believe pride of lions, something gives her

pause. Is that a gout of blood glistening on its abdomen? Is that a
laceration?

Poor little Bel-imperia Pinch. The urge to plunge her head into the
gash and rip out a morsel of meat is strong. Disconcerted, she takes a
deep breath and considers her predicament. Is she subject to the same
primitive instincts that afflict her cousins in the Serengeti, or is she a
sophisticated specimen? For a moment, she isn't sure.

She rephrases the question. Did she come to the boathouse to eat
this creature or to help prepare it for cremation?

She crushes the inappropriate instinct and reminds herself of her
responsibilities. But even so. The more she stares at the laceration,
the more she is conscious of an unpleasant feeling in the pit of her
stomach. Indeed, it's impossible to ignore the sensation that she isn't
alone. Is some predator skulking in the shadows? Is some godlike
creature looking down on her trespasses from above? She might
be reluctant to entertain the thought, but as she glances over her
scapulars and peers into the dark recesses of the boathouse, she is sure
she can make out the shape of a gaunt-looking scavenger perched on
top of the spice drawers.

'Father?'

He must have been here all along, the pious vulture, contemplating
the firm principles that set him apart from lesser forms of life.

'Do you intend to dine on the deceased, Bel-imperia?'

'No, of course not.'

'Then perhaps you'd care to explain the meaning of your
disgraceful behaviour: strutting up and down and shrieking like a
banshee – what was that about?'

'Nothing.'

'Nothing?' He plunges his head into his quill coverts and plucks out
a parasite. 'I suggest you recite the First Commandment, chick.'

'But Father—'

'The Commandment, Bel-imperia.'

She intones the Commandment in a solemn contralto: '*Thou shalt
not eat of any other exhibit. Neither shalt thou eat of the herbaceous borders.*
But I wasn't going to eat it. I was examining it, that's all.'

'Examining it?' He opens his wings with a whoosh and leaps into the air. Is he going to give her a clip across the lappets? She crouches on the marble – brace, brace – but he just glides over her head and settles on the dead thing's shoulders. 'Then in that case,' he says as he folds up his wings, 'I should imagine you'll have no difficulty classifying the specimen. The correct scientific nomenclature, please. Kingdom, phylum, class, et cetera.'

'But Father... ' She has no desire to be tested and found wanting.

'Daunted by a spot of classification practice?'

'No, not daunted. I'm just—'

'I suppose a little cautious trepidation is understandable.' Something in his tone has changed. 'Indeed, I must admit I would have struggled to classify a creature such as this when I was your age. But then, I didn't have the benefit of your education, did I, chick?'

'No, Father.'

He reminds her that he had to teach himself to read from an old spelling book that he found on a rubbish heap. 'Nevertheless, as soon as I'd mastered the alphabet, I consulted the bestiaries and gave myself a decent schooling. I assume you're acquainted with the medieval manuscripts that I'm referring to?'

Bel-imperia sighs. She is in no mood to be cross-examined on the contents of some dusty old bestiaries. Then again, compared to an afternoon of classification practice, the bestiaries are a doddle. 'I read that one you recommended, yes.'

'*The Book of the Nature of Beasts* – an excellent choice. And what did you learn?'

'Oh, I learned that the lion is the mightiest of beasts; I learned that elephants live for three hundred years; I learned that vultures don't indulge in the "c" word... '

Perhaps she shouldn't have alluded to the mating habits of their species. She can see that his lappets have turned bright red.

'I beg your pardon?'

'Copulation, Father.' She takes a deep breath. 'The subject might be distasteful, but I'm afraid it's central to the book's argument. You see, the author maintains that she-vultures conceive without losing their maidenhead; an improbable supposition, but—'

'Improbable?' Bel-imperia can tell that the adjective has ruffled

her father's feathers. 'Good gracious me, the natural world is full
of improbabilities, chick. Perhaps it might seem improbable to the
general public that the animals in these gardens manage their own
affairs. Or that we have done so since the Uprising.'

No one can remember the Uprising – least of all little Bel-imperia
Pinch – but she has studied the subject. And so she understands that he
is referring to the day the animals celebrate every year, the day their
ancestors rose up against mankind and laid down their lives for their
freedom.

'Yes, Father.'

'Perhaps it might seem improbable that some of us have taught
ourselves to read and write. But these things are true. Now, tell me,
have you read any other works of natural history?'

'No, but there's one book I'm most anxious to read. In fact, I
understand that some wise owls consider it a seminal text.'

'And what's that? *The Natural Histories* of Pliny the Elder? *The
Etymologies* of Saint Isidore?'

'*On the Origin of Species by Means of Natural Selection.*'

He seems displeased. Nothing is said, but she can sense his
displeasure all the same. It fills the silence that has settled on the
boathouse and makes her feel inadequate. Is he attempting to impress
on her that she has fallen short of the high standards he requires? Is
that the meaning of his distant stare?

She scutters a little closer to him, tries to get his attention. 'Of
course, I don't suppose there's a copy in the Bog-land Enclosures, but
I'm sure I'll be able to find one at the Cloist… '

'Yes?'

She should never have spoken. She should never have reminded
him that she has let him down. 'I'd been hoping to find the book at
the Cloisters if… '

He is glaring at her.

'If I'd been fortunate enough to get a scholarship.'

'I see.'

The Cloisters: the most prestigious quadrangle of cages in the
zoological gardens. She tries to picture its bell tower and black-capped
owls, its secluded colonnades and its babbling fountains, but she

cannot bring her imagination to bear on them, she cannot summon them up. She's sure she'd been able to picture them a couple of months ago when she was swotting up for her entrance paper. Then again, she remembers she'd also been able to imagine a carrier pigeon – not one of the second-class specimens that her father uses to deliver his business correspondence, but a first-class Columbine clutching an envelope embossed in gold: an offer of a scholarship.

Bel-imperia sighs.

She has been attempting to cling onto an image of the Cloisters all summer, attempting to picture its owls and its bookshelves, its manuscripts and its scribes, but as the pigeonless months dragged on, the image receded into the distance, reducing itself to a smudge, like the sepia-tinted photograph of the boathouse in the current edition of the *Official Guide*. Something on the opposite shore. Something impossible to see.

She glances over her scapulars at the old duchess dressing table. Is that the *Official Guide* she can see propped up against a can of motor oil? She isn't sure. She turns her attention to the wireless set standing on the cabinet where all the unopened bars of Pears' soap are stored. She'd love to give its big black button a good peck and make its needle move across the names of all the strange cities etched on the glass. Perhaps she might even be able to find a station broadcasting some big-band music. No, Father doesn't approve of the Glenn Miller Orchestra. She'd have to tune in to something educational: a discussion programme or a debate – anything to break the silence between them.

She glances up at him. His hunched-shouldered silhouette, his dreadful stillness. Silas Pinch: a respectable member of the Elders. She must be such a disappointment to him – there can be no doubt about that – but she has no inclination to concede defeat. She'll just have to make a more concerted effort to live up to his expectations, that's all. Perhaps if she tries hard enough she might be able to earn his respect and admiration, his love.

She has learned her lesson: she'll be careful not to mention the Cloisters again – not just the Cloisters; he didn't seem too pleased about *On the Origin of Species* either. Is the book salacious? Does it contain illustrations of chimpanzees and bonobos indulging in indecent behaviour? She cannot be sure…

On the Origin of Species by Means of Natural Selection. Interesting title. But she doubts that even the closest reading of its pages could shed much light on the origin of the specimen spread out on the marble. Neither does she suppose it could account for the flames that consumed the creature's coat. She steals a glance at the strange beast: its charred hide, its lacerated abdomen. What on earth could have reduced it to such a shocking state? Never mind some stupid old bestiaries, that's something she'd be interested to learn. But she has no desire to raise the matter, no desire to remind him that he has threatened to use the deceased as an excuse for a spot of classification practice, and so she just hangs her head in silence and listens to the lake sloshing against the boat slip. In the distance, she can hear the wind whistling through the trees on the escarpment. It sounds like it is gathering strength. Perhaps it might bring on a storm.

3

Of course, one is accustomed to attracting a large audience, but even so… Well, what a good turnout this evening! Why, I dare say there must be at least a dozen different species gathered around one's cage. Oh, and such magnificent specimens too. Is that a spotted pard I can see reclining on the slats of that bench? Is that a leopard seal slumped beside that urn of geraniums? I am sure it must be. One is delighted to learn that one still appeals to the masses, delighted.

Nevertheless.

I am afraid one can sense a certain disquiet in the audience all the same. Just like one's distant cousins on the plains of the Serengeti can sense approaching danger. One can feel it in one's bones. What was that? What was that? I didn't catch the question, dear.

Something about classification practice.

Then perhaps I should explain…

Father noticed that I was an inquisitive bird and directed that instinct. He encouraged me to examine the specimens that passed through the boathouse and come to a decision about them. Oh, I must admit he could be a strict taskmaster at times, but goodness me, it stood me in good stead.

I still find it fascinating, the classification of species. You see, it introduces a little order into the chaos of creation – a place for everything and everything in its place. Amphibians, reptiles, mammals… All in their proper place. Of course, a certain competence in Latin is required, but I used to receive private instruction in the language from a long-eared owl and so…

Yes?

The specimen squatting beside the Pallas cat. Over there in the rhododendrons. The toad.

You think that sounds expensive? Private tuition in Latin. You didn't realise that I had access to the same privileges as Bengal tigers and other endangered Carnivores?

I see.

Then let me make it quite clear: I had no privileges at all. Goodness me, no. Father was a creature of limited means. Oh, he had his small business, of course. 'Silas Pinch: Embalming, Obsequies and other Rites of Passage.' I suppose that must have turned a modest profit. But even so, I'm afraid he was obliged to scrimp and save to ensure that his daughter received a decent education. There's nothing wrong with that. There is not. One has a responsibility to provide for one's offspring. One cannot expect the zoological gardens to pick up the bill. Besides, long-eared owls aren't all that expensive. Indeed, I am told one can still get an hour's tuition in exchange for a decapitated mouse.

But of course, it can be such a demanding discipline. The classification of species. One had to examine the evidence and make up one's mind. One had to prove oneself again and again and again…

OLD HESPER HOUSE ᴀɴᴅ ZOOLOGICAL GARDENS

The Bog-land Enclosures

THE OLD BOATHOUSE

Grade II Listed Cage, Enclosure or Other Estate Building.
Preservation order pending.

KEEP OUT

So. The scent of SO_2 might not displease the little lappet-faced thing standing on the marble, but the foul odour escaping from the spice drawers is a different kettle of fish. Such an astringent confusion of cinnamon, cardamom – and what's that? Cumin? She steals a glance at the raptor perched on the dead thing's shoulders. Can he smell it too? But her sainted father has settled into such a sullen, brooding silence that she's reluctant to disturb him. Besides, she cannot afford to let her thoughts dwell on the stench a moment longer. Far better to concentrate on something else. She turns her attention to the mortal remains of the creature spread out beside her: its lacerated abdomen, its limp little tail. But as she struggles to calm the acid churning in her stomach, something sharp and acrid snags on the delicate mucus membrane that lines her gullet, making her retch.

'I beg your pardon?'

'I'm sorry, Father. It must have been the spices.'

'You must learn to suppress your instincts, chick. Instinct is the sign of an uncivilised animal. Good gracious me, it even compels our cousins in the Serengeti to defecate on their own legs. But no one comes to the zoological gardens to see something soiled in its own excrement, so we don't defecate on ourselves here. Neither do we retch.'

She hangs her head in shame.

'Besides, I don't have time to waste with weak stomachs. There's work to be done. The deceased must be scrubbed and disinfected. The embalming solution must be prepared... '

'Perhaps I can help,' she says, eager to please. 'Shall I open a new bar of soap?'

'I fear that would be a sinful extravagance.'

She glances around the boathouse: the cast-iron buckets set out to catch the rain, the clutter of cupboards and cabinets. There must be something she can do to earn his respect and admiration. 'I'll prepare the embalming solution, then.'

'You will do no such thing. Did I not make it clear that your first priority is to classify this specimen?'

'But Father... '

There is no time to appeal to his better judgement: he has leapt into the air and soared across the boathouse to his perch on the spice drawers. 'Let's get on with it, then, shall we? Kingdom?'

'Oh, but I'm not sure I... ' She is struggling to suppress her sense of apprehension.

'Come on, Bel-imperia. The deceased is clearly a motile, multicellular organism.'

'The specimen belongs to the kingdom of *Animalia*, Father.'

The classification has begun.

'Phylum?'

'Goodness me.' She darts a quick glance at the creature's dome-shaped head. 'Well, it's got a mouth, so I assume... ' She has no intention of lifting up its tail to check that it's also got an anus. '*Chordata*.'

'Subphylum?'

'*Vertebrata*.'

'Class?'

The classification continues apace. Before long little Bel-imperia Pinch has concluded that the specimen is a mammal and deduced from its useless nipples that it must be the male of the species.

'What species, though? That is the question.'

She hazards a guess: 'Is it an atlas bear?'

'No, of course not; atlas bears are extinct.'

She should like to point out that there are said to be dinosaurs in the Hall of Relics. And so it's not inconceivable that there might be an atlas bear too. But she cannot be confident about such things; after all, the Hall of Relics is on the other side of the zoological gardens, in a great conurbation of cages called Caer Lud. She's never seen the extinct specimens that it's rumoured to contain. Neither has she ever seen the Hall of Exhibits. Of course, she remembers reading that the Rt Hon Exhibits sit in the same building – just along the corridor from the Relics in the upper chamber – but she's never had the privilege of meeting one. Bel-imperia sighs. She should love to go to Caer Lud and admire the monumental buildings set out around Old Hesper House; she should love to see a Nile crocodile and a Bengal tiger. But she has never been outside the Bog-lands and their provincial parades of terraced cages.

'Don't be defeated, chick. Examine the evidence. Hop up onto the specimen's head.'

She does as she is told, but the deceased's charred coat is so coarse it feels as if she is standing on the bristles of a scrubbing brush.

'Now, take a closer look and tell me which order of placental mammals the creature belongs to.'

'Can I inspect its teeth?'

'No, let's leave its mouth closed, shall we? We don't want the thing gaping at us when we flush it out with embalming solution. Why don't you inspect its anterior limbs instead?'

It doesn't take her long to spot the peculiar organs. 'Goodness me, it's got hands! Look, Father, it's got fingers and fingernails too.'

'Order?'

'I suppose it must be a primate.'

'Suborder?'

It had not occurred to her that primates had been divided into suborders.

'Come on, chick. Does it look like a lemur?'

'I don't know what a lemur looks like, Father.'

She can see that he is shocked at this admission. 'Do you mean to tell me you haven't been schooled in prosimians? Good gracious me, I'm not surprised you failed to win a scholarship to the Cloisters.'

Ouch.

'There are lessons in Prosimian Studies at Hedge School, Bel-imperia. Would you like to go to Hedge School with numbats and sloths?'

She clambers down onto the marble in disgrace.

From across the lake-shore, the sound of an opossum or something screaming. Is that the rumble of distant thunder?

Caught in a sudden gust, the double doors creak open on their hinges. Bel-imperia gazes out across the lake, listens to the boathouse moan and groan. She remembers spotting a can of motor oil on the old duchess dressing table. Should she offer to pour a drop on the doors? She glances up at her beloved father. Still perched on the spice drawers, then. He calls them the spice drawers because he keeps cumin and other commodities from the East Indies in them – spices and oils to perfume the dead – but his daughter is sure she can remember him mentioning that the great chest of glass-fronted drawers once belonged to a haberdasher or something. Their height makes him seem even more remote than usual. He hasn't settled into another one of his unsociable silences, has he?

'Father?'

He subjects her to a disdainful stare. Bel-imperia meets his gaze, searches for some sign of affection. Nothing. Just disappointment and contempt. She had so hoped to please him. She had so hoped…

Is that a tear she can sense brimming up? Is that something damp spilling onto her lore? She hardens her heart, suppresses her gentle tears, but she cannot suppress the thought that it had been cruel of him to remind her of her failure to get into the Cloisters. She glances at the books piled up beside the old lacquered tea chest: *The Road to Serfdom*, *The Coming Struggle for Power*, something about chemistry. She might not have been schooled in prosimians, but it cannot have escaped his attention that she has a good grasp on a range of subjects. Or that she had done her best to prepare for the entrance examination. Besides, it's not as if the paper had been about lemurs; it had been about the Uprising. Not just the Uprising; there had been a question about the origins of the zoological gardens too – she is sure about that, because she can remember organising her answer into three elegant paragraphs: medieval hunting reserve, landed estate, private menagerie…

Did she spend too much time on the question? Is that the reason she didn't get a scholarship? Perhaps she should have just said that Lord Hesper started his private collection of exotic beasts after the Maharaja of Jaipur had sent him a Bengal tiger and left it at that. But she remembers she'd gone on to point out that His Lordship kept the cat in his mother's suite of apartments in Old Hesper House. At least her response to the second question had been more succinct. Indeed, she just needed a sentence to explain that Lord Hesper had constructed a dower house in the grounds because his widowed mother was reluctant to share her bedchamber with a tiger. No doubt she could have gone into more detail there.

The next question had been about the rapid expansion of His Lordship's private collection and the appalling conditions in his menagerie, but she cannot remember the answer she gave. Something about malnutrition? Something about an Indian elephant that contracted septicaemia due to the chafing of its chains?

There had been just one question on the Uprising itself. 'Name three specimens that laid down their lives in order to disarm Lord Hesper's gamekeeper.' She had named six. In Latin, of course. Perhaps that had been a mistake. Perhaps she should have paid more attention to the wording of the paper.

The last question had been about Lord Hesper's trial and execution, but she had spent so long on her previous answers that she only had time to dash off a short sentence about His Lordship getting his head bitten off before a spectacled owl swooped down from a bookcase and snatched her paper. She might at least have given the date; she might at least have scribbled 'on 30 January 1649'.

Could she have done better? Of course she could, otherwise she'd be preparing to take up her scholarship. The admissions office at the Cloisters doesn't send out pigeons at the last minute. There is no hope at all.

She glances around the cheerless boathouse. The jars of cedar-scented embalming oil and the unopened bars of soap. The mortal remains of some primate spread out on the marble. Is this her future, then? Embalming, Obsequies and other Rites of Passage? The disposal of the dead?

From the direction of the llama house, a terrible clap of thunder. Something inside little Bel-imperia Pinch snaps. She has had enough of standing on marble staring at the corpse spread out before her. She is getting impatient.

She shakes the sulphur dioxide out of her flight feathers, turns to her father. 'So the deceased isn't a lemur, then?'

'No.'

He proceeds to lecture her on the differences between prosimians and other primates, but just as he is dismissing ring-tailed lemurs and their cousins as primitive creatures, the heavens open.

'Family?'

'I beg your pardon, Father?'

He has to shout to make himself heard over the sound of the downpour. 'I shall be most displeased if you cannot tell me which family of simians the specimen belongs to. Do I make myself clear?'

It is an exacting question – there can be no doubt about that. True, she once spent an evening swotting up simians, but all she can remember from her studies is that some come from the Old World and others from the New. Just like vultures. But of course, vultures don't come in such a bewildering range. It isn't just a matter of choosing between a baboon and a mandrill, or a capuchin and a guenon. There are countless shades of red colobus to consider too – not to mention all the leaf-eating langurs. There are chestnut-bellied titis and black-bearded sakis. There are red-handed howlers and crab-eating macaques. She does her best to focus on the problem – of course she does – but it's impossible to concentrate in the confusion of the storm. She darts an impatient glance at the cast-iron buckets that have been set out around the boathouse. The sound of the rain dripping into them is intolerable.

'Come on, chick. I haven't got all afternoon.'

She has a hunch – more than a hunch: she has a strong impulse, an instinct. Indeed, it is so strong that notwithstanding the clamour of the rain she can almost hear it whispering – what? She can almost hear it whispering: 'It isn't a monkey, dear, it's an ape.'

But even so.

Instinct is the sign of an uncivilised creature. Vultures that defecate on their own legs. Besides, the specimen has got a tail, and apes don't have tails, do they? What is it, then? Not a pug-nosed macaque – she's sure about that because she can see that its nostrils are flared. Then again, appearances can be deceptive; after all, it isn't just spider monkeys who are masters of disguise. There are all the second-rate shape-shifters to consider too. The lion-tailed this, the pig-tailed that – poor imitations the lot of them.

'Your answer, Bel-imperia.'

'I'm so sorry, Father.' She glances up at him. There it is again: the disappointment and the contempt, the disdainful stare. She takes a deep breath, tries to articulate her emotions. 'I wanted to prove that I could do it; I wanted to… ' But it is a battle to suppress her tears.

She concedes defeat; she lets them tumble down her lores.

'Family?'

'I thought it might be an ape,' she sobs, 'but it's got a tail, and apes don't have—'

He spreads his wings, raising the dust that has settled on the spice drawers into a great cloud.

'Father?'

He leaps into the air.

For a moment, the thought crosses her mind that he might be about to comfort her. She imagines a gentle nudge on the lappets, the reassuring brush of a bristle feather. But he is careful to maintain his distance as he alights on the marble.

'For goodness' sake, stop sobbing, chick. Remember, our emotions exist to be controlled.'

'I can't help it,' she blubs. 'There are too many monkeys to choose from.'

'Never mind that. Forget about the classification. There's something I need to explain, something I can no longer postpone.'

She can tell from his trembling lappets that he's getting himself into a state. No doubt the subject he is attempting to broach must be important.

'Now, how can I put this?' He searches for an appropriate turn of phrase. 'In a month or so, I should imagine you'll experience some changes.'

'Changes? What changes, Father?'

'I am alluding to the physical transformation that takes place in a female prior to her first post-juvenile moult.'

'I see.'

'And when you go through this unpleasant metamorphosis...'

'Yes?'

'Well, it can be a confusing time for a bird. You might be troubled by certain urges. You might receive undesired attention from other... From members of the superior sex. Before this torment comes to pass, there's a delicate matter I am obliged to discuss. I must admit it's not the most agreeable topic of conversation, but I'm afraid there are certain basic facts that a female of the species needs to...'

'Yes?'

'And as your father, it's my duty to...'

She wonders what on earth she is about to learn.

'Let's not mince words. The time has come for me to tell you a thing or two about monkeys.'

'Monkeys?'

'That's right. Now, I don't suppose it'll come as a surprise to you to learn that monkeys are different from us – so much is obvious. But it's not just their grasping hands and their prehensile tails that set them apart from birds. There is something else. And it's much more unpleasant. In order to maintain a modicum of decorum, I shall refer to the organ in question as an appendage. Nevertheless, I am required to mention that it is located in a simian's nether regions. In between the hind legs. Of course, it's much more pronounced in the male of the species, but according to some authorities, the female possesses something similar too.'

She is glad to hear it. She has already made up her mind that she wants one.

5

Oh, dear. I'm afraid I am getting a little uncomfortable in this nest. Excuse me a moment. Let me remove this broken branch and make more room for this plumed helmet. Shall I discard these earth-pig bones? No, I'll just stuff them in here.

There. That's better. Now, where were we? Let me see if I can recollect...

No, it escapes me. Perhaps someone in the audience can remember? The bird perched on the arm of that iron bench. The buzzard.

What was that, dear? Did I ever give up on a session of classification practice?

Goodness me, no, Father used to expect me to get it right. Not just genus, but species and subspecies too. I must admit one sometimes felt so small. I remember a primate turned up in the boathouse once. Oh, and the classification of simians can be so problematic. But of course, I rose to the challenge: I inspected the specimen and used a little good old-fashioned common sense. Whatever happened to that, I wonder? It's such a shame. Who would have thought that common sense would end up on the scrap heap? Who would have thought that the classification of species...

Perhaps I should explain.

Consider the lappet-faced vulture. Consider me. When I was a fledgling it would have been taken for granted that I should be classified as a bird. But sadly, this is no longer the case. In fact, I understand that since birds are descended from dinosaurs I have been reclassified as a reptile.

That's right, dear, a reptile.

I have never heard such nonsense. I'm not obliged to slither around these gardens like a serpent. Neither am I cold-blooded. Goodness me, no. I don't have to lounge under an infrared lamp in the Reptile House in order to get going in the morning. I regulate my own body temperature; I get up and get things done.

Cold-blooded? Me? There isn't a shred of truth in the allegation. There is not.

29

Besides, I might be descended from some dinosaur that had the guile to snatch a lumbering iguanodon from the killing fields of the late Jurassic, but that doesn't mean I'm not compassionate, dear. Of course, sometimes one has to be cruel...

No, not cruel. Let me rephrase that: sometimes one has to be dispassionate to be kind. Yet even so—

I see some members of the audience are impatient to contribute to the discussion. The spectacled lizard in the geraniums. Your question?

No, no. Let me make it quite clear: I didn't accept this speaking engagement in order to discuss the dinosaurs in the Hall of Relics. Next question, please.

The bird perched on the roan antelope. The starling.

Something about compassionate Carnivorism.

Oh, I am afraid the Order of Carnivores seems to have repositioned itself for the scent-marking contest. But make no mistake: its members still believe that an animal must learn to stand on its own four feet.

What was that? What was that?

No, one doesn't lack compassion, dear. One attends the occasional funeral. One offers one's condolences to grieving relatives. I just don't drool and drivel about how much I care, that's all.

But even so.

I am afraid some specimens in these gardens – ruminants, rodents, that sort of thing – refuse to accept that I can be compassionate. Indeed, I seem to recall some old goat in the Order of Herbivores once stood up in the Hall of Exhibits and tabled a motion that I should be sent to a taxidermist. That's right, dear, a taxidermist. He argued that since I dined on carrion I represented a threat to his deceased relatives. I'm sure you can imagine how terrible that spiteful comment made me feel. Goodness me, it's astonishing, isn't it? That a natural inclination to consume a small portion of meat at mealtimes should inspire so much hatred? Oh, I can appreciate that Decomposing Carcass of Domestic Cat on a Bed of Maggots might be an acquired taste – of course I can – but I'm afraid an obligate Carnivore cannot be expected to subsist on a diet of dandelion leaves, dear.

Besides, it's not just Carnivores that require the occasional nutritious meal. I've never had much time for the Order of Omnivores – an Omnivore is neither one thing nor another; it's just indecision – but I am told that even an orange-bellied ground squirrel likes a little first-class protein on its plate from time to time.

Excuse me one moment. The creature sitting on the paving stones. The stoat. You're looking rather pale. Is there a problem, dear?

What was that? You cannot stomach the thought of dining on Decomposing Carcass of Domestic Cat? You're feeling...

Oh, dear.

I do hope you're going to lap that up when you're finished...

I must admit I had no inkling a short-tailed stoat could be so squeamish. Then again, I suppose it stands to reason that some of you might feel a little uncertain – a little ill at ease, perhaps – in the presence of a raptor that plunges her head into a carcass to rip out a lump of meat. I can understand this sense of apprehension – of course I can – but let me tell you how I see it, dear: I believe the most important thing about a creature is not its diet, not its species, not its class. What matters is what an animal believes in, what it has done with its life. Whether it has contributed to the zoological gardens or not. That's what I believe. And so, you see, there's nothing to be apprehensive about. Nothing at all.

Next question, please. The moustached guenon loitering in the magnolia tree.

You're apprehensive about – what? You're apprehensive about listening to the ramblings of a female of the species.

For goodness' sake, dear, it's 2010, not 1910. What's that phrase our pups and cubs like to use? Get over it.

Next.

Who do I think will win what? Who do I think will win the scent-marking contest going on at the moment?

Well, I must admit one is a little concerned that the Order of Carnivores might not be returned to its natural position at the apex of the food chain. True, the Order of Herbivores is exhausted. True, Ebenezer Bull and his administration are on their last legs. But even so, I'm afraid it hasn't escaped one's attention that some lily-livered specimens still have reservations about another Carnivorous era. And so it's essential that our Commander-in-Chief fights a good campaign. Essential. Never mind these newfangled debates. He needs to get out and do some good old-fashioned cage-to-cage campaigning. If not, I fear the result might turn out to be indecisive. Indeed, I suspect he might even be tempted to approach the Omnivores and cobble together some sort of consensus. Heaven forbid.

6

'But I don't understand, Father.'

She is still standing on the marble, still staring at the mortal remains of the specimen spread out in front of her.

'You don't?'

'This thing between a simian's hind legs... This appendage. What is it?'

'It's their undoing, Bel-imperia – that's what it is. It has a will of its own; it leads little monkeys astray.' He pauses to attend to a flight feather in need of preening. 'Oh, I dare say some species are less susceptible to its influence than others, but I shouldn't care to atone for the sins of a macaque – such rampant little rascals, such licentious little imps. And I'm afraid the female of the genus is no better than the male. You see, it's the female that leads us... that leads a he-macaque into temptation.'

His daughter isn't at all surprised to hear it.

'In fact, I met a she-macaque this morning that I suspect might be nothing more than a brazen harlot.'

Has he been frequenting harlots? Bel-imperia dismisses the thought. Inconceivable. But even so, she'd be interested to learn a little more. 'Where on earth... ?'

No need to prise the sordid details out of him. In fact, he seems

33

to be quite eager to unburden his conscience: 'Oh, I fear for the immortal soul of that simian, Bel. Indeed, I believe she's committed the most dreadful crime.'

'Why? What has she done?'

He glances over his scapulars at the double doors. Is he concerned that some snooping rodent might be standing on the boat slip in the rain, eavesdropping on their conversation?

'She has brought shame on these gardens, chick. She has dragged all our good names into the mud.' He pauses to admire his reflection in the mirror of the old duchess dressing table. 'Then again, I suppose some reputations can never be tarnished. Who knows? Perhaps the crocodiles might even give me a blessing for bringing her depraved behaviour to light. Of course, I do not seek that honour.'

'No, of course not, Father.'

'Neither do I make a habit of calling in at the macaque compound. But I'd heard from a gossipmonger that their matriarch had contracted consumption, so I decided to seize the initiative and drum up some business.'

Bel-imperia had suspected as much. He often descends on creatures that are close to death and leaves them a business card. In this instance, though, it seems the matriarch had recovered from her ordeal.

'And so I scoured the compound in search of another specimen that might soon be in need of our services. Sadly, I'm afraid the troop appeared to be in rude health. I remember I was just about to leave when I spotted a she-macaque that had just given birth in the long grass, and so I decided to swoop down on her and inspect the infant. Of course, I noticed at once that there was something queer about it.'

'Why? What was wrong with the creature?'

He scuttles a little closer to his daughter and hisses: 'It had chestnut-red legs and agouti-silver underparts. It bore no resemblance to its mother at all.'

'And so?'

'And so I asked her to tell me the name of its father. "His pops be Obadiah, sir," she said. "Is that so?" I replied. I turned to the other macaques in the troop. "If there's an Obadiah here present," I said, "could he please step forward?" But all the adult males just scampered into their boltholes as fast as they could.'

'What did you do then, Father?'

'I cross-examined the strumpet, of course. "Obadiah appears to be an absent father," I said. "He be an organ grinder's monkey, sir," she replied. "He comes and goes." I seem to recall one of the other she-macaques shouted: "He comes all right, love. We can see that."'

'I don't understand.'

'No, neither did I, but I suspect it might have been a joke.'

Bel-imperia is a little confused. She has never heard of such a thing. 'What's a joke, Father?'

'Oh, just some foolishness that idle specimens indulge in. We're above that sort of thing. We need someone to explain them to us. But even so, I could tell that I'd been ridiculed, so I rounded on the harlot. "Don't forget that I'm a member of the Elders," I said. "I am sure the committee is going to be most interested to learn that a she-macaque has given birth to an abomination."'

'What do you mean, Father? An abomination?'

'What do I mean? I mean neither one thing nor the other; neither toque macaque nor red-shanked douc. I mean the strumpet must have broken—'

'No.'

'Recite the Second Commandment, chick.'

'Of course, Father.'

Bel-imperia might not have managed to get the joke about Obadiah coming and going, but she is well aware that some creatures snigger at the Second Commandment. Indeed, she remembers glancing over her scapulars one morning at matins and giving the slender mongoose that sometimes sits behind her a disapproving stare for giggling at the phrase 'privy parts'. And so it does not cross her mind to smirk as she intones the Commandment: '*Thou shalt not mount any species other than thine own. Neither shalt thou nudge, sniff, stroke or otherwise interfere with the privy parts of any species other than thine own.*'

'Amen,' her father adds in a resounding baritone. Has the excitement of hearing the Second Commandment inspired him to lift up his heart in praise? She suspects that it might have done, because he sounds as if he is addressing a congregation of collared lemmings or something: 'For it is written,' he squawks, stepping up onto the dead thing's stomach, '*When lust hath conceived, it bringeth forth abomination…*'

Bel-imperia recognises the sermon. It's the one about the gnashing of teeth. The last time she heard it she had been sitting on the steps of the amphitheatre, staring out across the lake at the escarpment on the opposite shore. She remembers her father had gone to great lengths to remind the congregation of horrors that await them in Hades. Of course, the mongoose sitting behind her didn't seem convinced. 'It's all right, love,' the creature reassured his companion, 'we won't go to Hades for what we did behind the llama house last night. There ain't no such place.'

But it is quite clear that the gaunt-looking raptor perched on the deceased has no such misgivings. He turns to his daughter. Is that fire and brimstone she can see smouldering in his eyes?

'Make no mistake: that abomination is going to burn – burn in eternal torment. And so is its mother. Macaques don't have our strength of character. There's just one thing in these gardens that can lead decent, upright creatures like us into temptation. You must promise me, chick. You must promise me something important…'

'What's that, Father?'

'You'll never trust a prosimian, will you?'

'You mean a lemur?'

'Yes.'

'Oh, all right, then; I won't.'

'Is that a promise?'

'It is.'

But she can tell that a solemn oath is required. 'I swear on the Seven Commandments, I'll never trust a prosimian.'

'Good.' He scrambles down onto the marble, settles beside her. 'Now, where were we? We've done kingdom, phylum, class…'

She had been hoping he'd forgotten about the classification.

'That's right, family. Well, there was no need to get so upset about monkeys. The deceased isn't a monkey at all.'

'It isn't?'

'No, of course not. It's an ape.'

She remembers having a hunch that it might have been an ape. Perhaps she should have trusted her instincts. She reappraises the dead primate. 'But I don't understand, Father. It can't be an ape. Look, it's got a tail.'

'I am afraid that's the specimen's appendage, chick.'

'Goodness me.' She rearranges her facial features into an expression of disgust and averts her gaze from the little scrap of sausage meat in between its legs. She stares out through the double doors. Still no sign of a let up in the rain.

'Family?'

'*Hominidae?*'

'Genus and species. Then the classification is complete.'

Bel-imperia cannot recollect seeing a mature example of *Homo sapiens* up close and personal – the species tends to avoid the parade of sandbagged cages behind the Marsupial House where she exhibits herself to coach-parties of schoolchildren during opening hours. But even so, the deceased cannot be a man; after all, members of the general public don't come to the zoological gardens to be embalmed. Neither can it be an orang-utan: its curls are black not orangey brown. Is it a chimpanzee, then? Perhaps. True, she has never seen a chimpanzee in the flesh, but she can remember gazing at a photograph of one in the *Official Guide*. For some reason, the creature had been persuaded to pose beside some piece of equipment belonging to the Marconi Wireless and Telegraph Company. Perhaps it had been an advertisement or something – she cannot be sure. But she is quite confident that the specimen spread out before her is a primate of a different sort. There's just one option left, then; just one great ape remaining: 'It's a gorilla, isn't it? That's what it is.'

He isn't listening.

'It's a mountain gorilla. *Gorilla beringei.*'

He should be congratulating her on her performance. He should be expressing his pride and admiration. But he is just staring up into the rafters agape.

'Father?

37

Has he spotted a movement in the crossbeams and trusses? 'This intrusion is most unwelcome.'

'Intrusion?'

'Oh, bother! Be on your best behaviour, Bel-imperia. We seem to have the displeasure of an uninvited guest.'

He has never been able to summon up much enthusiasm for entertaining animals that turn up at the boathouse unannounced, but his daughter is quite excited at the prospect of an afternoon caller. Could it be a grieving relative? Could it be a gorilla? She turns her attention to the rafters, hoping to see a great ape clamber down onto the marble and cradle its loved one in its arms, but the intruder is just a pigeon.

Disappointed, she subjects the bird to a reproachful stare as it clatters down onto the deceased's chest. Of course, her father is more courteous, but instead of responding to his polite 'good evening', their guest just paces around in a circle, cooing. Perhaps it hasn't mastered the power of language. Perhaps it is a simpleton.

'Species?'

Not again. She is in no mood for another round of classification practice. She cuts to the chase. 'It's a carrier pigeon, Father. *Columba livia.*'

'That's right.'

Her thoughts turn to the Cloisters. Is it inconceivable that a letter could get lost at the pigeon cotes and end up in the clutches of a second-class pigeon such as this? Dare she hope that the piece of paper tied to this simpleton's leg is addressed to her?

'Father? You don't suppose—'

'Silence, Bel-imperia.'

He is setting an ambush for the specimen, tensing his long, S-shaped neck, like a cobra poised to strike. Is he going to grab their guest in his beak? Is there going to be pigeon pie for dinner? No time to reprimand herself for entertaining such a sinful thought. Before the bird can complete another pointless circle, her father lashes out at its legs and snatches the piece of paper.

The startled pigeon swoops across the boathouse and settles beside the can of motor oil on the old duchess dressing table.

'Oh, that's unfortunate. I'd rather hoped our guest would leave us in peace. I dare say a reply must be required.'

But his daughter isn't listening. She is glaring at the piece of paper on the marble. She should never have let herself get so excited; she should never have raised her hopes. She can see that it's addressed to Silas Pinch Esq, Master of Embalming, Obsequies and other Rites of Passage.

He pecks it open, spreads it out under his talons. 'Good gracious me, this is a turn up for the books. Black-edged mourning paper. It must be from the Dower House.'

'The Dower House?' Bel-imperia is astonished. It just doesn't make sense. The Dower House is the official residence of the creature responsible for managing the zoological gardens, the home of the Prize Exhibit. She gazes at the black border on the sheet of foolscap, the deep blue ink. 'Perhaps it's from the P Ex, Father?'

'Don't be silly, chick. I'm sure the Rt Hon W. L. S. Chartwell has more important things to do than dictate letters to the likes of us. Besides, I don't suppose he'd entrust his private correspondence to a second-class pigeon, do you?'

She is under no illusions: it is still a great honour to receive a letter from the Dower House. Second-class pigeon or not. But she can tell from her father's ruffled feathers that he is far from pleased. 'What's the matter? What does it say?'

Despite his apparent distress, his tone is calm and dispassionate: 'There isn't going to be an embalming – not this evening at least. The Order of Herbivores are adamant that the deceased doesn't deserve a decent funeral. They maintain that he should be cast onto the nearest compost heap and left to rot. The Prize Exhibit is going to be consulted. In the meantime, I'm permitted to douse the corpse in cedar-scented embalming oil, but I must leave it at that.'

Bel-imperia is outraged. 'No embalming? No obsequies? Goodness me, this isn't the Serengeti. I should like to remind the Order of Herbivores that it's precisely these tender mercies that set us apart from our cousins in the wild. How could they even consider dumping a dead gorilla on a compost heap and leaving it to rot?'

'What gorilla's that, chick?'

He must be confused. He must have lost the thread of the conversation. She scrabbles up onto the great ape's chest and stamps on its useless nipple. 'This gorilla, Father. This gorilla here.'

'I do not see a gorilla, Bel-imperia.'

'But...'

It had not crossed her mind that she might have been mistaken. It had not occurred to her that the deceased might not be a gorilla at all. She glances down at the specimen. She'd like a couple of minutes to gather her thoughts, but she isn't going to get them, because she has another surprise coming.

'Leave it out, eh? I ain't got time for all this crap about gorillas.'

She gapes in astonishment at the pigeon perched on the dressing table. Not a simpleton at all, then.

'I got loads o' other letters to get out tonight. Come on, I just need a scribble, guv'nor.'

'One moment, please.' He reminds the pigeon that its salvation requires the patience of the saints. He turns to his daughter. 'Now, get down from there this instant.'

'But Father...'

He glares at her until she clambers down onto the marble.

'I've never been so disappointed. Good gracious me, a numbat could have classified this specimen. What on earth made you think it was a gorilla?'

'Its broad shoulders? Its muscular limbs?'

'Did I not point out that the deceased has been blessed with an appendage? Did I not make it clear that his father had the good fortune to sire a male?'

She flinches. Does he have to be so hurtful?

'Is it surprising that a member of the superior sex should be strong and muscular?'

'No, I suppose not, but—'

'Be quiet. We'll discuss this after I've dealt with our guest.'

He drops down to the ground and scuttles across to the old lacquered tea chest. He prises it open and rummages through his collection of priceless treasures: his scrubbing brushes and his scouring pads, the old cigarette tin he uses to stash his beaten-copper groats. Is that a box of matches she can see?

'Here it is.'

He returns to the marble-topped contraption clutching a bottle of Quink.

His daughter stares at him as he tries to coax off the top of the cobalt-blue ink bottle. His gnarled scutes and his hooked talons. His bolt-cutter beak and his rasp-like tongue. No point in striving to gain his respect and admiration, much less his love. He has nothing to give. He pecks up the letter and sets it down beside the ink bottle. She is conscious that she shares his high standards, his meticulous attention to detail, but, in this instance, his behaviour is too fastidious, too exacting. Is it essential to align the black edges on the sheet of mourning paper at such a precise angle to the edge of the marble? Does it matter if some scrap of foolscap that has been strapped to the leg of a pigeon gets another crease in it? She can see the dotted line; all that is required is his signature. But he needs a quill. He inspects his remiges. No doubt he is going to use one of his secondaries. He pauses. Has he had a better idea? He lunges at his daughter, plucks a feather from her inside leg.

The pain is sharp, piercing. Struggling to suppress her tears, little Bel-imperia Pinch glances around the boathouse, searches for something to distract her. She considers the canisters of embalming fluid, the last drops of rain dripping into the cast-iron buckets, the steaming puddles of sulphuric acid on the flagstones. Is this miserable building all that Old Hesper House and Zoological Gardens has to offer a female of her species? Mistress of Embalming, Obsequies and other Rites of Passage – is that her purpose in life?

She scutters across to the edge of the marble, peers out through the double doors. She gazes at the mist rising from the lake; she gazes at the ruined amphitheatre cut into the hillside across the shore. Is that a cluster of pine trees she can see on the horizon? Or is it the pointed roof of some provincial parade in the Middle Gardens? She bristles with impatience. It might still be raining in the confines of the boathouse, but outside, the skies are starting to clear. The sun is coming out. In the distance, a snatch of big-band music, a ripple of laughter. She does not hesitate, does not dither. True, this is the most important decision she has ever made, but even so, it just takes a moment – a fraction of a second, nothing more. Sooner or later she is going to escape. Sooner or later she is going to leave Silas Pinch and his boathouse behind. For ever.

'You'll never succeed.'

'What?'

He is putting a final flourish to his signature. 'In this business. You'll never become a successful Mistress of Embalming, Obsequies and other Rites of Passage. You need to be able to tell the difference between one dead animal and another. How could the deceased be a gorilla? For heaven's sake, apart from the curls on its head and chest it's as hairless as a naked mole rat.'

'I assumed its coat had been burnt to cinders.'

It is an innocent comment, but she can see that it has unsettled him. He straightens his serpentine neck and stares out at the boat slip, senses alert to some approaching danger. The plumage on his mantle bristles. Has he spotted a pride of lions or something prowling through the long grass on the lake-shore?

'Here.' He stuffs the signed letter into her talons. 'Give that to the pigeon.'

'Father?'

'The pigeon, Bel-imperia.'

'Yes, but... ' She wants to ask him what's wrong. 'What's the danger?'

Too late. He has leapt into the air and soared out through the double doors.

She sighs. She is tired of being given instructions; it is explanations she needs. She pecks up the letter, sails across to the old duchess dressing table.

The pigeon says, 'So help me, Sol, I never had to hang around so long for a bleedin' scribble.'

She has a hunch. Call it instinct. 'Yes,' she says, 'I do apologise. Have we held you up? You said you had a lot of post to deliver this evening?'

'Yeah, one o' the lads found a load o' letters slipped down the back o' his nesting box.'

'Old letters?'

'Months old some o' them.'

She takes a deep breath, tries to remain calm and collected. 'I don't suppose there was anything from the Cloisters?'

'I dunno. The Pigeon Master General said we got to get them out tonight. "Fat chance," I told him. "It'll take us 'til the barnacle geese come home."'

'But the barnacle geese don't return until late October.' Perhaps she should call in at the pigeon cotes and make some enquiries. Perhaps she should speak to the Pigeon Master General. 'Well, I'd better let you get on with it, then.'

The Columbine clatters out through the double doors, disappears into the burnished light. Is the sun setting? Bel-imperia is sure that it must be. She turns her attention to her father. He is standing on the boat slip: a stooped figure silhouetted against the golden lake. Should she go out and join him? He is bound to object to her calling in at the pigeon cotes this evening, but so be it. Let him object. She has made up her mind.

Outside, the air smells fresh, clean. It might have stopped raining, but the branched bur-reeds on either side of the boat slip are still sagging under the weight of the water clinging to their tapered leaves. She peers into the lake. The tadpoles and the little fish. The damsel-flies. Is that an eel snaking through the mud, its semi-transparent skin glistening in the slime? It's almost as thick as the forearm of the ape on the marble. The snake-like thing disappears into the darkness. She forgets about it; she lets it go.

Bel-imperia is glad to be out on the boat slip. For the first time since she scuttled into the building behind her, she almost feels free. She remembers the Cloisters, her hope of a scholarship. She creeps a little closer to her father, musters up her courage.

'I thought I might call in at the pigeon cotes this evening.'

Silence. Did he hear? Is he listening?

'I said I thought I might call in at the pigeon cotes… Father?'

He is staring up at the spent rainclouds. 'Let's hope others do not come tonight.'

'Others?'

'You got one thing right I suppose: that great ape in there has been burnt to cinders. But he didn't lose his coat in the inferno; he just lost a leather jacket and some other old threads.' He pauses, perhaps to let the implications of his comment sink in. 'Species?'

'I think I've had enough of this spot of classification practice.'

'It's getting late, Bel-imperia. Let's get this done and dusted, shall we?'

'But it can't be a man. What about that laceration? What about those terrible burns? How could a member of the general public come to the zoological gardens and end up in such a frightful state?'

'Oh, the man on the marble isn't a member of the general public, chick. He didn't come here to admire the animals in these gardens. He came here to strip us of the freedom our ancestors died for in the Uprising. He came here to slaughter us like lambs.'

He glances up at the clouds, as if concerned that something dreadful might be about to emerge out of them, but his daughter can see nothing more disconcerting than a house martin, summer's guest, returning to its roost, the bright plumage on its underside muted in the diminishing light.

7

I am sure I mentioned that a middle-aged man came to see me. Unpleasant scar, tangled mane of hair? Claims to be a biographer. Well, he turned up again this morning. He said he was wondering...

What were his words? He was wondering what makes one animal become P Ex and another not. What makes a bird aspire to greatness.

'Oh, I didn't believe a bird could become Prize Exhibit,' I said. 'Not in the 1940s.'

'Perhaps not,' he conceded, pulling a packet of Old Holborn out of his bag. 'But that little lappet-faced thing that used to stand on the marble hanging its head in shame... What turned it into the Rt Hon Bel-imperia Pinch? What put all that iron in its soul?'

'Nutritious guts and livers?' I suggested. 'Oh, and a good education, of course.'

'Thing is,' he said, as he set about rolling a cigarette, 'it's not much of an education, is it? The occasional afternoon of classification practice.'

I reminded him that I studied a broad range of subjects in that old boathouse. I detailed some of the disciplines Father encouraged me to master: the practicalities of running a small business, balancing the books – that sort of thing. 'Oh, and I learned about death, of course. You see, in such an environment one soon comes to realise that life is short and that one has an obligation to use it to some purpose. That said, I remember our first obligation used to be to the customer.'

'The customer?'

'The deceased, dear. We didn't keep our customers waiting. We did not. We attended to their needs before rigor mortis set in. Well, I suppose we had to otherwise we wouldn't have been able to arrange them in the appropriate position. There are different positions for different species, you see. Thomson's gazelles are laid out as if leaping into the afterlife. Coral snakes are coiled into elegant spirals—'

He interrupted me. He asked me something about a man in his mid-twenties. 'What would be the appropriate position for a customer like that?'

'The mortal remains of a man?' I said. 'Goodness me, I cannot recollect a creature of that description passing through the boathouse, dear.'

'Is that so?' he replied, lighting his roll-up.

I suppose a couple of minutes must have passed. I remember him staring at me through a great plume of smoke: silent, accusing. I pretended not to notice. I plumped up the lining of my nest. Eventually, he attempted to rephrase his question.

'Is this essential?' I said. 'I'd been hoping to discuss the embalming procedure.'

But I am afraid he insisted: 'I'm not interested in Thomson's gazelles. Or coral snakes. The man on the marble. The Flight Lieutenant. Tell me about him.'

'I thought I made it quite clear: I cannot recollect... '

He mentioned something about the drone of a damaged engine, a distant explosion.

'Oh, I remember the sound of engines,' I said. 'I remember sheltering under a sheet of corrugated steel and listening to the screams of falling bombs. Goodness me, I should hope no one could forget that in the 1940s the animals in these gardens stood alone against mankind and his hideous apparatus of destruction. His great iron birds. His stub-nosed Messerschmitts. Oh, and I remember the hardship, too: no offcuts of mutton behind the counter at the cold store – nothing to eat apart from mouse tails unless one had enough coupons. In fact, I'm told some specimens had little to sustain them other than the marvellous leadership of our Prize Exhibit. Oh, but his courage and determination put steel in our hearts, make no mistake.'

He stubbed out his cigarette, consulted his spiral-bound notebook. 'The Prize Exhibit from 1940 to 1945? You mean that elephant seal?'

'That's right, dear.' I decided to remind him of the tone of Chartwell's leadership; I recited a short passage from one of his speeches: '*The animals in these gardens shall never surrender to servitude or shame. We shall defend our freedom whatever the cost might be. So lift up your hearts. All will come right. For out of the depths of sorrow and sacrifice will be born again the glory of animalkind.*'

I must admit I should have thought the experience of hearing one

P Ex deliver the lines of another might have encouraged a certain comparison, but he just said, 'Finest hour and all that, right?'

'I suppose it must have seemed like that at the time,' I replied. 'But of course, there have been other fine hours since then. Indeed, I seem to recall that on the odd occasion I managed to summon up a similar spirit.'

'Perhaps,' he said. 'But in the 1940s... '

'Yes?'

'Thing is, there are reports... '

'Reports?'

'This man. The Flight Lieutenant.'

'Did I not make it clear? I have no recollection... '

He explained that in the autumn of 1940 an iron bird came down in the Marshes – not a Messerschmitt: a medium-range reconnaissance bird or something. He seems to believe its pilot might have ended up in Father's establishment. From all accounts, some pheasant caught a glimpse of a man on the marble the night the boathouse burnt down.

'He must have been about the same height as me. Broader shoulders, perhaps. More muscular. Ring a bell?'

'Let me see,' I said. 'I do recall a large, ape-like primate passing through the boathouse once. But I am sure the creature must have been an orang-utan or a chimpanzee. The latter I should imagine.'

He seemed doubtful so I informed him that in the 1940s a disproportionate number of chimps used to end up on the slab.

'Of course,' I said, 'the species is supposed to be adept at using tools. But even so, I'm afraid some specimens struggled to operate the equipment that had been acquired – at no small expense I might add – from the Marconi Wireless and Telegraph Company. Indeed, I seem to recollect more than one incompetent chimp managed to electrocute himself before the creatures made their first successful broadcast. Such a shame. Then again, I suppose opposable thumbs are no substitute for common sense.'

'I guess it might have been a chimp, but—'

I reassured him that there must have been at least one death in the Ape House that autumn. I encouraged him to go and have a rummage through the zoological archives and leave me in peace.

But he insisted that he had scoured the archives. 'Fine toothcomb, remember?'

'Is that so?'

'Besides,' he added, 'the *Register of Births, Deaths and Extinctions* is missing. Perhaps the chimpanzees keep statistics. I guess I'll have to drop in at the Ape House again.'

I subjected him to a hard stare. 'What do you mean, "again"?'

'Oh, I called in there last night, but—'

'Last night?'

I suppose that must have been the moment I suspected he might not be one of us, the moment I realised I had been deceived. You see, when he applied for the position he went to great lengths to reassure me that he was working on a manuscript called... Oh, I forget the title, but I'm quite sure that it contained a reference to me. And so I had assumed that I was going to be its subject. Indeed, it hadn't occurred to me that I might be reduced to sharing its pages with another, more recent Prize Exhibit.

I decided to get to the bottom of the matter. 'You called in at the Ape House last night?'

'Yeah, that's right,' he mumbled.

I rounded on him. 'Let me make one thing clear,' I said, 'I cannot condone a member of the general public trespassing in the zoological gardens. Neither can I be held responsible if there should happen to be some misunderstanding.'

'Misunderstanding?'

I explained to him that during a scent-marking contest, the Order of Carnivores is bound to be out and about, campaigning from cage to cage. 'I should be most upset to learn that a middle-aged man clutching a notebook and pencil had been mistaken for a meal.'

'I'm not middle-aged.'

'Perhaps not,' I said. 'But I must advise caution all the same. There are some big beasts in these gardens, dear.'

'I stumbled into a square-lipped rhinoceros last night,' he admitted. 'Beasts don't get much bigger than that.'

Of course, I'd suspected as much. 'This rhinoceros,' I said. 'I assume the specimen must have been in the Ape House. Standing on a platform in the atrium I should imagine.'

'That's right,' he replied. 'The poor thing looked dead uncomfortable, so it did. In fact, I was worried it was going to charge.'

'I'm not surprised to hear it. Ebenezer Bull has never been at ease in the limelight.'

'Ebenezer Bull?'

'The Commander-in-Chief of the Order of Herbivores. The incumbent Prize Exhibit.'

'I thought I'd heard the name before,' he said, pretending to scribble it down. But I'm not blind. I could see that the lead of his pencil had snapped.

So insincere. So disingenuous. Heard the name? He'd called in at the Ape House to listen to that incompetent rhinoceros attempt to defend its record – I had no doubt about that. And so I made it quite clear to him: 'I didn't grant this audience in order to discuss Ebenezer Bull,' I said. 'Neither do I see the point of introducing him into the conversation. Goodness me, I'm sure no one is going to be interested in some old rhino that squandered his brief tenure as P Ex charging from crisis to crisis. There's no intellectual basis to his leadership. No coherent narrative to his life and times.'

'Perhaps not, but—'

I made him promise not to mention Ebenezer Bull in his manuscript. 'Not so much as a footnote, understand?'

He muttered something under his breath.

'Is that a solemn binding oath?' I said.

I remember he nodded. 'Seven Commandments,' he said. 'I swear.'

8

```
OLD HESPER HOUSE 𝔞𝔫𝔡 ZOOLOGICAL GARDENS

The Cages of Caer Lud

## THE APE HOUSE

Grade I Listed Cage, Enclosure or Other Estate Building.
(Completed 1697)
```

It is Thursday 15 April 2010. It is the evening that Ebenezer Bull has been dreading.

Inside the building, a couple of chimpanzees are still clambering about in the lighting rig, making last-minute adjustments to the direction of the spotlights, but otherwise the preparations appear to be complete. The enclosures on either side of the atrium have been given a spring clean, and a purpose-built platform has been constructed underneath the stained-glass cupola, as agreed. Designed to be dismantled and put into storage at the end of the scent-marking contest, the platform is simple, unadorned. Has it been reinforced with rolled-steel joists? Has it been tested to confirm that it can support 2¼ tonnes of square-lipped rhinoceros? Ebenezer Bull cannot be sure.

He snorts. Is he going to let the thought of a loose floorboard detain him? Of course he isn't, damn it. Besides, he has more pressing concerns on his mind.

He stomps up the steps and lumbers across the platform to his designated bale of bristle bent grass. He ruminates on his predicament. Should he squeeze out another turd in order to assert his territorial rights, or should he suppress the urge? He cannot decide. Is there no one that can advise him? Lucius, his second-in-command, perhaps? Sue?

Squinting into the bright lights, he peers out across the Ape House. No, no sign of his entourage, damn it. So be it. He'll just have to make an executive decision then.

He hoists up his tail and grunts. He concentrates on expelling an impressive splattering of dung. Despite a great deal of effort, though, he is disconcerted to discover that he can produce nothing more substantial than some anal acoustics. Has he done it again? The same old mistake that has dogged him since he became Prize Exhibit. Too much time spent coming to a decision instead of just getting on with it and getting the job done. He dismisses the thought, settles down to rehearse his opening statement.

Here he is, then, the Rt Hon Ebenezer Bull, P Ex – a great lump of square-lipped rhinoceros, solid and immense. Here he is, then, the Commander-in-Chief of the Order of Herbivores, doing his best to enthuse and inspire as he intones his lines. But his leaden performance cannot disguise the fact that he has no desire to be standing in the glare of the spotlights. He'd much rather be roaming the Northern Pastures alongside his loving she-rhinoceros and their little calves.

He scrapes his fore-hoof across the boards and snorts. He should never have accepted the invitation, damn it. He should have made it clear to his advisers that it's inappropriate for a creature of his stature to appear on the same platform as Dale FitzClarence – not to mention that little upstart, Nicholas Cobb. But it is too late to change his mind and stomp out of the Ape House in a rage. Someone is calling his name.

'Ebenezer Bull to Spruce Up, please. Ebenezer Bull to Spruce Up.'

He peers over the orange crates that have been set out for the audience to perch on, searches for the spangled coquettes that specialise in the removal of parasites. But the Ape House is a blur. He cannot see the she-gorillas staring back at him through the toughened panes of glass that separate their enclosure from the atrium. Neither can he see the she-rat that is scrabbling up onto the audio signal processor, eager to claim a sought-after position to scribble her report. He cannot see these things because, like all rhinoceroses, his small almond-shaped eyes aren't much cop at collecting light and converting it into a coherent image. In recompense, the species has good hearing and a sharp sense of smell, but Ebenezer's most impressive attribute is hidden under his sagittal crest. For he has the most magnificent brain. It is an organ that can empathise, an organ that can process long numbers, an organ that can grasp abstract concepts, such as 'tangible assets' and 'short-term liabilities', notions that might addle the mind of a lesser rhinoceros. But it is one thing to understand the implications of the annual profit and loss statements of Old Hesper House and Zoological Gardens Ltd and quite another to explain them to an armadillo or an opossum. Perhaps this evening he'll be able to make the animals understand that these are dangerous times. Perhaps this evening he'll be able to convince them that the Order of Carnivores cannot be trusted to get their calculations right.

'Ebenezer Bull to Spruce Up, please. Ebenezer Bull to Spruce Up.'

Here come the spangled coquettes, then. Here come the hummingbirds, darting in and out of the aluminium trusses that hold up the lighting rig, stopping a moment in mid-air to regroup, then speeding towards the square-lipped rhinoceros, their iridescent feathers glistening in the light.

Despite his reluctance to submit to the procedure, Ebenezer does his best to stand still so that the hummingbirds can flit around him and peck out the parasitic mites that dwell in the deep folds and creases of his hide. But he has no inclination to remain calm as the spangled coquettes lance the carbuncles on his shoulders. He scrapes his fore-hoof across the boards again. He snorts. Is it the humiliation of being spruced up that has unsettled him? Perhaps. He dismisses the hummingbirds: 'That'll do. That'll do.'

But he cannot dismiss the deep sense of unease that is tightening its grip on his heart. He can tell that another male is trespassing on his territory. He can smell that something slippery is insinuating itself into the room.

'Dale FitzClarence to Spruce Up, please. Dale FitzClarence to Spruce Up.'

It must be the Commander-in-Chief of the Order of Carnivores. It must be the Rt Hon Dale FitzClarence.

Ebenezer shudders as the smooth-coated otter scampers up the steps. He cannot see the light glistening on its coat, but he can hear its rudder-like tail thumping on the boards as it bounds across the platform to take up position behind its designated bale of bristle bent grass. He can hear its posh accent, too.

'I say, may I have a quick word?'

FitzClarence is explaining to the chimpanzee in charge of the proceedings that he has brought his own hummingbirds. Impeccable manners, Dale. But no amount of charm can disguise the sense of entitlement that sets this otter apart from the great herds that roam the Northern Pastures.

'Nicholas Cobb to Spruce Up, please. Nicholas Cobb to Spruce Up.'

Has the Commander-in-Chief of the Order of Omnivores scurried up on the platform, too?

Something squeaks: 'Good evening, Ebenezer. Good evening, Dale.'

Ebenezer grunts. He is in no mood to make conversation with an Omnivore, no mood to be gracious to little Nicholas Cobb; it is the smooth-coated otter that concerns him. He steals a glance at the creature: its perfect grooming, its slick coat. Dale FitzClarence might not be popular in the terraced cages of the Middle Gardens, but it's quite clear from the 48-sheet poster of an airbrushed otter that has been plastered up on the side of the Nocturnal House that the Carnivores have no shortage of groats to squander on their scent-marking campaign. There must be something Ebenezer can do to impress on his opponent that he intends to dominate the proceedings this evening.

He samples the air. Is that otter he can smell?

He should have been more decisive, damn it. He should have defecated on the platform as soon as he'd arrived. Is it too late to have another attempt at asserting his territorial rights?

He jacks up his tail and grunts. But just as his bowels are about to lurch into motion, a chimpanzee at the other end of the atrium opens a door and ushers in a representative audience of small mammals, reptiles and birds.

Ebenezer clenches his sphincter, glares at the discontented band of beasts shuffling towards the orange crates that have been set out for them. Is this a demographic cross section of the zoological gardens, then? He cannot be sure – the audience is just a shifting mass of mottled fur and feathers, nothing more – but he can smell Pantanal cat and mouse deer, porcupine and pheasant. His heart misses a beat. His legs labour to bear him up. Can he persuade these specimens to reinstate him as Prize Exhibit? Has he got the charisma to convince them that he deserves a second chance?

'Remember, the broadcast is going out live,' a chimpanzee clutching a clipboard is telling them. 'No snarling or hissing – not so much as a squeak, understand?'

But Ebenezer can tell that the audience isn't listening. He can hear them chattering: 'That's him,' a marmoset is muttering to its companion. 'That's the clapped-out old rhino that got us into this mess.'

Is that a barnacle goose glaring at him as if he is to blame for the strange cloud of ash that has been disrupting its migration plans? He suspects that it might be.

Of course, these creatures don't care for Dale FitzClarence – there can be no doubt about that. But Ebenezer is beginning to suspect that perhaps some of them might care for a certain square-lipped rhinoceros even less. He should have called a scent-marking contest as soon as he charged at his predecessor and chased him out of the zoological gardens, damn it. He had been popular then. But this is no time to ruminate on might-have-beens: a she-chimpanzee is shambling across the atrium towards him.

Is it a she-chimpanzee? Ebenezer cannot be sure: there's something rather masculine about the primate's collection of piercings, something butch about its swagger. He remembers that some chimpanzees have unconventional tendencies. He reminds himself that times have changed and that he is supposed to have an enlightened attitude to such things.

'Evening, Prize Exhibit.' The chimp places some minuscule object in the palm of her hand, holds it up for him to inspect. Is it something to eat? No, it is no bigger than a dung beetle, no bigger than a bug.

'It's the latest model, sir. The Marconi GSM.'

Ebenezer grunts. He has no desire to let the chimp attach the device to his horn.

'Come on, sir. Stand still. Dale FitzClarence didn't stomp up and down.'

Poor Ebenezer Bull. He cannot name the components in the gadget that the ape is clipping onto him, but he understands that it has been designed to convert his grunts and snorts into electromagnetic signals and send them to the transmitter on the escarpment. His mind reaches out across the great conurbation of cages clustered around the Ape House, out across the landscaped gardens and their provincial parades of terraced cages, out across the Northern Pastures, to all the specimens settling down in front of their second-hand transistor radio sets: the mammals and the rodents, the reptiles and the birds. He can almost sense the last dregs of self-confidence draining out of him.

His thoughts turn to his nemesis. His thoughts turn to his predecessor. No doubt he could have taken this evening in his stride. But Ebenezer is no charmer. Is he going to be able to turn in a decent performance?

'Starting positions, please. One minute and counting… '

He attempts to muster some courage. He reminds himself that he is Commander-in-Chief of the Order of Herbivores, damn it. He should be able to command a platform in the Ape House, then. But it hasn't escaped his attention that the big beasts in the Order are already sharpening their antlers and horns in preparation for his defeat. He scrapes the boards again and snorts. He cannot afford to let the thought that he might lose the scent-marking contest enter his mind. He must concentrate on his performance. He must persuade the audience to take another look at him, and then a long hard look at Dale FitzClarence. He must make it clear to them that the Order of Carnivores hasn't changed its spots. He takes a deep breath. Has he got all the facts and figures he needs at his disposal? He cannot be sure. But he's in no doubt that this ordeal is going to cost him dear. He can hear his heart pounding against his ribcage. He can hear a loose motion sloshing around in his bowels. No time to release it. The music is starting up. It has begun.

[II]

Mouse Tail Tangle

THE EVENING RODENT

LATE EDITION   **FRIDAY 6 SEPTEMBER 1940**   PRICE 2g

IRON BIRD BROUGHT DOWN

From Our Avian Correspondent

The following Department of Birdcages and Aviaries *communiqué* was issued by the Dower House at 10 o'clock this morning:

"At midnight on Thursday 5th September a medium-range iron bird was intercepted in the skies above the zoological gardens. Searchlights held the hideous creature in their beams as No. 2 Squadron of Buzzards and Spot-tailed Goshawks swooped in to attack. The battle that followed was protracted and fierce. Nevertheless, it has since been confirmed that all but one of our brave little goshawks managed to escape the intermittent bursts of machine-gun fire unscathed. The thoughts of all animals in these gardens go out to the long-legged buzzards that hurled themselves into the iron bird's engines. Their sacrifice, however, was not in vain, because moments later the mechanical bird came down in the Marshes and burst into flames. There are no reports of injuries to animals on the ground."

P. Ex. UNDAUNTED

In a statement to the Hall of Exhibits this morning the Rt. Hon. W. L. S. Chartwell, Commander-in-Chief of the Order of Carnivores and Prize Exhibit, insisted that the animals in the zoological gardens are united in their determination to resist the odious apparatus of mankind's aggression. Slobbering as he addressed a crowded chamber, the elephant seal argued that he would rather see our magnificent promenades of cages and enclosures reduced to rubble than the creatures that reside in them surrender to servitude and shame.

Turning to last night's aerial engagement, the P.Ex. expressed his regret that the animals cannot rival the mechanical resources of their aggressor. Nevertheless, he noted that our spot-tailed goshawks are more agile on the wing than the enemy's mechanical contraptions, and he is confident that in due course our command of the skies will turn the tide of this great conflict.

MORTAL REMAINS

Once he had paid eloquent tribute to the specimens that laid down their lives in last night's tragic trial of strength, the Prize Exhibit confirmed reports that the corpse of a man has been recovered from the iron bird that came down in the Marshes.

Dismissing a suggestion from the Herbivorous benches that the man's mortal remains should be dumped on a compost heap and left to rot, he reminded the Hall that it is tender mercies, such as embalming, obsequies and other rites of passage, that set the animals in these gardens apart...

(Continued page 3, column 1.)

(Continued from page 2)

...from their cousins in the wild, and announced that he therefore intends to issue instructions for the Flight Lieutenant's remains to be embalmed.

NOT THE BEGINNING

Then he came to this passage: "Of course, the aerial engagement that took place last night is just an overture to the great battle that lies ahead. It is not the beginning. It is not even the beginning of the beginning. But I am confident that as long as nothing is neglected — as long as each specimen does its duty — rather than dampen our spirits, this brutal assault on our freedom will kindle in our hearts an intense and universal flame.

"Our coats bristle against the prospect of invasion. Our claws are sharp, and our teeth are bared. Other institutions might have fallen, but we shall defend these gardens whatever the cost might be. We shall fight in the paddocks; we shall fight in the Nocturnal House; we shall fight in the bear pits, and we shall never surrender."

SCANDAL IN THE MACAQUE COMPOUND

In other news, allegations that a she-macaque has given birth to an abomination have surfaced after our lake-shore correspondent...

(Continued page 4, column 2.)

10

OLD HESPER HOUSE AND ZOOLOGICAL GARDENS

The Cages of Caer Lud

THE APE HOUSE

Grade I Listed Cage, Enclosure or Other Estate Building.
(Completed 1697)

The chimpanzee in charge of the proceedings is past his prime, but there's still a spring in his step as he bounds up onto the platform to greet the audience.

'Good evening, good evening. Tonight the Ape House is proud to host an historic Clash of the Commanders.'

He flashes a smile at an attractive he-ape hanging from the lighting rig; it has the same self-assured charm as the smiles of the cage-to-cage sales-primates that tramp up and down the zoological gardens peddling second-hand tail brushes and other grooming aids.

'Since the advent of audiotape there have been several attempts to persuade the leaders of the three great Orders to appear on the same platform during a scent-marking campaign. None successful. But all that is about to change, because this evening, the three creatures competing to become P Ex are going to thrash out their differences in front of an audience of small mammals, reptiles and birds.'

Unable to contain its excitement, a gelada baboon succumbs to a bout of enthusiastic screeching.

'And so please give a warm welcome to Ebenezer Bull, Dale FitzClarence – and of course, little Nicholas Cobb.'

Ebenezer does his best to rearrange his square lips into a natural-looking smile, but he cannot disguise his discomfort.

'Now, in a moment I'm going to ask… ' The chimpanzee slips on a pair of spectacles, squints at a scrap of paper in his hands. 'In a moment I'm going to ask Nathaniel Grub, a long-nosed armadillo that has just taken out an encumbrance on a starter cage in the Small Mammal House, to get the Q&A rolling. But before battle commences, a brief opening statement from each Commander. First up, the Commander-in-Chief of the Order of Herbivores, Ebenezer Bull.'

But Ebenezer is not listening. He is concentrating on the advice that Lucius Scuttleson, his second-in-command, attempted to drum into him during rehearsal. He must remember – what? He must remember not to dribble. He must remember not to give the impression that he is about to charge. He must remember...

'Ebenezer?'

'These are no ordinary times,' he says at last, his tone, perhaps, a little too doom-laden. 'And this is no ordinary scent-marking contest. We depend on the groats that the general public cough up to get into these gardens, but because of the sub-prime encumbrance crisis in the United Species of Animalia, we've seen the biggest drop in takings at the gatehouse for a generation. Fortunately, due to the prompt action I took – slashing the cost of an admission ticket, investing in more attractions – the turnstiles are moving again. But this is the defining moment: get the big decisions right and all animals can have a comfortable cage to curl up in at night; get the big decisions wrong and... Well, there will be a double dip in gatehouse receipts.'

There. He has said it. But is it enough to differentiate him from Dale FitzClarence?

'I'm not a privileged specimen. I didn't go to the Cloisters; I studied alongside the great herds that roam the Northern Pastures. But I am strong-willed and determined. I don't shun the difficult decisions: I charge up and down until something gets done. Perhaps there might be some aspects of the job that I'm still struggling to get right, but one thing is certain: I know how to govern these gardens in good times as well as in bad.'

'Thank you, Ebenezer.'

Did he turn in a decent performance? Did he manage to impress on the audience that he is still a square-lipped rhinoceros in its prime? Or did he come across as a specimen on its last legs, a battle-scarred bull, too tired to defend its patch of the Serengeti for much longer? There's no time to ruminate on the matter. The quizmaster is turning on the charm again: 'Righty-ho. And so it's over to Dale FitzClarence, then.'

The smooth-coated otter springs up on its hind legs, clutches onto its bale of bristle bent grass and strikes a debonair pose. Ebenezer cannot see the creature's water-repellent guard hairs, but he can smell that its pelt has been slicked in a generous application of the scented oil that oozes from a special gland in the region of its anus.

'Dale?'

'If you want a modern, compassionate Carnivore, go for a smooth-coated otter. That's me. I am it.'

Is FitzClarence suffering from stage fright this evening? Ebenezer is sure he can hear his tail trembling against the boards.

'Now, I love these gardens more than words can wield the matter. Dearer than I love hot pies and pasties. And so it breaks my heart to see the mess that Ebenezer has made of them. We can't go on like this. We've got to do more.

'First of all, the three great Orders have got to clean up their act. The moat around the warty pig enclosure brought great shame on the Hoggs, and like all those that do the right thing and cough up their cage tributes on time, I was appalled to see the duck house on the lake. The specimens that dipped their snouts into the trough have been named and shamed, but not enough has been done to restore confidence in our Rt Hon members – and I intend to do something about that.'

It sounds like he's getting into his stride.

'I also intend to do something about the overdraft that Ebenezer has run up to disguise the fact that he's presided over the biggest drop in takings for a generation. I make no bones about it. Some of us might have to struggle on a little longer before being put out to graze, but I'm not cold-blooded; I care about the cageless and the lame. And I am not alone. There are some big beasts behind me, impatient to be let loose. So please rest assured, if old age or ill health leaves you struggling to keep up with the others in your herd, there'll always be a Carnivore nearby to ease your suffering.

'Thank you, Dale.'

The smooth-coated otter drops down onto the boards and chillaxes. But Ebenezer is in no mood to lower his immense buttocks and loosen up. These are dangerous times – too dangerous to let FitzClarence's statement go unchallenged. He must make it clear to the audience that it is counter-productive to cut investment until the takings at the gatehouse perk up. He must remind them that the Order of Carnivores has refused to guarantee prompt treatment for distemper and mange.

'Can I just respond to that?' he says.

'Perhaps it can wait until the commercial break, Ebenezer. I'm sure little Nicholas Cobb is eager to make a short statement, too.'

Ebenezer snorts. He had forgotten about the Order of Omnivores. He had forgotten about little Nicholas Cobb. Should he apologise?

He squints at the orange-bellied ground squirrel as the creature scrabbles up onto its bale of bristle bent grass. He grunts. Not the most eloquent expression of regret, perhaps, but more than the specimen deserves. Besides, no doubt Nicholas Cobb is accustomed to being ignored; after all, despite his orange markings, he blends into the background. Not surprising, then, that since he took over the reins of the Omnivores he's been struggling to make an impression on the consciousness of the zoological gardens at large. But all that is about to change: the little he-squirrel is appearing on the same platform as the big beasts this evening – his moment has arrived.

Exposure. Ebenezer has been advised that this is something the Omnivores crave. But he had not expected to see their Commander-in-Chief sit up on his hind legs and expose his pert little penis to the audience. Neither had he expected to see the creature caress the offending organ. Is Nicholas Cobb pleasuring himself?

Ebenezer is tempted to curl up the corner of a square lip in disgust, but has no desire to come across as puritanical. And so he just gazes at the creature as it combs some sort of secretion into its tail. Strange behaviour. Even for an orange-bellied ground squirrel. What could the explanation be? Is Nicholas Cobb attempting to impress on the audience that he's done his bit to ensure the survival of his species? Is he attempting to remind them that he's admitted to mounting 'no more than 30' she-squirrels?

'Nick?'

Ebenezer dismisses the thought of the rodent's sexual conquests, tries to concentrate on its opening statement.

'So, what's it going to be, then?' it squeaks with a swish of its tail. 'The clapped-out old rhino that got us into this mess? Or the over-privileged otter that seems to think a reduction in cage tributes for his Carnivorous friends is going to get us out of it? Not much of a choice, is it? But this time there's an alternative to these old Orders that have been playing pass the parcel with the zoological gardens all these years. You see, I believe the way things are is not the way things have to be... '

Ebenezer is reluctant to admit it, but he had underestimated little Nicholas Cobb. His performance is impressive. It's not just that he is at ease in the limelight, or that his mouse-like mannerisms have a certain endearing charm; he seems to have cast a spell over the audience. Indeed, it's quite clear from their rapt silence that some sort of hocus-pocus must be going on. Is that a dingo drooling at the mouth? Is that a cottontail rabbit gazing up at its orange-bellied idol, starry-eyed? Ebenezer scrapes a fore-hoof across the boards and snorts. How could such a bland rodent have this effect on the audience? It cannot be the substance of Cobb's opening statement that has enchanted them, because apart from some claptrap about a fairer zoo, there is none. The secret must lie in his performance technique, then.

He squints at the creature as it caresses its genitals and combs its hands through its tail again. Is Nicholas Cobb using his sexual prowess to charm the audience? Is he producing some sort of pheromone down there?

There's only one way to find out.

Careful not to dislodge the radio mic attached to his horn, Ebenezer expels the excess mucus from his nasal passage and snorts up a lungful of air.

He can smell it at once, the sensual aroma of orange-bellied ground squirrel. Of course, it's not as alluring as the scent of a she-rhinoceros on heat. But even so, it does seem to be producing a rather intoxicating rush. Is the perfume's top note subsiding? Ebenezer is sure that it must be, because he can detect a deeper, more resonant chord: a bass note that lingers in the senses, promising a moment's relief from the pressures of being P Ex, a moment of pure pleasure. He snorts. Poor Ebenezer Bull. He might not have grasped that the scent has been refined to stimulate the melanocortin receptors in the brain, but he can sense that something in between his hind legs is starting to stir.

He tries to suppress his desire, tries to concentrate on the facts and figures he has memorised. There are some urges, though, that not even a rhinoceros in its prime is strong enough to resist.

He grunts as his engorged organ slops out of its protective sheath.

Did Dale FitzClarence just dart a sidelong glance at him? Suspecting he might have a rival for the squirrel's affections, Ebenezer lifts up his hind leg, lets the otter get a good look at his impressive member. He is tempted to snort, 'Stiff competition, eh, Dale?' But he restrains himself. He has no insecurities about his rhinoceroshood. Indeed, he is more than capable of pleasuring an orange-bellied ground squirrel – there can be no doubt about that. Who cares that the relationship is bound to end in tears? He must have this seductive little rodent. He must possess it.

But Nicholas Cobb has not finished his opening statement. 'How many times have these clapped-out Orders made the same old promises and broken them as soon as the scent-marking contest is over?'

Ebenezer can stand it no more. He must ingratiate himself with the squirrel. He says, 'I agree with Nick.'

11

I must admit I had a rather disconcerting experience this evening. Indeed, I am still a little distressed.

You see, I used to like this time of night; the stillness, the silence. I used to like burning the midnight oil at the Dower House – catching up on correspondence as the zoological gardens slept. But since that thing in November...

But since those disobedient dogs turned against me and stabbed me in the back, I no longer receive quite the same number of pigeons that I used to. Oh, one still gets reminders to settle one's cage tributes on time, of course. One still gets bills. I must confess, though, I don't have any pressing correspondence to attend to. And so this time of night has ceased to be magical. In fact, it has become something that needs to be endured.

More often than not I just sit here, plumped up in this nest of broken branches like an old cushion coming apart at the seams. I sit and stare out through the bars. And so it was evening. Make no mistake: I scoured this cul-de-sac of cages. I studied the blossoms of that magnolia tree caught in the moonlight; I squinted at those overgrown geraniums spilling out of their stone urns. Why? Well, I dare say I must have been searching for a sign that I had not been forgotten. You see, I could have sworn I had a speaking engagement, but I couldn't make out a single member of the audience. No, not so much as a common stoat. Not one.

I must admit I found the experience most upsetting. Until I peered into the crimson-tinted darkness of the rhododendrons and spotted a red panda staring back at me. I turned to the magnolia tree and noticed a pale-faced primate emerging out of its blooms. Oh, and look! There's a salamander shaped just like a clump of moss on that paving stone over there. I haven't been forgotten, then, have I? Let's make a start. Your questions please.

Something about Ebenezer Bull.

Did I not make it clear? I've no desire to discuss some bad-tempered old rhino that has squandered—

What was that? What was that?

Ebenezer's all right? His heart is in the right place?

Oh, I am sure it is, but good intentions are no substitute for strong leadership. Besides, it's not as if the eradication of a little malnutrition is much of an achievement, is it, dear? Oh, I dare say the odd specimen scratching about in the Northern Pastures might be grateful, but I am afraid there isn't much hope of a return on the investment as far as the zoological gardens is concerned. Goodness me, it's astonishing, isn't it? Considering that Ebenezer once had a reputation as a prudent custodian of our groats. Then again, the Order of Herbivores has never been able to resist the temptation to spend, spend, spend. Never mind malnutrition and mange. There's no point in having good intentions if the coffers are depleted. There is not.

Of course, this is something that the Scriptures teach us. Consider the Parable of the Good Goat—

What was that, dear?

Well, I'm sure the other members of the audience remember it. The one about the little lamb who went down from Jerusalem to Jericho and fell among wolves – wicked wolves who stripped him of his prime cuts and wounded him. Well, the goat who bathed his wounds had more than good intentions: it also had hard cash.

But I digress.

Forget about Ebenezer Bull. Forget about his short stint as P Ex. One cannot hope to be celebrated if all one does is muddle along responding to events; a Prize Exhibit must set the agenda, dear. Of course, that's something I understood at the outset. Indeed, I recall the morning I arrived at the Dower House and conjured up the spirit of Saint Francis - the morning I became P Ex - I had one deliberate intent: to make Old Hesper House and Zoological Gardens Ltd profitable again. Oh, no doubt some specimens have forgotten the plight we were in when I took over the helm, but I shall never forget it. You see, this great landed estate, this stately pile - Old Hesper House, the outbuildings, the grounds - this old menagerie, this maze of bars, this other Africa, demi-Congo, this fortress built against extinction at the hand of man, this happy band of beasts, this teeming womb of Carnivores, this breast, this teat, this zoo had been reduced – I rasp pronouncing it – to little more than a second-rate tourist attraction: a miserable collection of creatures dependent on handouts in order to make ends meet.

I put an end to all that. I turned these gardens into an institution that encourages self-reliant specimens; I rose to the challenge and got the job done. Oh, and I didn't do a U-turn when the going got tough. I did not. I said, 'U-turn if you want to; the birdy's not for turning.'

Ebenezer Bull has done nothing to compare to this. Nothing. Neither has he managed to master the iambic pentameter. Then again, he's never been much of an orator, has he? Just consider his performance at the Ape House last night. I got the impression he spent most of the evening ingratiating himself with that orange-bellied thing. Goodness me, I cannot remember the last time I heard something so sycophantic on the wireless.

What was that? What wireless?

Oh, dear. I see someone hasn't been quite so attentive as one might have hoped. I'm sure I mentioned that I had a second-hand transistor radio stashed in this nest. Here it is, see, hidden under the corpse of a cottontail rabbit that I shall be dismembering later if I get peckish. How times have changed! When I was a fledgling our wireless was too big to squeeze into our cage in the Parade, let alone conceal in a nest. Father had to keep it in the boathouse. Dear me, I shall never forget the afternoon it arrived. Oh, it was so exciting! I remember I scuttled down the cobbled path that leads to the lake-shore as fast as I could. Of course, it soon became part of our routine, that second-hand wireless set. When we'd attended to our obligations to the deceased, we'd turn it on and tune into a discussion programme or a debate. Father used to be so disappointed if he couldn't get a signal. In fact, I seem to recall on one occasion he—

Yes? Is there a problem, dear? Well, what is it, then? Come on, I am listening.

The same old song? I am not sure I understand. What on earth... ? Oh, I see. The same old song in praise of Father. I did have a mother, didn't I?

What a silly question! Of course I did. Mother was marvellous, marvellous. But Father and I used to discuss things. We'd listen to a programme and thrash out the issues that had been debated. Oh, I must admit we didn't always agree with each other. But that didn't matter. He taught me to argue; he taught me to stand up for my beliefs.

What was that, dear?

Not another question about Mother. Did she – what? Did she take part in those discussions?

No, Mother didn't disturb us at the boathouse. Oh, I suppose there might have been the odd occasion, but as a rule, she spent her afternoons cooped up in the Parade, tending the nest. I must admit that didn't stop us having the occasional heated discussion, though. There's nothing dysfunctional about that. There is not. I'm sure all fledglings go through a rebellious phase, and of course, I soon came to realise that other birds had more creature comforts than I did. You see, I'd heard that some specimens had tropical hardwoods to perch on. Intricate bowers. I wanted those things. 'Well, we en't situated like that,' Mother used to say. I can still hear her unfortunate accent now: 'We en't situated like that.' Oh, she used to be such a drain on the spirit. One kicked against it – of course one did. One argued, one rebelled. And not just against Mother; I remember one evening Father and I had the most terrible quarrel too.

What was that about?

Oh, I don't suppose I'll be able to recall the details, dear. Goodness me, it's such a long time ago. I do seem to recollect that I'd spent the afternoon in the boathouse, though. That's right, I'd just classified some primate that had been brought in. Who knows? Perhaps it might even have been that large, ape-like creature I mentioned earlier. I cannot be sure. But even so, there's one thing I'm quite certain about: I remember standing on the boat slip and staring up at a house martin returning to its roost. It's extraordinary, isn't it? That such an insignificant detail should end up embedded in one's mind, just like a piece of shrapnel. For some reason, though, I shall never forget gazing at that house martin as Father turned to me and sent me home to tell Mother that he'd be late for dinner. Oh, he gave me such strict instructions. Go straight back to the Parade. Don't do this. Don't do that. But I'm afraid I had other plans. I got into so much trouble. Goodness me, such a terrible argument.

You see, there are some creatures in these gardens that have reverted to their natural state, some creatures that decent, upright specimens never discuss...

But I have said too much.

12

OLD HESPER HOUSE ᴀɴᴅ ZOOLOGICAL GARDENS

The Bog-land Enclosures

LAPPET-FACED (or NUBIAN) VULTURE

Torgos Tracheliotus

This species is adapted to a diet of carrion. In its natural habitat, an individual can range several hundred miles in search of a meal. Once it has spotted a carcass, it asserts its dominance over other scavengers before settling down to dine. Despite a natural preference for carrion, in times of hardship, it hunts rodents and other small mammals. In most instances, the female of the species is larger and more aggressive than the male.

CAUTION: THESE BIRDS PECK

She can tell it must be late because the moon is rising. There it is, edging up over the ridge of the escarpment: a bomber's moon trailing a tattered camouflage of cloud. Is Father still in the boathouse sprinkling cedar-scented embalming oil on the mortal remains of some man? She hopes so. But as she scuttles around the corner of the Marsupial House into the Parade, little Bel-imperia Pinch is sure she can make out the familiar sight of his hunch-shouldered silhouette in the distance.

She pauses to take in the terraces of damp little cages on either side of the Parade: the mean-looking tenements pressed up against each other, the crumbling red-bricks and the rusting iron bars. Her gaze settles on the boarded-up cage of a couple of polecats that have fallen on hard times. Have the irresponsible creatures been evicted? She cannot be sure. She turns her attention to a barricade of sandbags stacked up outside the cramped lodgings of a long-tailed pangolin. Is the creature concerned that one of mankind's iron birds is going to drop a bomb on its blocked gutters and its open drains? No doubt she should be grateful her father decided to invest in a cage at the other end of the Parade, a respectable distance from such squalor. There it is, on the corner, in between a lime tree and a greenhouse-like structure containing a three-toed sloth. Careful not to be seen, she creeps across the cobblestones, comes to a cautious standstill behind another barricade of sandbags. She needs a moment to gather her thoughts before she steps into the gaslight and scuttles up to the semi-circle of cast-iron bars that she calls home. She should have been here an hour ago. Dinner is almost over.

'Delicious, darling.' Her father is perched on the boulder that doubles as their dining table. He is eating. 'I cannot remember the last time I had such a succulent mouse.'

'I'd as leave have a dish o' dead mice as an expensive cut o' meat.' Her mother, Bessie: a big-breasted bird, as stout as a Michaelmas goose.

'I agree.'

'Then have the last one, dear.'

'Oh, I think not, Bessie. Temperance in all things. It's a sin to overindulge.'

'That may be so, but it's daft to let a good mouse go to waste.'

'*Eat so much as is sufficient for thee lest thou be—*'

'Don't give me that cat-lap. Just eat the friggin' mouse!'

Is Father trembling? She should not be surprised: it's quite clear who rules the roost.

'Go on, dear,' her mother adds, all sweetness and guile. 'He's longing to be gobbled up, he is.'

'Perhaps just this once, then.' The gas lamp hanging above the boulder sputters as he lunges at the last mouse in the dish: a plump-looking specimen that appears to have lost its tail. He lifts his head and gulps. Is that a mouse-shaped bulge his daughter can see sliding down his long neck?

'Taste all right, does he? None too fresh I hope. He didn't have as long as them others to go reasty.'

'No, no, it's delicious, darling. Just beginning to turn.' He seizes a napkin-shaped scrap of brown paper, dabs his beak. 'You're a good bird, Bessie,' he says, placing his napkin back on the mosses and lichens that cling to the boulder. 'You're a godsend.'

Did he just nudge her on the thigh?

'Oh, give over, Silas.' Unable to conceal her pride, Bessie pushes out her big breast, plumps up her plumage. The lamplight catches her chipped beak, the battle scars on her sagging lappets.

'I don't know where I'd be without you, darling.'

'I just do what I can to make ends meet, that's all. Shame that good-for-nowt daughter o' ours weren't here to appreciate it. Bit o' a nowter she is.'

Bel-imperia Pinch has heard enough. 'I am NOT a nowter,' she says, stepping into the pale square of gaslight spilling out of their neighbour's greenhouse.

Perhaps she should have held her tongue; she can tell from her father's tone that he is displeased: 'I'll be the judge of that – and the jury. Your poor mother has worked her talons to the bone to put a nutritious meal on this boulder. The least you could do is turn up in time to eat it. Now, get in this cage this instant.'

'Of course, Father.' She squeezes through a gap in the semicircle of bars and scuttles across the cage to an offcut of patterned linoleum that has been rolled out on the ground like a rug.

Home.

She curls up the commissure of her beak in disgust as she glances around the cage: the patches of rust on the cast-iron bars that soar out of the soil and curve up overhead into an ominous clump of metal; the peeling oil paint on the huge mural that dominates the cage, its garish depiction of a Serengeti sunset providing a constant backdrop to her torment. Of course, her mother delights in reminding her that she's devoted to keeping the place spotless: as bright as a new pin. But Bel-imperia doubts this can be a time-consuming exercise; after all, compared to some of the other enclosures in the zoological gardens, their lodgings are bare: no branches to perch on – no trees at all other than the unconvincing acacia in the mural. Just an old tin bath tub and a scattering of damp boulders.

'Have a gleg at her, Silas. Standin' there wi' a face like a brass pancheon. Where's she been? That's what I want to know.'

'Your mother asked you a question, chick.'

'An' I'll give her a clout if she tells me fibs. She's a bigger liar than Tom Pepper she is.'

Bel-imperia ignores her mother: 'I called in at the pigeon cotes, Father.'

'The pigeon cotes?'

'Yes, that's right.' She remembers standing beside him on the boat slip as he stared up at the spent rainclouds. 'I'm sure I mentioned that I needed to speak to the Pigeon Master General. Some lost letters have turned up. I must admit I'd rather hoped one of them might be from the Cloisters.'

'And was it, chick?'

'Don't be daft, Silas. She might talk like she cut her beak on a brocken bottle, but she's just a common scavenger. Them black-capped owls at the Cloisters don't give scholarships to likes o' her.'

'You're quite sure about that, are you, Mother?'

'As sure as eggs is eggs.'

'Well, that's strange, because according to the Pigeon Master General, a second-class specimen delivered a letter here this afternoon. Of course, he couldn't confirm that it was from the Cloisters, but—'

'Is this true, Bessie? Did you receive a pigeon while we were at the boathouse?'

'Nah, I never got nowt.'

'I'm surprised to hear that, Mother. Because the Pigeon Master General introduced me to the Columbine in question. His name is Herbert.'

Bel-imperia can tell that her mother is getting into a fluster: her plumage is all at sixes and sevens.

'Ooh, I can feel one o' me turns coming on. I'm all o' a lillilow like an 'ot egg pie.'

'Well, that's a coincidence, because when he got back to the pigeon cotes, Herbert was shaking too. He said some big bird had pinned him down on a scrap of linoleum. He said the specimen gave him a sharp peck when it snatched the letter attached to his leg.'

'Is this true, Bessie?'

She is bustling about on the boulder, clearing up the dishes. 'I clean forgot. Summats did turn up i' the second post. Summats addressed to me. A note from them fummards been strugglin' to make ends meet.'

'Fummards? Father, help me, please.'

'She means those polecats that have fallen on hard times.'

'A note thankin' me for that dead frog I sent 'em. Ever so polite it were.'

'Where is it, then, Mother?'

'The frog?'

'The note.'

'Oh, I'm that fruggard I could pull out all me plumage.' She drops the last dish onto the pile, collapses onto the boulder. She sighs. Is this a defeated bird? Bel-imperia cannot be sure. But she is quite certain she can detect a look of disappointment in her mother's eyes. 'What did we do to be burdened wi' a brat like this, Silas?'

'I don't know, darling.'

'I think she's callin' her mam a liar.'

'You are a—'

'Silence, chick!'

'But she is a—'

'Silence, I said.' He bares his broad wings. He crouches, as if to leap into the air. Is he threatening to give her a clip across the lappets? 'Not another word – is that understood?'

Bel-imperia's instinct is to complete her sentence, to call her mother a liar, but instinct is the sign of an uncivilised animal. Besides, her desire for her father's love and approval is too strong. No use reminding herself that he has no love to give; she needs it all the same. She hangs her head and she hates herself for hanging her head. She stares at the gaudy pattern on the linoleum. In the distance, she can hear a nightingale singing: something about a certain night, something about magic in the air.

He closes his wings, settles back down on the boulder.

Her mother pipes up: 'Thou should ha' given her a good clout, Silas. Thou should ha' putten her shoulder blade out o' joint. She deserves it. Turnin' up 'ere this time o' night like summats the cat brought in.'

'There aren't any cats in the Parade, Mother.'

'That's enough, Bel-imperia.' He turns to his beloved Bessie. 'In all fairness, darling, I do seem to recall she did mention something about dropping in at the pigeon cotes. I suppose it must have slipped my mind. But even so, she should apologise for speaking to you like that. Come on, chick, say sorry to your mother.'

It is not in Bel-imperia's nature to apologise; it goes against the grain. 'Forgive me, Father' is the most she can manage. 'I had no intention of casting aspersions on Mother's spotless character.'

She is astonished he cannot hear the contempt in her tone.

'Right. Let's put this little misunderstanding behind us, then, shall we? Now, it's no short distance to the pigeon cotes. You must have worked up quite an appetite, chick.'

'I have rather, yes.' Her stomach has been gurgling all evening. She is ravenous.

'Well, why don't you hop up here and tuck into some supper, then?'

She clambers up onto the boulder, perches in between her parents. But the dinner plate balanced on the tablecloth of mosses and lichens is bare.

'Don't look at me daggers, madam. I called in at the cold store an' bought a big bag o' mice this morning. Thou should ha' see'd 'em. Plump little things. Nice bit o' meat on their bones.'

Bel-imperia might not have eaten since breakfast, but she has no intention of begging. She stares at the bone china dinner plate: the cracks in the glazing, the chip on the rim.

'Here's the bag the rascals came in.'

She steals a glance at the brown paper bag as her mother turns it upside down and shakes out some rodent droppings.

'Nowt but mouse charmings, see. 'Cos I gave all their meat to him.'

She darts a resentful glare at her father.

'Don't scowl at your da. He has a stiff row to hoe, standing up for his principles from dawn 'til darklins. Your need is greater than ours, isn't it, Silas?'

'I dare say it is.'

'But thou needn't worrit, madam. I'm sure I can find some belly-timber to bolster up a scrap o' a thing like thee.'

Bel-imperia is glad to hear it: she is starving. Her mother staggers up to the dinner plate, snatches a gulp of air.

'Don't forget to say grace, chick.'

She hangs her head and stares at the cracked glazing on her dinner plate. 'For what we are about to receive… '

'Go on.'

'But isn't it a bit early to say grace, Father? After all, I don't know what I'm going to receive yet, do I?'

Her mother belches. 'Beg pardon, pig in garden.'

'I'm sure you'll find out soon enough.'

He is right. She can hear the contents of her mother's gizzard churning. It cannot be long, then, until dinner is served.

'You're lucky to have such a marvellous mother, chick. Whatever's on the menu this evening is bound to be delicious.'

It had better be. She is in no mood for another plate of marinated cockroaches. She needs something more substantial: a generous portion of giblets perhaps, or, better still, a succulent rabbit. Her mother belches again. Is there a decent helping of giblets in that gizzard? Is there a cottontail rabbit sloshing around in the maelstrom of those digestive juices? Little Bel-imperia Pinch cannot stand the suspense.

Bessie lets out a deep groan, disgorges the contents of her stomach onto her daughter's plate.

Is this it, then? Is this dinner?

Bel-imperia stares in disgust at the steaming mound of mouse tails piled up in front of her, like so much spaghetti. 'Not again, Mother. Isn't it about time I had rabbit?'

'I didn't have enough coupons to get a rabbit.' She snatches a brown paper napkin, prises one last mouse tail off the commissure of her beak and drops it onto her daughter's plate. 'Or a prickly 'otchin.'

'Well, what about a brace of ptarmigan, then?'

'Ptarmigan? Hark at her. She's forgotten she's a common scavenger. She thinks she's some better-ma-sort o' bird – some endangered little thing, too hoity-toity to eat her mam's Mouse Tail Tangle. She should be grateful for what's putten on her plate, shouldn't she, Silas?'

'Yes, she should.'

But Bel-imperia is not in the least bit grateful. She inserts the tip of a talon into the moist cluster of mouse tails, pulls one out and inspects it. Shockingly, a small nugget of the rodent's rear end is still attached. Suppressing an urge to retch, she drapes the offending mouse tail over the edge of her dinner plate and considers her options. For some reason, her mind turns to the boathouse: the stench of East Indian spices and the scent of sulphur dioxide, the cast-iron buckets and the canisters of embalming fluid. She sighs. It isn't just the prospect of a career in Embalming, Obsequies and other Rites of Passage that she longs to escape from; it's also meals like this. She gives the mound of mouse tails an impatient prod. Enough is enough. She needs to find out if the letter her mother received came from the Cloisters or from some polecats that have fallen on hard times. She needs to discover the truth.

'Come on, chick. Tuck in.'

She has an idea. She cooks up a plan.

'I haven't got a napkin, Father.'

'Bessie?'

Her mother grabs the brown paper bag that the mice came in. 'Here, use this.'

Perfect.

In the adjacent cage, a twig snaps. Bel-imperia seizes the moment, snatches some mouse tails, drops them into the paper bag.

'Looks like him next door is up to no good,' her mother remarks.

'I expect he's just climbing down to his latrine, darling. It must be a fortnight since the poor chap last relieved himself.'

She darts a glance through the cast-iron bars, peers into their neighbour's greenhouse: a dilapidated building containing some ancient Suriname palm. Its occupant, the most decrepit-looking three-toed sloth imaginable, gazes back at her through a broken pane of glass. There's a long pause before he unlatches a limb from his tree: lethargic, ponderous. 'Perhaps if he emptied his bowels more often he might be lighter on his feet.'

'Shurrup. Us don't want to offend the neighbours.'

'Oh, he can't hear us, Mother. He's as deaf as a post – I can prove it.' She squawks good evening at the sloth, and as soon as her parents turn to look at the creature, drops another clump of mouse tails into her paper bag. 'Of course,' she adds, pretending to gulp down a tail, 'it's a shame he can't hear us. He needs a good talking-to. I mean, he's bone idle, isn't he, Father?'

'I'm afraid so.'

'Goodness me, I think he must be exhausted. Just look at him.' She pops some more mouse tails into the bag. 'I don't know why he bothers clambering down from that stupid tree. Why doesn't he just do his business up in the branches and save himself the effort?'

'I should imagine he's incapable of controlling his primitive instincts, chick. You see, sloths use a communal latrine in order to increase their chances of meeting a member of the opposite sex.'

She glares in horror at the sloth's latrine: the dried-up turds, the dung flies. 'It doesn't strike me as the most romantic spot for an intimate liaison.'

'Never mind him next door. Finish up them mouse tails, madam.'

Bel-imperia disentangles the last three tails on her plate.

There is a moment's silence. She can sense that her parents are looking at her. She isn't going to have to eat one, is she?

'I had a gleg at the *Rodent* afore dinner,' her mother says, making conversation. 'I see there be another scandal at the macaque compound.'

'Good gracious me, it isn't in *The Evening Rodent*, is it?'

Into the bag.

'It is that. An' I'm main troubled to think what's these gardens are a-coming to. That trollops should ha' read the Commandments afore tartin' herself up like a drape goose and poutin' at the langurs.'

'Yes, she should.' He tells Bessie about his experience in the macaque compound: the brazen harlot that has given birth to an abomination, the joke some macaque made about the infant's father coming and going. 'I didn't realise the strumpet had got herself into the *Rodent*,' he adds as his daughter drops the last mouse tail into the paper bag. 'I think I'll table a motion at Elders this evening. I'm sure I can persuade the Committee to issue a summons.'

'Never mind no summons. Thou should tell them Elders to get thee another chain. I gave that old one a spit an' polish this mornin', but it's fallin' to bits I'm telling thee. Table a motion about that.'

Her mother is referring to the chain of office that he takes such pride in draping on his pectorals before he attends meetings of the Elders. He seems to believe it adds a certain gravitas to his raptorial persona, but his daughter is less than convinced. Indeed, she once heard a rumour that there are identical chains hanging above the porcelain thrones in the Ladies' Convenience. Is it true? Do members of the general public dangle replicas of her father's chain of office over their latrines? She dismisses the thought, turns her attention to the brown paper bag beside her. Time to set into motion the second phase of her plan. Of course, she is under no delusions: she doubts she'll be able to slip out unseen. But even so, as long as she adopts a confident attitude, she's sure she'll be able to convince her father that her intentions are irreproachable. She steals a glance at him. He's still rambling on about summoning some she-macaque to appear before the Elders. This is the moment, then. Deep breath.

'May I have permission to leave the boulder, please, Father?'

He inspects her dinner plate. 'Yes, I suppose so. Now, where was I? That's right, the abomination… '

Bel-imperia snatches the paper bag, hops down onto the linoleum. No reaction from her parents. So far so good. Freedom is near – a short scuttle across the soil, nothing more. But just as she is approaching the onion-shaped gap in the bars of their cage, her mother lets out a loud squawk.

'Oi! Where do you think you're goin', madam?'

She'd been expecting this; she is prepared. 'Oh, I'm just popping out for a moment, Mother. I shan't be long.'

'Popping out?' Her father sounds indignant.

'Yes, Father. You see, while I was dining I found myself contemplating that passage in the Scriptures. You know, *And be ye kind one to another.* And I remembered a small act of compassion I'd been meaning to perform. Oh, I must admit it's an inconvenience – I'd been looking forward to spending a quiet evening at home – but I do feel it's essential to atone for one's sins before matins, don't you? I'll be back in half an hour.'

Has that taken care of the matter? She hopes so. No time to lose. She scutters across to the gap in the bars, but behind her she can hear the sound of something large and lumpen hurtling through the air.

Her mother crashes to the ground, blocking her escape. 'Thou should ha' clipped her wings when she were a weenun, Silas. She's as wick as an eel.'

'I'm nothing of the sort, Mother. Now, if you'll excuse me, I'm just going to help the poor—'

'Thou don't give two squawks for the poor.' Is she bulking up her plumage? Is she spoiling for a fight? 'What's in that paper bag?'

'Nothing much – just some scraps left over from dinner.'

'Scraps?' Her mother sounds outraged. 'Your daughter hasn't eaten her Mouse Tail Tangle, Silas.'

Bel-imperia glances over her scapulars, attempts to appeal to her father's better judgement. 'It's more blessed to give than to receive, isn't it?'

He looks like he is thinking about it. 'She's right, Bessie,' he says at last. 'If she's chosen to help those less fortunate than herself, it would be a sin for us to frustrate her efforts. Stand aside, darling. Let her pass.'

'You heard him, Mother.'

But Bessie seems reluctant to budge. 'Who's she goin' to give 'em to? That's what I want to know.'

'Who am I going to give them to?' Some instinct is telling her to deflect the question, but the temptation to assert her dominance is too strong. 'Who am I going to give them to? Oh, just some polecats that have fallen on hard times, that's all.'

Is that panic she can see in her mother's bulging eyes? 'You en't callin' in on them fummards.'

Bel-imperia leans closer, hisses into her mother's auricular feathers: 'Yes, I am. But don't worry, Mother. I'll remember to thank them for sending you such a polite letter this afternoon.'

She should never have spoken.

Her mother lunges at the paper bag and snatches it. 'No point. Them fummards have gone out gallivantin'. I'll take these round i' the morn.'

'Gallivanting?'

'They've gone to a dance.'

She glares at her mother in disbelief. 'The stupid creatures have squandered all their groats. Their cage has been boarded up. What have they got to dance about?'

'I told them to go. Thought it might cheer 'em up a bit.'

She's sure her mother is lying. 'Where is this dance, then? In the Majestic Flamingo Palace I suppose.'

'Nah, i' the Hunting Wood.'

She means the trees on the escarpment. She means the last acres of the medieval hunting reserve that once used to dominate the estate. Bel-imperia glances at her father. He looks a little on edge. Is his plumage bristling?

Her mother says, 'Them birds o' paradise are puttin' on a spectacle.'

'You mean a spectacular?'

'I know what I mean. That six-plumed bod has set up some sort of dance floor in a glade.'

'A six-plumed bird of paradise is performing?'

'So I been told.'

'Even better.' She snatches the bag back from her mother. 'I'll take these mouse tails into the woods and meet the polecats there. I'm sure they'll be grateful for something to nibble on during the performance.'

'Silas?'

Unable to disguise her excitement at the thought of an evening out, Bel-imperia gives her primaries a good shake. She rouses. It is just so thrilling. Who knows? Perhaps a ribbon-tailed astrapia might even be performing. She hopes so. Its iridescent tail feathers are said to be sensational. 'Now, if you'll excuse me, Mother... '

'Don't let her near that gap in the bars, Bess.'

'Nah, o' course not, dear.'

He swoops down from the boulder, touches down on the damp

soil beside his darling Bessie. 'Dancing like heathen in the Hunting Wood?'

'No, not like heathen, Father.'

'Listening to all that screeching and gibbering?'

'It's not screeching and gibbering, it's music.'

'It en't proper, is it, Silas? Shammockin' about in the trees.'

'No, it's not. Good gracious me, do you think I don't know what goes on in the bushes? Those performances are courtship rituals, Bel-imperia.'

'She'll end up with her behind on a muck heap.'

'No, I won't. Oh, please, Father. I'm sure lots of other little animals are going.'

He turns to her and subjects her to a hard stare. 'Never do something just because other animals do it. Never follow the herd.' She is going to remember this moment. She is going to remember this lesson.

'But Father—'

'I have spoken, Bel-imperia. There's nothing more to be said on the matter.'

He snatches *The Evening Rodent* and returns to his perch on the boulder. She stares at him as he spreads the pamphlet out under his talons: Silas Pinch Esquire, the male of the species, poring over some article entitled MORTAL REMAINS. No point in attempting to convince him to change his mind. He's made it quite clear that he considers the subject closed. Besides, he's too engrossed in the *Rodent*. So that's that, then. No polecats, no dancing, no escape...

Her mother lunges at the bag of mouse tails. 'Now then, let's see what we got here. Just as I thought. Have a gleg at this, Silas.'

'I'm reading, Bess.'

'She hasn't touched her Tangle. Not a single one.' She latches her chipped beak onto her daughter's right lappet, drags her back up onto the boulder.

Here she is again, then, little Bel-imperia Pinch, sitting between her parents, staring at the same chipped dinner plate.

'You're going to eat this meal, madam.'

'I'm going to do no such thing.'

Bessie tips the mouse tails out of the bag. No longer a tangle, the meal has congealed into a solid lump of gristle and mouse hair.

'It's inedible, Mother.'

'Nowt that a splash o' salad dressing won't mend.' The mouse tails relax into a tangle as she tosses them in a gob of spittle. 'There,' she adds, pushing the plate across the tablecloth of mosses and lichens. 'Eat up your orts.'

In the distance, the sound of a door squeaking on an unoiled hinge. Is some creature stepping out of the Marsupial House? Bel-imperia turns her attention to the Parade: the barricades of sandbags, the moonlight on the cobblestones, the terraced cages receding into the distance. There's the Marsupial House. She recognises its imposing door. Is that a possum chattering to – what? It looks like an adolescent tree-kangaroo or something. There is a ripple of laughter. 'Have a nice time, dear,' a mother is calling. Other animals, other parents.

'Eat up them mouse tails, I said.'

Poor little Bel-imperia Pinch. She can feel it rising up in her: the anger, the aggression. Is she conscious that these are primitive emotions? Perhaps. But she has no inclination to rein them in. Much better to let the savage beast out of its cage.

'I'm not touching the disgusting things,' she squawks, pushing the plate of mouse tails across the boulder to her mother. 'I refuse to be brought up on a diet of second-rate rodent parts. I demand something more nutritious. I need muscles and tendons; I need guts and livers.'

'Well, we en't situated like that, are we, Silas?'

He glances up from *The Evening Rodent*. 'You can spare us the temper tantrum, chick.'

'I am not a chick and I refuse to be treated like one. Oh, Father: I've seen things that no fledgling should see: I've seen a naked man; I've seen a limp appendage. Who cares about experiencing a post-juvenile moult? I'm almost an adult, and if I choose to go to a dance this evening I shall go to one, and that's that.'

Intoxicated on her anger, she swooshes out her wings. But she has drunk too deep on the emotion. Her head is spinning. Has she got the presence of mind to leap off the boulder and soar through the gap in the bars? Her instincts are telling her to do it, but something is holding her back. She appraises her father: his sinuous neck, his sharp beak. She hates to admit it, but she couldn't care less about going to some dance; she'd much rather have his respect and admiration.

He closes *The Evening Rodent*: deliberate, precise. He turns to her. 'Sit down, chick.'

Despite her unprecedented outburst, there seems to be no anger in his gaze. In fact, she cannot remember the last time he looked so calm, so collected. But his stillness is unnerving. She sits.

'Now, listen carefully, because I'm only going to say this once. And when I've finished we'll never mention the subject again. Do you understand?'

'I suppose so.'

'Birds of paradise are improper. There can be no doubt about that. But the thing that concerns me above all is the location that's been chosen for the performance. You see, the Hunting Wood is wild – wilder than the Serengeti. It's the last refuge for exhibits that have been cast out of their cages: creatures that have no respect for the Commandments, savages that have reverted to their natural state. That's why I refuse to let you attend this dance.'

She subjects him to an incredulous stare. 'And what sort of savages are those, Father? Pheasants? Rabbits? No, don't tell me – let me guess: some toothless old bear?'

Her mother stands up and pushes out her breast. 'Sit down and read the *Rodent*, Silas. Leave this to me.'

'No, it's all right, Bessie. I'm quite capable of—'

'Leave the friggin' brat to me, I said.' It sounds like she has decided to assert her dominance again. She turns to her daughter. 'Now then, listen here, madam. There's summats much more fearsome than a bear in them woods, an' it be strange and queer.'

'What's that, then, Mother? Some dinosaur?'

'Nah, but it be almost as old as summats from the Jurassic; an' it have long black hair, all cotted and tangled together; an' it comes crappelin' out o' its cave in the darklins. Limpelty lobelty. Limpelty lobelty.'

'That will do, Bessie.'

'An' you know what? It snorts up smoke and deals in spells an' things.'

'I said that will do.'

She shouts at him. 'Shurrup, Silas.'

For a moment, there is an embarrassed silence. Even the nightingale in the distance seems to have stopped singing. But Bel-imperia can sense that her father is determined to stand up to the old bird, determined to articulate his thoughts. His tone is hushed, hesitant. 'You seem to know an awful lot about this creature, Bessie. Our daughter might be forgiven for assuming that you've been to its cave and—'

'I done no such thing.' She seems quite adamant. Is she telling the truth?

'And so what is it, then, Mother? This beast?'

'It's a wim wam for a mustard mill an' a catcher for a meddler – an' if you don't look out it'll catch you.'

Perhaps she can get more sense out of the male of the species. 'Does it have a Latin name, Father?'

'It's not the sort of thing that decent, upright creatures care to discuss, chick.'

'Oh, it don't speak no Latin. It just spouts a load o' old cat-lap. It's as daft as a boiled owl. It's depraved.'

'But it must have a name, Father?'

'It does. It's called That Which We Do Not Speak About.'

'That can't be its name.'

'I am afraid it is.'

'Well, why's it called that, then?'

'You've been told once, Bel-imperia, and once should be enough: That Which We Do Not Speak About we do not speak about. Now, you'll get a clip across the lappets if you bring the subject up again. Is that clear?'

She still needs his love and approval. 'Yes, Father.'

He reminds her that he has to leave for Elders, instructs her to eat her mouse tails and get some rest. 'You've got a busy day tomorrow.'

'Have I?'

He tells her about some article he's read in *The Evening Rodent*. 'The Prize Exhibit is about to issue instructions for that chap in the boathouse to be embalmed. I shall require your assistance, chick.'

'Oh, but I won't have time. I've got other plans.'

'Other plans?'

She needs to call in on the polecats, perhaps speak to the Pigeon Master General again. She needs to find out if she has been sent a letter. But she cannot tell him that. 'I must admit I'd rather not spend so much time at the boathouse at all. To be honest, I'm starting to get a bit tired of the place.' There. She has said it.

'Tired of the boathouse?' He looks shocked. He turns his head to one side, coughs up a polite pellet of mouse hair: the indigestible remains of his meal. 'Impossible.'

'She could spend her afternoons here,' her mother suggests. 'She could help her mam tend the nest.'

'No, Bessie, she needs to learn the ropes if she's going to succeed in the profession.'

'Oh, but I'm not interested in a career in embalming, Father. What a waste of a life! Washing dead warthogs, scraping dung out of the hooves of Herbivores. Goodness me, no. I've been put in these gardens to do something much more important, I am sure I have. In fact—'

It comes out of the blue, the clip across the lappets. One moment he is sitting beside her on the boulder, the next he is hurtling through the air, legs outstretched, talons bared. The pain is sharp, agonising. He pins her down on the tablecloth of mosses and lichens. The dinner plate crashes to the ground.

'Good gracious me, I've never been so insulted.'

'Let me go… '

'Your behaviour this evening has been a disgrace. I've a good mind to clip your wings.'

'Just do it, Silas.'

'One more word out of her and I shall.'

'Clipping's cruel, Father.'

'No, it en't. Didn't do me no harm, did it, dear?'

'Oh, Mother, why don't you just—'

'One more word, Bel-imperia. I mean it. One more word.'

There is a word she's tempted to use – or to be precise, two words: the verb requires a preposition. But she's not quite convinced she understands its meaning. She's never heard her father use it, or her mother, come to that. Is it part of their lexicon? She cannot be sure. Yet even so, she has a suspicion that under the circumstances it might be appropriate. She learned it from the slender mongoose that sometimes sits behind her at matins. Indeed, she can remember hearing the creature muttering it under his breath after she'd reprimanded him for giggling at the Commandments. She can also remember his companion calling him a foul-mouthed mustelid. No doubt, it must be an insulting turn of phrase, then. She takes a deep breath. Has she got the courage to utter it? Perhaps. Is she going to utter it? No, of course not. It's not in her nature; she isn't that sort of bird. Besides, bad language is never going to earn his respect and admiration. Or his love. And so she just stares in silence at the spilt mouse tails and the shards of broken china until he decides to mete out her punishment.

```
┌─────────────────────────────────────────────┐
│                                               │
│  OLD HESPER HOUSE ᴀɴᴅ ZOOLOGICAL GARDENS     │
│                                               │
│          The Cages of Caer Lud                │
│                                               │
│            THE APE HOUSE                       │
│                                               │
│  Grade I Listed Cage, Enclosure or Other     │
│         Estate Building.                       │
│          (Completed 1697)                      │
│                                               │
└─────────────────────────────────────────────┘
```

Has Ebenezer Bull lost the strength to go on? He should have lumbered out of the building as soon as he'd delivered his closing statement, but he is still standing on the purpose-built platform that has been set up beneath the stained-glass cupola: a square-lipped rhinoceros staring out across the darkened atrium as if in a trance, a battle-scarred bull, indifferent to the moonlight spilling onto his cuts and bruises through the iron dome's pale shards of glass.

He snorts, disturbing the dust that has settled on the radio mic attached to his horn. Is he alone? He glances around, takes in the devastation. The DMX cables coiled up beside the dismantled lighting rig. The discarded clipboards and the scrunched-up clumps of gaffa tape. He might not be able to see the gorillas slumbering behind their panes of glass, but he can sense that night has reclaimed the Ape House. And not before time, damn it. He is glad to be standing in the moonlight, glad to be spared the uncompromising glare of the electrics. He has no desire to be scrutinised after turning in such an uninspiring performance.

Disaster.

He remembers his engorged organ, his unnatural urge to roger little Nicholas Cobb. True, he'd managed to restrain himself from mounting a ground squirrel, but even so, his desire for carnal knowledge of the creature's orange underparts had compromised his performance, making him reluctant to turn against the thing and challenge its cloud-cuckoo-land concept of a fairer zoological gardens. It had also compromised his self-confidence. Did the audience notice he had a hard-on? Is that the reason he became a target for their indignation? He remembers the armadillo that asked him to account for all the groats he had spent. He remembers the pipistrelle that cornered him and...

Disaster.

Fuck it.

Fucking disaster. Fuck.

He snatches a quick breath, struggles to calm down.

He needs to distract himself from the thought of his performance. He needs to concentrate his mind on something else. Time to tune into the sounds of the night, then. Normal sounds. Soothing sounds. Is that an orang-utan, snoring? Is that the chimpanzee that presided over the Q&A clambering up to his mezzanine-level sleeping platform? Ebenezer is sure that it must be. He recognises the idiosyncratic thump of the quizmaster's leaps and bounds, the sing-song of his banter. It sounds like he's attempting to seduce one of the muscular males that dismantled the lighting rig...

Oh. He must have succeeded. He can hear them groaning, the chimpanzees. He can hear the springs of their sleeping platform squeaking.

Suppressing an urge to remind them of the Commandments, Ebenezer attempts to convince himself that he's an open-minded rhinoceros. True, he might not have managed to put in a single appearance at the Hall of Exhibits on the 14-or-so occasions that its members debated buggery. True, he might not have got round to casting a single potsherd. But he should hate to be dismissed as less progressive than Dale Fitz-Fucking-Clarence. And so he listens to the groaning and squeaking in silence – not so much as a grunt of disapproval. He tolerates it.

Is he intruding? Of course not. He is the Rt Hon Ebenezer Bull, Commander-in-Chief of the Order of Herbivores and P Ex, damn it. Impossible to imagine, then, that his lugubrious presence might not be required. But even so, he's a little surprised to find himself attending a display of chimp-on-chimp action. He has no recollection of the spectacle being on his schedule. Indeed, he seems to remember his second-in-command telling him to lumber back to the Dower House as soon as he'd given his closing statement. Something about a post-mortem. But he needed a moment to gather his thoughts, a moment to patch up his pride after...

He hangs his head in shame. It had been so humiliating, his failure to placate the pipistrelle that had swooped down on him.

Disaster.

Fuck.

Nevertheless. He needs to get some sleep if he's going to resume his regal progress through the zoological gardens in the morning. His thoughts turn to the Dower House. No doubt his she-rhinoceros has turned down the corner of his four-poster bed and left him a little treat – a bunch of buffalo grass, or a sprig of bush jasmine. He glances at the door. Should he barge out into the promenades of Caer Lud and stomp home? The thought is tempting, but he is reluctant to lurch into motion. No sudden movements. Nothing to attract the attention of the black dog that has been hounding him.

He calls it his black dog: the sense of despair that renders him incapable of coming to a decision, the feeling of abject failure that feeds on his hopes and aspirations. Is it still skulking in the shadows, alert to the slightest movement? He shuts out the groans of the chimpanzees and concentrates... He is sure he can sense it, crouched in a corner of his mind, its sharp incisors glinting in the darkness as it snarls.

He hadn't expected his old companion to hound him tonight. Then again, neither had he expected some she-pipistrelle to give him a piece of her mind. He flinches at the thought of the creature's tirade. Did he manage to address her concerns? He'd done his best. He'd told her he'd been listening to members of her species. But he could have done so much better, he is sure about that. He can sense that the encounter is going to cost him dear.

He can also sense that he is no longer alone.

He scrapes a hoof across the boards and snorts, producing a delicate mist of nasal mucus that glistens in the moonlight. He cannot smell the creature that is approaching. Neither can he see it. But he can tell from the sudden chill in the air that something cold-blooded is about to make an entrance.

Can the chimpanzees sense an ominous presence too? The springs of their mezzanine-level sleeping platform have stopped squeaking.

Silence.

Ebenezer shudders.

The atmosphere reminds him of the mood that settled on the Dower House the night he glanced in the mirror on the mantelpiece and thought he'd glimpsed a ghost. It has the same threat of menace about it, the same sinister edge. It is the sort of silence that makes the hackles on a pampas cat rise for no apparent reason, the sort of silence that makes a porcupine curl up into a ball. Of course, some creatures might dismiss it as a sudden change in atmospheric pressure, or an inauspicious alignment of the planets, but not Ebenezer Bull. He understands its significance. It means that something has escaped from the Hall of Relics. Something that belongs to the late Jurassic, something that is supposed to be extinct. It means that a prehistoric reptile is approaching. It means that the Prince of Darkness is strutting into the room.

'Luce?'

Ebenezer is sure he can hear the sound of the dinosaur's sickle-shaped claws clicking on the ceramic floor tiles. He peers into the gloom, catches a glimpse of the moonlight glinting on its scales. There it is, strutting across the atrium on its hind legs, its stout, muscular tail held high in the air: an agile theropod, a feathered dromaeosaur. He can see its grasping hands, its lizard-like head. The prehistoric reptile pauses beside the gorilla enclosure and peers at its reflection in the polished glass. It parts its thin lips, inspects its impressive arsenal of incisors…

The Rt Hon Lucius Scuttleson, Second Relic of Reptilia.

It still astonishes Ebenezer that there should be specimens from the Jurassic hidden behind the locked doors of the Hall of Relics, specimens that according to some so-called authorities ought to be extinct. But there's no escaping the fact that Old Hesper House and Zoological Gardens has managed to amass a significant collection of oddities over the centuries. Indeed, the Hall of Relics is said to contain several creatures from the Cretaceous, not to mention the Triassic. From all accounts, there are representatives from the more recent past too: an atlas bear and a marsupial lion, a moa and a dodo. Is there an aquatic rhinoceros? It might be interesting to barge through the doors and have a look inside. Ebenezer dismisses the thought. He reminds himself that he is a member of the Hall of Exhibits. There are rules and regulations: the upper chamber is out of bounds.

Besides, he'll almost certainly be elevated to the Hall of Relics in due course; most ex-Prize Exhibits are granted that honour. Not his predecessor, perhaps. Not his nemesis. But even so, Ebenezer is quite confident that he'll be made First Relic of Rhinocerotoidea after another decade or so at the helm. Will he accept the role and take his seat next to the decrepit iguanodons and toothless Caspian tigers slumped on those fabled red benches? Or will he just accept the title and retire to some gracious cage behind the Small Mammal House, like the Rt Hon Bel-imperia Pinch, First Relic of Raptoria? He cannot pretend he's looking forward to making the decision, because once an animal has taken its seat in the Hall of Relics it's too late to have second thoughts: it cannot come out again unless a Prize Exhibit summons it and offers it a position on the Board of Beasts.

Ebenezer appraises the prehistoric reptile as it inspects its teeth in the glass of the gorilla enclosure.

He remembers he had been a little reluctant to summon a somethingosaurus from the Hall of Relics, reluctant to place his trust in a raptor that had been so close to his predecessor. But it had been a brilliant appointment. For there is nothing better than a cold-blooded reptile from the late Jurassic to sniff out the scent of sedition and silence a herd of conspirators. The creature is indispensable in a crisis too...

Crisis.

Ebenezer snorts. He can smell the scent of an approaching crisis. He can sense the threat of disgrace gathering on the horizon, just like his square-lipped cousins on the plains of the Serengeti can sense the first rains of the monsoon. His thoughts turn to the creature that had concerned him. The pipistrelle.

'Luce?'

The dinosaur tilts its head to one side, peers a little closer at its reflection. Has it spotted a slight imperfection? It picks a gobbet of meat out of its serrated incisors, flashes a grin at the terrified gorilla on the other side of the glass.

Here it comes, then, negotiating a circuitous route through the detritus of the debate: the upended orange crates and the cottontail rabbit droppings, the discarded trigger clamps and the tangle of cables snaking out of the audio signal processor. Here it comes, its green scales glittering like sequins as it struts past the blinking lights on the broadcasting equipment: Lucius Scuttleson, otherwise known as Lucy.

It says, 'What are we doing mooching around in here? It's done and dusted. You're wanted back at the Dower for the post-mortem.'

'No point in a post-mortem. Fucking disaster.'

'Oh, we're not down in the dumps again, are we? Come on, Ebs, chin up.'

But it is unnatural for a square-lipped rhinoceros to hold up its chin. Besides, Ebenezer is still thinking about the pipistrelle. 'I've got to get better at this communication thing, Luce.'

'But you *are* getting better at it, Ebs. You were brilliant, brilliant.' His lips part into a thin smile. 'Of course, yours truly spun it brilliantly too. Oh, it's bedlam down in spin alley, bedlam. Not just the usual collection of flea-bitten specimens. Dear me, no. I spun to that long-haired he-rat from *The Evening Rodent*. Oh, and that foxy, red-haired thing from *The Rat*. You should have seen them – so desperate for something to print in their pamphlets. I must admit I gave a magnificent performance. I put a gloss on the goss. Span it to them like a pro.'

Ebenezer doesn't doubt it. The feathered dinosaur has a natural instinct for the glib art of spin. It just has to unfurl the loose flaps of skin around its neck and strike that pose it adopts when it spits poison and the sound bites trip off its double tongue.

'Fucking disaster. Did you tell them that?'

'Oh, I wouldn't use that word, Ebs.'

'Fucking?'

'Disaster.' Lucius struts a little closer, gives Ebenezer a gentle nudge on his sagittal crest. 'Your performance wasn't without its redeeming defects.'

'Wasn't it?'

'No.'

Ebenezer is not sure he can believe his second-in-command. It is not in the nature of a somethingosaurus to tell the truth on a consistent basis.

'Of course, the rats have all got hard-ons for that little orange-bellied hottie. Don't be too disappointed if the pamphlets agree that the night belonged to him. He's such an attractive specimen, isn't he? But there's no meat on his bones. You might not have his bushy tail, but you've got substance, Ebs. You've got gravitas. Oh, I suppose there are certain adjustments that could have been made. The statistics could have been a little lighter, the sound bites a tad more spontaneous… '

But Ebenezer isn't listening. His thoughts have returned to the creature that cornered him, the pipistrelle. She said she used to support the Order of Herbivores. She said he made her feel ashamed.

'Disaster.'

'What was that, Ebs?'

She should never have been granted access to him, damn it. Perhaps she slipped into the building through a missing pane of glass in the cupola: 'I just popped in to catch some moths for me supper,' she had said. But of course, as soon as she caught sight of Ebenezer she forgot about her stomach and decided to have a go at him instead. He remembers she gave him such a hard time about the animals that have migrated to the zoological gardens to escape persecution in their natural habitat. Did he point out that it isn't just a matter of creatures coming in? Did he mention that several specimens have managed to escape since he became P Ex? He's not sure he can recollect.

'Of course, FitzClarence underperformed.'

Ebenezer turns to the dinosaur. He needs to discuss the pipistrelle, but it sounds like the somethingosaurus has got its teeth into the Order of Carnivores. The specimen might have been raised on great lumps of iguanodon, but there is nothing it hates more than another meat-eater.

'That otter's too smooth-coated for his own good. There's nothing for him to give.'

'Fucking disaster.'

'FitzClarence? Oh, I'm sure he will be. In fact, I shouldn't be surprised if he leads us into the most terrible crisis.'

'Not FitzClarence. Me.'

'Come on, Ebs. There's still hope.'

'No, there isn't. Not after that nocturnal thing had a go at me. Should never have been let into the Ape House – whose bright idea was that?'

'Don't know. Didn't see.'

'Sue, I think. Ridiculous.' He scrapes the boards and snorts. Where are his minions when he wants to shout at them? Where is Sue?

'Forget it, Ebs. Some nocturnal thing? The rat corps won't go with that one.'

'Yes, it will.'

'Why? What sort of creature was it?'

'Oh, just some bigoted old bat that—'

The dinosaur hisses. Is it about to spit poison? It is glaring at the radio mic that some she-chimpanzee attached to his horn. 'What's that? What's that?'

'Oh, the Marconi GSM or something. Latest model.'

'It's not still transmitting, is it?'

Ebenezer darts a nervous glance at the little green lights on the audio signal processor. 'Oh, Luce.'

14

> **OLD HESPER HOUSE AND ZOOLOGICAL GARDENS**
> The Bog-land Enclosures
>
> ## AMPHITHEATRE
>
> Set into the natural slope of the hillside, this ornamental amphitheatre is thought to be a small-scale replica of the Odeon of Herodes Atticus. Its lakeside setting offers an impressive panorama of this isolated region of the estate. Please spare a moment to appreciate the escarpment on the eastern shore and the Old Boathouse to the north.
>
> **CAUTION: STEPS CAN BE SLIPPERY WHEN WET**

It is September 1940. It is the morning after the night before.

'Father?'

Is that him hopping down into the semicircular arena, or is it another member of the congregation – a pelican, perhaps? Belimperia cannot be sure. Determined to arrive at the amphitheatre in good time, he had set a demanding pace, and as the distance between them had lengthened, she'd started to lag behind. But as she pauses to admire the panorama from the upper circle, she can see that his haste had been undue. For the lake is still little more than a gaping hole in the landscaped gardens, as black as a sheet of smoked glass, and across the shore, the ridge of the escarpment is all but indistinguishable from the deep blue–black of the departing night. It is too soon, then, for the crocodiles that chart the constellations to stir their cold blood. Indeed, there is still a slight chill in the air, a crisp hint of autumn that seems to have crept into the bones of the collared lemmings huddled in the upper circle, making them tremble as she bustles past. Should she have stopped to bid them good morning? She has never arrived at the amphitheatre alone before. She isn't sure.

Conscious that the steps can be treacherous, she negotiates them one at a time. She must be careful not to trip on a loose tendril of bindweed, careful not to lose her footing on the mosses that thread the arena's stones, and so she resists the urge to look up. But she can tell that the other animals in the congregation are staring at her. Is that some cat-like creature crouched in ambush? Is that an African hunting dog? She summons up her courage, tries to reassure herself that this isn't the Serengeti. Yet even so, she can sense she's too small to be running the gauntlet of these big beasts alone.

'Father?'

He is standing at the bottom of the steps listening to a long-nosed bandicoot confess its shortcomings. Is he going to make his excuses and escort her to her perch? In an attempt to attract his attention, she coughs up a polite pellet of gristle, but he just glances over his scapulars and subjects her to a disparaging stare.

Bel-imperia sighs. She had forgotten that she's still in disgrace. In retrospect, perhaps it hadn't been in her best interests to refuse to eat her Mouse Tail Tangle, to demand something more nutritious, to speak her mind. But she doesn't regret it; she'd meant the things she said. Besides, the sudden surge of anger that had gripped her had been rather exhilarating – all that instinctive aggression. Perhaps she should listen to her instincts more often. Her instinct at the moment, though, is to interrupt his conversation and insist that he accompanies her to her perch. Dare she do it? She glares at the long-nosed bandicoot. It is tempting. Then again, so is the thought of his forgiveness. She gets a grip on her impatience, bides her time until her father absolves the bandicoot of its sins and ushers her to their usual slab of stone near the front. But it is quite clear from his indignant silence that forgiveness is out of the question.

He puts down the piece of paper he is clutching in his beak and secures it in a clump of creeping buttercup. Unusual. He has never brought a note to the amphitheatre before. She steals a glance at the folded sheet of foolscap: FOR THE CROCS. Not his normal neat talon. Perhaps it is a hurried note, an aide-memoire scribbled in haste or something. She has no intention of asking him. Neither does she intend to enquire about the threats he made as he doled out her punishment. Is he serious about recruiting an assistant to take on her duties at the boathouse so that she can spend her afternoons helping her mother tend the nest? Is he serious about pinning an advertisement for the position onto the double doors as soon as possible? She turns to him. Not the best moment to broach the subject. But even so, his silence is unbearable. And so she searches her repertoire of polite conversation for some comment to reach out and span the distance between them.

'There seems to be quite a good congregation this morning, doesn't there, Father?'

No response. Not in the mood to exchange pleasantries, then.

She turns her attention to the night lamp balanced on the sundial that stands at the centre of the circular stage, studies the reflection of its dancing flame in the thin strips of copper set into the ground to represent the constellations: a ram, a lion, a scorpion. It looks like the lamp has attracted a passing moth. She watches the stupid creature singe its wings. She sighs. How much longer is she going to have to wait? Perhaps the crocodiles that peer at the heavens through their telescopes have introduced an error into their calculations. She shouldn't be surprised; after all, she can sense that the congregation is getting impatient.

She glances around the amphitheatre. There's no sign of the slender mongoose that sometimes sits behind her – or his companion, come to that – but she can see a palm civet standing up on its hind legs and staring out across the lake. Is that a spectacled owl perched in the upper circle? Is that Miss Scroop? Bel-imperia is sure that it must be. She recognises her spectacle-like markings, her imposing beige breast. The last time their paths had crossed Edna Scroop had been perched on a pile of paperbacks in the Hunting Tower, compiling a list of creatures that had taken out books and failed to return them in pristine condition. Such a disagreeable old spinster. Such a bad-tempered bird. Impossible to imagine her entertaining romantic aspirations. Is it true that she once courted some disreputable specimen, or is it just a rumour?

'Face the front, Bel-imperia. Your salvation lies in the east, not over your scapulars.'

She does as she is told.

'Is your conscience clean? Perhaps there's something you'd like to confess before the crocodiles arrive.'

'I don't think so, Father.'

But she can tell that he's hoping for a confession. 'Did you reread the Commandments last night as I instructed?'

It had been a strange sort of punishment. Once he had gathered up the spilt mouse tails and rammed them down her throat, he sent her up to the nest and told her to reread the Commandments and consider their implications on her behaviour. She remembers struggling to concentrate on the assignment, though. Indeed, it had been impossible to ignore the disgusting sloth in the adjacent enclosure. But at least the hideous creature's behaviour means that she has something to confess this morning.

'I am afraid I found the Fifth Commandment rather challenging.'

'You did?' He seems delighted to have discovered another defect in his daughter. 'And what's so challenging about loving the specimen in the neighbouring cage as thou dost love thyself?'

'Nothing, as long as the specimen in question isn't scrabbling about on its latrine. Oh, I tried to love that sloth, Father – of course I did – but I must admit I struggled to summon up much affection for the thing.'

He pauses to consider his daughter's confession. 'No one is at their most attractive on the latrine, chick. Is there something else about our neighbour that makes him unlovable?'

'You mean apart from the fact that he's not much to look at?'

'Yes.'

'Well, he doesn't contribute much to the success of these gardens, does he? Unless hanging upside down in a tree can be considered a contribution. He's bone idle.'

'And would you love yourself if you were to behave in a similar manner?'

'Goodness me, no. I don't suppose I'd care for myself at all.'

'Then in that case your conscience is clean.' He plunges his head into his plumage, dispatches a parasitic mite. 'There's no obligation to love someone who falls short of our own high standards, chick. The crucial phrase is *as thou dost love thyself.*'

'I see.' There's something about this interpretation of the Fifth Commandment that rather appeals to little Bel-imperia Pinch. 'Does this mean that it's acceptable to despise a sloth, then? Father?'

But she can sense that the moment has passed. He is staring out across the lake, scanning its surface for the slightest disturbance. He catches his breath. Has he spotted a tell-tale movement? It must be about the right time: sunlight is starting to seep around the eastern rim of the hemisphere and shape out the landscaped gardens. True, the lake-shore is still dim, the detail indistinct, but she can tell that the atmosphere in the amphitheatre has changed. Is that a mountain goat clattering to its feet? Is that a bighorn sheep bleating in anticipation? She peers at the lake, spots a ripple. Could that be them? She's sure she can make out the armour-plated predators that have caught her father's attention.

'Look to your soul, chick. The crocodiles are approaching.'

There are three of them gliding through the mist, their long tails lashing behind them like horsewhips: three slender-snouted gharials – a little more compact, perhaps, than the Nile crocodiles that are said to reside in the Reptile House, but no less streamlined, no less lethal.

She appraises the largest of the males as the creature lunges out of the lake and drags his dripping carcass up into the arena. His gaping mouth reminds her of a spring-loaded trap primed to catch the leg of a passing gazelle. Her gaze settles on his bulging eye. Is the disfigurement the result of spending too much time peering up at the heavens through the lens of a telescope? Perhaps. She darts a glance at the creature's subordinates – a pair of immature reptiles scrabbling into position: one stage left, the other stage right. But it is hard to ignore the great leviathan lumbering up to the sundial. He hauls himself up onto his hind legs, startling the moth that had singed itself on the night lamp. He pauses, perhaps to concentrate on the insect's movements, snatches it out of the air, and then, licking his lips, turns to the congregation and says, 'I beseech thee, repeat after me, this, our penitential rite.'

It has begun, then, aurora matins.

'Forgive us, most merciful Sol,' the crocodile intones. 'For we are no better than wild beasts. We struggle to suppress our primitive instincts and abide by thy Commandments. There is no health in us: we are diseased.'

Hanging her head in contrition, Bel-imperia adds her solemn contralto to the drone of the other animals in the amphitheatre: 'There is no health in us: we are diseased.'

'Almighty Sol, have mercy upon these miserable specimens.'

'Have mercy upon us, Sol.'

'Let us plead.'

She stares at a clump of creeping bindweed as she pleads for salvation: 'Most merciful Sol, the remembrance of our sins is grievous to us. Deliver us from the darkness of our shame: put upon us the armour of thy light. Amen.'

'Amen.'

And so it continues, the crocodile rambling on in his monotonous baritone. Please sit. Please stand. Let us contemplate our depravities. Let us plead. Until at last it is time for the morning madrigal.

'Please stand.'

Bel-imperia springs up like a jack-in-the-box, glances over her scapulars as the other members of the congregation rise to their feet: the collared lemmings and the mountain goats, the bighorn sheep and the palm civets.

It is a mistle thrush that begins the madrigal, setting down a simple song-phrase; a little sad perhaps, but a blackbird soon picks up the tune and elaborates it into something more cheerful. Is that a chiffchaff producing those ascending scales? Is that a common starling? On the other side of the lake, a second chorus counterpoints, and soon the morning is full of birdsong. Bel-imperia sighs. She should like to join in, but the crocodile conducting the madrigal has made it clear that unless a specimen can sing like a nightingale it must remain silent. Her thoughts turn to the nightingale that sometimes sings in the Parade. Its song about magic in the air. There are rumours the creature is going to Caer Lud to sing to an audience of lions and tigers. Big beasts. Of course, she should be delighted that one of her peers has managed to escape from the cages behind the Marsupial House, but as much as she hates to admit it to herself, she is more than a little envious. She should love to put on a performance for an appreciative audience. In fact, she suspects that in due course she might make a good prima donna. Can she sing like a nightingale, though? She isn't sure. Concentrating on the morning madrigal, she attempts to counterpoint the song of a blackbird. Pianissimo. But her pitch is too shrill, her tone too strident.

'For goodness' sake be quiet, Bel-imperia.'

Can she do nothing right? Perhaps she might need some private tuition from a songbird before she can command the stage. She stands in silence, stares out across the lake. On its northern shore, she can make out the timbered façade of the boathouse through the thinning mist: desolate, menacing. Her thoughts turn to the man on the marble, the prospect of preparing his corpse for cremation. Scrubbing brushes and dried-up scraps of soap. Cast-iron buckets of embalming solution. Perhaps her father's threat to appoint an assistant is a blessing in disguise. Perhaps she should be pleased that he seems determined to advertise the position. She lets the thought go, turns to the limestone escarpment that lurches up from the lake on its eastern shore: the outcrop of boulders on its jagged ridge, the silhouette of a juniper tree. Is that a thin column of smoke rising from its summit? She cannot be sure. She can see that the promise of sunlight is beginning to sculpt out the landscaped gardens, though. Indeed, it is such a beautiful morning it deserves to be praised. Tempted to have another bash at the morning madrigal, she steals a glance at her father. He is staring at the piece of paper he brought to matins: solemn, pensive. Is something troubling him?

'Father?'

Snatching it in his beak, he swoops down onto the stage.

She studies the crocodile-priest as he shakes the letter open and spreads it out on the sundial: his long slender snout, his needle-like teeth. 'I'll see that it's done, Silas,' he mutters: hushed, conspiratorial. 'Have no fear.'

His bulging eye swivels in its socket. Is he subjecting her to a disapproving stare?

He turns to her father, tells him there's no point in going back to his perch. He isn't going to ask him to give a sermon, is he? Bel-imperia hopes not. She is in no mood to sit through another lecture on Hades. But it seems she's been spared that ordeal.

The crocodile clears his throat, addresses the congregation: 'And so the hour has come to examine your conscience.'

Is that a ripple of excitement she can sense passing through the amphitheatre? She should not be surprised; after all, this is the best part of the morning ritual.

'Please remain standing,' the crocodile continues. 'Unless.'

There's no need for him to finish his sentence, no need to elaborate on the meaning of 'Unless'. It is something that mountain goats learn in their nurseries, something that palm civets instil in their litters at birth: an article of the catechism. It means unless the sins on your back are too heavy for you to bear. It means unless you have done something too terrible to confess to an Elder before the crocodiles arrive. It means unless your only hope of salvation is to be publicly shamed.

The crocodile pauses to give them a chance to consider their shortcomings.

Confident that her conscience is clean, Bel-imperia stands as straight as she can. Is no one going to sit down and be shamed this morning? She stares over her scapulars at the other members of the congregation. She hopes she isn't going to be disappointed. Surely some miscreant must have broken the First Commandment, or committed some other unmentionable crime.

Is that a strangled gasp of surprise she can hear? Someone must have sat down.

She scours the upper circle of the amphitheatre. Of course, she must be careful not to seem too interested, careful not to give the impression that she lacks the strength of character to resist the sinner's raffish allure, but even so, there can be no harm in practising her reproachful stare on the specimen. Where should she direct her indignation, though? Who is this creature that has looked into its conscience and discovered something so disturbing that it deserves to be shamed? She cranes her neck, tries to peer through the legs of the roan antelope standing behind her. Sometimes in a large congregation it can be difficult to see the reprobate that's been compelled to sit down, but this morning it couldn't be easier. In fact, she just needs to turn her head in the same direction as the other animals to spot the degenerate sinner, because the creature is spread out prostrate, his lappets laid down in the dust that has settled on the stage.

'Father?'

She gapes at him in horror. Silas Pinch, Master of Embalming, Obsequies and other Rites of Passage. Silas Pinch, a respectable member of the Elders. Impossible.

No doubt the crocodile-priest is as shocked as the miscreant's daughter. Faltering as he attempts to summon up his baritone, he instructs the congregation to come down onto the stage and make their offerings to Sol.

Poor little Bel-imperia Pinch. She is conscious that the other animals are clomping down the steps – she can hear their clattering hooves, their hushed conversation – but something inside her is broken. She is incapable of reacting to the surge of movement. She is looking down on herself from above: a little lappet-faced thing standing in the middle of a stampede, a daughter staring at her respectable father spread out across the ground like the contents of an overturned litterbin. What on earth has he done to warrant such a public display of shame? What is his sin?

It looks like a long-nosed bandicoot is scuttling up to him. The rodent-like marsupial hacks up a gob of phlegm and spits on his lores. Poor Father. Should she go to him and help him up onto his feet, or should she join the decent, upright specimens shuffling in a queue around him?

There's no time to make the decision: some primate is scampering up to him. She peers at the creature... Not an ape; she can see that it's got a tail. Not a red colobus, or a black-bearded saki. Just some stocky grey monkey with a whorl of hair on its head. Just some common low-ranking thing.

The creature holds out its hand, helps him onto his feet. Is it brushing the grit out of his flight feathers? Is it touching him? There is a brief exchange of pleasantries. Did it just call him 'sir'?

Bel-imperia studies the simian as it bounds up the steps to reclaim its seat in the upper circle. She has a hunch it might be a toque macaque – the female of the species, judging from the infant clinging to its chest. Infant or abomination? Is this the brazen harlot her father met that morning he called in at the macaque compound to drum up some business? Do strumpets get up before sunrise to go to aurora matins? It seems doubtful. She remembers that the classification of primates is a complicated matter. Too many monkeys to choose from. Perhaps she is mistaken, then. Perhaps the specimen is just a baboon or a langur.

'Bel-imperia?' He is staggering up the steps, dust on his lappets, a lump of bandicoot phlegm on his lore: a broken bird.

She goes to him.

'Oh, Father. What on earth… ?' She wants to ask what possessed him, what made him make such a spectacle of himself, but she just says, 'Why?'

'I'll explain later, chick. Go and make an offering.'

But she's unable to move. She stares at him as he stumbles back to his perch. He isn't going to disgrace himself again, is he? It seems not. Once he has settled down, she toddles on stage and takes a place in the queue behind – what is it? A collared lemming or something.

'Next.'

There goes a bighorn sheep.

'Next.'

There goes the collared lemming.

'Next.'

Here goes, then. Time to shuffle up to the sundial and choose an offering for Sol. Time to select one of the teacups that the subordinate crocs have removed from the tabernacle. But all the best pieces of bone china have been claimed. Bel-imperia inspects the miserable collection of chipped teacups. There isn't one that hasn't sustained some minor damage: a missing handle here, a V-shaped chip there… Decisions, decisions.

'There are mammals in this queue, missy,' the palm civet standing behind her says.

Ignoring the creature, she takes her time before choosing a pale-blue teacup that has lost its handle. At least it contains a burning tea light: a little flame to encourage His light to shine.

Careful not to spill its precious cargo, she shuffles up to the edge of the amphitheatre and plops the teacup into the lake. Is it going to sink to the bottom like the cup that the miserable-looking lemming standing beside her must have chosen? She holds her breath. Her piece of china might be listing to one side, but it doesn't appear to be capsizing. Confident that her offering has been accepted, she subjects the envious lemming to a condescending smile. Is the stupid thing sobbing? No time to tell it to pull itself together: her teacup must be caught in a slipstream; it looks like it's about to be dashed against the amphitheatre. She gives it a gentle nudge, sends it sailing across the lake to join the other vessels in the flotilla of second-hand china. Thank goodness for that.

Satisfied that a maritime disaster has been averted, she returns to her perch and settles down beside her father. There's an uncomfortable silence as he struggles to articulate his thoughts. 'Oh, Bel-imperia,' he mumbles at last, 'I am afraid... '

She glances up at him. He is hanging his head.

'It's all right, Father.'

'I am afraid that late last night... '

Is he attempting to account for his decision to disgrace himself? Is he about to confess the shocking sin he must have committed?'

'I am afraid late last night as I scuttled back to the Parade after Elders, I succumbed to an urge to—'

She interrupts him. 'I said it's all right.'

'You mean... You don't want an explanation?'

'What's there to explain? You committed a sin. You broke a Commandment.'

'Yes, but—'

'We are all frail, Father. Why, just last week I saw that waterbuck over there defecate on the cobbled path in defiance of the Seventh Commandment.'

'You did?' He hazards a disapproving glare at the creature.

'Besides, this disgrace isn't a permanent stain on our species, is it? Let's be pragmatic: tomorrow morning another member of the congregation will sit down – and the day after that another. This lot have short memories; the incident will soon be forgotten.'

'But I need to confess—'

From the direction of the sundial, the sound of breaking china. Someone must have dropped their teacup.

'There's no need to confess the sordid details to me, Father. In fact, I'd rather not know.'

There is a moment's silence as he takes this in.

'I still feel I should—'

'Let it be, Father.' She changes the subject. 'Goodness me, look at all the sacred vessels on the lake.'

He glances up at the armada of bobbing teacups.

She says, 'Perhaps a moment of quiet contemplation to prepare for the coming of the Lord?'

'Yes, of course.'

But the moment isn't as quiet as she had hoped: a mountain goat is clattering up the steps. As soon as the creature has settled down, the crocodile-priest returns to the sundial, scrabbles up onto his hind legs.

'We beseech thee, Sol,' he thunders in his resounding baritone, 'accept these humble offerings. Deliver these miserable specimens from eternal darkness. Wash them with the mercy of thy light.'

'Sol, come in glory,' she says, a split second before the rest of the congregation.

'We beseech thee, Sol, save W. L. S. Chartwell, our P Ex. Shine upon him as he wrestles against the rulers of the darkness of this world.'

'Sol, come in glory.'

'We beseech thee, Sol, protect us from the ghosts that haunt these gardens. Banish them to Hades with thy transcendent light.'

'Sol, come in glory.'

'We beseech thee, Sol… '

Silence.

She wants to squawk: We beseech thee – what?

112

'One moment, please.' The crocodile turns to his subordinates. 'How much longer?'

'Not sure, Padre. I should imagine a minute or so, perhaps less.'

Bel-imperia sighs. It can't be all that difficult to look up the precise time of sunrise in an almanac and coordinate a couple of 'Sol-come-in-glories', but the crocodiles never seem to get the timing right. Could she make a better job of it? Of course she could. She'd never be reduced to padding out the service until sunrise, repeating the same old 'Sol-come-in-glories' again and again. She'd burn the midnight oil to make sure she had the relevant details at her disposal. This morning, though, the crocodile-priest glances down at a scrap of paper spread out on the sundial and recites some 'Sol-come-in-glories' that little Bel-imperia Pinch has never heard before.

'We beseech thee, Sol, protect our chicks from creatures of the night. Lead them not into the Hunting Wood. Smite those savages that have reverted to their natural state.'

'Sol, come in glory.'

She's sure she can sense her father attempting to muster a reproachful stare.

The crocodile squints at the piece of paper. 'We beseech thee, Sol, protect our little lappet-faced things from false prophets. Tempt them not to scuttle into caves. Bring down thy wrath on That Which We Do Not Speak About.'

'Sol, come in glory.'

Bel-imperia is astonished. She glances at the clump of creeping buttercup beside her, remembers her father slipping the note he'd brought to matins under its fronds. 'For the Crocs,' it had said. Yet even so, she hadn't expected it to contain some 'Sol-come-in-glories' aimed at her. Did he compose them himself? She should not be surprised. Protect our little lappet-faced things from false prophets? Tempt them not to scuttle into caves? It's just the sort of thing that he delights in scribbling late at night as he sits under the gas lamp in their cage. She squints at the scrap of paper that the crocodile-priest is clutching in his reptilian hand. She'd like to swoop down and snatch it out of his scales. She'd like to take a close look at the spelling. Does it say That Which We Do Not Speak About or That *Witch* We Do Not Speak About?

'We beseech thee, Sol… '

No time to think about the creature of the night, the creature in the cave. Here it comes at last, inching up over the ridge of the escarpment: the most spectacular sunrise.

'Behold,' snorts the crocodile, jabbing a stout forefoot at the rising sun, 'He cometh with clouds and every eye shall see Him.'

Of course, sometimes He cometh with a great deal of cloud indeed. But not after such a clear night, not this morning. It is unfortunate, then, that the prehistoric reptile looming over the sundial has positioned himself between little Bel-imperia Pinch and her god. She cranes her neck, tries to escape the crocodile's long shadow.

'Lift up your hearts to Sol, the Everlasting Light.'

'We lift them up to Sol.'

The croc snorts on the night lamp, snuffs out the flame. 'Now, let us proclaim the Most Sacred Tenet of the Faith.'

It's a simple piece of dogma, the Most Sacred Tenet of the Faith, but it sets the animals in the zoological gardens apart from their cousins in the Serengeti – savages that haven't seen the light. Nothing could be more important, then. This morning, though, rather than intone the solemn phrase, one member of the congregation is standing in silence. True, just like the others, she is staring out across the lake, but Bel-imperia isn't gazing up in rapture at the rising sun. Far from it. She is peering into the thin gauze of mist that shrouds the oaks and beeches on the escarpment; she is searching for an outcrop that might conceal the mouth of a cave. Of course, she's aware that the others are proclaiming something, but their bleating is nothing more than background noise, nothing more than a distraction. Because she is listening to the call of her instinct – not intuition, not an idle hunch, but the most urgent gut instinct. She takes a deep breath. She accepts the challenge. So be it, then. It is decided. If she's going to escape a career in Embalming, Obsequies and other Rites of Passage, she needs to give her father the slip and creep into those oaks and beeches as soon as the sun goes down. If she's going to get into the Cloisters, she needs to summon up her courage, and trespass into That W**ch We Do Not Speak About's lair.

'He had set, but He is risen and He shall rise again.'

Let him set. She is not interested in the garish sun. It is darkness she craves.

[III]

Less Than a Mother's Hope

15

One might be in one's dotage, but make no mistake: one still commands the respect of the Order of Carnivores – more than respect: I am an icon to them.

But that is not all.

I also command the respect of the general public that come to this great institution to gaze at me. Imagine approaching the bars of this cage as I sit here staring out across the zoological gardens like an iron statue on a monument. This hooked beak and these bloodstained talons. This intimidating stillness. One is accustomed to being appreciated, accustomed to being admired.

Nevertheless.

I'm afraid some members of the general public aren't as respectful as one had hoped. I am alluding, of course, to a certain middle-aged man that claims to be a biographer – I forget his name: Robin or Robert or something. You see, I'd expected him to be more – what's the word? Pliant. Oh, but he can be so argumentative at times. Indeed, the thought has occurred to me that perhaps he might have an axe to grind. Sadly, his questions this morning did nothing to allay these concerns.

'Right,' he said, as soon as he'd settled down on a bench and pulled out his spiral-bound notebook. 'So this creature that the crocodiles dismiss as a false prophet—'

I interrupted him. 'Crocodiles?' I said. 'Do not underestimate their importance, dear. Goodness me, the spirit of these gardens is Crocodilian. After all, crocodiles give us standards – not just standards: crocodiles provided the inspiration that emboldened me to make the zoological gardens a better place.'

'False gharials? Prehistoric reptiles spreading superstition and delusion? Please.'

'There's nothing superstitious about it at all,' I replied. 'Oh, I suppose some simpletons might still believe that the sun rises each morning because of our penitential rite, but most of us are more enlightened. We accept that the zoological gardens is spinning through the cosmos on a great lump of rock. That's something science has taught us. Do not forget that I studied science. I can cite the molecular formula for sulphuric acid; I can transmute base metal into gold. But science doesn't alter the fact that there is such a thing as good and such a thing as evil. Neither does it offer moral guidance to an animal that might be struggling to choose between them. Some specimens need a crocodile to help them make up their minds.'

'Fine,' he conceded. 'But I'm not interested in crocodiles. Tell me about this creature in the cave, this creature of the night.'

'Let me make it quite clear,' I said, 'I didn't become Prize Exhibit because of some nocturnal specimen that dabbles in the occult. I did not. I became P Ex because of the conflict between good and evil. I wanted to make sure that good triumphed, dear.'

'So the creature is nocturnal, then?'

I decided to deflect the question. 'Of course, I'm afraid sometimes the emphasis on a strict Crocodilian upbringing can be exaggerated. Indeed, I remember Father's insistence on attending matins used to set me apart from the specimens that I called friends. Oh, and all those Commandments! Thou shalt not do this. Thou shalt not do that. I must admit it could all be a bit much at times. But I have no regrets. I still believe in the things I learned on the steps of that amphitheatre. And one of the wisest things the crocodiles instilled in me was: That W**ch We Do Not Speak About we do not speak about. Do I make myself clear?'

I stared out through the bars at his tangled mane, his hideous scar. I thought he might have had the courage to return my gaze, but he just rummaged through his bag and pulled out a packet of Old Holborn.

'Thing is,' he said, stealing a glance at me as he rolled a cigarette, 'I heard a rumour about some confrontation in the creature's cave. Something about a birdcage and—'

I nipped his sentence in the bud; I changed the subject. 'I must confess,' I said, 'one is also reluctant to discuss one's spiritual convictions. Does one believe in Hades? Does one aspire to return to these gardens as a ghost? These things can be misinterpreted. But that doesn't mean I don't have faith in the immortal soul. Goodness me, no. One has to believe there is more to life than sitting in this roost and staring out through the bars at this desolate cul-de-sac. One has to believe one has some hope of salvation.'

'Salvation?' he said.

'Deliverance. I should like to be delivered.'

'You mean like a letter?'

'No, of course not, but… '

'Yes?'

'I should like to receive a letter. Let me share a little secret: I am expecting something in the post. Oh, I don't suppose it'll be more than a couple of lines – a short note scribbled on a sheet of black-edged mourning paper, perhaps. But even so, I'm most eager to receive it. I expect it'll arrive after the scent-marking contest, once things have settled down a bit. It's bound to get here sooner or later, isn't it? I mean, it's not as if the zoological gardens doesn't need me. Goodness me, there's no one else that could rise to the challenge. There is not. No one has strong convictions; no one believes in anything any more.'

'What about Dale FitzClarence?' he mumbled as he lit his cigarette. 'He hugs huskies. He claims to believe in things.'

'Oh, I am sure he does, dear,' I said. 'But nothing too much. Make no mistake: there's an absence of conviction in that otter. Indeed, he seems to be more interested in rebranding the Order of Carnivores than standing up for something that a Bengal tiger can believe in. Let's not mince words: I suspect he might have Herbivorous inclinations; I suspect he might not be one of us.'

I waited while he scribbled something in his notebook. In the distance, at the entrance to the cul-de-sac of cages, I spotted a couple of old-age pensioners: members of the general public dressed in, my goodness me, the most unseasonable overcoats. I glared at them as they admired the geraniums.

'Of course,' I added as soon as the couple had shuffled out of sight, 'one hopes one is mistaken. Perhaps FitzClarence is just pandering to progressive opinion because of the scent-marking contest. I mean, he does seem rather desperate to become P Ex, doesn't he? I should imagine it must be the trappings of the role that attract him: living in the Dower House, sleeping in a bed with sheets – all of that. Yet even so, I'm afraid there are limits. And apologising for the clause I introduced to ban the promotion of certain practices is one of them.'

'Certain practices?'

'Chimpanzees and bonobos that indulge in indecent behaviour.'

'You mean the natural behaviour that dare not speak its name?'

I almost coughed on his cigarette smoke. 'There's nothing natural about it at all,' I replied. 'There is not. Oh, I can understand that the odd subordinate male might turn to a member of the same sex for companionship – of course I can. Be under no illusions: it hasn't escaped one's attention that some specimens find a dominant female intimidating. But that's no excuse to indulge in indecent behaviour. One must consider our impressionable pups and cubs.'

He told me that attitudes have changed. Such nonsense.

'The Commandments do not change,' I reminded him. 'FitzClarence should spend less time holding court and go down to the amphitheatre more often. I'm sure no one who attends aurora matins on a regular basis could fail to recognise that the Commandments are the most fundamental expression of the difference between right and wrong. Of course, one cannot always live up to them. One does one's best, but... '

'But?'

In retrospect, I dare say I should never have started the sentence. But I didn't flinch from his accusing stare. I held his gaze and said, 'Let me make it quite clear: I have never broken... '

'Yes?' he said, stubbing out his cigarette under the seat of the bench.

'Oh, I suppose there might be the Fourth Commandment... '

'Which one's that? Remind me.'

'*Thou shalt not speak to a member of the general public unless thou art a parrot.* I'm afraid I had to set that one aside in order to have these delightful conversations.'

'Who cares about the Fourth Commandment? What about—'

I interrupted him: 'One moment, please. You asked the most fundamental question. It's gone to the gut; it's gone to the jugular. Now, let me finish... I care deeply about the Fourth Commandment – of course I do. But there is such a thing as choice, dear. Indeed, it's the essence of ethics; after all, the concept of good and evil is meaningless unless one is free to choose. The Order of Carnivores understands these things. We believe in choice. We believe a creature should be free to make choices – to make mistakes, to be generous and compassionate. We believe—'

'If I might get a word in edgeways,' he said, rudely. 'And so the Commandments are something a fledgling could just pick and choose?'

'No, of course not.'

'Well, what about the First Commandment, then? With respect, what excuse did you come up with for setting that one aside?'

'The First Commandment? *Thou shalt not eat of another...* Goodness me, no. Under no circumstances could I condone dining on... '

'The mortal remains of a man?'

'Oh, I see.'

'Well?'

I subjected him to a disparaging stare. 'With respect,' I said, 'I have made it quite clear: sometimes I forget things, dear.'

16

OLD HESPER HOUSE 𝔞𝔫𝔡 ZOOLOGICAL GARDENS

The Bog-land Enclosures

THE OLD BOATHOUSE

SITUATION VACANT   sure or Other Estate Building.
Embalming Assistant   order pending.
(Part-time)
The successful candidate will   P OUT
be competent with a bar of
soap and have an aptitude for
removing stubborn stains
from a challenging range of
orifices. Previous experience
of working with the dead
useful, but not essential.
Remuneration according to
species, sex and experience.
Apply Within

She stops on the boat slip and shakes the sulphur dioxide out of her flight feathers. Perhaps a brief moment to prepare herself for the ordeal that lies ahead...

She glances up at the notice: Situation Vacant. 'Of course, chick,' she remembers him muttering as he Sellotaped it to the door, 'I shall require some assistance until a suitable candidate can be found.' Naturally, she attempted to impress on him that she had other demands on her time. Considering the disgrace he'd just made of himself at matins, she'd hoped to exploit his self-doubt, but he seemed desperate to reassert his authority, and so she reluctantly agreed to meet him at the boathouse as soon as the zoological gardens had closed.

She sighs.

Here goes, then. She summons up her strength, scuttles through the gap between the double doors.

'Father?'

She had been expecting to find him siphoning out the embalming fluid or something, but apart from the mortal remains of the man on the marble she appears to be alone. Then again, appearances can be deceptive. Besides, she can sense a sinister presence. Is some predator sizing her up? Perhaps it might be sensible to conduct a quick search of the building. She dismisses the thought. She is quite confident that there's no godlike specimen perched on the spice drawers this afternoon: the sunlight streaming into the abandoned boathouse through the colander of holes above her head is bright, dazzling. It dances in the mirror on the old duchess dressing table and sparkles in the puddles of sulphuric acid. No dim recesses for a predator to hide in, then. Unless...

She peers up into the crossbeams and trusses, squints at the ropes that are used to hoist cumbersome creatures up onto the marble. Is that a tinge of green? For a moment, she is sure she caught a glimpse of something slipping out of sight – a brief shimmer, a subtle hint of spots. Nothing. It must have been an optical illusion, reflected sunlight.

She is alone, then. Thank goodness.

She releases the tension in her serpentine neck and loosens up. She is pleased there's no one to squawk at her. She's tired of being given instructions. 'Bring me a bar of soap, Bel-imperia. Pass me another scouring pad.' She glances up at the marble-topped contraption. The thought of helping her father prepare the corpse of some strange man for cremation disgusts her.

But still.

The deceased is producing such an appetising aroma.

Conscious of a sense of déjà vu, she hopscotches over the puddles of sulphuric acid and hauls herself up into the air. This afternoon, though, there is no lapse of concentration, no miscalculation as she alights on the marble. She congratulates herself on a perfect landing – no mean achievement, given the state of the man's remains. Is the poor chap in the throes of some metamorphosis? She should not be surprised. For his skin is marbled, and his stomach so distended it looks like he might be about to give birth. Fascinated, she scuttles a little closer.

Of course, she's accustomed to the occasional odd-looking specimen turning up in the boathouse, but this is unprecedented. Then again, it's also unprecedented for her father to receive a pigeon urging him to postpone an embalming. Thank goodness he's been issued further instructions. Thank goodness he's been told to get the job done. The flies the corpse is attracting are beginning to test her patience. She attempts to snatch one out of the air, but the insect's reactions are too sharp. Determined not to be defeated, she studies its movements, tries to predict its behaviour. Is it going to settle on the dressing table? No. The bluebottle changes direction, darts across the boathouse to the man's abdomen, disappears into a swarm of identical insects. Is there something in particular attracting them to the area? She clambers up onto the deceased to investigate.

It doesn't take her long to spot the laceration. No doubt the pressure of the gas in his bloated stomach must have torn it open. Careful not to step on his appendage, she scutters up to the gaping hole and peers inside. Is that his pancreas she can see peeking out? Is that his liver glistening under all those maggots? The digestive juices in her stomach gurgle. Poor little Bel-imperia Pinch. She hasn't eaten since…

She remembers her mother's Mouse Tail Tangle, compares it to the nutritious banquet spread out before her. She might be struggling to suppress an instinct to dine on the deceased, but suppress it she must. She recites the First Commandment: '*Thou shalt not eat of another exhibit. Neither shalt thou eat—*'

Strange. She is sure she can detect a breath of cold air on her auricular feathers, sure she can hear a subtle hiss. Is someone whispering into her ear?

She glances over her scapulars: nothing, no one. It must have been the wind whistling through the oaks and beeches. It must have been the lake sloshing against the boat slip.

She repeats the Commandment: '*Thou shalt not eat of another exhibit. Neither—*'

This time the hiss is louder. 'But this chap isn't an exhibit, is he, old girl?'

She leaps into the air, soars up to the spice drawers. 'Who's there?'

She can hear the creature, but she cannot see it. 'This man came here to slaughter us, remember? He deserves to be gobbled up.'

She steadies her nerves, tries to bring a little logic to bear on the situation. Something must be responsible for the hissing. Is it a disembodied spirit? Is it a spectre? True, she has never had the dubious pleasure of being haunted, but she is quite confident that ghosts are a nocturnal phenomenon. She is also confident that the intruder cannot be projecting its hiss from the second-hand cupboards that clutter the boathouse: she had felt its cold breath on her lappets. Is it camouflaged, then?

From her perch on the spice drawers, she inspects each detail: the sunlight gleaming on the lacquer of the tea chest, the neat pile of Pears' soap, the bloodstains on the marble. But still no sign of the creature that is hissing at her.

'Besides, I should imagine the species is delicious. Tastes just like pork I'm told.'

There it is. She can see its reflection in the mirror of the old duchess dressing table: a large snake looped around the crossbeams, like a length of mooring rope. She glances up at the rafters to get a better look at the reptile, but all she can make out is a shimmer of green; a disturbance in the sunlight, nothing more. She turns her attention to the mirror again. The serpent is still strung up in the rafters. She can see the spots on its scales, the stripes on its head. The image is sharp and clear. So? The creature's camouflage is excellent, there can be no doubt about that. For some reason, though, it cannot disguise its reflection in a looking glass.

'Just consider that nutritious liver, all those plump maggots. Yum. Yum.'

She peers into the mirror, appraises the intruder. The serpent is much bigger than the grass snakes that slither through the pond sedge on the lake-shore. Indeed, judging from the droop of its coils, it must be at least three times as long as the man on the marble, and almost as thick as his thigh. Is it a boa constrictor or an anaconda? Bel-imperia isn't sure, but she can tell that the creature is an ambush predator. She looks up at the rafters and down at the mirror again. Is it adjusting the pigmentation of its scales as it breathes in and out? Is that the reason for the occasional shimmer?

'Come on down, old girl. Dinner is served.'

She ignores the invitation. The reptile could crush her in its coils in an instant. Has it come to the boathouse to eat her? Is that its plan? She decides to confront the thing.

'Impressive disguise, but it isn't much use in a looking glass, is it?'

It darts a glance at its reflection. 'Mirrors, damn and blast them. Such a nuisance.' The snake must have stopped pumping pigment into its cells because it is slipping into focus. It is a green anaconda: the male of the species. 'I suppose an introduction is in order. The name is Draco, Draco Stanford Middleton Coil.'

'Goodness me, what a lot of names!'

'Sign of good breeding, old girl. But I must confess I am sometimes called other things.' The serpent loosens its coils, drops down onto the marble. 'This chap used to call me Dog. Said I smelt like one.'

Is this anaconda an acquaintance of the deceased?

'Oh, I should like to snake around his ribcage; I should like to squeeze the life out of him.'

'I think it might be a little late for that.'

'Indeed.'

There is a moment's silence. Bel-imperia studies the serpent. Is she in danger? Can she trust the creature? For some reason, she seems to be listening to her instincts. It takes her ten seconds to make up her mind.

She glides down onto the marble and introduces herself. 'Just three names I'm afraid: Bel-imperia Hildred Pinch.'

'*Enchanté*.' He slithers around her in a circle, treats her to a glimpse of his forked tongue. Is he tasting the molecules in the air she's breathing out? 'Such courage. Oh, and it isn't a bluff, is it? I detect a fighting spirit in that delicious breast. I do like a little fight in the specimens I dine on.'

Did she make the right decision? Is he going to crush her in his strapping coils? She trusts her instincts, holds her ground. 'So do I.'

'Unusual, though. I tend to put the fear of Sol into most fledglings.'

'Oh, but I'm not a fledgling. I happen to be on the cusp of a post-juvenile moult.'

'Is that so?'

'Besides, I'm not frightened of snakes in the grass.' She gives Draco a defiant stare, dares him to contradict her. 'I am not. In fact, I'm rather fond of cold-blooded reptiles.'

'But I sometimes eat birds for breakfast.'

'Well, that's something we have in common, then. I'm a carnivore too.'

'Not a Carnivore with a capital C. Not a member of the Order.'

'No, but... ' She glances in the direction of the double doors. 'But I'm hoping to join the League of Young Carnivores if I get into the Cloisters.'

'The Cloisters?' Draco recoils, puckers the scales around his lips into a sneer. He seems to find the concept of a quadrangle of cages dedicated to academic achievement distasteful. 'You won't be popular I'm afraid. The Cloisters is a den of closet Herbivores. Indeed, I remember most of the black-capped owls that taught me turned out to be radical Animalists.'

'What's an Animalist?'

'Someone who believes all animals are equal.'

'Goodness me, I've never heard of such nonsense. What a silly thing to believe! How can a three-toed sloth be equal to... ' She searches for an appropriate example. 'Equal to an anaconda?'

'Quite.'

'I don't care if it makes me unpopular, I intend to stand up for my convictions. Oh, I'll make mincemeat of those radical Animalists... ' She remembers her entrance examination, her pigeonless summer; she hangs her head and stares at the marble. 'If I get in.'

'If?' The serpent slips under the man's shoulder and snakes out the other side. 'It's a bit late for ifs and buts: Michaelmas Term starts on Monday.'

She tells Draco about her predicament; the letters the pigeons discovered behind their nesting box, her hopes of receiving one.

'One?' he hisses. 'There should be more than one, old girl. Oh, and rather attractive letters too. The Cloisters sends all its correspondence in Nile-blue envelopes embossed in gold.'

'More than one?'

He explains that the secretarial owls in the admissions office are sticklers for protocol. 'First, an offer of a scholarship, and then another letter containing the admissions papers – that's the important one.'

'I see.' She pauses to take this in. 'There's still hope, then?'

'There might be.' He darts a sidelong glance at the gash on the man's upper abdomen, gives her a piercing stare. Bel-imperia can tell that she's being sized up. Is he attempting to decide if he can trust her or not?

She stands up straight and meets his gaze. 'Might be?'

'Our battle against mankind means that communications are essential. One rogue pigeon in the roost could compromise the defence of these gardens.'

'I can imagine.'

He slinks a hair's breadth closer, hisses into her ear: 'Then you won't be surprised to learn that there are reptilian agents in the pigeon cotes.'

'Reptilian agents?'

'Undercover chameleons. Specimens that use their camouflage to gather intelligence… ' He is squinting at the second-hand cupboards and cabinets. Is he concerned that a chameleon might have infiltrated the boathouse? 'It's all rather hush hush I'm afraid. But even so, I might be able to instruct one of our agents to put some pressure on the Pigeon Master General, perhaps even persuade him to send a letter here this afternoon.'

'Oh, Draco, I'd be so grateful.' She should like to wrap her wings around the serpent and hold him in her embrace; she should like to recruit him to fight her corner. Of course, she has no idea that in a couple of decades or so Draco Stanford Middleton Coil is going to be her closest adviser, no intimation that he is going to champion her campaign to seize control of the Order of Carnivores, but she can sense that she'd been right to listen to her instincts and place her trust in him.

'Consider it done, old girl.' The man on the marble lurches as the snake slides under the arch of his spine. 'Of course, I shall require a small favour in return.'

'Anything. Just say the word and I'll do it.'

Draco tightens his grip on the corpse, gives it a gentle squeeze. The deceased's liver bulges to the surface, spilling a squirm of maggots across the marble.

'Eat.'

It is a tempting sight, there can be no doubt about that: an appetising liver, glistening in blood and gore. But she is a sophisticated specimen, not some savage on the Serengeti. Besides, there are bound to be consequences. She'll never earn her father's love and approval if she consumes one of his customers; she'll be reduced to an object of hatred, something to be reviled. She hesitates.

Can Draco sense her indecision?

'Let me share another secret, old girl. See those cities? See those names etched on that wireless set? Well, I've snaked through their avenues and boulevards. I set an ambush in Le Jardin Zoologique; I fought to defend us from mankind. He captured me, this chap. He put me in a crate and transported me to a place called Das Museum Für Naturkunde. He locked me in the basement, imprisoned in Room IVc.'

'Goodness me.'

'Oh, there are such horrors in that room, Bel-imperia; such monstrosities. Crocodile eggs in cardboard boxes. Unborn pups and cubs suspended in glass jars. I even discovered the remains of a turtle that had been prised out of its shell.' He pauses, perhaps to observe a moment's silence for these unfortunate specimens. 'And so I decided to escape.'

'Escape from Das Museum? Had it ever been done?'

'Never. Indeed, it is said to be impossible. But I had the good fortune to come across a chameleon in a detachment of reptiles en route to the taxidermist. I rescued the creature and persuaded it to teach me that little disappearing act. I must admit I had to devour it in order to acquire the requisite genes; I had to practise. Nevertheless, as soon as I'd mastered the art of disguise, I gave this chap the slip and returned to the zoological gardens.'

'You're quite sure this is the same man?'

'Smells the same: stale tobacco and cheap cologne.' Draco recoils from the corpse in disgust. 'He deserves to be punished for his crimes.'

'Yes, I suppose he does.'

'But I haven't got the stomach to digest a meal that's started to decompose. I need a specialist to assist me, a bird adapted to the task.'

'I see.'

He tightens his grip on the man. There is a gentle plop as the deceased's liver slips out onto the marble.

Bel-imperia stares at the meal that has been set before her. Dare she eat it?

'You have strong instincts.' The serpent's hiss is subtle, insinuating. 'Natural instincts. The time has come to trust them, old girl.'

Perhaps the anaconda has a point. Perhaps she does need to trust her instincts more often. She remembers the classification; she remembers attempting to smuggle the bag of mouse tails to the polecats. On both occasions her instincts had been spot on, and on both occasions she had ignored them. She has no intention of making the same mistake again. Besides, her appetite is sharp. She can hear it screaming in the pit of her stomach. It demands satisfaction. Never mind Father. Never mind his love and approval. She must leave all that behind; she must have something more nourishing. The time has come, then, to step up and start acting like a member of her species. The time has come to dine.

She lunges at the man's liver. She slices through the common hepatic duct and rips off the right lobe.

She is pure instinct, unrepentant and uncompromising. She is Bel-imperia Pinch.

She lifts up her head and eases a lump of liver into her gullet. Is she conscious that she has passed the point of no return? For a moment perhaps. But she refuses to entertain doubts. Doubts are traitors. Doubts are Quislings. She has made her decision and she's going to see it through until the bitter end.

She plunges her head into the porta hepatis and tugs off the quadrate lobe. She shreds the left lobe into strips and uses her rasped tongue to ram the goujons down her oesophagus. She eats and eats. She gorges.

Of course, no scavenger has a sophisticated palate. Yet even so, she's quite certain the meal must be more nourishing than her mother's Mouse Tail Tangle. Isn't liver supposed to be rich in a range of minerals? Copper, phosphorus and zinc perhaps. She cannot be sure; she cannot taste them. But she can sense that iron is entering her soul.

She gobbles up the caudate lobe, glances down at the mess on the marble: the man's bitter gallbladder, some scraps of bile duct. She has eaten all the best bits. Is that it, then? Is that the end of the banquet?

She takes a sip of blood, dispatches a squirming maggot. But her appetite is still not satiated. There must be something else she can nibble on. Nothing too substantial – she has no desire to be bloated. Just a delicate morsel to refresh the palate. She is sure she can remember seeing some little scrap that she fancied. Now, where was it?

Of course.

She scuttles up to the man's crotch and pecks off his appendage. She slices into the shaft and slashes through the penile urethra. There's no need to shred the organ into bite-sized chunks: it is the perfect fit for her throat. Down it goes, like a smoked sausage. Delicious. Now, what will it be for dessert?

She scrambles up onto the deceased's abdomen to inspect the items on the menu: a slither of omentum, perhaps. Or a portion of spleen? No. She makes a decision and plunges her head into the man's abdominal cavity, but just as she is about to help herself to a loop of colon, she catches a glimpse of something luminescent glistening in the gore. She squints at the pale orb. Is there some sort of growth on his pancreas? She gives it a gentle peck. No, it cannot be organic: it's as hard as a stone. And so it must be a foreign object – something the deceased ate before he died, perhaps. Should she leave it there, or should she remove it? She'd like some advice.

'Draco?'

Silence.

She glances around the boathouse, but there's no sign of the anaconda. Nothing, not even a reflection in the mirror. He must have slithered out through the double doors. Never mind.

She seizes the object in her beak and gives it a gentle tug.

It appears to be some sort of string: a long chain of pea-sized globules, dripping in blood and gore. She drops it into the nearest cast-iron bucket and jumps down onto the ground. She gives it a good rinse, drapes it over the rim of the pail.

'Goodness me.'

She has never been so astonished. Is there a logical explanation? No doubt there must be, but this isn't the moment to contemplate it. She is too amazed to organise her thoughts.

It is a strand of precious stones, a silver clasp. It is a string of pearls.

17

Can I make a confession? One is beginning to tire of sitting in this roost, staring out at the rhododendrons, tire of admiring the blossoms on that magnolia. Nothing changes in this cul-de-sac of cages: the stone urns and the iron benches – they're always the same. Oh, but there are going to be some changes around here this evening, make no mistake. Indeed, I don't suppose it'll be long until the scent-marking stations close and the results start to come in. Just imagine the excitement in Carnivorous Central Office. Just imagine the—

What was that? What was that? I am sure I heard a noise.

Oh. One seems to have an audience this evening. Well, what a pleasant surprise! Let's get started, then. The barnacle goose loitering near the geraniums. Your question, dear?

I don't understand. We don't seem to have mastered the English language, do we? Oh, I see. We've just arrived from the wild. We're a recent migrant. Well, have another stab at it, then.

Something about the marquee that has been put up outside the Small Mammal House.

What? No, of course it isn't a reception centre for immigrants. It's a scent-marking station. Next question, please.

Yes? Oh, not another barnacle goose. I do hope these gardens aren't going to get swamped. What was that? Gobbledegook. Could someone translate, please?

It's almost – what? It's almost summer. Couldn't the scent-marking contest be held in the open air?

Goodness me, no. This is a respectable institution. Scent-marking is something one is brought up to do in private. Indeed, I should imagine a specimen might find itself unable to perform if it caught a glimpse of a peeping Tomcat in the bushes. There is no peeping under the canvas of a scent-marking station. There is no intimidation.

Next question. The creature crouched on the litterbin. The raccoon.

You'd like to have a look inside one of the marquees?

Don't bother. It's not an attractive sight. Unless one happens to find the spectacle of three animals drenched in urine appealing. Of course, three is the norm – a representative of each Order – but I'm afraid one might also have the misfortune to come across a red-throated loon or some other extremist. Thank goodness there's no conversation. Oh, I suppose the candidates might sometimes grunt at each other, but it's against the rules and regulations to campaign for a creature's scent at this stage in the contest. One must leave the scent-marker in peace to come to a decision and anoint its chosen representative accordingly.

Yes? The Tasmanian devil. Your question?

Do I mean—

Would you care to rephrase that? The expletive is not a term I recognise.

Do I mean urinate on them?

Well, it all depends on the scent-marker concerned. You see, some have special glands that can be rubbed against their chosen candidate. In red deer and moose, these are located on the hind legs. In otters and civets, I am told one can find them a little higher up, near the... Near the base of the tail. But in the absence of such an organ a drop of urine is acceptable, yes. Or at least it's supposed to be no more than a drop. In practice, I'm afraid most specimens like to make sure their bladders are full before setting off for their local scent-marking station. Next question, please.

The marbled cat crouched behind – what is it? Some rodent.

Have I been out to cast a squirt of scent today?

Well, what a coincidence! Someone asked me the same question this afternoon.

What was that?

Oh, I am afraid that disagreeable man came to see me again: the chap that claims to be a biographer, remember? He seemed to be interested in the scent-marking contest too. 'Been out to cast a drop of scent, then?' he said.

I made it quite clear to him. 'There's no point in me calling in at a scent-marking station,' I replied. 'I am not equipped for the purpose, dear.'

'Not equipped?'

'One is reluctant to discuss one's internal organs.'

'Oh, go on.'

'No, I don't think so.'

'Is something missing?' he said, giving me an insolent glare. 'Let me guess... a heart, perhaps?'

I told him I resented the accusation.

But of course, he insisted. He accused me... He accused me of dining on the remains of some poor creature that had passed through the boathouse. 'The man on the marble. The Flight Lieutenant.'

'Not him again. I thought I'd explained: sometimes I forget things, dear.'

He said he found that – what was the word he used? Convenient.

I remember I had to suppress an urge to give him a sharp peck. 'Convenient?' I said. 'There's nothing convenient about it at all. There is not. Be under no illusions: it's the most distressing affliction. You see, nouns are the first to go: the correct term for a certain cut of mutton in the cold store, the right name for the beaten-copper groat that's missing from one's change. One is reduced to referring to the item that one requires as a something-or-other or a thingummy. It's humiliating. But of course, that's just the beginning, because then one might discover that one has forgotten the subject of a conversation, or lost the thread of an argument – and I do love a good argument, so that can be most frustrating. I am told the condition is degenerative, incurable. That said, I've been reassured that the distant past should remain intact until... until the end. Indeed, I understand in some birds old memories are sharper than usual. No doubt I am one such specimen. Did I not recollect standing on the boat slip and staring up at a house martin returning to its roost? I seem to recall that I did. But I cannot remember this man on the marble, dear. I cannot.'

There must have been a short silence. Perhaps he needed a moment to take in the horror of one's affliction.

'Fair enough,' he said at last. 'Let's leave the Flight Lieutenant to rest in peace. What about that Coil character? The anaconda. Can you remember him?'

'Draco? Oh, I shall never forget Draco Coil. He lived for his convictions and he died for them – died in such atrocious circumstances. Goodness me, I can still hear the sound of that explosion echoing through the corridors of the Hall of Exhibits. Some devils got him – sheep and goats, separatists from the Norn Iron Farmstead. Never mind the peace agreement that Ebenezer's predecessor signed. I shall never pardon them. Never.'

I remember I had to take a deep breath. You see, I'd hoped to speak at length about the atrocities committed in these gardens – the assassination attempt on me, the device that detonated as I was putting the finishing touches to a speech – but I'm afraid he insisted on changing the subject. 'You mentioned a missing internal organ?' he said.

I decided to confess: 'I don't have a bladder, dear,' I replied. 'No bird does. Indeed, I don't suppose I'd be able to get off the ground if I had to lug all that useless liquid into the air. Natural selection has eliminated the need for excess baggage. One doesn't produce urea. One excretes an odourless deposit instead.'

He reached into his bag, pulled out a packet of Old Holborn. 'Odourless? Doesn't that make it difficult for birds to participate in the scent-marking process, then?'

'Not at all,' I said. 'Birds are entitled to approach a mammal of their choice and instruct the specimen to produce a squirt of scent on their behalf. Of course, an egret might use the hippopotamus it perches on, an oxpecker might use an ox, but I find the scent of such creatures a little too delicate. Much better to make one's intentions clear in no uncertain terms. Much better to use a skunk.'

'Sounds like an unpleasant experience,' he said, reaching for his cigarette papers. 'For the candidates.'

'I'm afraid it can be at times. But of course, some members of the Hall of Exhibits consider it an honour. Indeed, I believe there might still be a stubborn old mule in the Order of Herbivores that refuses to bathe from one scent-marking contest to the next. In practice, though, most candidates are more pragmatic. In the Order of Carnivores, it's standard practice to recruit a doppelgänger to take one's place. In fact, I remember I managed to persuade a Cape Barren goose to step into the breach for me.'

'But a goose is nothing like a lappet-faced vulture.'

'Oh, once I'd plucked the thing and draped a string of imitation pearls around its breast no one could tell the difference.'

He glanced up at me as he rolled his cigarette. 'Your pearls aren't imitation, then?'

'Imitation?' I said. 'Let me make it quite clear: there's nothing imitation about mother of pearl. There is not. It is strong and resilient – just like me. Oh, and the craftsmanship! Do not underestimate the care that has gone into protecting those pearls over the centuries. Goodness me, I shudder at the thought of stringing them around the neck of some goose.'

'Not posh enough, a Cape Barren goose? Too common?'

'Oh, I am not as posh as I sound, dear. I am not grand at all. We are reluctant to put on airs and graces. We are an undertaker's daughter. Besides, I don't have the plumage to strut up and down like a peacock. Of course, I remember when I was a fledgling I used to long for a little more glamour. But there's no escaping the fact that one is brown, or that one's tail is short and wedge-shaped. One just has to make the most of the other attributes one has been given – and I do have other attributes; after all, I have the most magnificent pair of lappets.'

He told me that a lappet-eared bat had moved into the Nocturnal House.

'Has it?' I said. 'The specimen must be a migrant I assume. Be under no illusions: I am most eager to inspect the little thing. But I don't suppose its lappets amount to much: a nip of loose skin, perhaps – nothing more. I doubt it has fold upon fold of paper-thin flesh hanging from either side of its face. Then again, it isn't a lappet-faced vulture, is it, dear?'

'Perhaps not,' he conceded, as he fumbled through his pockets for a lighter. 'But––'

'Let me finish,' I said. 'Now, I mentioned one has an obligation to make the most of one's attributes? And that's the thing about a good string of pearls. Their luminescence sets off the lappets, gives the commissure of the beak a gentle lift. Oh, I must admit the effect isn't quite the same in a fledgling – a bird needs to be in her prime to pull it off. Yet even so, I shall never forget the afternoon I first tried them on; I shall never forget… '

'Yes?'

'The sensation. Call it instinct, but it felt as if that string of pearls had been made for me. I remember looking into the mirror on the old duchess dressing table and realising that the little lappet-faced thing staring back at me could no longer be dismissed as just another example of her species, just another specimen; she demanded to be seen as an individual. I suppose I must have understood that I'd been set apart from birds that lack ambition, birds that tend the nest. I must have understood that I'd been chosen.'

'Chosen?' he mumbled as he lit his cigarette.

'That's right, dear. Oh, I was so excited I could have danced.'

18

OLD HESPER HOUSE AND ZOOLOGICAL GARDENS

The Bog-land Enclosures

THE OLD BOATHOUSE

SITUAT~~ION~~ Cage, Enclosure or Other Estate Building.
Preservation order pending.

KEEP OUT

Instead of clearing up the mess on the marble, she gives the big black button on the wireless set a sharp peck and tunes into a station broadcasting big-band music. She might be no nightingale, but she attempts to sing along.

'*Who's the* something something dum–de–dum diddy–dum.'

She cannot resist the urge to dance.

'*What a* something something dum–de–dum diddy–dum.'

The string of pearls dangling on her breast lurches from side to side as she quicksteps across the boathouse in a little routine based on the courtship ritual of the great crested grebe. She shimmies up to the tea chest and pouts at her reflection in the lacquer. Is she as graceful as the grebes that sometimes perform on the lake? She suspects she might be.

She sidesteps a puddle of sulphuric acid and spins off the chains and couplings that hang from the marble-topped contraption. She leaps over a small scrap of fallen liver.

'*In the mood* de–dum–de–dum–dum.'

Poor little Bel-imperia Pinch. She is so engrossed in the Glenn Miller Orchestra that she cannot hear the double doors creak open on their hinges. Neither can she see the horrified expression on the face of the gaunt-looking specimen that has marched into the building.

He has to shout to make himself heard above the trumpets and trombones: 'What on earth is the meaning of this spectacle?'

Bel-imperia is disconcerted to see her mother standing beside him. 'She were struttin' up an' down like a common trollops – that's the meaning on't.'

'I wasn't strutting, Mother. I was… ' She steals a moment to snatch a gasp of air. 'I was dancing.'

'Dancing?' There is a bundle of old rags strung around his scapulars. He pecks at its strings, sets it down on the flagstones. 'And is it respectful to dance in the presence of the deceased?'

'Perhaps not but… ' She's quite sure that dancing is more respectful than eating the deceased's appendage.

'This song's smutty, isn't it, Silas? It's about copulation.'

'No, it's not, Mother. Lots of animals listen to—'

He interrupts her. 'I didn't invest in a second-hand wireless set so that we could waste our time listening to light entertainment. It's for discussion programmes and debates. Now, turn it off this instant.'

There is something threatening about the silence that replaces the sound of the Glenn Miller Orchestra. Bel-imperia cannot describe the precise nature of the threat, she cannot put a name to it, but she can sense that something bad is going to happen. She considers her predicament. It cannot be long before her parents discover the mess on the marble. She should have mopped up the man's spilt blood; she should have disposed of his uneaten gallbladder. Perhaps it might be sensible to slip outside and make herself scarce. She shuffles around the marble-topped contraption, saunters across to the double doors…

'Laws-a-massy-me, what's she got snick-snarled around her neck?'

'It looks like some sort of gaud to me.' He hoists up his tail and reverses into the doors, slamming them shut. No escape, then.

'It's not a gaud, Father. It's just a string of pearls, that's all.'

Her mother says, 'Pearls bring tears.'

Bel-imperia glances down at the precious stones resting on her breast. Is that true? Do pearls bring tears? She suspects she might be about to find out.

'Where she gotten 'em from? That's what I want to know.'

'Oh, I found them on the lake-shore, Mother.' It isn't a lie: the boathouse is on the lake-shore and the man is in the boathouse. But even so, it hasn't escaped her attention that a dead man's gut is an unusual place to discover a string of pearls. There's bound to be a logical explanation, a series of events that led to them being there. Did a careless she-surgeon drop them during some operation? Improbable. Did someone creep into the boathouse and slip them into the man, then? She remembers the laceration looked like it had been torn open – the pressure of the gas building up in his bloated stomach, she had assumed. Perhaps she'd been mistaken. Perhaps someone forced it open in order to push the pearls inside. But who would do such a thing and why?

No time to consider the questions. Her mother is squawking: 'It en't finders keepers in these gardens, is it, Silas?'

'No, it isn't.'

'But Father––'

'Silence, chick.' He tells her about some magpies that have set up a small business trading under the name of Lost & Found, suggests she takes them there.

'Where's this?'

'In the Cages of Caer Lud.'

Caer Lud. Bel-imperia's heart misses a beat at the sound of the name. There's nothing she'd like more than to see the bright lights of the great conurbation of cages clustered around Old Hesper House: the majestic promenades, the monumental animal houses. But she has no intention of surrendering her pearls to some thieving magpies.

'The thing is, Father… '

'Let me have a look at them.'

He lunges at his daughter, snatches the pearls in his beak. Is he going to break them? She resists the urge to struggle; she lets him remove them.

He drapes them over the lid of the old lacquered tea chest.

'Pearls indeed.' His tone might be disparaging, but the precious stones look stunning in the sunlight that is streaming into the boathouse. She scutters up to the tea chest. Just a little closer. Is there a subtle difference in the luminescence of each delicate orb? Is that a sign of craftsmanship? She cannot be sure, but she is quite certain that she must get them back at all costs.

'These aren't pearls at all, chick. What woman would wear her best string of pearls to the Bog-land Enclosures? What member of the general public would leave them on the lake-shore? There's no point in taking them to those magpies in Caer Lud. The necklace is just imitation – a cheap piece of tat.'

'Then in that case can I keep it, please, Father?'

'Keep it?' He seems undecided. 'Well, I'm not sure I... '

'Just chuck 'em in the lake, Silas.'

Bel-imperia glares at her mother. She's pecking at the bundle of rags that the couple brought to the boathouse, attempting to open it.

'Please, Father.'

He drops the pearls into the tea chest, slams the lid shut. 'I shall have to give the matter some thought.'

'Just give her a good clout instead.'

Her mother has managed to untie the bundle. Is that a laddered stocking she is pulling out? Is that the sleeve of an old cardigan or something?

'What's she doing here, Father?'

'Your mother knows what's required of her, chick. Now, we've wasted enough time. We have a customer who needs attending to.' He instructs her to help him prepare the embalming solution. 'Six buckets should be enough. Come on, let's make a start.'

She scuttles around behind him searching for suitable buckets, but it's impossible to concentrate on the chore: her mother is clambering up the spice drawers, trailing a laddered stocking behind her. It cannot be long, then, until she glances over her scapulars and spots the mess on the marble: the discarded gallbladder, the pool of blood... Bel-imperia musters her inner strength, tries to prepare for the performance she'll need to put on, but her self-confidence is thin. Is she going to be able to convince her father that she hasn't set foot on the marble-topped contraption all afternoon? She isn't sure.

Bessie grabs a brass handle in her gnarled talons and gives it a sharp tug. Is that a bag of cumin she is removing?

'Father?' He seems to have discovered a leaking bucket. She helps him turn it upside down. 'Shouldn't she be at home tending the nest?'

'Your mother has another nest to prepare this afternoon, chick.'

Bessie stuffs some rags into the glass-fronted drawer and plumps them up. 'There, that should keep the little bastard snug as a bug.'

'Language, darling! The correct term is abomination.'

'Don't tell me I gone an' putten "putten" where I should ha' putten "put". I know where the word "bastard" goes.'

'Now, then, Bess. I'd be the first to admit that macaques have loose morals, but… ' He explains to her that the creature he'd dismissed as a brazen harlot helped him up onto his feet after he'd disgraced himself at matins. 'She brushed the grit out of my feathers. She called me "sir".'

'And so?'

'And so I don't think we should use the "b" word to refer to her infant.'

'Well, I'm not afeard o' callin' the babby o' some trollops a bastard… '

Bel-imperia couldn't be less interested in her parents' discussion. Who cares about the correct term for the offspring of some disreputable macaque? She tries to tune out of their conversation, but it's impossible to ignore her mother if she has a piece of gossip that she's determined to spread.

'I heard the harlot's been told her babby's going to die.'

'Die?'

'Not sure as I should be gabbin'.' She darts a pointed glance at her daughter. 'Little pigs have big ears.'

'I'm not a pig, Mother.'

'Be quiet, Bel-imperia.'

She scuttles across to the nearest bucket and pretends to inspect it.

'Go on, darling.'

'I heard the trollops 'as been to see the beezum.'

'The beezum?'

Her mother must be referring to the specimen that no one cares to talk about: the creature in the cave.

'You know, that thing that skulks i' the darklins and comes

crappelin' out, limpelty lobelty. That W**ch We Do Not Speak About.'

'I see.'

'I heard the beezum snorted up some smoke an' had one o' its turns; I heard it made a prediction. From all accounts, it told the trollops her babby's going to die on't Sabbath.'

So the creature must be some sort of prophet, then. It makes sense. 'Protect our little lappet-faced things from false prophets,' the crocodile-priest had said. 'Tempt them not to scuttle into caves.' Belimperia remembers standing in the amphitheatre and staring across the lake as the other animals intoned the Most Sacred Tenet of the Faith. It still nags at her mind, the instinct to seek out the creature in the cave, but so does the instinct to reclaim her string of pearls – and of course, she also needs to find out if she has been offered a scholarship or not. There's so much that needs to be done. Yet here she is, cooped up in the boathouse staring into a cast-iron bucket. It's so frustrating. She takes a deep breath and counts to ten, tries to calm her irritable temper, but it's impossible to concentrate on the exercise: her mother is squawking like a parrot.

'Laws-a-massy-me! Never mind them buckets, Silas. Hop up on't marble an' have a gleg at the dog's dinner your daughter's made o' the deceased.'

This is it, then: the moment she has been dreading.

'Bel-imperia Pinch, come up here this minute.'

'Goodness me. What on earth… ?' Her astonishment is genuine. She cannot remember leaving the man in such an appalling mess. His stomach appears to have deflated, disgorging an assortment of organs onto the marble. Is that his pancreas sitting in a pool of gore? Is that his spleen?

'I cannot see his liver, chick.'

'No, neither can I.'

The judicial process is much as she had imagined: his unsubstantiated allegations, her emphatic denials. Of course, she is obliged to be economical as far as the truth is concerned, but as soon as she's sworn on the Seven Commandments, as soon as she's under oath, she is careful not to tell deliberate lies. Besides, it's quite true:

she arrived at the boathouse to find the double doors ajar, she sensed the presence of an intruder, she caught a glimpse of something in the mirror, she glanced around the building but the creature had gone.

'I must admit there's no incriminating evidence.' He is inspecting the bristle feathers on the commissure of her beak. 'No bloodstains.'

'Of course not.' Thank goodness she plunged her head into a bucket to give the pearls a thorough rinse.

'I suspect it might have been a black-capped jackal.'

'Yes, so do I.'

He scuttles around a pile of spilt entrails. 'Good gracious me, the culprit has eaten... ' He must have spotted that the man's appendage is missing.

'Father?'

Is he going to look up? Is he going to subject her to an accusing stare? It seems not. No doubt he cannot bring himself to contemplate the thought of such a prim and proper creature gorging on a penis.

'Or perhaps,' he mutters to himself, 'it might have been a hyena.'

Is that it, then? Have the judicial proceedings been concluded? Confident that she's about to be acquitted, little Bel-imperia Pinch rouses, shakes the stale air out of her flight feathers. For a moment, she is almost content. But she has forgotten that there is another member of the judiciary perched on the spice drawers.

It passes judgement: 'She's a bigger liar than Tom Pepper.'

'I resent that allegation, Mother.'

'Thou hast sore need o' a pottle o' brains, Silas. Just have a gleg at her belly. She's fatted like a bacon-pig.'

'I doubt she'd devour the deceased's manhood, Bessie. Good gracious me, she's not much more than a fledgling.'

'Poison goes in a small compass.'

'For goodness' sake, Mother.'

'Make her boak up the scraps in her gizzard. That'll settle the matter.'

'Father, please.' She attempts to appeal to his better judgement. Insisting that there is nothing in her stomach to regurgitate, she reminds him that this isn't the Serengeti, that it's impolite to retch. He seems to be in agreement. Indeed, she can sense that he's reluctant to make her undergo such a humiliating ordeal. He turns to his beloved Bessie: hesitant, uncertain.

'Just friggin' do it, Silas.'

'Yes, of course, dear.' Is he incapable of standing up to the tinpot general perched on the spice drawers?

He bends his daughter over the man's leg and instructs her to evacuate the contents of her stomach. She can imagine his reaction to some scraps of regurgitated liver. It doesn't bear thinking about. She consents to a delicate cough. 'I'm afraid that's all I can manage, Father.'

He inspects the little lump of phlegm she has produced. Could he be less impressed?

'Happen this'll make her boak,' her mother says, snatching a bag of cumin and slinging it across the boathouse.

He catches it in his beak and slashes it open, releasing the offensive odour. He places the bag under his daughter's nares and tightens his grip on her mantle.

Bel-imperia tries to ignore the stench – of course she does – but even so, she is soon conscious of an undulating sensation in her gizzard. She can also detect an uncomfortable tightness, a blockage. Is a lump of liver obstructing her isthmus gastris? No, it can't be liver. It must be the last thing she ate; it must be the man's appendage.

She belches. 'Pardon me.'

The pressure building up behind the blockage is intense. Is she going to shoot a penis across the boathouse like a torpedo? She should like to aim the projectile at her mother. She imagines the moment of impact, the bulbous head of the organ detonating in an explosion of gore. She imagines her mother sinking down onto the spice drawers like – what? For some reason, the image of a stricken battleship comes to mind. Gotcha.

'Come on, Bel-imperia. I haven't got all afternoon.'

She banishes the thought of torpedoes and battleships – another time, another place – and concentrates on suppressing the urge to regurgitate. She should never have given in to the temptation to lunge at the man's liver; she should never have listened to—

Draco?

She can sense that there is something up in the crossbeams. She steals a glance at the rafters, catches a glimpse of the intruder: no, not an anaconda. Just a common carrier pigeon. But even so, perhaps the creature means salvation.

'You're beginning to try my patience, chick.'

'But Father, isn't it bad manners to regurgitate in the presence of a guest?'

'Guest? I am in no mood to receive guests.'

Is he ever?

Undaunted at the prospect of a hostile reception, the pigeon clatters down into the dappled sunlight, settles on an upended bucket.

'Not another second-class specimen.'

But Bel-imperia can tell that this is a first-class Columbine: it has dark stripes on its remiges, an orange nostril cere. Besides, there's nothing substandard about the Nile-blue envelope that the creature is clutching in its beak.

She tries to get a better look at it, tries to crane her neck, but she's still pinned down over the dead man's leg. And so she cannot see if the letter is embossed in gold or not. Yet even so, she's quite certain that it must be from the Cloisters.

She thinks, Thank you, Draco.

The pigeon spits out the envelope, places it on the bucket. Does it contain an offer of a scholarship – or, better still, a bundle of admissions papers? Or is it just a polite rejection? It looks like she might be about to find out.

'Right, then. Sorry to break up the game o' Happy Families, but the Pigeon Master General insisted that I gotta get a scribble.'

'Bring me a bottle of Quink, Bel-imperia.' He releases her from his grip.

'No, not you, guv'nor. This one's addressed to the female o' the species.'

Never mind the Quink. There's no time to lose.

She scuttles across the marble, leaps into the air, but no sooner is she airborne than she can hear the sound of some large object hurtling across the boathouse. She can also hear an alarm bell in her head ringing DANGER: MID-AIR COLLISION. Primitive instinct? She chooses to trust it all the same. She pulls up in a curve to the right, returns to the marble-topped contraption.

Did she make the right decision? Of course she did: the object's wings were clipped when it was a fledgling; it is incapable of executing an evasive manoeuvre, incapable of controlled flight.

There is a dreadful clang as her mother snatches the startled pigeon out of the air and crashes into a cast-iron bucket.

'Bessie, darling... '

She pins the carrier pigeon down under her talons. She plunges her beak into its breast and plucks out its heart.

'Oh, Bessie!'

Bel-imperia gazes in astonishment at the merciless predator crouched over its victim: its mantled wings; its wild, staring eyes. She had no idea her mother could be so brutal, so magnificent. Has she reverted to her natural state? Has she gone feral?

She glances at her father. The colour has drained out of his lappets.

'Don't stand there gatherin' gape seed, Silas. The general public don't come to these gardens to gleg at common pigeons. One more, one less, it's swings an' roundabouts.' She extracts the Nile-blue envelope from the carnage and squints at it. 'Just as I thought, addressed to me.'

'I don't think it is, Father.'

'I am... I am so shocked, Bessie.'

'Shocked at the death o' some pigeon? You're as soft as a bladder o' lard, Silas Pinch. It were a clean kill. Thou should ha' heard that mouse that ended up on your dinner plate last night – that one that didn't ha' time to go reasty, remember? Laws-a-massy-me, how he squealed!'

'You've been hunting mice? Oh, Bessie... '

'How dost thou think I make ends meet? Fool.' She plumps up her breast, turns to her daughter. 'I'll tell thee summats, madam: he en't no saint.'

'He is to me.'

'Well, you're a bigger fool than he is, then. Why dost thou think he sat down on his arse in the middle o' matins? Why dost thou think the other animals gossip about him?'

'Enough is enough.' He sounds like he has lost his patience. 'Get out of this boathouse this minute, Bessie. And don't bother coming back unless it's to apologise.'

There is a chilling silence as her parents glare at each other. Is he going to swoop down from the marble and give his beloved Bessie a clip across the lappets? Bel–imperia's never seen them at loggerheads like this before; she isn't sure.

Eventually, her mother says, 'Well, I know when I'm not wanted.' Is she sobbing? Is that a tear on her lore?

He seems to think it must be. 'Oh, come on, darling, there's no need to cry. Hop up here and I'll forget about this quarrel. Let's preen and make up.'

But it doesn't look like she's in the mood to be preened. She reverses into the double doors, bouncing them open, and stomps out onto the boat slip, the bloodstained envelope clamped in her beak.

'Bessie, darling… '

Later, he is going to brood on this moment; he is going to reconstruct the details in his mind and return to them again and again: the sunlight slanting into the boathouse through the half-open doors, a bluebottle settling on the remains of a slaughtered pigeon. Poor Silas Pinch. He's never going to forget catching this last glimpse of his beloved's tail feathers disappearing out of sight. He's never going to forgive himself for hanging his head and gazing at the marble. Never. Not even in the 1960s; not even in old age. 'You should have gone after her, Silas,' he'll mutter to himself. 'You should have made her see sense.' This afternoon, though, he has no inkling that she has just barged out of the door for the last time, no inkling that he is never going to see her again. Neither has his daughter.

'Father?'

He is still staring at the marble. 'I'm concerned that something cold-blooded has been let loose in this boathouse, Bel.'

'Cold-blooded?'

'First the mortal remains of the deceased, butchered like the carcass of a common goat. And then that poor pigeon… '

This is the moment. She seizes it: 'You know I'd never break the First Commandment, don't you, Father?'

'Of course I do, chick.'

There's a short silence. In the distance, the sound of some small mammal screeching.

'That letter… I don't think it was addressed to Mother.'

'No, neither do I.'

'I suspect it might have been from the Cloisters.'

'Yes.'

She can sense that he's got something to tell her. Is he searching for a suitable turn of phrase?

'Your mother… '

'Yes?'

'She's no spring chicken. She has stopped laying. Her… What are they called, those tubes in her tummy?'

'Ovaries?'

'Her ovaries are exhausted. She has run out of eggs.'

Bel-imperia isn't surprised to hear it.

'Of course, she used to have plenty, but I'm afraid… Well, I wanted to build up the embalming business, get some groats behind us before we settled down to raise a clutch of chicks. And so I resisted the urge to… You know, the "c" word.'

He means copulate.

'Time passed. Breeding seasons came and went. Until one night she hoisted up her tail feathers and said, "Tha'd better get on with it, Silas, 'cos I only got one egg left."'

'I see.'

'I consented, of course; I obliged. Oh, I remember she took such care of that egg. The most attentive incubation. Turning it at just the right moment, keeping it at just the right temperature. You see, she'd set her heart on… She'd hoped… '

'She'd hoped that it contained a male of the species.'

'Yes.'

Bel-imperia gazes at the remains of the man's amputated appendage. The scrotum, the stump. 'So I'm a disappointment to her?'

'Yes, but I tried to comfort her. "We'll just have to make the most of our misfortune," I said. "She seems quite bright. For a member of the inferior sex. We'll invest in some private tuition. Who knows? Perhaps she might turn out to be almost as successful as a male."'

She can feel it rising up in her: the anger, the aggression. Should she release it, or should she bottle it up and put it in the cellar to age?

'Your mother doesn't share our love of learning, though. She insists that the female of the species isn't adapted to academia. She thinks it's daft to squander good groats on educating something that's destined to tend a nest.'

'For goodness' sake… '

'Don't hold it against her, Bel. Your grandparents couldn't afford to give her much of a start in life. Oh, she had a couple of months at Hedge School, of course; just enough to get to grips with the ABCs, but no private instruction in Latin, no hope of a scholarship to the Cloisters.'

'She's jealous.'

'Perhaps.' He shuffles along the edge of the marble.

'You'll put her in her place this evening I assume?'

He is gazing at the dead pigeon. 'Her place?'

'You'll make her give me that letter?'

'Oh, I don't suppose… ' He steals a sheepish glance at his daughter. Is Silas Pinch Esq too henpecked to stand up to the old harridan? 'You know what your mother's like when her dander's up. Besides, I expect she's already burnt it.'

'Burnt it!' She imagines her mother stuffing the letter into an incinerator. 'What am I going to do, then?' She reminds him that Michaelmas Term starts on Monday. 'That's the day after tomorrow, Father.'

'You could traipse across the zoological gardens to the Cloisters and make some polite enquiries.'

'Over the weekend?' She is starting to panic. 'The admissions office is bound to be closed.'

'Call in at the Hunting Tower, then. I heard that spectacled owl on reception has been moonlighting at the Cloisters. She might have a list of the successful candidates.'

'Not that disagreeable old spinster? Not Miss Scroop?'

'That's the one.' He darts a glance at the spice drawers, mentions something about a book he has reserved. 'You can collect it for me while you're there.'

But his daughter isn't listening. She is contemplating the prospect of confronting Edna Scroop and persuading her to surrender a list of the successful candidates. The mission is daunting, there can be no doubt about that. Has little Bel-imperia Pinch got the courage to rise to the challenge? Of course she has.

She shakes the sulphur dioxide out of her remiges and leaps into the air. She glides across to the old duchess dressing table and inspects her reflection in its looking glass. Is she presentable enough to take on such an obnoxious owl? Just a quick preen, perhaps.

Done.

'I'll speak to Miss Scroop at once, then.'

'You'll do no such thing.'

'But it's getting late, Father. The Hunting Tower closes at sunset.'

'And opens again tomorrow.'

'No, it doesn't. Tomorrow's the Sabbath.'

He explains that the Elders have instructed the owls to open the building all the same. 'I argued against it, of course, but it seems the animals in these gardens need something to take their minds off mankind and his Messerschmitts. I was persuaded that reading is better than dancing.'

'But Father... '

'The deceased is decomposing, Bel-imperia. And so is that pigeon.' She's tempted to point out that the pigeon hasn't had time to decompose, but she can tell that he's in no mood to be contradicted. 'Your presence is required here. There should be no need to remind you that I still haven't decided what to do with that cheap string of beads.'

She strikes a bargain: she agrees to assist him in exchange for the pearls.

'Right. Let's make a start, then.' He drops down onto the ground. 'First, the pigeon.'

'Shall I look up the recommended amount of solution?'

'No, I haven't got time to embalm a common Columbine. Besides, it's not as though its relatives have given us their commission. Who would I send the invoice to?'

'The Pigeon Master General?'

His nerves seem to be on edge. Is he concerned he might be asked to account for the pigeon's disappearance? 'No, I think in this instance a simple funeral is more appropriate. One hesitates to use the phrase "dispose of the evidence", but… '

'I understand.'

He gives the dead bird a gentle nudge. 'I suppose it's about the same size as a man's liver, isn't it?'

She is too smart to get caught out. 'I don't know, Father; I've never seen a human liver.'

'I am sure it must be.'

He snatches the pigeon and stuffs it into the man's upper abdomen.

'There,' he says, stepping back to admire the achievement. 'Now, I suspect there might be just enough room to ease these entrails back inside.'

His daughter helps him gather up the spilt organs, but as she scrabbles up onto the deceased something makes her stomach turn. Is it the bitter tang of the gallbladder she is clasping in her beak? Perhaps. She slips it back into the man, returns to the marble to collect his spleen. Dare she let her tongue explore the ridges on the organ's surface? Delicious. It cannot be these delicacies that are upsetting her stomach, then. Is it something she has eaten? The thought occurs to her that it might be a pellet. Under normal circumstances, there is nothing improper about expelling the indigestible remains of a meal. Indeed, it's quite acceptable to turn one's head to one side and cough up a discreet pellet of rabbit teeth or rodent gristle. But these aren't normal circumstances: her pellet is bound to contain incriminating evidence.

'Bring me a surgical needle, Bel.'

She attempts to concentrate on holding the seams of the laceration together as he places a series of cross-stitches in them, but it is impossible to ignore the sensation that something is lodged in her oesophagus. She suppresses a belch. Is that the man's appendage she can taste repeating on her? She hopes not.

Time to prepare the embalming solution. No need to read the label on the canister: she's been told a thousand times that its contents are inflammable. She siphons a pint or so into a bucket, pauses to peer inside. Is that going to be enough to turn the deceased's soluble albumins into a gel-like substance? She cannot be sure: it's getting late; the light is beginning to fail.

'Shall I get out the candles, Father?'

Silence.

'Father?'

He is up in the rafters, pecking at the ropes hanging from the crossbeams. He threads one through the handle of an old-fashioned flat iron, ties it in a knot and nudges the iron off the edge of the beam.

'Stand clear!'

She watches with awe as the weight descends with a whoosh, taking up the slack in the rope attached to the man's arm. Although she's been schooled in the basic principles of a block and tackle, it still gives her a start to see the dead man raise his right hand and point at her, accusingly. But the deceased is nothing more than a puppet on a string. One more rope, one more counterweight, and he is soon in the appropriate position for a large primate to meet its maker: arms folded across the chest.

'There, that's much more dignified, isn't it?'

She agrees that it is.

'Right. Let's give him a good scrub, then.'

He swoops down onto the tea chest and overturns it, spilling its contents across the flagstones: the cigarette tin and the box of matches, the scouring pad and the tail thinner. Is that her string of pearls she can see caught on the bristles of some old scrubbing brush? She disguises a sudden urge to rescue them, but she cannot disguise her impatience. She glares at him as he rummages through the debris. It's almost dark. Will she be able to give him the slip and call in on That W**ch We Do Not Speak About, or is she going to be here all night attending to the needs of the man on the marble?

She belches.

'Pardon me.' She can taste it in her mouth again, the man's appendage. It repulses her.

'Here it is!'

He snatches a stocking that has been tied into a knot and slings it into a saucepan. Bel-imperia cringes. It is her mother's creation, the soap-stocking – a collection of a dozen soaps stuffed into the toe of a laddered stocking. Soaps? Dried-up scraps that have been prised off the basins of the Gentlemen's Convenience. Pastel-coloured ovals that ought to be thrown out. 'Waste not want not,' Bessie had said as she presented the object to him. 'That'll save thee using all the Pears'.' But over the months, the soap ends have congealed into a grey gloop that oozes out through the mesh of the nylon and gets caught on the barbs of a bird's feathers. She leaves it soaking in the saucepan, offers to scrape the dirt out of the man's fingernails instead.

'Of course,' her father announces as soon as the deceased has been scrubbed and disinfected, 'one can tell a lot about an institution such as ours from the tender mercies it administers to its dead; one can measure the moral character of the creatures that run the establishment… '

But his daughter isn't listening. She's losing her battle against the object inching up her oesophagus. She needs to get out of the boathouse. Soon.

'Father?'

He has disappeared into a cupboard. No time to lose. She cranes her head over a cast-iron bucket, but before she can cough up the offending organ, he re-emerges, dragging out the embalming machine. Despite its castors, the contraption is difficult to manoeuvre. Does he need some help? She scutters along behind him, tries to gather up the clear plastic tubes that trail from the motor, but she is unable to stop them slithering through the odd puddle of sulphuric acid.

He snatches the shortest tube, plunges it into a bucket of embalming solution, seizes another and carries it up to the marble.

'I just need to make a couple of incisions.'

Wielding the tip of his hooked beak like a scalpel, he scratches an 'x' into the man's charred skin.

'I'm afraid I might spill some blood – not an appropriate sight for an impressionable chick to behold. Take that tube out onto the boat slip and put it in the lake.'

Thank goodness.

She scuttles out through the gap between the double doors,

dragging the tube behind her. She drops it into the lake, glances back at the boathouse and retches. Up it comes. Up it rises. She can feel it shooting up her neck, squeezing through her throat, bumping over the corrugated ridges on her rasp-like tongue…

There's a gentle thud as the man's undigested penis lands on the timbers of the boat slip, a little plop as it disappears through the gap between the slatted boards and drops into the lake. Bel-imperia peers at the sunken organ. It looks so small, so insignificant – just a scrap of tissue and tubing, nothing more. Does this make one sex superior to another then? She recoils in disgust. She has no desire to put such a disagreeable object in her mouth again, no ambition to acquire such an organ. In fact, she's delighted to be rid of the thing. She leaves it for the little fish to nibble at, and scuttles down to the end of the boat slip.

In the distance the sun is setting: orange, scarlet, rust. She rouses, shakes the smell of death out of her flight feathers. She is pleased to be out in the open air, pleased to put the soap-stocking and the buckets of embalming solution behind her. Should she make good her escape? She glances up at the bulging clouds: the sunlight on their bellies, the tempting gaps of blue. She is sure she can hear them calling her, urging her to come up and soar high above the zoological gardens. She inspects her underwing coverts. Is that a scrap of infantile down? How much longer until she's completed her first post-juvenile moult? Disappointed, she folds up her wings. Perhaps it's a blessing in disguise. The impulse to take to the air might be strong, but she's no fool: she can see that the boat slip is too short. No time to accelerate to the required ground speed, then. Besides, she has no intention of making a spectacle of herself. Someone is approaching.

Here comes the creature, strutting around a clump of branched bur-reeds. 'All right, love. Hope I'm not too late.'

Bel-imperia appraises the bronze-tailed she-pheasant: her ample breast and her burnished plumage, her slender legs and her graceful tail – an attractive specimen, it cannot be denied.

'Interviewing someone else, is he, love?'

'I don't think I've had the pleasure?'

The pheasant's plumage bristles. 'Fannie Hodgson. Pleased to meet you I'm sure.'

Bel-imperia squints at the bird. There seems to be something unnatural about Fannie's appearance: the commissure of her beak is too sharp, the edge of her lore too pronounced. 'Are you wearing make-up?'

'Just a spot o' kohl, love. Oh, and a dab o' red amaranth from the hothouse. Wouldn't dream o' going out without putting the damage on, not with an important interview an' all.'

She must have spotted the advertisement for an embalming assistant and gone back to the pheasant house to get spruced up.

'You been waiting long, then, love?'

'I'm not waiting; I just came out onto the boat slip to... ' She darts a glance through the slatted boards at the little fish tucking into their snack. She has no inclination to admit that she stepped outside to cough up a penis. 'I just came out to get some air.'

'Oh, dear. Bad as that, was it? I heard he can be a one.' The specimen shuffles up to her, gives her a gentle nudge. 'You all right, love?'

'Of course I'm all right. Why wouldn't I be?'

'Just asking.' Fannie recoils. Is she offended? She struts down to the end of the boat slip, gazes at her reflection in the lake. 'So, the candidate he's got in there at the moment... an attractive bird, is she?'

'He isn't interviewing a candidate.' Bel-imperia explains that her father is preparing a customer for cremation. 'You can't go in until he starts up the embalming machine. Is that clear?'

But she can tell that Fannie isn't listening. Something in the branched bur-reeds seems to have caught her attention.

'Ooh, I'll have that.' She pulls out a pale blue piece of china, places it on the slatted boards. 'Shame about that chip. Not in bad nick, though, is it, like? Considering.'

It is the teacup that Bel-imperia launched onto the lake at aurora matins. It is her offering to Sol.

'I hope you're going to give that back to the crocodiles. Some mornings there aren't enough to go around.'

'No, I'll put a candle in that – a candle and some scraps o' meat. I'm proper skint. I could use me a little good fortune.'

'Teacups don't bring good—'

'I'll take it up to… ' Fannie hesitates, peers at Bel-imperia. Something about her stare reminds her of Draco. Is she attempting to decide if she can trust her or not? 'Some of us leave offerings in teacups, love. Offerings to appease the whatchamacallit.'

'What whatchamacallit?'

'You know, That W**ch We Do Not Speak About.'

'You've seen it?'

'No, but I've been to the mouth of its cave. Up there, near the top.'

The pheasant is gazing at the ridge of the escarpment – a great bastion of solid rock rising above the treeline, like the ramparts of a medieval citadel. Bel-imperia is sure it must be three thousand trotters high, perhaps more. But even so, she is still determined to go there. The problem is that she is also determined to reclaim her string of pearls. Her instincts are pulling her in both directions at once. Time to make a decision, then.

Fact: her father is never going to surrender the pearls if she slopes off in the middle of the embalming. She glances over her scapulars at the double doors, tries to picture the precious stones caught on the bristles of a scrubbing brush: their luminescence, their lustre. Still holding the image in her mind, she turns to the escarpment, and tries to picture That W**ch We Do Not Speak About, but it's impossible to conjure up a coherent impression of the creature. Can she trust her instincts? Perhaps it is dangerous. Perhaps it's a charlatan – a false prophet, the crocodile-priest had said. Her thoughts turn to her mother. She calls it a beezum. She said it predicted that the macaque's infant is going to die on the Sabbath. It's almost the Sabbath; just one more night. Better to postpone the expedition, then. Better to test the creature in the cave. If the infant dies, That W**ch We Do Not Speak About isn't a false prophet, simple as that.

She scuttles up to the pheasant, pretends to be making conversation. 'I wonder what it is, the whatchamacallit.'

'I dunno, love. I heard a rumour she's the last o' her species, like those things in the Hall o' Relics. But I'm not sure.'

From inside the boathouse, the sound of a motor coughing and sputtering. It's a simple piece of equipment, the embalming machine – just a small pump, and some parts salvaged from an old lawnmower or something – but it produces more than enough pressure to force embalming solution into the specimens that pass through the boathouse and flush out their blood.

'Can I go in, then, love?'

'I suppose so.'

Bel-imperia bundles the bird through the doors and scutters down to the end of the boat slip. Just a moment to gather her thoughts, then she'll go back inside.

The sun has gone down and the lake-shore is shedding light, losing its sharpness as it casts off colour. She glances up at the escarpment. Is that a full moon rising behind a juniper tree on its desolate ridge? Is that a bomber's moon? She hopes not. She has no desire to spend the night cooped up in some iron bird shelter listening to the drone of engines overhead. She lets the thought go, turns her attention to the darkening mirror of the lake. She doesn't believe in spirits and daemons and all that hocus-pocus, but she can tell that it's magical. This place. This moment. She catches a glimpse of a sudden movement in the depths. Is something rising out of the gloom? Yes, she is sure she can make out the dim shape of some creature not dissimilar to the man on the marble. More sinuous, perhaps. More graceful. Is that a hand reaching up? Is that the ripple of a forefinger disturbing the surface of the water? She peers a little closer.

No. It must have been her imagination.

She can see nothing apart from the man's blood gushing out of a clear plastic tube and billowing into the darkness, like a cloud.

19

```
┌─────────────────────────────────────────────────┐
│                                                 │
│   OLD HES        OUSE Ⱥ         LOGICAL GARDE    │
│                                                 │
│              The Escarpment                     │
│                                                 │
│                    YE                           │
│                                                 │
│             la Madagascariensis                 │
│                                                 │
│        CAUTION: THIS ANIMAL          S          │
│                                                 │
└─────────────────────────────────────────────────┘
```

Here she is, then, That W**ch We Do Not Speak About. She sits, slumped in the nest she has built beneath the dripping stalactites: a canopied throne of brambles and gnarled branches. Sometimes she scratches her flea-bitten coat, or reaches out to stoke the embers of the fire that burns in front of her, but she seldom clambers out of her throne. She just sits and bides her time.

Occasionally, she might sing. She sings about the Last Judgement; she sings about the slaughter of mass extinction. Is she the last of the species, just like the dinosaurs in the Hall of Relics? Perhaps there might be another of her kind in the southern hemisphere – she cannot be sure – but she is quite certain that she's the eldest. Indeed, no doubt she should have shuffled off her mortal coil centuries ago. Yet here she is, clinging on at the edge of existence, just three score zodiacs short of her third millennium. Not bad at all. For an animal that is sometimes dismissed as a primitive primate.

She glances up at a limestone boulder caught in the firelight. The stalagmites and the soaring arches. The meander niche. Is this going to be her last resting place? Is she going to be reduced to a pile of bones on the floor of this cavern – a pair of rodent-like incisors, the odd shard of postcranial matter? Not if she can help it. From 1000BC to AD2000: that is her allotted span. And so she must seize the moment that is approaching, then, if she's going to cheat the Fates.

And seize it she must, otherwise she'll end up extinct: as dead as a pug-nosed crocodile or a pantanodon, as dead as a proverbial dodo.

She scratches her shaggy coat, digs at a sore. Is she starting to shrivel up? She suspects she might be. For she is old, and even though she has been to Hades and scampered among the dead she isn't immortal.

But she can still hold a tune.

Is she going to be able to make her song heard above the drone of the iron birds that are coming? She's been told that sometimes on summer nights the odd fragment of her song gets carried across the zoological gardens on the breeze. She imagines the music drifting out through the cast-iron bars at the mouth of her cave, out over the chipped teacups that the faithful leave to placate her. Earlier this evening, some pheasant brought her another teacup, another offering. She appreciates the gesture, but doesn't need placating. For even though she possesses a godlike gift, she isn't a goddess. She is at most a half-glimpsed movement in the mouth of a cave, a long hand reaching out through the bars to seize a squirming grub, a pair of all-seeing eyes that glint for a moment in the darkness and then are gone.

But even so.

She remembers that on the island of Madagascar she used to be considered an ill omen; a harbinger of death, according to mankind. In fact, if the Fates had not lured her into a trap and transported her across the seas and oceans to Ostia, perhaps she, too, might have been drenched in oil and set alight like her sisters – all nine of them.

From Ostia to Rome. *La sua Roma. Bellissima.* Ostia? Rome? Is she in her right mind? So much has happened since the rise of the Roman Empire, she sometimes gets confused. Did she use the proceeds from the books she sold to Tarquin the Proud to set up residence in Cumae? Or did she squander them on bark beetles and other succulent grubs? She cannot recollect, but she is quite sure she can remember munching on cicadas as she sat for Michelangelo.

She gazes into the smouldering embers of the fire in front of her, flinches at the sight of the hot coals. She has not forgotten the pain she endured before she managed to escape the Supreme Sacred Congregation of the Roman and Universal Inquisition, an escape that meant another sea, another ocean.

Neither has she forgotten the morning she arrived at the zoological gardens in a crate. Of course, a moustached guenon allocated her a cage in the Nocturnal House, but she struggled to adapt to exhibiting herself to the general public. She kept her head down. She pretended to be just another something-or-other curled up in the corner of its cage, just another thingummy that refuses to react to the sound of a set of knuckles rapping on the glass. She endured the experience. Until the other animals in the Nocturnal House turned against the harbinger of death in their midst. Until the *idioti* ganged up on her and chased her out into the glare of the sunshine.

She is an outcast, then. She is an impish hobgoblin, a daemon cloaked in a dark mantle of dishevelled hair. She is That W**ch We Do Not Speak About, but she doesn't bear a grudge against those that refuse to pronounce her name. Let them stumble in the sunlight: the pious, the self-righteous. Let them fumble from the past to the future, ignorant of the Fates. She has no need of their acceptance. For she has a godlike gift: she does not move through time like the other animals in the zoological gardens. She comes and goes as she pleases.

She glances down at the precious object she is clutching in her arthritic hands: a Nile-blue envelope embossed in gold, a Nile-blue envelope spattered in pigeon blood. She turns her attention to the great birdcage constructed out of scrap metal. Its bars and its perches. Its glinting blades. Is everything going to go according to plan? For a moment, she isn't sure. Perhaps she should cast a sprig of nightshade into the flames and practise her potent art. In an instant, she could leap into the future. But she needs to resist the urge, she needs to conserve her strength. The night she has been waiting for is almost at hand. The preparations are complete, nothing has been neglected. The she-macaque has given birth and the Elders have agreed to issue a summons. Bessie has built a nest in the spice drawers and the Flight Lieutenant has been embalmed. The iron birds have been refuelled and their pilots are resting. It is just as the Fates have decreed. There is nothing that remains to be done, then, other than maintain a tight grip on the present moment.

One more sunrise, one more sunset, and there is going to be such a blaze.

One more sunrise, one more sunset, and the supplicant is going to stumble into the inner sanctum, nursing the cuts and burns on its little lappets.

Bel-imperia Hildred Pinch. Imperatrix.

One more sunrise, one more sunset.

She nudges a smouldering ember back into the fire. She settles back into her throne. She bides her time.

[IV]

The Ghost in the Glass

20

I am afraid he had another go at me this evening: Robin or Robert or something – a middle-aged name for a middle-aged man.

'I've been rummaging through the zoological archives,' he said as he sharpened his pencil. 'Remember that missing Register of Births, Deaths and Extinctions? Thing is, I managed to find it. Turns out it had just... Never mind. Listen, I'll grasp the nettle.'

'Please do.'

'Your mother—'

'Oh, Mother was marvellous, marvellous.'

'Yeah, sure,' he replied: dismissive, insincere. 'But she isn't in the Register. I tell a lie. There's a record of her birth – I mean her hatching. Bessie Crust. Hatched in an incubator, 1888. Changed her name to Pinch after she plighted her eggs to Silas. But nothing else. No mention of her death or extinction.'

'Extinction?' I said. 'One hesitates to entertain the thought of Mother being elevated to the Hall of Relics. The Rt Hon Bessie Pinch, First Relic of Foul Language? Imagine her maiden speech. Goodness me, no.'

'Fair enough,' he conceded. 'But even so. There's no record of her dropping off her perch. She is dead, isn't she?'

'I should hope... I should hope her ghost is at peace. Yes.'

He made some disparaging comment. He insisted that there is no such thing as a ghost.

'Isn't there?' I said. 'Oh, no doubt some spineless creatures might be reluctant to accept that the spirits of the dead roam these gardens, but I'm not spineless, dear. I am not. Neither am I unaccustomed to the sensation of being haunted. Indeed, I shall never forget I once had the most peculiar experience... But I have said too much.'

Of course, he begged me to go on, but I declined.

I told him I had no intention of being reduced to an object of ridicule. 'Besides,' I said, 'it's not just the dead that can give one the creeps. I'm afraid the previous Commander-in-Chief of the Order of Carnivores used to haunt me like a ghost. Oh, and such a lugubrious apparition too. Be under no illusions: there's never been a gorilla as sullen and morose as Egbert Curmudgeon. He never forgave me for ousting him from office. He never got over losing command of the Order to a bird. Never. Then again, he didn't seem to be all that attracted to birds, did he? I suspect he might have had more sinister inclinations. Oh, it used to send a shiver down the spine to catch a glimpse of him slumped on a bench in the Hall of Exhibits, staring at me in contempt during P Ex Qs. But I digress. Your question?'

'Your mother?'

'Oh, I've never seen her ghost. Thank goodness.'

I seem to recall he consulted his notes. 'She didn't die in that blaze at the boathouse, did she?'

'No, of course not,' I said. 'Mother never came to the boathouse. Oh, I suppose there might have been... '

'Yes?'

But I couldn't complete the sentence. I... I could feel the tears brimming up. 'Forgive me, dear,' I sobbed. 'I still find it upsetting.'

'Your mother's death?'

'Father's business going up in flames like that. The unopened bars of Pears' soap, the expensive consignments of spices from the East Indies, the priceless treasures in his tea chest – all reduced to ashes. Such a terrible tragedy! I'm sure your readers will weep. In retrospect, though, I suppose it had to happen sooner or later, didn't it? The second-hand cupboards and cabinets, the embalming fluid – it all burns.'

'But not Bessie Pinch?' he said. 'She didn't burn?'

'In Hades?'

'In the boathouse.'

'No one died in the boathouse. No one apart from... Oh, it's such a long time ago; I cannot be sure. Besides, I seem to recall being cooped up in an iron bird shelter the night of the blaze. Oh, I shall never forget huddling under those sheets of corrugated steel and listening to the falling bombs. The stale air, the condensation. Of course, one didn't let it dampen one's spirits. One had the Prize Exhibit to strengthen one's resolve. But even so, it isn't an experience I should care to go through again, make no mistake. Thank goodness the zoological gardens is at peace. Imagine if those iron birds were to return tonight with their incendiaries and bombs. There's no P Ex to give an inspirational speech. Or scramble a squadron of spot-tailed goshawks.'

'There's Ebenezer Bull,' he said. 'He might have lost the scent-marking contest, but he's still Prize Exhibit.'

'He's nothing of the sort,' I replied. 'He's just a stubborn old rhinoceros squatting in the Dower House. He has no mandate to manage these gardens, dear.'

'Neither does Dale FitzClarence.'

'No, I am afraid it is a rather disappointing result. FitzClarence should have stuck to tried and tested Carnivorous principles. Never mind all that nonsense about compassionate Carnivorism. He should have emphasised his credentials as a meat-eater. But of course, I don't suppose he'll detain us for much longer. I should imagine the Order is bound to turn against him after a scent-marking contest like this.'

'Not sure that's on the cards,' he mumbled. 'I heard he's been sniffing around that ground squirrel.'

I assumed he must have been alluding to Nicholas Cobb, the Commander-in-Chief of the Order of Omnivores.

'I thought I could smell the stench of consensus in the air,' I replied. 'Oh, I do hope Dale doesn't make that rodent his second-in-command. I'm not an expert in the orange-bellied ground squirrel, but it's not the sort of thing that can be described as a flagship species, is it, dear?'

He mentioned something about a pact, a binding agreement between Carnivore and Omnivore. 'Most Carnivores accept that the Order has got to give ground,' he bleated.

'Lesser specimens,' I said. 'Earth pigs and pangolins, not true meat-eaters. I regard such creatures as Quislings. Let me make it quite clear: there's no point in abandoning one's beliefs in order to cobble together a consensus that no one can believe in. There is not. These gardens need a Board of Beasts that can get things done. FitzClarence should consider the example that I provide – not that I have ever been in such an unfortunate predicament, of course. Goodness me, no. The animals in these gardens had full confidence in me. I've never been defeated in a scent-marking contest. Oh, those traitors in the Board of Beasts might have stabbed me in the back, but I still inspire the affection of the masses; I am still adored.'

'I'm not sure about that,' he said, sheepishly. 'You see... Well, word has gone round that I'm working on a novel about—'

I interrupted him. 'A novel?'

'I mean an account,' he replied.

'I should hope so too,' I said. 'Novels are for specimens like Mother – birds that have nothing better to do. I'm not interested in fiction; I'm interested in facts and figures. Now, give me some facts. You said word has gone round... ?'

He informed me that some animals are eager to contribute their opinion.

'I am not surprised to hear it,' I said. 'Indeed, I suspect one might have become a zoological treasure. Is that true?'

He just said, 'No.'

'Well, what do they say about me, then, these animals?'

'Oh, that Bel-imperia Pinch is pig-headed.'

'Pig-headed?'

'Yeah, I believe that was the phrase.'

'Who says that?'

'Oh, just ordinary creatures. You know, in conversation.'

I rounded on him: 'I'm an ordinary creature,' I said, 'and don't you forget it. Where did these conversations take place?'

'Down at the watering hole. In the queue at the cold store.'

'I thought you'd just come from the archives.'

'This isn't the first time I've been here.'

'Well, what sort of creatures were they?'

'You know, mammals, reptiles, birds... '

'That's not an answer,' I said. 'That could be anyone. Would you please tell me their names and where they exhibit themselves?'

Of course, he couldn't name one miserable specimen. Not one. But he claimed some marsupial said that if different species are going to share the same gardens there needs to be compromise.

'Compromise?' I said, outraged.

'It's no use being inflexible.'

'Oh, I am not ashamed to admit that I'm inflexible about certain things,' I replied. 'I'm inflexible about defending the freedoms that our ancestors laid down their lives for in the Uprising: the freedom to exhibit oneself in a cage of one's choosing, the freedom to have the zoological gardens as one's beast of burden and not one's mahout. But freedom requires regulation. If nothing is prohibited it can deteriorate into licentiousness – the 1960s taught us that. Felines must be discouraged from developing an addiction to catnip. Primates must be persuaded to restrain themselves from fornicating during opening hours. And so I am also inflexible about upholding the rules and regulations that govern an animal's behaviour. That's not pig-headedness. It is not. It's leadership, dear. And the specimens in these gardens need strong leadership. Oh, I do hope FitzClarence can provide some. If not, I… '

'Yes?'

'If not, I shall be tempted to descend on him and give him a piece of my mind.'

21

OLD HESPER HOUSE AND ZOOLOGICAL GARDENS

Bog-land Hill

THE HUNTING TOWER

Grade II Listed Cage, Enclosure or Other Estate Building. Completed in 1348, this medieval Hunting Tower must have once provided an impressive vantage point for Ladies to admire the spectacle of the hunt. In the late 1500s, however, depleted game reserves led to the decline of the sport, and the building fell into disrepair. It remained in ruins until the 1850s, when it was converted into an owlery. Although not as prestigious as the collection of owls at the Cloisters, the Hunting Tower contains some curious specimens, including the SPECTACLED OWL *(P. perspicilata)* and the FOREST OWLET *(A. blewitti)*.

NO ADMITTANCE TO THE GENERAL PUBLIC

Inside the building, there are other signs, other notices. There are long lists of Rules and Regulations. There are posters reminding the patrons to *Look Out In The Blackout* and *Make Do And Mend*. There are Directions to the Nearest Iron Bird Shelter. But it's the sign hanging above the old department store counter in the reception area that has caught the attention of little Bel-imperia Pinch:

SILENCE
IN THE HUNTING TOWER

Silence? It is as silent as a morgue. Is there no one in the Hunting Tower this evening? She scutters across the faded heraldic motif on the floor tiles, peers into the reading room. Is that a crocodile she can see buried under a mound of manuscripts? From the shape of the creature's snout, she suspects it might be one of the subordinate males that sometimes officiates at matins, but she cannot be sure – the dim Anglepoise lamps do little to dispel the gloom. She cranes her S-shaped neck, catches a glimpse of a sheet of corrugated steel bathed in a gentle blue light. Has someone built an iron bird shelter behind the shelves of liturgical calendars and medieval bestiaries? She dismisses the thought. So much for *090: Manuscripts & Rare Books*.

There is no one in *110: Metaphysics*, no one in *128: Humankind*.

Is that a primate crouched under an Anglepoise in *130: Parapsychology & Occultism*? It looks like it might be the interfering simian that helped her father to his feet after he'd humiliated himself at the amphitheatre – a she-macaque or something – but Bel-imperia cannot be sure. The creature turns the page of the book propped up in front of her, glances down at the infant clinging to her chest: a bundle of skin and bones, nothing more. Impossible to imagine a member of the general public stopping to admire such an odd-looking specimen; after all, there's nothing endearing about it. Yet even so, its mother must have managed to summon up some affection for the thing, because she is cooing at it in the most revolting manner: 'He be me little Rapscallion. He be me little Scamp. Oh, his mam do love him so.'

Is this a brazen harlot, then? Bel-imperia suspects it might be, but she's conscious that the classification of simians is difficult. Perhaps the specimen isn't a macaque at all. Perhaps it's just a langur or something. She decides to give it a disapproving stare all the same. For good measure.

She turns her attention to the soaring bookcases, gazes up at *290: Other Religions*; up again to *320: Political Science*; up past all the disintegrating gold leaf and leather until she comes to *997: Atlantic Ocean Islands* at the top of the tower. She imagines the Cloisters must be similar to this – more impressive, perhaps: more interesting books, more sophisticated owls. These are just provincial specimens. Some long-eared owl nesting in the middle of a rolled-up map. Some little owlet gliding across the building in silence, the serrated edges of its primaries slicing through a golden shaft of light. Golden? No doubt the sun must be setting. Not long until the Hunting Tower closes, then. No sign of Miss Scroop. Has the irritable old spinster tidied up her desk and clocked out? Has she popped down to the cold store to get a mouse for her supper? Bel-imperia is not sure.

From the direction of the reading room, the sound of a bunged-up crocodile expelling something unpleasant from its snout.

Here goes, then…

She hops up a staircase of books – large, leather-bound tomes stacked up like steps – and scuttles onto the reclaimed department store counter that the owls use as a reception desk. Ah, Edna Scroop is perched on a blotter, staring at the crocodile responsible for the disturbance. Deep breath. She must be careful not to ruffle her feathers. She must be polite.

'Good evening, Miss Scroop.'

In less than a second, Old Scroopers turns her head through an unnatural 180 degrees, glaring as if she'd just spotted a mouse that she intended to dispatch. Bel-imperia shudders. It is a stare to examine the soul, a stare to determine if a mouse's conscience is clean before it meets its maker. She takes up the gauntlet and meets the owl's gaze.

Can she give as good as she gets? Can she hold her nerve? The last time Miss Scroop stared at her like this she ended up conceding defeat, but she isn't the little lappet-faced thing she used to be; a decent helping of liver has put some iron into her soul. She stands and stares: steadfast, resolute. Is that a lapse of concentration she can detect, a moment's distraction at the recollection of some blighted hope? Bel-imperia is sure that it must be. Does this mean that the rumours that have been going round are true, then? Is there a broken heart in that stout breast?

Flustered from her defeat, Edna Scroop turns her attention to the pile of loose papers beside her blotter, pretends to shuffle through them. 'I hope this isn't going to take long, Pinch. The Hunting Tower is about to close.'

Spectacled owl. The name must be on account of the circular markings around the eyes – an impressive pair of spectacles indeed. But it looks like Miss Scroop must have swooped down on an unsuspecting member of the general public and helped herself to another pair. Bel-imperia appraises the reading glasses dangling from a chain strung over the owl: the prescription lenses, the discoloured lump of Sellotape holding their tortoiseshell frames together. She smiles to herself. Does this make Old Scroopers a spectacled spectacled owl?

'Don't stand there smirking, creature.'

'Miss?'

'What do you want?'

What does she want? Well, she wants to know whether or not the rumours are true. Did Miss Scroop once have romantic expectations? Of course, it is impossible to imagine such a bad-tempered old bird being in the mood for muggin' and huggin', or whatever it is that owls do, but at least the scandal might explain why she has been moonlighting at the Cloisters. What does she want? She wants to know whether she has been awarded a scholarship or not.

'Out with it, Pinch. Some of us have better things to do.'

'The thing is, Miss… '

But it is a delicate matter. Bel-imperia must be careful not to allude to Miss Scroop's straitened circumstances, careful not to remind her that she's been reduced to touting her secretarial skills around the zoological gardens in order to make ends meet. Perhaps something less personal to break the ice.

'The thing is, miss, I understand Father sent a pigeon to the Hunting Tower. He asked the owls to set aside—'

'Reservations? One moment, please.' Old Scroopers slips on her spectacles, starts to rummage through the pile of correspondence on her desk: a loose scrap of parchment and a manila envelope, a postcard from Le Jardin Zoologique and an expensive-looking sheet of Nile-blue paper.

The sound of a male tu-whit tu-whooing: 'Did she mention a pigeon, Edna?'

Bel-imperia inspects the little owlet that has just alighted on the rung of a ladder, admires its hammer-shaped head and the understated spots on its mantle.

'Yes, but I can't seem to find the reservation.'

'Perhaps it hasn't arrived. I heard a rumour that the pigeon service is short-staffed.'

'I don't listen to malicious rumours, Reginald.'

'It isn't malicious. In fact, the Pigeon Master General is rather concerned. It seems a first-class Columbine has gone missing.'

Bel-imperia pretends to be interested in the scratches on the counter.

'Missing?' Edna Scroop sounds upset. 'Is that a euphemism for 'absconded', Reginald? Am I to assume that some scoundrel has abandoned his devoted she-pigeon?'

'No, of course not.' The little owlet hops down onto the counter and gives his colleague a nudge. 'Oh, Eds, I wouldn't dream of alluding to—'

'Reginald!' She darts a pointed glance at the SILENCE IN THE HUNTING TOWER sign. 'Not in front of the customers, please.'

The rumours must be true, then. Poor old Scroopers. Of course, she had it coming. She should have used some common sense before entering into such an inappropriate courtship ritual. Bel-imperia remembers meeting Miss Scroop's suitor – a disreputable-looking specimen called Cecil. She shudders at the recollection of him scuttling up beside her. His chestnut-brown underparts. His slicked-backed supercilia. What on earth made Edna fall for such a creature? Did he bribe her with a bouquet of dandelions to line her nesting box? Did he woo her with dead mice? Whatever Cecil's technique, it must have worked, because the couple were soon witnessed indulging in a spot of mutual preening behind the llama house. Oh, and then, of course, after a fortnight of chaste billing and cooing, the scoundrel moved on to the next phase of his plan: he asked Old Scroopers to elope with him to Le Jardin Zoologique. 'Oh, just imagine it, Eds,' he must have said, 'we could start a new life over there. You've studied the lingo. We both eat frogs. We could copulate and raise a clutch of chicks.' No doubt Miss Scroop let out a shocked hoot when he said the 'c' word. Perhaps she even sent him home to his nesting box in disgrace. From all accounts, though, Cecil called in at the Hunting Tower the next morning to find her perched in *445: Grammar of Standard French*. 'I'm just brushing up on the future perfect, dear,' she hooted. The couple started making plans. Cecil offered to go out ahead and build their love nest. 'Of course, I'll need a deposit to put down on a cage,' he must have said. So she gave him all her hard-earned groats. And as soon as he arrived at Le Jardin Zoologique he changed them into centimes and spent them on a more attractive specimen instead.

Stupid old Scroopers. *La folie de l'amour.*

Is she still searching through her correspondence?

'Here it is!' She pulls out a scrap of paper and scutters across the counter to a pile of books labelled 'Reserved'.

Bel-imperia tilts her head to one side, tries to read the lettering on their spines. She cannot remember the last time her father consented to the sinful extravagance of sending a second-class pigeon to the Hunting Tower. It must be a title he is eager to read. Some sacred tome about the Commandments? Some scientific paper on the latest innovations in embalming?

'Got it!' Miss Scroop pecks out a small cloth-bound publication and carries it back to her blotter. She dribbles a ribbon of spittle onto her endorsing pad and steps into the ink. Is she going to open the book on the right page? It should be a fortnight; it should be page 22. 'There,' she says, hopping off the book to admire the impression of her talons, 'due back on the 22nd – no later than sunset, Pinch, or I'll issue a fine.'

'There must be some mistake, miss.'

'Mistake? I never make mistakes.'

'Why would Father want a manual about——'

'*Breeding Monkeys in Captivity Vol. II: Baboons, Mandrills and Macaques* – that's the book he ordered.'

She'd like to pass comment on the old bird's secretarial skills. She'd like to suggest that she should invest in a new pair of spectacles. But she resists the urge. There's something much more important she needs to discuss.

'That will be all, Pinch. You can go.'

'In a moment, miss. There's just one more thing… It's about the Cloisters.'

She explains her problem. Couching her request in polite language, she steers clear of the phrase 'moonlighting in order to make ends meet'. She implies that Miss Scroop has been 'persuaded to accept a part-time position'. Can she tell her if she has been awarded a scholarship or not?

'I am sure the successful candidates have been notified, Pinch.'

'Edna?' The square-headed owlet is attempting to hoot something into his superior's auricular feathers.

'I haven't been notified, miss. Neither have I received a letter of rejection.'

'No, I am aware of that.'

'You are?'

She's beginning to suspect that Old Scroopers knows more than she is letting on.

'Edna?'

'What is it, Reginald?' she snaps.

'The Cloisters sent us a list of the successful candidates. I pinned it on… '

The noticeboard.

Bel-imperia soars across the reception area, scours the confusion of notices pinned to the board: *See The Blue Light: It Means Shelter At Night*, a list of instructions explaining What To Do If Fire Breaks

Out, something reminding the animals that *Careless Squawking Costs Lives*. Just the usual montage of faded posters. Nothing from the Cloisters. Nothing at all. She spots a suspicious-looking rectangle of bare noticeboard. Has someone taken the list down?

She returns to the counter. 'Where is it, miss?'

'Perhaps some scatter-brained owlet removed it to make room for something else.'

She can tell that Miss Scroop is expecting her colleague to confess, but Reginald just says, 'I'm not scatter-brained, Eds.'

Is Old Scroopers to blame? Did she rip the notice down? Bel-imperia turns to the owlet. 'I don't suppose you can remember any of the names on the list, sir?'

'Let me see. There are three scholarships and so I imagine… '

'There must have been three names?'

'Yes, three names printed on a blue sheet of paper. Orson Brusque – I remember he got in. Orson Brusque and… ' He hangs his hammer-shaped head. Clearly, he's forgotten the other successful candidates.

'Scatter-brained, Reginald, just as I said. I'm a good judge of character.'

Bel-imperia cannot resist saying, 'Oh, I'm sure you are, miss. As long as the character in question doesn't have chestnut-brown underparts and slicked-back supercilia.'

The old bird lets out a little hoot. Is she trembling? No doubt she's struggling to keep the sluice gates closed. For a moment it looks like there might be an embarrassment of tears, but there is just one. There it is, trickling down Miss Scroop's facial disc. There it is, seeping into her blotter. Poor old Scroopers. Perhaps Bel-imperia spoke in haste. Should she have held her tongue? Examining her conscience, she is disconcerted to discover the tender shoots of a sensation that resembles remorse. She nips them in the bud. She has no inclination to apologise.

'Shall I ask her to leave, Edna?'

'No, it's all right, Reginald, I'll do the honours.' She snatches a small brass bell, rings it three times and screeches: 'The Hunting Tower will be closing in ten minutes. Would all patrons please return their books to the correct shelf and proceed to the exit.'

In the reading room, a pampas cat stirs. Is that a porcupine?

'The door is open, Pinch.'

Bel-imperia is staring at the pile of correspondence on the counter: the loose scraps of parchment and the torn manila envelopes. If she has ten minutes she intends to make good use of them: 'Oh, but I'd like to take a book out before I leave, assuming that's not too much trouble, Edna.'

It had better not be too much trouble. She is sure she can remember catching a glimpse of a sheet of Nile-blue paper in that pile. She plumps up her plumage, tries to make it clear that she expects to be served, but the bird on the blotter seems to be more interested in hooting to its colleague: 'She just called me Edna.'

'Even so. You can't refuse to lend her a book, Eds.'

'No, I suppose not.' She turns to her customer. 'Come on, then. Title?'

'Let me see… ' It needs to be something unusual, something to send Old Scroopers scuttling along the counter to her box of index cards. 'I'd like a book about false prophets, please.'

'False prophets?' No doubt she finds the subject distasteful. 'There's a guide to seers, augurs and other charlatans in *130: Parapsychology & Occultism*. You'll have to make do with that.'

'I am afraid another patron is reading it, Eds.'

Miss Scroop glances over her mantle at the macaque in the reading room. 'Who let that brazen harlot into the Hunting Tower? Chase her out, Reginald. She'll bring this establishment into disrepute.'

So the simian in *130* must be the infamous harlot, then – a strumpet, a Jezebel, a loose macaque. Bel-imperia scurries along to the end of the counter to get a better look at the creature. And so this is the specimen her father met the morning he called in at the macaque compound to give their matriarch his business card. And so this is the specimen that helped him to his feet in the amphitheatre, the specimen that the Elders have been discussing. Not an unattractive thing. Shame about all that lipstick and mascara, though. Is she attempting to ape the glamour of the she-apes in the magazines that the general public read in the Refreshment Rooms? Perhaps. But she's no Marlene Dietrich, no something-or-other Garbo. She is a toque macaque.

Bel-imperia turns her attention to the harlot's infant, glares at the thing as it clambers up onto its mother's shoulders. Is it neither one species nor another? Is it an abomination? She cannot be sure. She remembers standing in the boathouse, pretending to inspect a cast-iron bucket as she listened to her parents' conversation: 'I heard the trollops been to see the beezum,' her mother had said. Bel-imperia sighs. The creature of the night might have predicted that the infant is going to die on the Sabbath, but the little simian doesn't look like it's about to drop down dead. And there are just three or four hours of the Sabbath remaining. She scowls at it as it clambers about on its mother. No, it's far too agile for a specimen that's about to meet its maker. Does this mean That W**ch We Do Not Speak About is a false prophet, then? Presumably the infant's mother has been asking herself the same question. Hence the book about seers, augurs and other charlatans. But at least she must have been to the creature's cave, at least she must have seen the thing. Bel-imperia has a good mind to soar into the reading room and interrogate the strumpet, but there is no time: Miss Scroop is ringing her bell again.

'The Hunting Tower will be closing in five minutes... '

Five minutes to distract Old Scroopers and ferret through her correspondence. Five minutes to find out if she has been offered a scholarship or not.

The spectacled owl says, 'It seems Reginald is having a spot of bother persuading the patron in question to leave the premises. Shall I snatch the book, Pinch?'

'No, I'd rather not touch pages that a harlot has been turning.'

For once, Edna Scroop is in agreement. 'Yes, harlots spread diseases.'

'Perhaps something else instead.'

'Title?'

'Let me see... ' She is sure there had been some magnum opus she'd been meaning to read.

'Come on, Pinch. I haven't got all night. I'm moonlighting this evening.'

'*On the Origin of Species by Means of Natural Selection.* Charles Darwin, miss.'

'I shan't be long.'

Seizing the moment, Bel-imperia creeps across the counter, studies the edge of the pile of correspondence: manila, lilac, cream…

'Daniel, D'Annunzio, Dante… ' Miss Scroop is still riffling through her index cards.

Is that a scrap of Nile-blue parchment? Could that be the list of successful candidates? Careful not to make a sound, she eases the sheet of paper out of the pile, but it's just a letter from Snag, Snarl & Scapegrace, Jaguars at Rules and Regulations. 'On behalf of our client, Edna Scroop… ' Something about stolen groats. She pushes it back into the pile, catches another promising glimpse of blue. Is that a pinhole in the corner? Is that the letterhead of the Cloisters? No time to pull it out.

'Here it is, *On the Origin of Species.*' Miss Scroop stuffs the index card into a spring-loaded canister and releases a catch.

Bel-imperia stares at the gleaming canister as it shoots into the reading room. There it goes, gliding over the she-macaque like a little cable car. Did the ingenious mechanism come from the same department store as the counter that the owls use as a reception desk? Perhaps. Up, up it goes, zigzagging from *200: Religion* to *400: Language*, pausing in between each class of books so that an owl can inspect its contents before sending it soaring up to the next level. It comes to a standstill at *500: Science*. But Bel-imperia can tell that something is amiss. The owl responsible for the 500s should be dropping the book she's ordered into a chute, not sending the canister back again. She glares at the cable car as it zigzags down from *300: Social Sciences* to *100: Philosophy & Psychology*. Has the creature slipped something inside the contraption?

'Oh, dear.' Edna Scroop opens the canister and pulls out a small pamphlet. 'That's a shame, isn't it?'

'Miss?'

Old Scroopers stamps the pamphlet on page 22 and slides it across the counter. It's too thin to be a magnum opus.

'Don't just stand there, Pinch. The Hunting Tower is closing in less than a minute.'

'But this is *On the Origin of Species: a Crocodile's Contention*. This is illustrated with cartoons.'

'That's right. For the junior reader.'

Bel-imperia is seething. She might have ordered the book to distract Miss Scroop, but she resents being palmed off with some second-rate pamphlet. Besides, she has a hunch there might be something important in Mr Darwin's masterpiece, something fundamental that she ought to learn; she can feel it in her bones. She makes a mental note to get her talons onto the adult edition, complete and unabridged. Is there such a thing at the Cloisters? No doubt there must be. And so she has another reason to find out if she has been awarded a scholarship, then. She steals a glance at the pile of correspondence. If she could just get Old Scroopers to scuttle across to her index cards again...

'You have outstayed your welcome, Pinch. Please go.'

'In good time. I'd better get something for Mother, too – a romantic novel, as usual, please. Large print.'

Miss Scroop seems surprised. Has she heard that no one has seen Mother since she slaughtered a pigeon and stomped out of the boathouse? Bel-imperia hopes not.

'Bessie isn't going to be able to read a novel.'

Bessie, is it? Does this mean that Edna and her mother are on first-name terms? 'Oh, I'm sure she'll manage. Just give me a Mills & Boon. Or something about mothers and sons; she'll love that.'

'Perhaps she might, but she isn't here to read it, is she? Now, run along, Pinch. Oh, and remind your mother to call in and see me as soon as she gets back from Le Jardin Zoologique.'

Bel-imperia is astonished. 'You must be thinking of another specimen, miss. Mother's never been to Caer Lud, let alone Le Jardin Zoologique.'

'Well, I should imagine she must be having a wonderful time, then.' Is that a note of resentment in the old bird's tone?

'But miss—'

'Of course, I don't suppose she'll care for the cuisine – a little too sophisticated for Bessie's palate – but no doubt she'll be pleased to see her sister.'

'Sister?'

'*Sa sœur française*, Pinch.'

'Mother hasn't got a sister.'

Old Scroopers lets out another shocked hoot. Is she trembling again? 'No sister? But Bessie promised——'

In the distance, a sudden bout of gibbon song: raucous, clamorous. Bel-imperia can tell that it's coming from the direction of Caer Lud. She concentrates on the riotous outburst as it rips across the zoological gardens. It is so resonant, so sonorous, that she imagines it can be heard from one end of the estate to another. From the turnstiles of the gatehouse to the chicken coops in the Norn Iron Farmstead. From the boulders on the ridge of the escarpment to the clumps of purple small-reed in the Marshes. She gapes at Miss Scroop, exchanges an expression of concern. Never mind the list of successful candidates. Never mind their mutual distrust. This bloodcurdling alarm call has bound them together, united them in the same battle. For it is the song of the siamang – and that means just one thing: an iron bird is approaching.

In the reading room, the other animals are attempting to set an example, attempting to remain calm and collected: the pampas cat and the porcupine, the crocodile and the macaque. But little Bel-imperia Pinch can sense their fear; she can smell it contaminating the air. She can also smell spilt urine. Has someone lost control of their bladder? She gives the porcupine an accusing stare, but the creature just curls up into a ball.

She turns to Miss Scroop. She is the most senior bird in the building. Despite her contempt for the customers that frequent the establishment, shouldn't she be showing some leadership instead of searching through her index cards?

'Forget about Mother's novel, miss.'

'This is for me, Pinch.'

'But the iron birds——'

'Here it is.' She snatches a card and stuffs it into the spring-loaded canister. What on earth could be so urgent? Bel-imperia glances at the contraption as it shoots into the reading room. There's no time to watch it whizz up the tower: a toothless old dingo is limping into the building.

'Is this some sort o' shelter?'

Ignoring the canine, Old Scroopers swoops along the counter, seizes her bell. 'The Hunting Tower is closed. Bolt the door, Reginald.'

'But Eds… '

'For goodness' sake, Reg, just do it before there's a stampede. We don't want a herd of swamp buffalo clomping into the building.'

'Let me make it quite clear, miss: I refuse to be locked up in here during an iron-bird raid; I refuse to be… '

But it's too late to rebel against the spectacled dictator: the owlet has bolted the door.

'Our shelter is *un peu petit*, Pinch. Maximum: six small mammals, nine reptiles and birds.'

'What shelter?'

'See the blue light?'

'No.'

'*090: Manuscripts & Rare Books.*'

Bel-imperia leaps off the counter, soars into the reading room. It doesn't take her long to spot the sinister heap of corrugated steel skulking behind the cases of liturgical calendars and medieval bestiaries. She settles on a mound of manuscripts and inspects the incongruous object. Some practical-minded owlet might have inserted a blue light bulb into an Anglepoise, but the misshapen lump of scrap metal bathed in its glow is never going to save its occupants from a bomb.

'This isn't going to protect us, miss.'

'Nonsense. It's an Anderson shelter – standard issue.'

'Who brought it in here? Who bolted it together?'

'We hired some rag-and-bone baboons to put it up, didn't we, Reginald?'

'Well, I hope you didn't pay them; it should have been buried under six trotters of soil.'

'I told you, Eds.'

'We've had this discussion, Reginald. I'm not having soil traipsed into the building. We've got enough on our plates with the muck our patrons bring in on their hooves.'

'I think there might be room for some more muck on your plate, Eds.'

'What are you insinuating?'

'Well, you're not the one who has to clear it up… '

While the owls bicker among themselves, the gibbon song continues: relentless, spine-chilling.

Bel-imperia interrupts. 'This shelter needs to be reinforced, miss. Urgently.'

'Oh, I'm sure it'll do its job.' She rings her bell again. 'During an iron-bird raid, all animals must proceed to the nearest shelter. Rules and regulations. Come on, everyone. Quicksticks.'

But the creatures in the reading room seem reluctant to approach the menacing mound of corrugated steel.

Cautious, stomach slung close to the ground, the pampas cat creeps up to the entrance, peers inside. 'I ain't getting in there,' it says, springing back from the shelter. 'The thing's a death trap.'

The porcupine quivers. 'Yeah, but what if them iron birds got a Satan bomb?'

'We'll be blown to Kingdom Come,' says the dingo. 'That's what.'

Someone loses control of their bladder again. Someone gasps for air.

Here she is, then, in the midst of the crisis: little Bel-imperia Pinch. She is conscious of the atmosphere of panic in the reading room – of course she is; but at the same time she's detached from it, like the still point at the centre of a storm. She lets the tempest swirl around her. She remembers her favourite poem and keeps her head as others lose theirs. Indeed, she is so calm and collected that she can almost sense the particles of iron coursing through her bloodstream, almost hear some deep-seated instinct calling her to action. Is it a primitive instinct? Should she suppress it? She dismisses the thought. There's nothing primitive about asserting one's dominance. There is not. Besides, someone needs to step into the breach and give these simple-minded specimens the benefit of a little leadership.

She soars up onto the counter, snatches Miss Scroop's bell.

'I heard he's planning something big. Operation Sea Lion he calls it.'

'He's planning to invade, he is.'

'What'll we do then, eh?'

She rings the bell three times and delivers an impromptu speech: 'What will we do if mankind invades? We will defend these gardens, of course. Let me make it quite clear: I have come amongst you, as you see, at this, our darkest hour, not for my recreation or disport, but being resolved, in the midst and heat of the battle, to live and die amongst you all; to lay down for Sol, for these gardens, for our animals, my honour and my lappets. Even in the dung.'

She pauses to glance around the astonished animals.

'Oh, I know I have the body of a weak, feeble bird; but I have the heart and stomach of a lion – and a lion from the Lion House too – and I pour foul scorn on any man that dare invade this estate. I'm sure that if we all do our duty, we shall prove ourselves able to defend this old menagerie, to ride out this storm, to outlive this tyranny, if necessary for years, if necessary alone. And even if Operation Sea Lion turns out to be successful, even if we find ourselves subjugated and starving, there are forces more powerful than mankind's cruelty. For man might chain us, but he cannot chain our mind; he might enslave us, but he cannot enslave our spirit. Make no mistake, then, the time will come when the anger of the animals is so great that it can no longer be contained. And then the edifice cracks, the mortar crumbles, and the freedom that our ancestors laid down their lives for during the Uprising is ours again.'

There is no applause; just a shocked silence as the animals gaze up at little Bel-imperia Pinch, some in admiration, others in horror at the creature that has emerged in their midst. For a moment, even the gibbons are dumbstruck. Eventually, the pampas cat says, 'Yeah, but how will we defend ourselves? We ain't got no incendiaries or bombs. We ain't got no iron bird.'

She wants to say, 'Yes, you have; you've got me,' but she resists the urge. Instead, she says, 'Well, we'll just have to make the most of the strengths we have, then, won't we? And we'll start with this shelter.' She turns to the she-macaque: 'You, what's your name?'

'Lola, ma'am.'

She cannot believe the creature just called her 'ma'am'. 'Right, Lola. Grab those old leather-bound tomes from *130* and stack them up like sandbags around the shelter. You, get those bestiaries down from the shelves. You, get those paperbacks and stuff them into the gaps. The books will protect us. Come on, look sharp.'

No one questions their orders, no one refuses to pitch in; even the crocodile obliges, scooping up an entire set of encyclopaediae in his long snout. Supervising from a stepladder, Bel-imperia cannot fail to notice that the porcupine's contribution leaves a lot to be desired, but she is delighted to see that the brazen harlot is putting her back into it.

She instructs the animals to step aside so she can inspect the shelter.

'That should do the job. Now, I'm not going to put up with any nonsense about death traps. Come on, get inside.'

But Miss Scroop appears to have no intention of joining the other animals; she is perched on the counter, staring up at the spring-loaded canister.

'I'm going to close the door, miss.'

'There's a pamphlet in that canister, Pinch. I just need to––'

'During an iron bird raid, all animals must proceed to the nearest shelter. Rules and regulations, Edna. Come on. Quicksticks.'

To Bel-imperia's surprise, Old Scroopers does as she is told.

Inside, it is like a chicken coop: Spartan, utilitarian. A bare light bulb, an upended orange crate.

'Now, all we have to do is wait.'

She settles beside the pampas cat, attends to a spot of preening, but it's impossible to ignore the oppressive atmosphere of her surroundings. Is that condensation dribbling down the corrugated steel? She stares at the rivulet of exhaled breath as it courses across the floor and pools in a blocked drainage sump. She turns her attention to the abomination slumbering in its mother's arms: the chestnut-red blotches on its legs, the agouti silver stain on its underparts. She can tell from the rise and fall of the specimen's chest that it's still alive. She glances at its mother, suppresses an urge to interrogate her about the creature in the cave. Not in front of the other animals.

Outside, the gibbons have fallen silent. Have the iron birds returned to base?

'He needs to bomb Caer Lud before he can invade. He needs to burn it down.'

'Let me make it quite clear: Caer Lud is never going to burn. Never.'

The decrepit old dingo pricks up its ears. Perhaps the dog has detected the drone of a distant iron bird. Do dingoes have good hearing? Senses alert, the animals listen.

'Here it comes.'

She can hear it approaching, the grinding engine. Is it a Messerschmitt? Has it entered the exclusion zone?

The pampas cat's coat bristles. The porcupine curls up into a ball.

In an unexpected contribution, the crocodile attempts to lead the animals in a special plea: 'Oh, Sol, thou hast provided this shelter for us in our hour of need. Put upon us the armour of thy light, and protect us against the darkness of this world… '

But the dingo is having none of it. 'Pleading ain't no good. If a bomb's got our names on it, it'll get us, shelter or no.'

The roaring engines are getting louder. Bel-imperia peers up at a loose bolt that has started to rattle; the Messerschmitt must be soaring over the Hunting Tower. Is that the screech of a Satan bomb falling to the ground? She darts a glance at the pampas cat, the crocodile. Whose name is written on this one, then? Her gaze settles on the brazen harlot. Let it be hers. Please, Sol. Let it be hers.

The sound of an explosion ripping through the air. The sound of someone's cage being reduced to rubble. The shelter rattles like a tin of beaten-copper groats. Outside, in the reading room, the thump, thump, thump of a thousand books falling from their shelves. The light bulb sputters out.

In the darkness, the second bomb is even more intimidating. Bel-imperia listens as another cage is laid to ruin. She hopes it's just someone's cage – not the amphitheatre, not the boathouse. She remembers her pearls. She should have insisted on taking them home after the embalming last night. She should never have decided to leave them in the lacquered tea chest for safekeeping.

There is one more bomb, one more dull thud, before the droning engines recede into the distance. And then at last another bout of gibbon song – not the siamang, but the short song phrase of a lar gibbon: the all-clear.

Impatient to escape their imprisonment, the animals push and shove. Someone steps on the tail of the pampas cat. Someone stumbles into the quills of the porcupine.

In the reading room, the she-macaque is scrabbling across the bomb damage, such as it is – a small mound of rubble, some shards of broken glass. For some reason, the creature seems upset to discover that the entire contents of *800: Literature* have fallen from the tower. She pulls something called *Pride and Prejudice* out of the debris, tries to bend its buckled corners back into shape. But Bel-imperia has more important things to do.

She leaps into the air and sails across the ocean of storm-tossed literature. She alights on Miss Scroop's blotter. No sign of the spectacled owl. Time to seize the moment. Time to search through the old spinster's scattered correspondence: manila, lilac, cream. Is there nothing Nile-blue?

Bel-imperia sighs. This means she'll have to traipse across the zoological gardens to the Cloisters and make some enquiries there. It's going to take all night to scuttle such a distance. She remembers that Michaelmas Term starts in the morning. She imagines turning up at the admissions office and joining a queue of successful candidates. The embarrassment of being informed she has failed to get in. She pictures herself trudging back to the Bog-land Enclosures: defeated, despondent...

So be it.

She shakes the condensation out of her remiges, but she cannot shake off the fear of failure that is clinging to her. Perhaps one last look around the building. She glances over her mantle as Miss Scroop swoops down on the spring-loaded canister and pulls out a small pamphlet: *Guide Officiel du Jardin Zoologique*. No point in hanging around. There's nothing to detain her here. She hops down the improvised staircase of books and scutters across the heraldic motif on the floor tiles.

'Come back here this minute, Pinch.'

No doubt Old Scroopers is going to remind her that she's forgotten her father's book about breeding baboons, but Bel-imperia has no intention of retracing her steps. She slips out into the night.

Is that a pall of smoke drifting across the cobblestones? Is someone's bomb-damaged enclosure smouldering? She is not sure. It's impossible to make sense of her surroundings in the gloom of the blackout. She stumbles into the crocodile, scrapes the bridge of her beak on its scales.

'Ouch!' She has a good mind to tell the reptile it has no business loitering in the dark. Then again, given its sharp incisors, perhaps a polite exchange of apologies might be more appropriate: 'Pardon me.'

She'd been expecting the specimen to make a similar noise, but it seems to have more pressing concerns on its mind. It mumbles something about deliverance. Is it intoning some special plea?

She notices the dingo. 'There ain't no such thing as the devil.'

'It can't be another iron bird, brother,' the crocodile replies. 'The lar gibbons have sounded the all-clear.'

'I ain't scared o' no monster,' the dingo insists, disappearing into the smoke, but Bel-imperia can tell that the other creatures on the cobblestones are reluctant to return to their cages. For no apparent reason, the pampas cat arches its back and spits. The porcupine darts under a rhododendron bush and curls up into a ball.

Is there some dangerous beast hiding in the darkness? Perhaps she should seek refuge in the Hunting Tower until the moon rises. Bel-imperia glances over her scapulars at the dim light spilling out of the building, spots the she-macaque stepping into the night.

Lola.

Here she comes, cradling her sleeping infant in her arms. The simian scampers across the cobblestones: purposeful, determined. Is she clutching a piece of Nile-blue paper?

Lola slides the sheet of paper under Bel-imperia's talons. 'That be from the bird in the specs, ma'am. Edna something. She said she'd had a change of… ' She stops short of finishing her sentence. No doubt she can sense the sinister atmosphere, the threat of impending danger. 'What be going on?'

'Oh, just some nonsense about another iron bird.' Bel-imperia pecks up the piece of folded paper, scuttles back towards the Hunting Tower, back towards the light.

'It isn't an iron bird, sister.'

In the distance, the dingo barks: 'Friggin' hell, something's escaped from the Hall o' bleedin' Relics.'

Did the pampas cat just cry 'Pteranodon' or 'Pterodactyl'? Impossible to hear above the sound of the commotion. Bel-imperia resists the urge to glance up. She's in no mood to be distracted: she has something important to read.

She shakes the piece of paper open, spreads it out under her talons.

No time to peruse it. The other animals are right: that sounds like the whoosh of some prehistoric pair of wings. She peers into the darkness.

There it is, descending in a great pall of smoke, like an avenging angel: a gaunt-looking dinosaur, its grasping talons outstretched. Is it a pteranodon? Bel-imperia cannot be sure. But she is quite certain she can make out the shape of the reptile's wings wrapped around Lola. Is it grappling with the she-macaque? Is it attempting to rip her infant out of her arms? There's still no moonlight; she cannot make sense of the desperate struggle, the terrible screams.

She glances over her scapulars in the direction of the light. Should she snatch up her scrap of paper and scuttle back inside? Too late.

Something is thrashing at the air – strong downward strokes. She stares into the great cloud of dust rising from the cobblestones, catches a glimpse of a pair of reptilian legs as the dinosaur disappears into the night, the limp corpse of Lola's infant dangling from its talons like a rag doll.

The she-macaque scrambles up from the cobbles. More shrieking and screaming. The harlot is hysterical. In an attempt to distract herself from the unbearable din, Bel-imperia turns to the scrap of paper spread out under her talons:

THE CLOISTERS

DONEC RURSUS IMPLEAT ORBEM

The Cloisters is pleased to announce
that in recognition of their exceptional
grades in our annual entrance paper,
the following candidates have been
awarded a scholarship:

BRUSQUE, Orson
U. arctos horribilis   A -

CURMUDGEON, Egbert
G. Gorilla   A -

PINCH, Bel-imperia
T. tracheliotus   A +

```
OLD HESPER HOUSE ᴀɴᴅ ZOOLOGICAL GARDENS

The Cages of Caer Lud

THE DOWER HOUSE

Grade I Listed Cage, Enclosure or Other Estate Building.
Built in the mid-1600s, the Dower House has been the
official residence of the P. Ex. since 1735.

NO ADMITTANCE TO THE GENERAL PUBLIC
```

'Ebenezer?'

He is staring out at the back garden – a ruin of cabbage stalks and rotten cucumber frames. Is that an old boot buried in the soil? Is that a discarded pair of antlers tangled up in the rosebushes? He squints into the late-afternoon sunlight. He cannot distinguish more than the crown of the antlers, the tattered remains of their tines, but he recognises them all the same. No doubt the previous P Ex must have left them there. Strange, though. It's not as if his predecessor used to shed his antlers in the garden. He liked to have an audience. He liked to exploit the moment to underline some point about being New Herbivore – or use it to impress on the animals that he had no intention of leading them into a crusade against some despot. What was it he said as he shook off his antlers at the climax of that crucial speech? 'Conflict is not inevitable, but disarmament is.' His predecessor, Bambi.

Ebenezer glances around the drawing room. The broken armchair and the dismal oil paintings. The pianoforte and the faded carpets. He remembers barging in here and having a dump on the chaise longue in order to remind Bambi of his territorial claim. 'When the fuck are you going to honour that deal we made down at the watering hole?' he had said. 'When the fuck are you going to prance out of here?'

He hangs his head in shame.

His conduct had been unbecoming, undignified. Couldn't he have exercised a little restraint rather than let the primitive urge to assert his dominance get the better of him again and again? He is ashamed of his behaviour. He should never have clomped up the cantilevered staircase in the middle of the night. He should never have revealed his engorged member to Bambi's doe.

But still. This afternoon he has a chance to rise above all that unbridled ambition, a chance to make amends...

He peers at the sheets of black-edged mourning paper on the backgammon table: the crossed-out paragraphs, the underlined sentences. More than the final draft of a resignation speech, an act of atonement: simple, dignified. He has learned his lines. He just needs to lumber out of the front door and deliver them, then he can hold his head up again.

'Ebenezer?'

But all the same. That it should come to this.

He remembers the morning he announced that he'd been persuaded to charge at Bambi and chase him out of the zoological gardens. His coronation as Commander-in-Chief and P Ex. 'I shall be strong in purpose,' he had said. What purpose, though? What had he hoped to achieve? He's sure he must have had some ambitious agenda, some grand master plan, but as he gazes out at the garden, the precise details escape him. Something about affordable caging? Something about malnutrition and mange? He cannot recollect.

He snorts.

Perhaps his short stint as P Ex had been doomed from the outset. Could another Prize Exhibit have made a better job of the difficulties that beset him? The subprime encumbrance crisis in the United Species? The drop in receipts at the gatehouse? He'd prevented Old Hesper House and Zoological Gardens Ltd from going into receivership, damn it. What went wrong, then? What made the animals give him such a drubbing? Was it because he struggled to get his ideas across? He remembers his behaviour in the Ape House, the word he'd used to describe the pipistrelle that had cornered him. He's not just a penitent sinner. He is ashamed. He gazes at the sheets of paper on the backgammon table again. Perhaps this time he might be able to turn in a decent performance. Has he got it inside him to rise to the challenge? Can he get this job done?

'Ebs?'

He snaps at the somethingosaurus that has crept up beside him: 'What the fuck is it, Lucy?'

'I think that little orange-bellied hottie might have sent us another pigeon.'

He glances around the room again. The dust on the grand piano. The cobwebs strung up in the Bohemian glass chandeliers. He cannot see a pigeon.

'On the mantelpiece, Ebs.'

It is perched beside a carriage clock.

'Shall I do the honours?'

Ebenezer appraises the prehistoric reptile as it struts across the room on its hind legs, like a member of the general public in a pair of stilettos. Bambi's spiritual guru. His Holiness, the High Priest of New Herbivorism. The master architect of the magnificent edifice that has just come crashing to the ground. Is the creature going to miss all this excitement once it's been sent back to the Hall of Relics? Is it going to pine in a corner, longing for some desperate P Ex to summon a dromaeosaur so that it can bask in the spotlight again? No time to ruminate on the matter. The feathered dinosaur is unfurling the flaps of loose flesh around its neck.

It fluffs them up into a ruffed collar and spits a dart of poison at the pigeon. 'There. That should do it.'

Has it blinded the bird?

It snatches the letter attached to the pigeon's leg and glares at the disorientated Columbine until it drops off the mantelpiece, dashing its brains out on the coal scuttle.

'Whoops-a-daisy. I suppose the poor thing must have lost its balance. What a shame!' The dinosaur darts a glance at Ebenezer, genial but poisonous. The thinnest of smiles. 'Of course, it would be tragic if our comrade's sacrifice…'

Ebenezer grunts, pretends to admire the cabbage stalks in the garden. He has no desire to witness the spectacle of some prehistoric raptor gobbling up a pigeon. But it's a struggle to ignore the sound of the bird's bones breaking. Or the slurping noise as Lucius laps up – what? Some spilt blood, some spilt brains? It occurs to him that perhaps the Order of Herbivores might have fared better if its champions had been a bit more... What's the word? Herbivorous?

'Just as I thought, Ebs.' The dinosaur is clutching the letter in its bloodstained talons. 'Nick still hasn't signed the prenup. He's hoping to agree a better deal before he offers his backside to FitzClarence. He needs more time.'

'Do I have more time?'

Lucius struts across the threadbare carpet, peers out at the garden. 'Not much. It'll be dark soon.'

'What fucking difference does that make?'

'Image. Why creep out under the cover of darkness like a cat burglar when you can make a dramatic exit as the sun is setting behind the stained-glass cupola that stands atop the Ape House?'

Ebenezer snorts. It hadn't occurred to him that he might still need to consider his image.

'Besides, that ground squirrel is using us. Unless he's going to dump FitzClarence and offer himself to the Order of Herbivores we've got to assume that it's a done deal.' Lucius casts a glance at the sheets of paper on the backgammon table. 'You need to make a decision, Ebs.'

For once there is no hesitation, no dithering. It's the easiest decision he has ever made. 'I've been humiliated enough.'

'You mean... ?' The colour is draining out of the reptile's scales. Is it surprised to see its Commander-in-Chief showing some leadership?

'Ignore Nick's pigeon. The animals in these gardens have lost their patience and so have I. Come on, let's do it.'

Ebenezer stomps across the drawing room and barges into the hall. He summons one of the emperor penguins that staff the Dower House and instructs it to arrange for an old tin bath tub to be brought down from the attic so that FitzClarence has something to splash around in until a more permanent solution to his semi-aquatic needs can be found. He ignores his instinct to shout at the specimen. He is calm, but determined.

'You did all right, Ebs.' Lucius has scuttled up beside him.

'What? What did I do all right?'

'I've been around a bit – late Jurassic and all that. I've seen squillions of Prize Exhibits come and go. You did great.'

'I did?'

'One of the best. You rescued these gardens in one of their darkest hours. Not just us; other institutions too. That required leadership. No one else could have done it. Not Bel-imperia Pinch, given her agenda. Not Dale FitzClarence, given his. It took courage to invest in all those attractions and get the turnstiles moving again. Courage and compassion.'

'The animals didn't seem to appreciate it.'

'Perhaps not, but most of them didn't appreciate Chartwell either. Not in the scent-marking stations, not in '45.' The somethingosaurus struts across the chequered floor tiles, slips its lizard-like head under the net curtains and peeps outside. 'Now, remember, it's all been choreographed.'

Ebenezer lumbers past a line-up of penguins, apologises to a relative of one that had been trampled on as urgent business compelled him to charge from room to room in something that might have resembled a rage. Is that a thin strip of sunlight slanting into the building under the front door? He clomps up to it and snorts. He can smell long-haired he-rats and slender-tailed she-rats. He can smell endangered cotton rats and common shithouse specimens.

'Quick rehearsal, Ebs?'

'No need. I've a hunch I'm going to get it right this time. In fact, I suspect I might turn in a fucking brilliant performance.'

'Fresh pastures, then?'

'Yes, fresh pastures.'

The dulcet tones of the female of the species: 'Don't forget me, darling.'

His she-rhinoceros is clomping down the cantilevered staircase. He gazes up at his beloved as her rump brushes against a sepia-tinted photograph of some moustached guenon from the 1880s. Is it his imagination or is something about the portrait not quite right? He turns his attention to the snapshots of other, more recent Prize Exhibits: Egbert Curmudgeon, Jepson Pug, Jeb Moses... Their garish Polaroids are in correct chronological order. But still. Didn't that regal portrait of the Rt Hon Bel-imperia Pinch used to hang above the third step from the top? Ebenezer is sure that it did. He searches for Bambi's grinning selfie. Not in the correct place either. Has some minion moved all the photographs down a step in order to make room for a mug shot of a square-lipped rhinoceros?

He can sense the anger rising up in him. He glances around for someone to shout at, some lesser creature to blame. Sue, perhaps. Or one of the emperor penguins? No... There's no point in losing his temper. He's bound to regret it. He dismisses his anger. He lets it go.

His she-rhinoceros saunters up to him. 'Not that black dog again, dear? Is it snarling?'

'No, I think it might be dead.'

She busses him on his square lips. The touch of her bristles is calming, supportive. This is what he wants. This is what he needs.

'Have the calves been spruced up?'

'Of course, dear.'

He imagines the gasps of amazement as his stub-horned little ones stumble out into the sunlight at the climax of his speech. He imagines cantering down the paving stones alongside his she-rhinoceros, their little calves trotting along beside them, excited at the prospect of fresh pastures. Perhaps it's not as bad as all that, being put out to graze.

'Come on, then. Let's do it.'

He butts the door open and lumbers out into the golden sunlight. He clomps up to the flea-bitten rodents corralled behind the barricades and clears his throat to speak.

23

OLD HESPER HOUSE **AND** ZOOLOGICAL GARDENS

The Bog-Land Enclosures

THE OLD BOATHOUSE

SITUATI... ~age, Enclosure or Other Estate Building.
Preservation order pending.

KEEP OUT

'Father, I've been awarded a scholarship to... ' She chokes on the sentence. Poor little Bel-imperia Pinch. She has never had such an unpleasant surprise.

Of course, she had sensed she might be intruding. Indeed, she remembers some instinct had told her to announce her arrival before barging through the double doors. But she'd been so excited to learn about the Cloisters, so impatient to tell him about the A+, that she refused to listen to it. The scholarship had been something to make him proud, something to merit his respect and admiration, perhaps even his love. She had imagined celebrating. She had pictured him promising her something special for dinner – some goujons of goat perhaps, or a litter of stillborn rabbits. She had been planning to get preened up for the occasion and put on the pearls. But it's quite clear that there are going to be no celebrations tonight. Intruding? It couldn't be more obvious that her presence is unrequired.

She comes to a standstill beside a cast-iron bucket. Will she ever be able to expunge the sight on the marble-topped contraption from her memory? The mortal remains of the man: lugubrious, squalid. The she-pheasant bent over a mortar and pestle, her burnished plumage shimmering in the moonlight, her bronze tail hoisted up in the air.

The pious raptor pressed up against the pheasant's rear end, his beak latched onto her nape, his thighs poised mid-thrust.

Here he is, then, Silas Pinch, Master of Embalming, Obsequies and other Rites of Passage, rubbing his cloaca against his assistant. Here he is, then, Silas Pinch Esquire, a respectable member of the Elders, fucking a pheasant from behind.

'Father?'

'Oh, good Lord.'

In an imperious gesture that makes no concession to his humiliation, his daughter turns her head to one side, the commissure of her beak contorted into an expression of disgust. Is this the reason he decided to sit down and disgrace himself at aurora matins? His desire to indulge in the pleasures of the flesh. Is this the reason her mother said, 'Why dost thou think the other animals gossip about him?' Bel-imperia is sure it must be. She steals a glance at him. He should be uncoupling his cloaca and scrambling down from the simpering pheasant, not standing there like a lemon. Perhaps he's too embarrassed to dismount. Yet embarrassing or not, it's quite clear that someone needs to bring a little leadership to bear on the situation.

Careful not to send the bucket beside her clattering across the boathouse, little Bel-imperia Pinch flexes her pectoral girdle and unwraps her wings.

'Right,' she announces, as soon as she's settled on top of the spice drawers, 'you have one minute to regain some composure, Father. One minute. Is that understood?'

She attends to a spot of preening as he clambers off the pheasant and stuffs his cloaca out of sight. If he had a pair of long johns, this is the moment when he'd be pulling them up and popping his limp member back inside.

'Bel-imperia, I… '

'Silence, Father.' She turns to the pheasant. 'Fannie Hodgson, isn't it?'

'Yes, ma'am.'

She is delighted to hear another specimen call her ma'am. 'Well, what's the meaning of this spectacle, Fannie?'

'I didn't solicit copulation, love. Honest.' The pheasant struts across the marble, no doubt in an attempt to put a respectable distance between her rump and its admirer. 'I just stooped down to grind up them spices and he took me from behind.'

Bel-imperia takes in the upended mortar, the spilt cumin seeds. Is the bird telling the truth?

'Oh, he's a one, he is. He said he wanted to learn me what to do with that pestle thing.'

'Did he indeed?' She suspects her father might have had a different lesson in mind. 'Well, I'm sure there must have been some misunderstanding. Father? Would you care to explain what you were doing when I came in?'

'He was pressing his advantage – that's what he was doing, love.'

'Is this true, Father?' She can tell that it is: his lappets are as red as a scarlet ibis. 'Come on, out with it. What were you doing to little Fannie Hodgson?'

'Nothing.'

'Nothing?' She plunges her head into her quill coverts, plucks out a parasite. 'I suggest you recite the Second Commandment, Father.'

'Bel-imperia, please.'

'The Commandment, I said.'

'*Thou shalt not...* ' He seems a little distressed. Is that a tear brimming onto his lore? '*Thou shalt not mount any species other than thine own...* '

'And the rest.'

'*Neither shalt thou nudge, sniff, stroke or...* ' But he cannot bring himself to pronounce the words 'otherwise interfere'. He surrenders to his tears.

'For goodness' sake, Father, pull yourself together. Remember, our emotions exist to be controlled.'

She turns her attention to the pheasant. The spectacle of Silas Pinch sobbing his heart out seems to have made an impression on the foolish creature.

'It's all right, love. Let him be. I don't suppose he meant no harm.'

'No, neither do I.' She leaps into the moonlight, sails down onto the marble. 'Indeed, I doubt he'd have succumbed to temptation if a certain bronze-tailed temptress hadn't led him on.'

'Hang on a minute, love; I didn't lead him on.'

'No? Strutting in here all preened up like a splendid bird of paradise? "Yes, sir. No, sir. Whatever tickles your fancy, sir."'

'I didn't make him the thing he is. He's got a reputation for touching up the birds.'

'He's got nothing of the sort.' She hops up onto the man's mortal remains, rounds on the pheasant. 'Let me make it quite clear, strumpet: Father is a pillar of Old Hesper House and Zoological Gardens.'

'Strumpet, am I? You watch your tongue, madam, or I'll tell the world what he did, I will.'

'Who will believe you, Fannie? Silas Pinch is a respected member of the Elders, and he has an expensive chain of office to prove it. He also has a profitable business and a long list of influential clients eager to avail themselves of his services. Whereas little Fannie Hodgson is just a common pheasant that—'

'I'm not common; I've got a bronze tail.'

'So has his beloved Bessie. He must have mistaken you for my mother. Your eyesight's not what it used to be, is it, Father?'

'No, it isn't.'

'A regrettable error, but the fact remains that I'm about to go up to the Cloisters and I have no intention of letting the good name of our species get dragged through the mud. And so make no mistake: mention this unfortunate misunderstanding to another living soul and I shall have no hesitation in informing every eligible he-pheasant in these gardens that little Fannie Hodgson is nothing but a brazen harlot. Oh, and I shall also remind them that harlots spread diseases. Do I make myself clear?'

The pheasant nods.

'Now, drag that gaudy tail out of this establishment and don't bother bringing it back until it's time for it to be embalmed.'

'But I got a position here, ma'am. I'm his assistant.'

'You're nothing of the sort, Hodgson. This specimen has been relieved of its duties, hasn't it, Father?'

'Yes, it has.'

'You can't do that, sir. You can't give me the chop.'

'Of course he can, Fannie: conduct unbecoming. Now, get out of this boathouse before we decide to have broiled pheasant for our supper. Go on, shoo!'

Bel-imperia lunges at the bird, but it leaps into the air before she can give it the sharp peck that it deserves. There it goes, clattering out through the double doors. She turns to her father, but he seems too ashamed to meet her gaze. She takes in his hunch-shouldered stoop, his sagging lappets. He appears to have aged. She has a sudden urge to slip out of the boathouse and leave him here, staring at the marble in disgrace. Instead, she says, 'That's that, then. No more Fannie.'

He opens his beak and closes it again, unable to articulate his thoughts.

'I don't think she'll chirp.'

'Thanks, Bel. I appreciate it.' He hazards a cautious glance at her. 'The soul is... '

'Come on, Father. Spit it out.'

'The soul is imprisoned in a dungeon of flesh. Our instincts are primitive, unreliable.'

'Yours, perhaps. Mine are spot on.'

'Yes, of course.' He hangs his head again. Could he be in more disgrace? 'Oh, Bel, I am no better than our cousins in the Serengeti.'

'Enough is enough, Father. I've no desire to discuss the matter. Your reputation is intact. No damage has been done. There's nothing to discuss. Let's put the sordid episode behind us, shall we? I do not intend to allude to it again.'

'You mean you're not going to... ?'

'What?'

'Tell your mother.'

She subjects him to a penetrating stare. Is he trembling at the thought of his beloved's rage? 'No, of course not. Mother and I have nothing to say to each other. Besides, she isn't here, is she? She's disappeared.'

'Yes.' Hesitant, he shuffles across to the edge of the marble, gazes out through the double doors. His daughter can sense that his thoughts have returned to the moment her mother stomped out onto the boat slip leaving a dead pigeon behind her. 'I wish I knew where she was, Bel.'

She tells him about her conversation with Miss Scroop.

'Le Jardin Zoologique? I doubt it. She's never been able to stomach the taste of snails.' He pauses, steals a glance at some brown paper parcel propped up against the spice drawers. 'Oh, I do hope no harm has come to her.'

'I am sure she's big enough to——'

'I've had some posters printed.'

'Posters?' He must have managed to persuade a rat to let him use the printing press at *The Evening Rodent*.

'That's right.' He drops down onto the ground, pecks at the strings of the brown paper parcel, pulls something out. 'I got a gopher to design them,' he explains, spreading one out on the marble. 'It's quite a good likeness, isn't it?'

Bel-imperia inspects the crude poster. 'Missing: Lappet-faced or Nubian Vulture' under an amateurish sketch of Bessie Pinch (née Crust). 'A Substantial Discount on Your Embalming as a Reward.'

'That's her chipped beak, see.'

'Charming.' It's not the most flattering portrait. But then, her mother is no oil painting.

'I was planning to put them up tonight. You... ' He hesitates, as if searching for the self-confidence to finish his sentence. 'You can help me if you like.'

'Me?' She'd sooner help him slop out a sloth's latrine. 'No, Father, Michaelmas Term starts in the morning.'

He takes this in.

'You got a place, then?' The question is emotionless, prosaic. There's no suggestion of pride in his tone.

She remembers some unfinished business she needs to attend to before she leaves for the Cloisters.

'Bel?'

Ignoring his appeal for attention, she scutters across the marble and peers outside. Such a still night – not so much as a ripple on the surface of the lake. But she suspects that the stillness might be deceptive. Indeed, there seems to be a sense of tension in the air, as if the fabric of the landscaped gardens has been stretched to breaking point. In the distance, the broadleaved trees on the escarpment shimmer as a gentle gust disturbs their branches. Is this an invitation? The birds of paradise might not be scheduled to perform this evening, but she can tell that her presence is required in the thickets and glades; she can feel it in her bones. She glances up at the ridge of the escarpment. It looks as though the moon is about to retreat behind a tattered cloud.

'Light a candle, Father. I think it's going to get dark in here.'

But she can see that he is trembling too much to open a box of matches.

'Oh, give them to me. I'll do it.'

She pins the matchbox down on the marble and starts to peck at it, but her hooked beak has been adapted to slashing through the tough hide of a sun-baked carcass, not sliding open a box of Bryant & May's Flaming Fusees. She loses her patience and applies too much pressure, sends the matches shooting across the marble. Snatching one, she strikes it on the dead man's toenail and lights the taper that her father is clutching in his beak. He turns to the nearest candle.

'No, not just one, Father. Let's push the boat out tonight. Light them all.'

He does as he is told. There he goes, scuttling around the deceased, lighting all the candles that his disgraced assistant must have set out: long, romantic dinner candles soaring out of Robertson's jam jars; short, stump-like candles stuffed into bottles designed to hold disinfectant or embalming oil. Their flames hesitate, as if uncertain, before summoning up the confidence to bathe the boathouse in light.

'Blast! This one's gone out.'

Ignoring him, she turns to the old duchess dressing table, admires the reflection of the dancing candles in the glass. Something else is moving in the mirror, though. Is it some reptile slipping in and out of focus? Is it Draco?

Confident that she is capable of seeing through the anaconda's disguise, she peers up at the rafters, searches for the tell-tale shimmer of his scales. But she can sense that no one is coiled around the crossbeams. She turns to the mirror again, catches another glimpse of the creature – some reptile rearing up out of the flames. Is it a serpent trapped in a circle of fire? Is it a cobra? No time to focus on the apparition. No time to tell. It has dissolved into the candlelight.

Nevertheless.

She has a hunch that the specimen might not have been a reflection at all. It seemed to have been on the inside looking out, not the outside looking in. Could it have been something trapped in the mirror, something imprisoned in the glass?

Impossible.

Putting the experience behind her, she turns her attention to the man on the marble: his broad shoulders, his muscular limbs. She remembers the afternoon she scuttled into the boathouse and discovered his mortal remains. For the first time, the thought occurs to her that he must have once been a rather magnificent beast. Is it the shimmering candlelight that has transformed him into something more dignified than a lump of decomposing meat? Or is it the scented oils and the East Indian spices, the embalming procedure? She suspects it must be the latter. For the deceased hasn't just been dumped on the marble, he has been laid out; he hasn't just been scrubbed and disinfected, he has been cleansed. Isn't it about time, then, he was sent down the boat slip to meet his maker?

She turns to her father. 'Shouldn't he have been cremated this evening?'

'Oh, I had second thoughts while I was dousing him in paraffin. I daren't cremate him during a blackout, Bel. The iron birds might return.'

'Of course.'

'I'll do it in the morning. In fact... ' He pauses, scuttles a little closer to his daughter, cautious, circumspect. 'In fact, I thought I'd ask the crocodiles to incorporate a short service into matins. You... You could read the lesson, if you like.'

Bel-imperia shudders. The man might seem presentable in the candlelight, but she has no desire to attend the funeral of something that came to the zoological gardens to slaughter the animals. She remembers gorging on his liver, his appendage. 'No, I don't think that would be appropriate. Besides, I shan't be here in the morning. I'm going to the Cloisters, remember?'

'You were lucky.'

'Lucky?'

'To win a scholarship.'

'I wasn't lucky; I deserved it.'

'Of course.'

There is a moment's silence. In the distance, some nocturnal primate squeals. The timbers of the boathouse moan.

'Oh, Bel, I shall… ' He seems to be upset about something: he is struggling to form a coherent sentence again. 'I shall… I shall miss you, chick.'

He sidles up to his daughter, perhaps in an attempt to give her a gentle nudge on her lappets. She takes a step back, changes the subject. 'There are some loose ends I need to tie up before I go.'

'Loose ends?'

'I came here to collect that string of… beads, remember?'

'I see.'

He swoops down to the old lacquered tea chest and rummages through his treasures. 'I'm sure I put them in here.'

He pulls out the soap-stocking and slings it onto the floor.

'For goodness' sake, Father, I can see them.' The pearls are still caught on the bristles of an old scrubbing brush. He untangles them, drops them at his daughter's feet like an owl presenting a dead mouse to its mate. Her thoughts turn to the disreputable specimen that deceived Miss Scroop. 'Not like that, Father. Put them on me.'

She is conscious of a sense of reconnection as he places the pearls around her neck, as though a bond is being reaffirmed between the precious stones and some fundamental aspect of her nature. She concentrates on the moment, attempts to sear it into her mind. Is she going to be able to remember it? She hopes so. She should like to look back on this evening and think of the pearls as a present from her father. She should like to forget that she found them in——

She tries to banish the thought of the man's intestines, the blood and the gore, but she cannot help wondering what sort of creature would slip something so precious into a corpse. She hopes whoever it was has no intention of returning to the boathouse to retrieve them. Perhaps she should make her excuses. Perhaps she should leave.

'Do them up at the back, please, Father.'

She can tell that he is struggling to fasten the clasp. 'Ouch!'

'What's wrong now?'

'Nothing. I just caught a bristle feather in the blasted thing.'

It seems so insignificant: a bristle feather caught in a clasp of a string of pearls – just one of those things. Bel-imperia cannot imagine the ramifications the incident is going to have. She lets it slip out of her mind; she moves on.

'There! Done.'

She glides across to the old duchess dressing table, admires her reflection in the looking glass: the lustre of the candlelight on her lappets, the delicate shimmer of the pearls. Is that a bruise on the bridge of her beak? She peers closer at the blemish.

Poor little Bel-imperia Pinch. She has no inkling that she is about to get such a shocking surprise. Of course, she recoils in horror as soon as the hideous specimen lunges at her, but she cannot avert her gaze from its penetrating stare. She gapes into the mirror as if caught in a spell. She holds her ground until the apparition recedes into the reflected candlelight.

Shaken, she turns to her father. Did he see it too? No – he might still be recovering from his recent embarrassment, but he seems quite composed. 'You must have got a good grade to get a scholarship, chick.'

'What?'

'What grade did you get?'

She pushes the apparition out of her mind. She pulls herself together, tells him about her A+. 'Of course,' she adds, returning to the marble-topped contraption, 'science is a demanding discipline, but I'm sure I'll rise to the challenge.'

'So am I.'

'Father?'

'Yes.'

But there is nothing more to be said. 'I suppose I'd better be going.'

This is it, then. The moment she has been longing for. Escape. She pauses to savour the experience. One last glance around the boathouse, one last look at all the clutter: the battered cupboards and the chipped cabinets, the canisters of embalming fluid and the unopened bars of Pears'. Should she try to commit it to memory, or is it better just to forget?

She hops across to the edge of the marble and spreads out her splendid wings.

'Don't leave me, Bel.'

She darts an impatient glance at him over her scapulars. 'I have no choice in the matter. I must.'

'But you haven't met our guest.'

Guest. It's just a common noun, just a scrap of language, but it detonates in her mind like an exploding bomb. Guest? Does this mean that some peeping Tomcat has been loitering in the building? Does it mean that some gossipmonger has seen him tupping little Fannie Hodgson?

'For goodness' sake, Father. What guest?'

'Up there. Second spice drawer from the top.'

She soars up to the glass-fronted drawer. Is something curled up on the collection of old rags that her parents brought to the boathouse? She snatches the brass handle in her talons, gives it a good tug.

She perches on the corner of the open drawer and inspects the specimen languishing on its bed of laddered stockings. Not much meat on its bones. Indeed, the little thing isn't much more than a morsel: an offcut of skin stretched over a ribcage, a porcelain doll that is losing its hair. She recognises it at once.

'The abomination!'

She remembers the last time she caught a glimpse of the creature: not long ago – an hour or so, perhaps. She remembers standing outside the Hunting Tower, peering up at the infant dangling from the talons of some dinosaur, like a rag doll. Bel-imperia sighs. Can she be confident that she caught sight of a dinosaur? Is that the correct interpretation of the incident? 'Something's escaped from the Hall o' bleedin' Relics,' the dingo had said – a pteranodon, or some such reptile. On reflection, it does seem improbable, though. Improbable that a specimen from the late Cretaceous should be on the loose in 1940. Improbable that such a creature should snatch a mere morsel, such as Lola's infant, rather than a dingo or a pampas cat – much more

215

substantial meals. Can she trust her judgement, then? She remembers stumbling into a crocodile and bruising the bridge of her beak: the darkness had been impenetrable. True, she had glimpsed something descending out of a great pall of smoke – she is sure about that – but in retrospect, she has a hunch the creature might have been a raptor; a bird of prey, not a prehistoric reptile. She turns to her father: a respectable raptor mired in disgrace, but a raptor all the same. Is this the monster that tore the screaming macaque out of its mother's arms? Her gaze settles on his reptilian legs, his prehistoric talons. No doubt it is. No doubt it must be. Dismissing the thought of dinosaurs, she hops into the cumin drawer and gives the simian a prod. No reaction at all.

'Is it dead?'

'Good gracious me, I hope not.' He leaps over a long dinner candle and takes to the air, dislodging the candle from the base of its jam jar as he whooshes over it. Does his daughter notice that it is leaning a little too close to the man's mortal remains? For a moment, perhaps. But she is so surprised to see her father in such a panic that it slips her mind. Does it matter if some abomination has died or not?

He alights on the spice drawers. 'No, no, it's just sleeping, thank goodness.'

She remembers staring at the creature in the iron bird shelter. It had been sleeping then too. 'Is that all it does, sleep?'

'No, sometimes it cries for its mother.'

Bel-imperia tries to imagine herself in a similar position, tries to empathise, but she cannot picture herself shedding a tear for Bessie Pinch. Is the infant feeble-minded? She scowls at it as it thrashes about in its sleep. It appears to be trembling. Perhaps it is having a bad dream. Perhaps it is reliving the horror of its abduction.

'What's this abomination doing in the boathouse, Father?'

'Let's not call it that, Bel.' His lappets are turning red again. Bright scarlet ibis. Is he embarrassed? She shouldn't be surprised; after all, she just caught him attempting to beget an abomination.

She says, 'Well, I can think of another word, but I'm reluctant to use it in polite company.'

'Why don't we just call it a macaque?'

'Very well, then. What's this macaque doing here? Why did you snatch the infant from its mother?'

He goes back to the beginning: the morning he descended on the macaque compound to drop off his business card. 'I couldn't let the brazen harlot bring the zoological gardens into disgrace. I had an obligation to raise the matter at Elders.'

That must have been the night Bel-imperia's mother served up Mouse Tail Tangle. She remembers them discussing the abomination. She remembers her mother mentioning his chain of office.

'Of course, the Elders are most concerned. Lola has been summoned to appear before us this evening. She claims the infant's father is a specimen called Obadiah – another toque macaque, she says. If she can produce him, she can come here and collect this creature, but if the Elders conclude that she's broken... ' His lappets are looking even redder. He hangs his head.

'Oh, come on, Father. Spit it out.'

'If she's broken the Second Commandment, the infant is going to be bundled into a crate and shipped to another institution.'

She gives him a hard stare. 'You still haven't answered my question. Why did you abduct the creature? What's it doing here?'

He explains that Lola is rather attached to the thing. 'From all accounts, she calls it her little Rapscallion, her little Scamp. The Elders were worried she'd abscond with it before her hearing. And so I was instructed to confiscate it in order to give her an incentive to turn up.'

'I see.'

'The thing is... '

'Yes?'

'I've been asked to attend Lola's hearing, but I should hate to leave the infant here on its lonesome. It might get up to mischief; it might come to harm. Of course, I'd intended to ask Fannie to step into the breach, but... ' He pauses, perhaps to muster up his courage. 'Oh, Bel, I don't suppose you'd consider... '

She has had enough of this. She stands up straight, plumps out her plumage. 'Let me make it quite clear, Father: I have no aspirations to spend the evening monkeysitting.' She glances out through the double doors, catches a glimpse of the escarpment reflected on the surface of the lake. 'I have more important things to do.'

'I daren't leave the little nipper all alone.'

'For goodness' sake, just lock it in the cumin drawer. It's sound asleep; I'm sure it'll be all right.'

But the macaque appears to have had all the sleep it needs. It opens its bleary eyes and blinks, as if in disbelief. Is it horrified to find itself in the presence of such a respectable pair of raptors? It starts to scream.

Bel-imperia subjects the specimen to a disapproving stare, all the better to impress on it that she's in no mood to tolerate the din it's making, but it just screams all the louder. Has it been eavesdropping? Does it understand that, chances are, it's going to be stuffed into a crate and sent to Le Jardin Zoologique, or some other institution that is lacking in morals? She turns to her father. 'What's wrong with it? Why's it making such a terrible racket?'

He has to squawk to make himself heard over the screaming. 'I expect it needs feeding. Did you collect that book I ordered?'

He must mean *Breeding Monkeys in Captivity Vol. II: Baboons, Mandrills and Macaques.*

She has no inclination to tell him about her evening in the Hunting Tower. 'Out on loan.'

'Never mind. It can't be all that difficult.' He plunges his head into a small cardboard box that has been sitting on top of the spice drawers and pulls out a miniature milk bottle. 'Just prop this up in the corner of the drawer and put the rubber teat into its mouth.'

She recoils in disgust. 'Oh, I am not sure I... '

'It'll stop the screaming.'

In desperation, she grabs the bottle and stuffs the teat into the macaque's mouth. The commotion subsides, but it's impossible to appreciate the silence: the simian is making the most revolting noise as it slobbers at the teat. Is there no end to its repertoire of sound effects? Bel-imperia squints at the bottle. The infant has guzzled at least a third of a pint. She is sure that milk must be expensive. She decides that enough is enough.

'Don't snatch the milk! Good gracious me, where are your maternal instincts?'

'I thought instincts were supposed to be the sign of an uncivilised animal.'

'Not maternal instincts, Bel.'

'No?'

'No.'

Perhaps she ought to acquire some, then. She gazes at the abomination, tries to summon up some affection for the thing. Chuckling, it reaches for the bottle and says, 'Milky-wilky.'

'Oh, dear,' she says, stuffing the teat back into its mouth, 'the specimen seems to have acquired some rudimentary language.'

Her father's tone is grave. 'Yes, and I fear it might have grasped more than it is letting on. I do hope it didn't witness... You know, that unfortunate misunderstanding earlier.' He seems to be concerned that the reputation of their species might be in danger. He asks her to cross-examine the creature, find out if it has cottoned on. 'I shan't be more than half an hour, Bel. One last favour?'

She glances out through the double doors: the moonlight on the lake, the shimmering reflection of the escarpment. She can still sense some instinct calling her, but does she have to leave this minute? Is half an hour going to make a difference? Besides, she's not at all convinced that her instincts can be trusted. Perhaps there's no point in trespassing into the thickets and glades in search of some cave; after all, she has achieved her objective, she is going to the Cloisters, she doesn't need a charlatan to tell her that she is destined for greater things. And it must be a charlatan, it must be a false prophet, because the abomination is still alive.

'Oh, all right. Not more than half an hour, though. Is that clear?'

Silence.

'Father?'

He is no longer perched on top of the spice drawers. Neither is he on the marble. He must have leapt into the air and soared out through the double doors.

Bel-imperia sighs. It had not been quite as she had imagined, their leave-taking. She should have been the one to disappear into the night, not him. She turns her attention to the abomination, inspects the blotches on its legs, the blemishes on its hands. Is it pure macaque or is its blood tainted? Perhaps its imperfections are nothing more than birthmarks; after all, the infant isn't quite as abominable as she had imagined. In fact, there's something rather endearing about its impish charm.

Endearing? Disconcerted to catch herself entertaining such a thought, she pushes it out of her mind. Time to interrogate the thing.

She snatches the milk bottle and pins the primate down under her talons. 'Right. Let's make a start, then, shall we?'

But the specimen appears to be under the impression that it is being tickled. It squirms about in the cumin drawer, giggling. It gazes up at her and says, 'Mamma.'

'Oh, dear,' she replies, tightening her grip on its abdomen. 'I do hope you're not implying that I'm a harlot.'

It giggles again.

'You cheeky little monkey!'

Of course, she has no intimation that this little simian, or something so similar that it could be its brother, is going to rise up through the ranks of the Order of Carnivores and become her dearest friend. And so she is tempted to lunge at the thing and give it a sharp peck, but something in its gaze brings her up short. For it seems to be staring at her in the most peculiar manner. Is it expressing affection? Is it offering her love? Bel-imperia recoils. She cannot recollect requesting a gift of this nature. True, she can remember sobbing her little heart out during an afternoon of classification practice, she can remember longing for the reassuring brush of a bristle feather, but she has changed; she is not the bird she used to be.

Yet even so.

Perhaps there might still be the odd fragment of that little lappet-faced thing in the pit of her stomach. Indeed, she is conscious of a desire to accept the macaque's love and offer it some crumbs of affection in exchange. Is this a defect in her character? She is sure that it must be, because it is rather disturbing. Then again, so is the prospect of not being loved; after all, she should hate to be dismissed as a cold-blooded carnivore, a mother lacking the merest scrap of maternal instinct, a milk-snatcher. She should hate to be despised. Perhaps it might be opportune to display a little love and affection, then. Is she capable of such a thing? Confident that she can rise to the challenge, she releases the infant from her talons and coos at it, lovingly.

But the creature on the receiving end of her gushing devotion seems ill at ease. It gasps in amazement at the sound of its intestines gurgling. It defecates.

Bel-imperia turns her head to one side in disgust. The stench is most disagreeable: rich, almost sweet. She disciplines the culprit: 'You're going to clean that mess up in a moment, dear. Understand?'

No. She can tell that the thing isn't listening. It is gazing at her breast, spellbound. It is admiring her pearls.

'I'm so pleased you like them. They're not imitation, you know. In fact, I suspect… '

She leaves the sentence unfinished. Underneath the sharp tang of the simian's ordure, she can detect another, more acrid stench. Is something unpleasant poisoning the air? For a moment, she almost manages to pin a name on the smell, but the correct term for the odour disintegrates as her mind reaches out to grasp it. Her thoughts turn to a cremation she once attended – a Thompson's gazelle that passed through the boathouse in the spring. For some reason, she remembers standing on the lake-shore as her father set the creature's mortal remains alight. She snaps out of her reverie. Does the stench mean that someone's hide is starting to smoulder? Is it the smell of burning flesh?

She remembers the burning candle that her father clipped as he leapt into the air, but before she can glance over her scapulars at the marble-topped contraption, the abomination reaches up and grabs her pearls.

'Let go of them this instant.'

But it is quite clear that the macaque has no intention of doing as it's been told. It likes this game.

'Don't tug on them. You'll break the thread.'

Time to teach the thing a lesson. Time to give it a sharp peck on the back of the hand.

'Let go of them I said.'

It releases the pearls at once. It squeals like a pig in an abattoir.

Ignoring its cries, she inspects the precious stones for damage. None, thank goodness. But even so. Better put them back in the tea chest, out of the infant's reach.

She drops down to the ground and scuttles across the boathouse. She slings the pearls into the old lacquered tea chest and closes the lid.

Strange. She is sure she caught a glimpse of something bright reflected in the lacquer. From the direction of the spice drawers, the sound of some small mammal scrabbling about. No time to glance up at the marble: the macaque is clambering out of the cumin drawer. She soars up to the abomination and gives it another peck. She bundles it back onto its bed of laddered stockings and slams the drawer shut. There. Done.

Thrashing at the air, she hauls herself up onto the top of the spice drawers – a brief respite, a perch – but as soon as she turns around and glances down at the man on the marble she can see that her ordeal has just begun.

Fire.

She snatches the soap-stocking and tries to beat out the insignificant blaze before it can claim possession of the dead man's upper thigh. Despite the uncomfortable heat, she's quite confident that she can defeat the troublesome flames. Just one more thump from the congealed bars of soap, perhaps.

There.

But it soon becomes clear that she has underestimated her opponent. For the man has been steeped in so much embalming solution and paraffin that no sooner does she manage to crush one riotous insurrection of flame than another smouldering rebellion ignites. The smoke catches in her gullet. She spits out the soap-stocking and coughs. This is getting out of control. She must put out this fire. She must quench these flames.

She drops down onto the ground, grabs the handle of the nearest iron bucket – too cumbersome to heave into the air. She needs a hosepipe; she needs a pump. The embalming machine?

She plunges a plastic tube into the brimming bucket. She seizes the cord that starts the motor and gives it a sharp tug. The machine shudders into action. It coughs and sputters. It dies. She pulls the cord again: sharper, stronger. Nothing.

She glances up at the burning man. The blaze has spread to his stomach, his chest. She soars up to a second-hand cupboard and snatches a glass bottle. Is cedar-scented embalming oil inflammable? No time to read the small print on the label. No time to dither. Swooping down from the cupboard, she glides into a column of smoke and releases the bottle.

It explodes.

In the searing heat of the blast, the man's biceps contract, producing convulsive spasms in his burning arms. Is he about to exact his revenge on the culprit that ate his liver, his penis? Is he about to reach up and snatch little Bel-imperia Pinch out of the air? For a moment, she's convinced that he's going to grab her legs and drag her down into the blaze, but of course, the man is nothing more than a lump of burning meat; he has no inkling that his manhood has been compromised, no grasp of the concept of revenge. Neither does he have the slightest intimation that – providing she makes the right choice this evening – there are going to be other men determined to bring her down, other explosions. For he is incapable of imagining a device primed to detonate in the dead of night as she is putting the final touches to a speech. He relinquishes his role to his successors, relaxes his agitated limbs. She beats the scorching air into submission and rises like a phoenix from the flames.

But it's impossible to breathe these ashes, these embers. Impossible to—

She spirals out of control, crashes onto the old duchess dressing table: a heap of legs and lappets.

Scrambling up onto the soles of her scorched feet, she catches sight of a cascade of molten debris spilling off the marble: burning oil and clumps of organic matter, scraps of flesh and shards of broken glass. She gazes in horror as it courses along the flagstones like a river of molten lava, igniting all the clutter in its path: the Flaming Fusees, the discarded soap-stocking, the posters offering a discounted embalming in exchange for information about Bessie Pinch (née Crust).

But it is the burning man that commands her attention. He is no longer solid. His arms, his shoulders, his chest are merging into one as he melts in the blinding light. Her gaze settles on his upper abdomen. For a split second, she is sure she can make out the contours of a bird – a pigeon roasting in the oven of his gut. She peers up through the soot at the great cloud of smoke billowing into the rafters. Is there nothing she can do to prevent the boathouse burning to the ground?

She darts a glance at the undercarriage of the marble-topped contraption: the cogs and gears, the iron couplings and the rusting chains. Is that the lever her father releases before a cremation? Should she brave the cascading debris and send the thing trundling out onto the boat slip, or should she just get out and leave the building to burn? The blaze is threatening to claim the second-hand cupboards and cabinets, the old lacquered tea chest. She remembers her pearls: the sense of reconnection she felt as her father placed them over her head, the perfection of each precious stone. She cannot let them be reduced to a string of blackened beads. She assesses the distance, charts a safe flight path through the flames – not simple: the ropes hanging from the rafters are ablaze, and there's a curtain of fire fluttering up the side of the spice drawers.

The spice drawers. The macaque.

She is sure she can remember hearing the creature screaming a couple of minutes ago, but it seems to have fallen silent. Is it dead? No, she can hear it coughing. There it is, thumping its little fists on the glass-fronted cumin drawer. She must soar across the boathouse and save it. She must let it ou—

There is a deafening boom.

She hurls herself down on the dressing table as the blast rips across the building. Did a canister of embalming fluid just explode? She stands up, catches a fleeting glimpse of her reflection in the mirror, but before she has a chance to focus on her scorched lappets the image dissolves. Is she melting into the flames?

There is a ripple on the surface of the mirror, a disturbance in the glass. The feathers on her mantle bristle. She can sense that something terrible is going to happen. She can feel it in her gut. But she's too astonished to take flight, too mesmerised to avert her gaze.

Here it is again, then, the hideous specimen that has been haunting her all night. Here it is, surrounded by flame like some daemon in Hades: the damned soul in the mirror, the ghost in the glass.

Time seems to stand still.

Poor little Bel-imperia Pinch. She clings onto the line of strength that runs like a seam of iron through the bedrock of her being, she holds her nerve, but no amount of courage can protect her from the spectre's penetrating stare. It pierces the heart. Can this grotesque ghoul see all her secrets, all her lies? She is sure that it can.

In desperation, she glances around for something to sling at the mirror, something to shatter the glass. No, second thoughts, better not break the spell, better not let the hideous creature out. For even though it is old and haggard, she can tell from its battle scars that there's nothing it likes more than a fight. She can also tell that, despite its cold-blooded stare, it isn't a reptile at all. It is the ghost of some great bird. It is a she-raptor.

Bel-imperia trembles. The spectre might have an alarming, chalk-like complexion, as if it had plastered some strange substance on its face before going out to find someone to haunt, but she recognises the species all the same, because it has the most magnificent pair of lappets: fold upon fold of paper-thin flesh dangling from either side of its face like a pair of papier-mâché earrings. Fold upon fold of sagging leather.

From the direction of the marble, the sound of breaking glass – a jam jar shattering in the heat of the blaze. Something brittle shoots across the boathouse, grazes Bel-imperia's right lappet. She can tell that the cut is deep, but she doesn't flinch at the pain. Neither does she glance down at the gouts of blood dripping onto the dressing table. She just stares in astonishment at the scar that is appearing on the corresponding lappet of the ghost in the glass.

Is this the damned spirit of Bel-imperia Pinch that Bel-imperia Pinch is staring at? Has she slipped out of Hades to haunt herself?

The ghost glares at her and says, 'Let me live, dear. Let me live.'

It sounds like her and it doesn't sound like her. Has it had elocution lessons?

'Who are you?'

'I seem to recall we both know the answer to that question.'

Little Bel-imperia Pinch shudders. Is this happening? Can it be real? She has never had the slightest inclination to give credence to ghosts, but there's no escaping the evidence in the mirror: she is standing in the burning boathouse, gaping in horror at the ghost of her older self. Why, why would she want to haunt herself, though? What does this damned spirit want?

It speaks: 'Let me make it quite clear: in a moment another canister of embalming fluid is going to detonate, and this time the explosion will bring that crossbeam crashing down. Let the boathouse burn. You need—'

'But I must—'

'Silence!'

Has this ghost slipped out of Hades to save its own life?

It clears its gullet. 'Tonight the future of the zoological gardens hangs in the balance. You need to get out of this building, or else we're both going to meet a premature end. And then our legacy will be unravelled.'

'What legacy?'

'All the great things I've... All the great things we've achieved. They'll be undone.'

'What have we achieved? What is it that I've been put in these gardens to do?'

'There's no time to explain. You know where you need to go.'

'You mean the escarpment? That W**ch We Do Not Speak About?'

'That's right.'

'Oh, but I've had second thoughts.'

'Nonsense. We never have second thoughts. We are always firm and resolute.'

'There's no point in traipsing up there. Don't you know? I've... We've got into the Cloisters; we've escaped.'

'We need our admissions papers or else our place will be given to someone else.'

Is this ghost telling the truth? 'You mean that Nile-blue envelope? But Mother stole—'

'Mother?' The ghost spits. 'Forget about her. The creature in the cave will explain. You just need to make the right choice.'

'What choice?'

From the spice drawers, the most terrible scream.

'The macaque or the pearls. There's no time to save both. One or the other. You must choose.'

'But I love the macaque.'

'You do? I don't remember that.'

'It's an impossible choice.'

The ghost seems to be looming closer. Has it remembered that little Bel-imperia Pinch is struggling to make up her mind? 'Come on, dear. You're a Carnivore. You believe in freedom of choice.'

'Do I?'

'Yes, and the time has come to exercise that freedom. Remember, good and evil are meaningless unless a creature is free to choose. And our choices dictate our character. We are what we choose. And so look deep down inside and make a decision. Choose what we are, Bel-imperia. And be quick about it. The pressure in that canister is building up. I shall count down from ten. Nine. Eight... '

Bel-imperia glances at the tea chest: the smouldering lid, the blistering lacquer. She turns her attention to the spice drawers: the screaming macaque's little face pressed up against the glass.

'Four. Three. Two.'

She makes her decision and leaps into the air.

[V]

The Visit

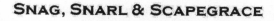

SNAG, SNARL & SCAPEGRACE

JAGUARS AT RULES & REGULATIONS
(EST. 1889)

THE SPOTTED PARD ENCLOSURES
THE CAGES OF CAER LUD
OLD HESPER HOUSE & ZOOLOGICAL GARDENS

8 June 2010

<u>PRIVATE AND CONFIDENTIAL</u>

Our Ref: CS/BHP/2010

Dear Mr Woodshaw,

<u>re: THE IRON BIRD</u>

Please be advised that due to other, more pressing concerns, our client, the Rt Hon Belimperia Hildred Pinch (ex-P Ex and Member of the Hall of Relics), is no longer available to indulge in idle conversation through the bars of her cage. Consequently, her generous contribution to the aforementioned account of her life and times must therefore cease, and you are hereby instructed to desist from loitering in the vicinity of her humble residence in the cul-de-sac of cages and enclosures behind the Small Mammal House.

Naturally, our client regrets that despite having granted an unprecedented number of private audiences, she has NOT been afforded the opportunity to provide an insight into the circumstances surrounding her awe-inspiring ascent to the giddy heights of the PrizeExhibitship, or, indeed, detail her numerous achievements in the role. Nevertheless, she assures us that over recent months she has generously donated more than enough material for even the most mediocre biographer to cobble together a short coming-of-age narrative that could, no doubt, prove a source of inspiration to other lappet-faced fledglings destined for greatness (should such creatures exist).

It remains for us to stress that our client retains her right to inspect the finished manuscript prior to publication, and that Justice Pongo Preamble, the orang-utan, can see no objection to granting a zoological injunction, should the result of your efforts fail to meet with the full and unconditional approval of all concerned.

Yours sincerely,

Cornelius Snag

Panthera onca onca, Dip Rules and Regulations (Hons)

25

I gave clear instructions to Snag, Snarl & Scapegrace: a restraining order, I said. Yet even so, I am afraid he turned up again and started to harass me. He didn't settle down and roll a cigarette. He just strode up to the bars.

'What's the meaning of this, then?' he shouted, shaking a sheet of paper at me. '"Please be advised that due to other, more pressing concerns"?'

'There's no need to read it out aloud,' I said. 'This isn't Hedge School.' I told him to turn the letter around so that I could see the signature. 'Oh, Cornelius! He must be getting long in the tooth. I'm so pleased to see that his pigeon arrived.'

'Yes, but what does it mean?'

'I'd rather hoped the meaning might be clear. Perhaps it contains too much legalese. Shall I put it into plain English, dear?'

'Just give me an explanation,' he replied.

I suppose I must have hesitated.

'Come on, I thought we had an agreement. What's going on? What are these "other, more pressing concerns"?'

I inspected his crumpled garments, his uncombed mane. From the stench of his breath, I could tell that he'd been drowning his sorrows in intoxicating liquor. I said to him, 'Oh, I do understand this must be a terrible disappointment – of course I do. Our conversations have been delightful, delightful. Indeed, I am sure I shall miss them too. But I no longer have time to sit here brooding on the past. Goodness me, no. There's just too much work to be done. Now, if you'll excuse me, I really must be getting on. One cannot insist on punctuality in one's subordinates unless one sets an example. One has no intention of being late.'

'Late? Late for what?'

'Did I not make it clear? I am pressed for time; I am not at leisure to—'

He interrupted me. 'I deserve an explanation. Please?'

Now, I'm not a hard-hearted bird. I am not. Deep down inside, I'm just an old softie. And so I decided to put him out of his misery. 'Oh, all right, then,' I said. 'I don't suppose there's any harm in letting you in on my secret; after all, it's bound to be plastered across the front page of the pamphlets in the morning. Indeed, I shouldn't be surprised to see a commemorative edition of *The Rat*...

'Dale FitzClarence has invited me to dine at the Dower House tonight. That's right, dear, the Dower House. No more sitting in this roost of broken branches. No more staring out through these bars at this cul-de-sac of cages. I am going back to the Dower; I am going home.

'It arrived this morning, the invitation. Here it is, see? Of course, I recognised the black-edged mourning paper at once – I used to scribble notes on it all the time. Let me read it again: *Dear Bel, Sorry I haven't been in touch since the scent-marking. Pressures of being P Ex and all that. You know how it is. But enough about me. Let's cut to the proverbial. Why don't you come round to the Dower for a country supper this evening? The kitchen is being ripped out at the mo', but I reckon I can persuade Snowy to rustle something up.* That's his she-otter, Snowy. I have no idea why she's called that.

'He goes on: *Have you heard? She's expecting another litter! Someone's been hard at it, eh? And so I guess she'll hit the holt once she's dished up supper, but at least that'll give us a chance to have a good catch up. Hope you can make it, Bel. There's something important I need to discuss. Shall we say eight?* Oh, look, I've just noticed... He's signed it LOL. I wonder what that means.'

'Laugh out loud?'

'Don't be ridiculous. Why would he be laughing out loud?'

'Because he's smooth-coated. Because he's insincere.'

'He is nothing of the sort. Dale FitzClarence is—'

He interrupted me again. He accused me of describing FitzClarence as 'not one of us'.

I made it quite clear to him: 'Nonsense,' I said. 'I'm delighted to see a member of the Order of Carnivores in the Dower House again.'

'Even though he had to compromise on his Carnivorous principles in order to get his snout in the door? Come on, admit it. His position in the Order is tenuous. Forget dinner. He just needs the approval of a real Carnivore, so he does. Someone the big beasts respect.'

'I am sure his intentions are nothing but honourable.'

'Honourable?' he said. 'Yeah, about as honourable as Silas Pinch, about as honourable as your father.'

I rounded on him. 'I think you'd better explain that snide remark.'

'You must remember the rumours. Does the name Fannie Hodgson ring a bell?'

I told him it didn't; I encouraged him to drop the subject. But I'm afraid he insisted on alluding to some allegations that a rat put to me in the 1990s.

'Your sainted father used to touch up his assistants,' he said. 'He used to abuse——'

'He did no such thing. Now, how do I look?'

'What?'

'It's a straightforward question,' I said. 'Just give me a straightforward answer.'

But he seemed hesitant.

'Of course, one is told one is a handsome bird; one is told one is well preened. But I must admit it can still be disconcerting to discover that one's lappets have started to sag. Nevertheless, one has no intention of letting oneself go. Perhaps a dab of ceruse this evening... '

'A dab of what?'

'Ceruse,' I repeated. 'There's no need to look so shocked, dear. Other birds use it. Oh, and it's such a simple procedure. Let me see if I can remember the recipe... That's right, three tablespoons of white lead and a dash of white wine vinegar.'

I ignored his incredulous stare and blended the ingredients in a second-hand saucepan I keep for the purpose.

'Fiddlesticks!' I said, as I squinted at the instructions on the packet. 'It seems that in order to give the finished application a glaze, one needs to fold in the white of a medium-sized egg. I don't suppose you have an egg on you, do you, dear?'

But of course, he had come unprepared.

'Never mind. Perhaps a drop of spittle instead, then.' I dribbled into the saucepan and combined the mixture into a paste. 'There's no need to leave it to set; it can just be daubed straight onto the face using a damp rag. Like so.'

He muttered something under his breath.

'There!' I said as soon as I'd finished. 'And so? What do you think? I find an alarming, chalk-white complexion sets off a bird's features and enhances a penetrating stare. Do you agree?'

Silence.

'What's the problem? I haven't overdone it, have I? I do hope not. One must never look like mutton dressed as lamb. Never.'

'No, it's not that. It's just—'

'Oh, I understand. Don't be embarrassed. You'd like a dab to hide that hideous scar.' I peered into the saucepan. 'Well, it's quite expensive, but I'm sure I can spare a little.'

For some reason, he refused.

I told him he could do as he pleased. 'It makes no difference to me,' I said. 'You've been served a restraining order, and so I won't have to look at you for much longer, will I? Now, I think I'll wear the pearls this evening – it's a special occasion, after all. Would you mind doing them up for me, dear?'

I'm afraid he had to be persuaded to reach through the bars and oblige.

'Well?' I said, as I gave him a twirl. 'How do I look?'

'I'm not sure I… '

'Oh, don't be such a shrinking violet. Your honest opinion. I can take it.'

'Honest?'

'Honest.'

He said that I'd plastered on too much slap.

'Slap?' I replied.

'Damage.'

I told him I prefer to think of it as warpaint. 'Not that I'm expecting to encounter much resistance. Who could resist me? No red-blooded male I am sure. Too much slap? Dear me, no. One wouldn't dream of exhibiting oneself on the steps of the Dower House without a dab of ceruse. Unlike Bambi's doe. You see, the rat corps is bound to be corralled behind the barricades, impatient to report one's triumphant return. Just imagine the headlines in the morning: "REJOICE, REJOICE!" Oh, and there's going to be such jubilation. Make no mistake: the animals in these gardens are just going to love it. "Thank goodness for that," they'll say. "Bel-imperia's back. She'll clear up the mess the Order of Herbivores have left behind. She's done it before, she can do it again." Oh, it's just so exciting. In fact, if I might share another secret, I can't remember the last time I had so much to live for.'

He seemed astonished. 'Bel-imperia's back?'

'Yes, that's right, dear, The Mummy Returns. Now, if you'll excuse me—'

He interrupted. He pointed out that the animals didn't get a chance to anoint me in the scent-marking contest.

'Perhaps not,' I said. 'But I'm still a member of the Hall of Relics, and Dale's entitled to have at least one Relic on his Board of Beasts. Indeed, I seem to recall I had several in mine. Oh, I'm so looking forward to building another nest on that board table and getting into a good argument. Of course, I shall insist on reduced rations all round. But Dale's committed to that. He'll help me finish the great work I started. Forget about Bambi. Forget about Ebenezer Bull. It'll be as if I'd never left.'

'But FitzClarence is Prize—'

'Yes, I'm well aware that Dale is P Ex. In name. But he hasn't got the experience to steer a straight course through this crisis. He needs a mature specimen looking over his shoulder. He needs a backseat driver. Of course, one shall require a title that's commensurate with one's stature. One has no intention of accepting Grand Exhibit for Garden Maintenance.'

'Is there something in particular you have in mind?'

'Well, I would have thought De Facto Prize Exhibit and Undisputed Power Behind the Throne would be appropriate, wouldn't you? Now, if you'll excuse me, I think I hear my carriage. Good night.'

26

OLD HESPER HOUSE ᴀɴᴅ ZOOLOGICAL GARDENS

Escarpment Edge

THE HUNTING WOOD

These 3¼ acres of deciduous woodland are all that remain of the medieval hunting reserve that once used to dominate the estate. Consisting of oak, beech and other broadleaved trees, it still supports a small population of deer, and a number of indigenous carnivores, including stoats and pine martens.

PRIVATE

NO TRESPASSING

It must be medieval, then – an *ancien régime* of gnarled roots and creeping mosses clinging to the slope of an escarpment. Or is it primeval? Little Bel-imperia Pinch cannot be sure. But as she wriggles under the barbed wire and scutters into the trees, she can sense that she is stepping into another world. For it is as though a door is closing behind her, shutting out the landscaped gardens and their reassuring promenades of cages and enclosures, shutting out the light.

She had not expected it to be as dark as this. Indeed, she is sure she can remember a bomber's moon looking down on her as she swooped out of the burning boathouse. It is the trees that are to blame. Still canopied in summer green, it is the oaks, beeches and hornbeams that are blotting out the light.

She scuttles under the bough of some great oak. Conscious that the thing is immense, she resists the urge to glance up and admire its crown. She must concentrate on negotiating the damp mulch of mud and acorns beneath her little feet. Is that beechmast? Something squelches in between her toes – a slug? Or was it a small tube of bile, the inedible remains of the last bird to pass through this place? She shudders at the thought. She has no inclination to surrender her precious nutrients to some predator. 'Let me live, dear,' the ghost in the looking glass had said, but she can tell that these trees are indifferent to the hopes and aspirations of the little lappet-faced thing scrabbling beneath their contorted branches.

Is she trespassing here? Perhaps.

She stops to consider her options. Up ahead, she can see the moonlit surface of some limestone outcrop; she can see stars. She must be near the edge of the escarpment. She creeps up to the rock formation. Careful not to lose her footing, she clambers up onto a boulder, peers down at the lake.

'Goodness me.'

She had not realised she had climbed so high. Beneath her, she can see the boathouse burning, like a beacon in the night. She gazes at the reflection of the flames in the lake. Is that Father she can make out caught in the light of the blaze? She can tell that it is. He is mantled over some mammal-shaped smudge on the lake-shore. He seems to be struggling to restrain the desperate creature. Is he attempting to stop it entering the burning building? She catches a brief glimpse of a primate's thrashing limbs. From the sound of its screams, she suspects the specimen might be a she-macaque. The abomination's mother, Lola.

Bel-imperia glances down at the string of pearls slung around her breast, admires their elegance, their grace. Did she make the right decision? She pushes the question out of her mind. She reminds herself that she must have the courage of her convictions.

From the lake-shore, the sound of a crossbeam or something crashing to the ground. There it goes, her father's business reduced to ruins, burnt to the ground, like some corner shop in a riot. His lists of eager customers, his profit and loss statements, his tin of beaten-copper groats... all gone. She sheds a tear. She lets it tumble down her lore. Should she go back and help him rebuild the firm? She banishes the thought. She cannot bring herself to countenance the prospect of turning. It is against her instincts, against her nature. She abandons the boulder and soldiers on.

But as she scurries up the slope of the escarpment, she is conscious that she isn't in her natural element. She should be circling above these trees, not creeping through the undergrowth like a dormouse: it is dangerous on the ground. She remembers the night her mother served Mouse Tail Tangle. Didn't Father mention something about creatures that have no respect for the Commandments, savages that have reverted to their natural state? She tries to muster up her courage, but the thought of some nocturnal predator crouched in the bushes has made her susceptible to the spell of the thickets and the glades. It isn't something she can reason against; it's an ancestral terror and it's tightening its grip on her. She picks up the pace, crashes through the brambles like a thing possessed.

Never mind the thorns. Never mind the long canes thrashing against her little lappets. Is that a clouded leopard behind her? She glances over her scapulars, stumbles on the exposed roots of a gnarled oak. No time to beat at the air. No time to control her descent. She tumbles into a clearing, comes to rest in a clump of stinking hellebore.

Silence.

This is the moment a predator is going to choose to pounce.

Nothing. No clouded leopard. Nothing.

She pulls herself up onto her feet, glances around the clearing. The spore-bearing stalks of adder's tongue. The creeping lady's tresses. Is that a light shimmering in the distance?

She creeps closer.

Teacups. There must be at least eight, no, nine of them: nine chipped teacups arranged in a semicircle at the entrance to a cave. Inside each one, a burning candle and an offering: a spoonful of rice, a squirming grub. She remembers the she-pheasant that led her father into temptation: 'Some of us leave offerings in teacups, love.' Offerings to appease That Which We Do Not Speak About.

Or is it That *Witch* We Do Not Speak About?

She peers through the cast-iron bars cemented across the mouth of the cave. Despite her trepidation, she should like to catch a glimpse of it skulking in the darkness: the creature of the night, the prophet that has been proven not to be false. But the candlelight is too dim to reach into the depths of its subterranean lair. She can smell the thing, though. It smells of stale urine. It smells repugnant.

She turns her attention to the rust-speckled sign tied to the bars. Impossible to read. Something *madagascariensis*. 'CAUTION: THIS ANIMAL—' What? There's an 's'. This animal scratches? This animal bites? She's tempted to remove the sign and scrape off the rust. Perhaps if she clambered up onto—

Something is approaching. She can hear it rumbling, like distant thunder. The thought crosses her mind that it might be a pride of marauding lions, but the roaring is too sustained, too mechanical. From the other end of the zoological gardens, a sudden bout of gibbon song. Is it an iron bird?

She glances around the clearing. There are no rabbit holes to bolt into, no badger setts to shelter in. Besides, she can tell from the rattling teacups that there's no time. She holds her ground, gazes up in defiance at the stub-nosed Messerschmitt soaring over the treetops. The bird isn't a lone predator. Here comes another – and another. Is this mankind's strategic fighter elite? Is this Operation Sea Lion?

The mechanical birds glide over the oaks and beeches in perfect formation, like a flock of metallic geese, the moonlight glinting on their blunt-edged wings. The din is appalling, of course, but high above the droning engines, Bel-imperia is sure she can hear a soprano singing – not the undulating song of a siamang, not a she-gibbon, but a single note, pure and untainted. Is it coming from some underground chamber?

The note hangs in the air until the lungs producing it can hold it no longer; a moment's respite, and then a long, complicated song-phrase building to a crescendo that rises above the sound of the receding engines and echoes through the glades. The cast-iron bars cemented across the mouth of the cave creak open: a hidden door. She does not hesitate. She steps over the chipped teacups and scuttles inside.

27

Don't look at me like that – I am not in the mood. Neither am I presentable. Dear me, one dreads to think of the state of one's ceruse. No doubt the glaze is cracked. No doubt the plaster is crumbling. Oh, I should imagine I must look the most terrible fright…

Let me make it quite clear: I have no inclination to entertain an audience this morning, no desire to put on a performance.

But I must admit one's distress does seem to have attracted some curious spectators. What a bizarre collection of oddities! Who would have thought the zoological gardens had such creatures in it? Why, it is almost as if some deranged specimen had conjured up this morning's audience in their imagination. You look like the sort of beasts that might lurk in a troubled mind. Is that a sabre-toothed tiger skulking in those rhododendrons? Is that a green mamba strung up in that magnolia tree? Ambush predators. Well, make no mistake: I have no intention of being ambushed this morning. As I said, I'm not in the mood.

What was that? What was that? The spider the size of a dinner plate. What are we? A goliath birdeater I presume. Well, out with it, then.

You understand my reluctance to take questions? You're sure it's bound to be a time-consuming business, orchestrating such a triumphant return?

Oh, it's not that I don't have time this morning. Goodness me, no, I have all the time in the…

No.

I don't suppose I do have all that long to be honest – another summer, another spring, perhaps. But let's not dwell on the inevitable. One might be in one's dotage, but one has no desire to contemplate the bitter end. Not this morning. One hasn't had breakfast. One hasn't slept.

Yes? The specimen sitting beside the orange-rumped agouti… There. On that paving stone.

No, of course I haven't been up all night rejoicing. I am afraid the celebrations have been cancelled. That's right, dear, cancelled. No commemorative edition of *The Rat*, no jubilation... But I have said too much.

Oh, perhaps I might consent to one last question. Just one. The hippopotamus. That's right, I said the hippopotamus. You.

Something about the celebrations. You are sure the Order of Carnivores will want to mark the return of their spiritual leader? You are confident a Bengal tiger can be persuaded to slaughter a goat?

Stop it! This is too cruel.

There's nothing to celebrate. There, I have said it. There's nothing to celebrate because Dale FitzClarence is under the delusion that he's capable of repairing this broken zoo alone. Of course, I tried to impress on him that he's going to need more than an orange-bellied ground squirrel to strengthen his resolve. Oh, but he's so complacent. He couldn't care less that most meat-eaters resent having to accommodate the Order of Omnivores. He could not. Neither does he seem to be bothered that sooner or later the Board of Beasts is going to turn against him, just like it turned against me. Or else he'll ask the animals in these gardens for their scent and get an unpleasant surprise. 'You'd better watch out,' I said to him. 'They'll replace you with that bear.'

What was that, dear? What bear?

Oh, I'm not sure I can recollect the specimen's name. That dishevelled-looking polar bear – messes up his coat on purpose to maintain his shambolic image, so I am told. You know the one: born in the United Species, spouts all sorts of nonsense in ancient tongues, uses humour to sugar the pill. Fancies himself as a circus animal – rides a bike, has aspirations to perform some ridiculous stunt on a zip wire...

That's right, Bojo de Pfeffel.

'Oh, I suppose he might get into the occasional scrape,' I said to FitzClarence, 'but Bojo is an honest bear. He'd never tell a deliberate lie. Bojo lie? Perish the thought. He'd never invite me to the Dower House under false pretences. Never. Or serve up such an unappetising dish. Indeed, I shall be delighted to accept his invitation as soon as he becomes P Ex.'

I must admit FitzClarence didn't appreciate that last comment. In fact, I seem to recall he looked rather upset. Or perhaps he might have been blubbing because I'd just given him the fright of his life – I cannot be sure: he was cowering behind the chaise longue at the time. Oh, I gave that smooth-coated otter such a shock! But make no mistake: he deserved it. Goodness me, I've never been so insulted. Leading me to believe he intended to offer me a seat on the Board of Beasts and then bringing up such an offensive subject. Let me make it quite clear: I shall never forgive him. Never.

28

```
OLD HES        OUSE A        LOGICAL GARDE
                The Escarpment

                    YE

              la Madagascariensis

          CAUTION: THIS ANIMAL        S
```

Inside, the air is like November: damp, cold.

Bel-imperia shudders. The rocks beneath her talons are smeared in so much slime that it feels as if she is trespassing into the mouth of a caecilian, or some other great amphibian. Should she retrace her steps? She glances over her scapulars at the cluster of teacups, the candlelight trembling on the cast-iron bars. It's tempting. But retrace them to what? The smouldering remains of the boathouse? Her parents' cage in the Parade? She strangles the thought. This is no time to entertain doubts. She needs to make good her escape; she needs to get her admissions papers.

She scrabbles over a heap of broken bedrock, totters deeper into the cave. Is the light bleeding out of the cream-coloured bands in the limestone? She is sure that it is. Undaunted, she continues to stumble along the catacomb–like corridor of rock until the darkness is total, absolute. Poor little Bel-imperia Pinch. She can no longer sense the gutting blade on the tip of her beak, or the calami of her flight feathers. Has she been absorbed into the gloom? Like a small steam locomotive, she comes to a standstill. But the magnificent engine of her mind is still chugging: the intricate cogs and gears, the great pistons. She recalibrates it. Ignoring the hum of a distant iron bird, she concentrates on the creature's song, listens to each note as it bounces off the rocks and redoubles in the echo chamber of the cave.

'*Judicii signum tellus sudore madescet...* '

Using the mournful plainchant to construct a mental picture of the subterranean maze, she surrenders to the pull of some primitive instinct and lets the music guide her. Up, up she climbs, clambering over some slab of residual limestone, creeping across the slit of some dried-up riverbed. In the distance, a fleeting glimpse of firelight dancing on the surface of a boulder. She readjusts her inner compass, presses on. The song seems to be getting louder. She must be nearing the source of the music. She must be nearing...

The singer.

She remembers her mother described it as strange and queer. 'It be almost as old as a dinosaur,' she said. 'An' it comes crappelin' out in the darklins. Limpelty lobelty. Limpelty lobelty.' She called it an old hag, a beezum. Is it a carnivorous old hag? Does it scoff the squirming grubs that Fannie Hodgson and other heathens leave to placate it, or does it use them as bait to catch something bigger?

Perhaps it eats birds.

She tries to suppress the thought, tries to concentrate on the haunting music, but she can tell that the creature is singing about some terrible torment. Is it a siren's song? Is it luring her into a trap?

'*Sic anime cum carne ader—*'

The specimen cuts short its dirge. No cadence to bring the song to an agreeable end, no coda to give it a sense of resolution. For a split second, a broken crotchet hangs in the air, trembling as it fades into silence. Bel-imperia stops. The absence of sound is even more intimidating than the absence of light. 'What now?' she whispers.

The answer comes in a subtle hiss. 'Ritual purification, old girl.'

'Draco?'

Up ahead, the sound of a branch creaking. The smell of burning juniper. Is that the crackle of a fire she can hear?

The hiss of a serpent again. 'Let there be light.'

'Goodness me.'

She gazes in astonishment at the great buttress of bedrock caught in the blush of some distant fire. Embedded in the rock, the petrified remains of an ancient tree, its roots shaped like a door-frame – a portal to the creature's lair.

She glances around, tries to get her bearings. Is this some sort of antechamber? She is standing at the edge of a rimstone pool. 'Ritual purification,' the anaconda had said.

'Draco?' She is sure she had heard him. She peers over her mantle. Some crumbling slabs of limestone. Some deposits of calcium. But no sign of the serpent that hissed in her ear. 'Don't do that disappearing act again, Draco. Not here.'

She studies the mirrored surface of the pool, searches for a glimpse of the snake's reflection, but she can sense that he has slithered out of the antechamber. She is alone.

Right. Ritual purification, then.

Cautious, hesitant, she dips a raptorial toe into the pool, rippling its mirror. Not as cold as she'd imagined. In fact, it is rather refreshing. Fanning out her tail feathers, she lowers her undercarriage into the water and sets about performing her ablutions. She soaks the soot out of her remiges and rectrices; she sluices her private parts. Is this ritual purification? Has she been made pure? For some reason, her mind turns to the little macaque locked in the spice drawers. Its terrible screams. Has the decision she made in the boathouse sullied her? She crushes the thought.

Confident that her conscience is clean, she gives her precious string of pearls a good rinse. There. Done.

She scrambles out of the pool and shakes the water out of her wings, her tail. Is she presentable? Perhaps a last-minute preen...

But even so, it is a bedraggled bird that scuttles through the portal of petrified roots into the creature's cavern.

Cavern? More like a subterranean cathedral.

She stops beside a stalagmite in the north aisle of the nave, takes in the great basilica of limestone. The semi-transparent speleothems hanging like canopies in the apse. The shaft of moonlight sloping down from a rent in the ceiling of stalactites. Splendid. No doubt some enterprising creature should open this up for the general public to marvel at these soaring pinnacles and pointed arches. No doubt an asset such as this could be sold. She sets the idea to one side. This isn't the moment to give it the consideration that it deserves: some big, bell-like structure has caught her attention.

She creeps along a colonnade of stalagmites to get a closer look at the strange object suspended from a rope in the south transept. Is it a birdcage? Bel-imperia suspects that it might be, even though it looks big enough to hold an eagle – not that she can imagine such a creature being comfortable behind its bars, because it has been cobbled together out of bits and pieces of scrap metal: a sheet of corrugated steel, an assortment of barrel hoops, an old cast-iron bedstead... Is that the blade of a scuffle hoe gleaming in the moonlight? She cannot be sure. But she is quite certain she can see a Nile-blue envelope impaled on a roasting spit.

Her admissions papers.

For a moment, she is tempted to soar into the birdcage and snatch them, but she isn't stupid: she can sense that the great bell jar of scrap metal is a trap. She can also sense that something sinister is staring at her. Is she being sized up?

Here goes.

Conscious that she is making an entrance, little Bel-imperia Pinch holds up her head as she approaches the great throne of broken branches in the chancel – a contorted structure silhouetted against a sheet of mineral deposits.

Is that it, then? Is that the creature no one cares to mention, the creature of the night? She curls up the commissure of her beak in disgust at the misshapen lump of foul secretions slumped against the arm of its throne. In the dim moonlight, the thing isn't much more than a disturbance in the darkness, an ominous concentration of black, about the same size as a small bear, perhaps. She cannot assess the length of its limbs, she cannot discriminate its head from its shoulders, but she can see its eyes – eyes as large as teacups, eyes that burn like boiling cauldrons. Is the creature catching the light of the smouldering campfire at its feet and casting it back across the cave, or is there some diabolical blaze raging in its soul?

Careful to keep a safe distance, Bel-imperia stops under a cluster of stalactites in the crossing of the subterranean cathedral.

'Vieni più vicino, pulcino.'

She is surprised. She had not expected the damned thing to pronounce its curses in such a strange tongue.

'Come closer, closer. There is nothing to fear.'

'Oh, I'm not afraid.' In order to convince the creature that she is telling the truth, she subjects it to a defiant stare.

'Come closer, then.'

She takes a couple of tentative steps towards the throne. Outside, the drone of a distant engine.

'Just one more step. *Dai, sbrigati.*'

She might not understand the disagreeable language that the specimen keeps slipping into, but she can tell from its tone that the request is urgent. She consents to one more step.

'You'll be all right now.'

The droning engines are getting louder. Is another squadron of iron birds soaring over the ridge of the escarpment? She can tell that it must be: the cluster of stalactites on the ceiling is trembling like a cut-glass chandelier.

'What do you mean, I'll be all right?'

'Stand as still as a statue – *una statua, capisci?*'

There is a loud crash: the sound of something brittle hitting the ground and shattering into smithereens. Bel-imperia glances over her scapulars, glares in horror at the broken shards of stalactite. 'My goodness me, I could have lost my head.'

'Yes, I've cheated the Fates; I've pointed them in another direction. You might want to commission a statue at some stage. Let some disaffected specimen decapitate that instead. The Fates don't like being cheated.'

'Oh, I don't think anyone would want to decapitate a statue of me.'

'You'd be surprised.'

She considers the creature as it rearranges itself in its throne. So is this the genuine article – a bona fide fortune-teller? Or is the stalactite routine just a cheap conjuring trick to impress a potential client, all sound effects and sleight of hand? She remembers the afternoon she discovered Draco in the boathouse. She'd trusted her instincts and made up her mind about him in ten seconds, but this is much more complicated, because one instinct is telling her that the creature means no harm, and another that she is being lured into a trap. She steals a glance at the sinister-looking birdcage in the south transept: the shards of metal and the sharp-edged barrel hoops, the assorted blades.

Both instincts cannot be right. Can she trust this specimen, then? She peers into the impenetrable darkness, tries to make sense of the indistinct shape slumped on its throne, but That W**ch We Do Not Speak About is almost indistinguishable from the gloom of its cave.

In the distance, the dull thud of an exploding bomb, a commotion as some ungulate screams in terror. Despite the precautions of the blackout, it seems the iron birds have managed to locate their target. Bel-imperia remembers clambering up onto an outcrop and gazing down at the boathouse burning like a beacon in the night, the flames reflected in the lake. She should have put out that fire as soon as she'd smelt it. She should have extinguished that blaze. Is she responsible for these bombs? She attempts to articulate her thoughts: 'The iron birds... '

It sounds like the creature is scratching its flea-bitten coat. 'You're not to blame, *pulcino*. Some things are destined to burn. Boathouses. Flight Lieutenants. Macaques.'

'Macaques?' She refuses to flinch from the old hag's accusing stare. She has no intention of admitting that she condemned the infant to death in the spice drawers. 'What macaque is that?'

The thing mutters some incomprehensible curse in its strange tongue. 'We both know what macaque we're talking about. She came here to see me, *la mamma. Come si chiama?* Lola. I consulted the Fates. I warned her that her firstborn would die on the Sabbath.'

Bel-imperia remembers her mother: 'It told the trollops her babby's going to die on't Sabbath.' And so it came to pass. Does this mean that the old hag isn't a false prophet, then? She cannot be sure. But it's quite clear that the little macaque's death is no secret. She searches her conscience, prepares to defend her decision to leave the infant to fend for itself and rescue her pearls. 'It wasn't a macaque; it was just an abomination.'

'Not true. *Il suo padre*––'

'Padre?'

'The infant's father, Obadiah. He might be an organ grinder's monkey, but he's a toque macaque. The same species as Lola.'

'He is?'

'*Si.*'

'I didn't make the right choice, then? I should have saved the little thing?'

'It had reached the end of its allotted span.'

'That might be so, but… ' She remembers the ghost in the glass: its sagging lappets, its penetrating stare. 'Why did I have to make such a difficult choice? Why was I put in that position?'

'Your character could only have been formed in a crucible of fire, *pulcino*.'

'But I caused such grief. The brazen harlot… I heard her screaming.'

'Lola isn't a harlot.'

'No?'

'*Porca miseria*.' The creature sounds displeased. 'You shouldn't speak of our sex in such terms. Harlots and strumpets. Spinsters and hags. It's limiting; it oppresses us. In a troop of toque macaques, the female of the species—'

'Oh, but I'm not interested in other females. I prefer the company of the superior sex. You see, Father and I—'

'We are the superior sex. Consider lions. Who does all the hunting? And raises a litter of cubs. Yet it's the male that calls himself King of the Beasts. And uses offensive language to suppress us. *Basta chiamarci puttane*. I am sick of it.'

'Even so, the brazen—'

'*Ho detto basta!* Lola isn't a harlot. Far from it. She's going to have a successful career. She's going to be the first she-macaque to have a column in *The Evening Rodent*.'

More of the beezum's predictions.

'It'll be quite popular, her column. She'll share recipes. She'll tell anecdotes about her son's antics.'

'Her son's antics?' Has the old hag lost the thread of the argument? 'But her son is dead.'

'Not the son that lost his life in the boathouse. His brother.'

The creature explains that Lola is going to seek out Obadiah and persuade him to make an honest macaque out of her. Once the couple have plighted themselves, she'll have another son, and she'll call him Rapscallion Scamp – the same name as the little thing that died in the boathouse. 'He'll grow up to be called the Rt Hon Rapscallion Scamp, but there'll be nothing honourable about his behaviour. *Dio mio,* he's going to be such an infamous member of the Order of Carnivores.'

'He is?'

'Oh, and such a good-looking specimen. So athletic. Imaginative too. He'll make his fortune telling tales. He'll get himself a... *Come si dice Olivetti?*'

'Olivetti?'

'*Una macchina da scrivere?* It's a machine. It has letters of the alphabet on it. He'll sit in front of it for hours, bashing away the keys. Like monkeys do. He'll make up stories about the Fates. Fables about thieves and fortune.'

'You mean novels?'

'Yes. He'll rise up through the ranks of the Order of Carnivores. Oh, but he'll tell such terrible lies. *Mamma mia, che bugie.* It'll get him into so much trouble, his little appendage.'

The old hag cackles. Is that a pair of rodent-like incisors Bel-imperia can see glinting in the moonlight?

'It'll lead him astray. It'll get him locked up in the clink.'

'You don't know all this.'

'You'll consider him a friend. You'll ignore his indiscretions. For a time.'

'Me?' Bel-imperia cannot believe she'd ever associate with such a disreputable specimen. Indeed, she is beginning to suspect That W**ch We Do Not Speak About is not in its right mind. She decides to cut to the chase. 'I am not interested in macaques. Neither have I come here at this time of night to discuss them. I just need to collect the Nile-blue envelope in that cage. I believe it's addressed to me.'

From behind the chancel, the sound of an animal stirring. Is some beast skulking behind that crumpled sheet of mineral deposits?

'What was that noise?'

'I'll ask the questions, *pulcino.* And if you give me the right answers, you'll get your admissions papers.'

'What questions?'

'The correct Latin nomenclature, please.'

'No.'

'You don't want to go to the Cloisters?'

'Of course I do.'

'Then the time has come for a spot of... *Come si dice?* Classification practice.'

Bel-imperia glances at the great birdcage suspended in the south transept. Is that the chassis of an old pram? Is that a pair of gardening shears? She squints at the length of rope the hideous clump of scrap metal is hanging on. It appears to be anchored to a boulder beside the creature's campfire. Loosen it and the cage is going to crash to the ground. She has no intention of soaring into the thing to snatch her admissions papers. She has never seen such a conspicuous trap.

'*Dai, cominciamo.*' The specimen snatches a couple of sprigs of juniper and drops them onto the fire. 'Kingdom?'

29

Of course, I should have seen it coming, I should have realised as soon as he met me on the steps that he had dishonourable intentions. But he's so charming. Oh, he has breeding, FitzClarence – I'll give him that.

He pretended to be pleased to see me. He scampered up to me and kissed me. Not just once but twice, brushing his bristles against each lappet like one of those frog-eating things in Le Jardin Zoologique. Perhaps he'd been hoping to impress on the rat corps that he's a cosmopolitan otter, but the mischief of rodents corralled behind those barricades couldn't have been less interested in him. Goodness me, such excitement! I can still see those rats scrabbling over each other to get a closer look at me. 'How does it feel to be back, Bel-imperia?' said one. 'Have you got any advice for FitzClarence?' said another.

'As a matter of fact, I've got a great deal of advice. For one thing—'

But before I could give them the benefit of my opinion, Dale snouted me in the scapulars and bundled me through the front door.

I remember I almost slipped on a bar of soap as I scuttled across the hall – some overpriced, citron-scented product, not Pears'. FitzClarence apologised, of course. He said his she-otter had been attempting to scrub the last threads of rhinoceros dung out of the grouting. The smell upsets her stomach it seems. But I couldn't smell rhinoceros. Furniture polish, perhaps. Oh, and potpourri. It brought it all back to me. The smell.

I'm afraid there have been some minor alterations – the décor isn't quite as tasteful as I left it – but the atmosphere hasn't changed: the clatter of pigeons, the sense of purpose; it's just as thrilling. In fact, I must admit it felt as if... It felt as if those ungrateful beasts had never...

But I digress.

FitzClarence offered me a guided tour.

'Tour?' I said. 'Oh, I don't need an otter to escort me from room to room and waylay me with anecdotes about the stains on the carpets.

I know my way around here better than you do, Dale.' I gave him a hard stare to make it quite clear that I'd come home to roost.

'Of course,' he said, hanging his head in shame. He stared at the floor tiles.

'Missed a bit, did she?'

'No.'

'Good. Well, let's get down to business, then.'

'Business?' he said.

I remember he seemed reluctant to assert some leadership, so I seized the initiative and ushered him into the drawing room. In retrospect, I suppose I should have chosen a different setting for our tête-à-tête. You see, the drawing room hasn't changed since that thing in November. It's just the same as... Just the same as the night those traitors turned against me: the spiders in the Bohemian glass chandeliers, the broken springs in the chaise longue. It brought it all back to me...

Oh, there had been a contest that November, of course. Some dead sheep stood up in the Hall of Exhibits and delivered... Goodness me, the most seditious speech. Some lion that had been in exile came bounding back to Caer Lud to announce his intention of challenging me. And so it began. And so the Order of Carnivores turned against their Commander-in-Chief.

I must admit I didn't get quite the number of potsherds that I'd hoped in the opening round, but I'm not a quitter. I am not. 'I shall fight on,' I said, 'and fight to win.' Oh, and I would have won too if those ungrateful dogs hadn't turned on me like that. Curs that I'd raised on prime cuts of mutton. Sons of mongrel bitches that I'd trained to be obedient. I shall never forgive them. Never.

You see, I still had so much to do.

I'm afraid standing in that room again brought it all back to me. I could see them snarling at me, the dogs. I could see them lunging at me and breaking... Something so precious. I told FitzClarence I needed a moment; I told him I had to sit down.

He splashed about a bit in some old tin bathtub that had been brought down from the attic, and then settled down opposite me on the chaise longue. He leaves puddles, dear. He leaves damp patches on the carpet.

What was that? What was that? I didn't catch the question.

Our conversation?

Oh, I seem to recall an uncomfortable silence. In fact, I should imagine a minute or so must have passed before Dale turned to me and muttered something about his she-otter rustling up dinner.

'I do hope she's managed to find a decent recipe for orange-bellied ground squirrel,' I said. 'I don't suppose the species has much meat on its bones. Perhaps she might need to add a ginger rodent to make it go around.'

I noticed that FitzClarence looked rather upset. Indeed, I suspect he might be struggling to suppress unnatural urges as far as that squirrel's hindquarters are concerned. Naturally, I made some polite enquiries about his inclinations, but I'm afraid that just resulted in another uncomfortable silence.

In desperation, I glanced around the room and spotted an expensive-looking edition of *On the Origin of Species* stuffed under the leg of a broken armchair. I pointed it out to him. 'You'd better remove that,' I said. 'We might need to consult it from time to time.'

But of course, he insisted that he'd read it from cover to cover. And so I asked his opinion on Chapter IV.

'Chapter IV?' he said.

'"Natural Selection; or the Survival of the Fittest",' I replied. I reminded him that I'd gone to great lengths to put Mr Darwin's theories into practice. I told him he needed to forget all that nonsense about compassionate Carnivorism and encourage the animals to compete against one another. 'Oh, I suppose those that fail to adapt might find themselves in danger of extinction, but the fittest are bound to prosper.'

He tried to change the subject, but before he could complete his sentence an emperor penguin sounded the dinner gong. Not a moment too soon, I might add. Indeed, I seem to remember being rather peckish. 'Shall we withdraw to the dining room?' I suggested.

'Oh, no,' he said. 'Let's have supper in here.'

But supper isn't the word I'd use to describe the dish that was set before me. Let me make it quite clear: I have never been so insulted. Never.

Next question, please.

```
┌─────────────────────────────────────────────┐
│  OLD HES      OUSE ẋ      LOGICAL GARDE       │
│             The Escarpment                    │
│                   YE                          │
│             la Madagascariensis               │
│        CAUTION: THIS ANIMAL      S            │
└─────────────────────────────────────────────┘
```

'Kingdom?'

Little Bel-imperia Pinch is speechless. She has never seen anything quite so repulsive as the hideous gargoyle caught in the glare of the burning sprigs of juniper. Indeed, the beast is so grotesque it should be clinging to the guttering of some gothic cathedral, not slouching on a throne of broken branches. But she doesn't recoil from the thing. She is fascinated. Its ugliness is so pure, so untainted, that it is almost beautiful.

'Come on, *pulcino*. Kingdom?'

She snatches a gulp of air, answers the creature's question: '*Animalia* I suppose.'

'Phylum?'

She can see that it has a mouth and she can smell that it has an anus. '*Chordata.*'

'Class?'

Simple. The specimen is cloaked in a mantle of hair – all cotted and tangled together, just as Mother had said. '*Mammalia.*'

'Order?' It scratches at an infestation of parasites in its black coat. '*Stai attenta*, the last visitor to attempt to classify me came to grief at this point.'

Bel-imperia isn't surprised to hear it. The thing looks like it has been stitched together out of bits and pieces stolen from other, more familiar mammals: the ears of a bat, the long chisel-like teeth of a beaver.

'Can I have some more light, please?'

The creature groans as it reaches for another sprig of juniper. Has it been holed up in this cavern for centuries? She shouldn't be surprised. She can tell that it is old: the skin on its long, skeletal hand is so thin that she can see its bones. Hands! It's got hands.

'You're a primate.'

It drops the sprig of juniper onto its campfire, collapses back into its tree-like throne. Behind the contorted branches of the structure, a thin sheet of mineral deposits shimmers in the firelight: delicate, transparent. Is that a ghost-like shape Bel-imperia can see on the other side of its translucent membrane? Is that the silhouette of a second beast skulking in silence? She cannot be sure. She remembers the ghost that appeared to her in the burning boathouse. Perhaps this place is haunted too. Perhaps the tormented spirit of some predator... No, no, one thing at a time. Suppressing the thought of a second beast, she turns her attention to the hideous specimen she is attempting to classify.

'Suborder?'

The creature is nothing like a chimpanzee, nothing like the man on the marble. Neither does it resemble the macaque that met its maker in the spice drawers. It is more rodent-like, more primitive. She hazards a guess. 'You're a prosimian. You're a lemur.'

'The correct term is *Strepsirrhini*.'

'Yes.'

Bel-imperia might not have been schooled in Prosimian Studies, but she remembers she once came across a list of lemurs in the *Official Guide*. She appraises That W**ch We Do Not Speak About. It cannot be a ring-tailed lemur, because its tail is black. Is it an indri, then? Do indris have black tails? She has no idea. For a moment, she almost hangs her head in shame, but she crushes the urge before it can take hold of her. This isn't the boathouse and she isn't some innocent lappet-faced thing standing on the marble – she has burnt that bridge. She steals a glance at the sinister object suspended from a rope in the south transept with its sharp edges and gleaming blades. Classification or not, she needs to retrieve her admissions papers. Dare she trespass into the birdcage and snatch them?

'Come on, *pulcino*.'

She can tell that the creature is starting to lose its patience: it is tapping its finger on the arm of its throne – a thin, elongated middle finger. It cups its bat-like ears and listens: rat-a-tat-tat, rat-a-tat-tat. It sounds like the branch is hollow. Is the old hag using echo location to piece together a mental picture of its chambered pith? Is the lemur hunting? Judging from its intense concentration, it looks like it might have found something. Using its incisors as a chisel, it rips off a strip of bark, pokes a probing finger into the branch and pulls out a succulent morsel.

'I'll settle for genus and species,' it says as it munches on the squirming grub. 'No?' It glances up at the birdcage. 'Never mind. The Fates told me I'd end up keeping that letter.'

'One moment, please.' Bel-imperia might have missed out on Prosimian Studies, but she's been schooled in Percussive Foraging and other Unusual Hunting Techniques. 'You're an aye-aye. *Daubentonia* something.' She remembers the sign at the mouth of the cave. 'Of course, *madagascariensis*.'

'Oh, that sign is... *Come si dice?* Inaccurate, mistaken. I am a giant aye-aye. The last of the species I should imagine.'

She has studied that too. '*Daubentonia robusta*.'

The creature hisses something incomprehensible into the palm of its hand: '*Ma che brava*.'

More gibberish.

'I suppose that primitive language is spoken in Madagascar, is it?'

'No, in the Apennines. I sought refuge there after I fled from Cumae.'

The Apennines? Cumae? Bel-imperia has never heard of these places. She lets the subject drop. 'I got it right, though, didn't I? You're an aye-aye.'

The creature nods.

'Good.' Time to get out of here. Time to set off on the long march to the Cloisters. 'Give me my admissions papers, then.'

'No.'

'But you promised… '

'*Fammi toccare le perle prima.*'

'Pardon?'

'The pearls. Let me touch them.'

'Pearls?' She has no intention of letting the thing get its hands on the precious stones strung around her breast. 'Oh, I think there must be some misunderstanding. These are just beads, cheap imitations. I found them on the lake-shore.'

'Don't lie to me, *pulcino.*' The creature drops another sprig of juniper onto the fire, gives her a chilling stare. 'The time has come to speak the truth.'

'The boathouse is on the lake-shore. That is the truth.'

'*Ti prego.* Did it take long to rinse off the blood? Did it take long to pick out the scraps of human remains?'

Bel-imperia gapes in astonishment. Does the old hag have access to all her secrets? 'I don't tell deliberate untruths. Oh, I must admit sometimes I can be a little evasive, but… ' She hangs her head, stares at a scattering of shingle on the ground. She regresses.

'*Fa niente.* You were weighed in the balance. You were not found wanting.'

'What balance? Who weighed me?'

'You broke their First Commandment.' The creature cackles as if it had nothing but contempt for the Seven Commandments. '*Thou shalt not eat of another—*'

Something inside little Bel-imperia Pinch snaps. She stands up straight, plumps out her plumage. 'I resent that allegation. I didn't break the First Commandment. I did not. The man on the marble wasn't an exhibit. He came here to slaughter the animals in these gardens.'

'No, he didn't. He was on a reconnaissance mission. He was returning to base.'

'He came here to bomb us.'

'*Non è vero.* He was outside the… *Come si dice?* Exclusion zone. He was heading away from us when he was brought down.'

'He was in an area which was a danger to our animals.'

'He was on a bearing of 280. He was heading west.'

'He came here to intimidate us. You accept that, do you?'

'No, I don't.'

'Well, you must. My goodness me, nothing could be more important than defending the freedom that our ancestors laid down their lives for during the Uprising. Nothing.'

'That's the spirit! *Brava! Brava!*' The aye-aye is clapping its skeletal hands. 'I shouldn't be surprised if the Fates insist on a repeat of that performance. *Bravissima.*'

It smiles at Bel-imperia. Is it pleased about something? Is it satisfied? It scrambles out of its throne. Here it comes, shambling up to some residual limestone boulder. Limpelty lobelty. It snatches the rope secured to the boulder and gives it a sharp tug, perhaps to test its strength. In the south transept, the great birdcage jangles. Cackling to itself like a crone, the creature hobbles around a heap of broken branches, settles beside its campfire.

Cautious, tentative, Bel-imperia scuttles closer. Dare she sit next to it?

'You made the right decision, *pulcino*. Eating that man's liver. Your instincts are strong. You must remember to trust them.'

'Don't worry; I shall.'

'You deserved to find the pearls.'

She is glad to hear it, but even so, she's quite sure no one saw her pull them out of the man. 'How do you know where I found... ?' She leaves the question hanging in the air, unfinished. The jigsaw puzzle is coming together. The picture is beginning to make sense. 'You put them there!'

'I collected them from their custodian, but I didn't slip them into—'

'You pushed them through that laceration.'

'Not me. *Il serpente.*'

The serpent. 'Draco?'

'He came to see me – a month ago *più o meno*. He'd been offered a position in... ' The creature shudders as if a black-capped jackal had just stepped on its grave. 'He'd been offered a position in the Reptilian Services. Chameleons that use their camouflage to gather intelligence.'

'Yes, he mentioned something about them.'

'He needed some advice, so I consulted the Fates. I burnt a sprig of belladonna and slipped into a trance.' The old hag darts her a sidelong glance: shrewd, cunning. 'I was transported to 1974.'

'Don't be ridiculous. 1974 is—'

'One of our darkest hours. This great landed estate, this old menagerie, this maze of bars... It's destined to become a second-rate tourist attraction.'

Bel-imperia is outraged. 'Nonsense. I am quite sure this great institution is never going to be reduced to—'

'I asked Draco to test a little solution the Fates might have to the problem.'

'Yes? What solution's that?'

'You.'

Is the specimen out of its mind? 'Me? Oh, I doubt I'd be able to save the zoological—'

'Draco has been imprisoned in Das Museum Für Naturkunde. He understands the meaning of... *Come si dice?* Freedom. He loves these gardens. He agreed to help.' The creature pauses to pluck out a parasitic mite.

'Help?'

'He put the pearls into the man. He prepared the test. You demonstrated you had the mettle. You passed.'

Bel-imperia recoils from the ragged old lemur. She doesn't believe for a moment that the thing is capable of transporting itself to 1974. The date so far in the future it feels like something out of a novel. Science fiction – speculative, implausible. She attempts to bring the conversation back onto firmer ground. 'I thought I heard Draco hissing at me in that antechamber as I came in.'

'*Può essere*. He called in to see me earlier this evening. I completed the reading.'

'He didn't stop to have a conversation. He just slithered out.'

'I expect he was upset.' In the distance, the drone of another engine. 'Upset?'

'I'd just revealed his fate to him; I'd just told him he's destined to meet an atrocious end.'

'Then it must be prevented.'

'No, *pulcino*. Draco's fate has been pronounced. *Come posso spiegare?*' The creature glances at the shattered remains of the stalactite that fell from the ceiling. 'Sometimes the Fates cannot be cheated. Sometimes there is nothing I can do. Draco's final destination is inevitable.'

'What did you tell him? What will be his fate?'

Outside, a bomb rips through the night, shakes the subterranean basilica of rock.

Silence.

The decrepit old prosimian prods the embers of the smouldering campfire. Its mood seems to have changed. It is solemn, pensive. It says, 'Your fates are similar. There is... *Come si dice?* There is a common thread. But you have the pearls for protection. You must remember to wear them. Even late at night. Even when putting the finishing touches to a speech.'

'And Draco? What does he have for protection?'

It just shakes its head.

'Tell me what's going to happen to him.'

'Draco's reading is confidential. I cannot reveal it to another supplicant. There is a code of conduct in my profession.'

'For goodness' sake.' She still thinks the creature might be a charlatan. 'You have professional standards, then?'

'*Si, certo.*'

Bel-imperia shudders. 'It's getting cold.'

The prosimian pushes a charred log back into the embers. 'It is almost autumn; it is the middle of the night. Time... Time is of the essence. Come on, *è ora di cominciare.*' It springs to its feet, scampers around the fire to its throne.

'What do you mean, time is of the essence?'

'Over here. There's something I need to show you.'

But Bel-imperia is gazing at the firelight dancing on the thin gauze of mineral deposits behind the throne. She is sure she caught another glimpse of some monstrous shape: a pair of hunched shoulders or a set of horns. The second beast.

'*Dai, sbrigati.*'

The aye-aye removes a branch from the base of its throne and drags out an antique campaign chest about the same size as the old lacquered tea chest in the boathouse, but carved out of ash, corners clad in iron. It inserts its long, probing middle finger into the lock and opens the lid. Bel-imperia peers over the creature's shoulder as it rummages through its treasures. She can see a tarnished goblet, a blunt pair of pruning shears, a dagger. Is that the skull of a domestic cat or something?

'*Ecco ci siamo.*' It is holding a familiar-looking object in its slender hands. 'These are almost the same. Look!'

It is a string of pearls: a single strand of precious stones, identical to the delicate orbs strung around Bel-imperia.

'Let me have a look.'

'Roman pearls. Oh, I suppose some craftsmanship must have gone into them, but they're just little balls of alabaster.'

'You mean... ?'

'Your pearls are *madreperla*. Pure nacre. These are nothing. These are just imposters, cheap imitations.'

'But there's a glaze to them.'

'Fish scales.' The creature holds the imitation pearls up in the moonlight. '*Guarda.* There's no lustre, no luminescence, see?' The prosimian is standing too close. Bel-imperia can smell its foul breath in the air. 'You must learn to tell the difference, *pulcino*. No lustre, no luminescence. It's important, understand? *Importantissimo.*'

'Why?'

It darts a pointed glance at the crumpled sheet of mineral deposits behind the throne. 'Your fate is going to depend on it, *capisci?*'

'I thought as much. You mean to tell me there's some monster skulking be—'

The aye-aye lays a chappy finger on its lips: 'Shh.'

31

First he insulted me and then he brought up... Goodness me, the most disagreeable subject.

I should explain. Dinner at the Dower House is supposed to be an elaborate affair. Let me see if I can recollect the menu the last time I'd dined there... There must have been an amuse-bouche. That's right, a plump maggot squirming in a schiuma of cuckoo spit. Oh, and then I seem to recall a real treat: Carpaccio of Caterpillars on a Bed of Crisp Lettuce. Of course, the lettuce is just for presentation – I had been reassured that one is not expected to eat it. But, I remember, as I pushed it to one side, I noticed that one of the caterpillars had little lappets attached to its abdomen. I made some polite enquiries and learned that the larva of the lappet moth had been added to the ingredients as a tribute to me. I mention the episode merely to indicate the standard of cuisine one is accustomed to. The attention to detail. But I am afraid FitzClarence didn't rise to the occasion. He served sardines.

That's right, dear, sardines.

He made some comment about me being partial to first-class protein out of a tin: salmon, ham, ox tongue – that sort of thing. He reminded me that I was once accused of hoarding it. Of course, Snowy sent down a note to apologise. Some lame excuse about the kitchen not being to her liking. But even so. Three sardines on a bone-china dinner plate. Three sardines swimming in oil...

Dale had four. I counted them as he gobbled them up. My goodness me, he's such a greedy little thing. Oh, and his table manners aren't as impeccable as one might suppose either. Don't sit opposite him at a banquet, dear. He slumps in his chaise, subjecting his guests to the sight of the cascading folds of fat on his underparts. It was most unpleasant. In fact, I must admit I was a little worried... Well, I was worried his appendage would pop out. Let me make it quite clear: one has no desire to inspect that particular organ. Or dine on it. Oh, I suppose the thing might make an entertaining amuse-bouche, but one is reluctant to put something into one's mouth unless...

No, no, I have said too much. Besides, it's just a rumour that's been going around the Order of Carnivores. It's not supposed to come out. Ever.

What was that? What was that? The specimen over there in the rhododendrons. The creature curled up beside the one-striped opossum. You.

Oh, I see. You'd like me to go on. You'd like me to finish that earlier sentence.

Well, as you asked so politely, I shall oblige: one is reluctant to put something into one's mouth unless one knows where it's been.

And I am not alluding to Snowy.

Of course, one hesitates to entertain the thought of Dale FitzClarence clambering up onto a dining table at the Cloisters and inserting his little scrap of sausage meat into a... No, no, no. Nevertheless, I am afraid I did catch him leering at my uneaten sardines in the most lascivious manner.

'I could put those to good use,' he said. Indeed, I suspect he might have made some comment about their accommodating mouths – I cannot be sure. But I am quite certain I heard him use the phrase 'a snug fit'. And so before he had a chance to get excited, I pushed the plate to one side and told him to sit up. You see, the meal might have been a disappointment, but I still had certain expectations; I still hoped to be offered a seat on his Board of Beasts.

'Let's talk about the scope of the position,' I said.

'What position's that?' he replied, licking a stray sardine scale off his lips.

'Your invitation?' I reminded him. 'You mentioned there was something important you wanted to discuss?'

'Oh, that,' he said, glancing down at the threadbare carpet. 'Listen, Bel, it's not urgent. You must be feeling tired after all this excitement. Let's leave it, eh?'

'Tired?' I said. I made it quite clear to him that as long as the zoological gardens needs me I shall never be tired.

But he just muttered something about a delicate matter and clammed up.

'Come on, Dale,' I said. 'Fortune favours the brave. Spit it out.'

Oh, how he wriggled! How he squirmed! 'Well... ' he said. 'It's the funeral arrangements.'

'Whose funeral arrangements?' I said.

His answer was blunt. He said, 'Yours.'

32

```
OLD HES        OUSE ᴁ        LOGICAL GARDE
            The Escarpment

                    YE
            la Madagascariensis

        CAUTION: THIS ANIMAL          S
```

'*Dai, cominciamo.*'

The creature snatches a clump of belladonna, drops it onto the smouldering campfire. Confident that she's going to get another glimpse of the second beast, little Bel-imperia Pinch concentrates on the thin membrane of mineral deposits behind the throne. For some reason, though, there's no firelight to alleviate the darkness. She darts an impatient glance at the feeble fire. Is the belladonna damp? It appears to be producing nothing more than smoke. Perhaps the prosimian should have snatched a sprig of juniper instead. Bel-imperia glares at the specimen as it clambers up onto its throne and settles down.

'*Porca miseria*, I'm too old to get into the lotus position.' That W**ch We Do Not Speak About mumbles something about a half lotus, crosses its hind legs. Is that some hideous callus on the sole of its foot? It sits up straight and curls its long tail over its head like a shaman's headdress. It inhales a breath of smoke.

'What on earth are you doing?'

'*Silenzio*. I must slip into an altered state of consciousness; I must concentrate.'

She can tell that the thing's breathing has changed. Is the darkness draining out of its frightful face?

It takes another drag of belladonna, holds the smoke in its lungs, breathes out. 'Now, give me your pearls, *pulcino*. Let me sing the Fates.'

But Bel-imperia has had quite enough singing for one evening. Besides, she's still not convinced that the creature can be trusted. She glances up at the great birdcage suspended in the south transept, at the sheets of corrugated steel, the cast-iron bedstead, the prongs of an old rake. Is her host using this hocus-pocus about the Fates to entrap her? Is it a false prophet? She remembers the terrible screams of the little macaque. The stalactite that came crashing to the ground. Nothing false about those prophecies. Perhaps she should give the specimen the benefit of the doubt. She slips off her pearls, drops them into the palm of its hand.

'*Dio mio, l'energia è forte.*'

The creature looks a little disconcerted. It tilts its head to one side, scowls at the chaplet of stones. Is something amiss? It plucks a bristle feather out of the clasp and discards it. Bel-imperia gazes at the offending feather as it drifts to the ground. It looks rather long. She hasn't started to sprout masculine bristles, has she? She hopes not. She turns her attention to the prosimian. Has the specimen slipped into a trance? No doubt it must have done. It is foaming at the mouth, like a rabid dog; it is trembling. Perhaps she should cushion its head until it recovers from the seizure. She dismisses the thought. She is reluctant to approach its thrashing limbs. Besides, she suspects it might be about to regain consciousness, because it has started to emit the most terrible groan: an ululation from the depths of its being, a moan that bounces off the rocks and boulders and makes the stalactites sing. It sounds like an orchestra tuning up.

Silence.

The creature catches its breath, drops the pearls onto the ground and speaks: 'You will be great – as great as Chartwell.'

From behind the chancel, the sound of something sniggering: scornful, dismissive. But Bel-imperia is unconcerned. She can hear the laughter and she cannot hear it; she is present and she is absent: she is standing beside the campfire staring up at the prophet, and at the same time, she is up in the stalactites looking down on a little lappet-faced thing from above. Forget about barging into the boathouse and catching her father *in flagrante delicto*. Forget about the terrible sight of the ghost in the glass. She has never been so shocked. She tries to speak...

'Me? As great as Chartwell?'

The prosimian raises a skeletal hand and points at her. 'Hail Bel-imperia Pinch, all hail to thee, Rt Hon Member of the Hall of Exhibits. Hail Bel-imperia Pinch, Commander-in-Chief of the Order of Carnivores. Hail Bel-imperia Pinch, P Ex hereafter.'

'Goodness me, no.'

'*Perché no?*'

'I don't think a bird is going to become Prize Exhibit – not in my lifetime.'

'*Non è vero*. I saw it come to pass.' The creature seems a little shaken. Is it still coming to its senses? 'I saw... '

'Yes?'

'Rats.'

'Rats?'

'Outside the Dower House. *Mamma mia*, such a great plague of rodents: smoke-bellied rats and bulldog rats; slender-tailed rats and—'

'The rat corps?'

'Yes. I sensed the excitement, the atmosphere of anticipation. I could see the animals corralled behind the barricades: a mongoose, some baboons, a gorilla. The shouting and the cheering. You arrived with an escort of wolves. You turned to the rats and made a statement. You said, "I am very excited, very aware of the responsibilities that await me as I scuttle through this door, and I can assure the animals in these gardens that I'll strive unceasingly to fulfil the trust and confidence that has been placed in me." You took some questions. You said you owed your success to your father.'

'Father? What on earth did he have to do with it?'

'I don't know, but then you said, "Now, I should like to remember some words which are rather apt at the moment." You had a scrap of paper clutched in your talons, a page torn out of *The Collected Pleas of Saint Francis*. You glanced down at it and recited something.'

'What was this plea? What did I say?'

'"Where there is swill may we bring sustenance; where there is ruminant may we bring hay; where there is… " I couldn't hear the rest. Something about predators? The mists of time… *Come si dice?* Clouded over. I came out of the trance.'

'I see.'

Bel-imperia consents to a surge of contentment, raises her feathers and shakes them back into place.

There is a moment's silence. In the distance, the sound of engines. Is that a colobus or something screaming?

'You're quite sure about all this? You're quite certain?'

'Nothing is certain, *pulcino*. Fate is the most probable expression of the potential that exists in the present, the strongest thread. But there are thousands of threads, thousands of possible outcomes. You must seize the right thread again and again. You must make it happen.'

She could not be more determined. 'Be under no illusions: I shall.'

She struts across to the south aisle of the nave, stares up at the birdcage. Her admissions papers are still impaled on an old roasting spit.

'You must be alert to danger, *pulcino*. Your enemies are strong.'

'What enemies?'

'You'll have enemies within and enemies without. You'll have enemies in the coteries of black-capped marmots, enemies in the Norn Iron Farmstead, enemies in the Order of Carnivores. You can trust tigers, but not lions. You can trust serpents, but not—'

'Serpents? You mean Draco?'

'Yes. He'll champion your campaign in '75. He'll teach you a mantra to summon up a ghost. You must learn to use it. Your enemies have weaknesses. There are… *Come si dice?* Chinks in their armour. But the battle will be protracted. You'll need to go on and on, P Ex, until the Millennium.'

'You mean 2000?'

'2001. And the battle begins tonight.'

'Oh, I don't think I'll be fighting the good fight this evening.'

'You'll need a weapon.' The creature clambers down from its tree-like throne and opens its campaign chest. 'Now, where did I put it?'

Is she going to be given a sword and breastplate? Is she going to be armed? She tries to control her excitement, but she can feel the feathers on her mantle bristling. What is she going to be given? It had better be something more substantial than the Sword of the Spirit and the Breastplate of Righteousness. She imagines having cannons and catapults at her disposal, cauldrons of burning oil. She pictures herself putting on a plumed helmet and leading a herd of scimitar-horned oryx into battle.

'*Ecco ci siamo.*' The specimen is pulling something out of its hoard of treasures.

Bel-imperia creeps a little closer. She can tell that the item is too small to be a sword. Her thoughts turn to more sophisticated munitions: a detonation device and a secret code, a test tube containing a lethal dose of some contagion. She peers over the creature's shoulder, catches a glimpse of a steel cross-guard, a double-edged blade.

'Is that a dagger?'

'Shh.' It places its elongated finger on its lips, darts a sidelong glance at the gauze of mineral deposits. Bel-imperia squints at the speleothem, snakes her head from side to side. She cannot see the second beast, but she is in no doubt that something must be skulking behind the structure. Does the dagger mean she's going to have to stab some monster in the heart? She hopes not.

The aye-aye slides the dagger under a pile of broken branches. 'I'll leave it here in the belladonna.'

'Yes, but—'

'In the belladonna, remember?' The creature hobbles under the rope descending from the birdcage, shambles up to her. 'You'll need the luck of the devil, *pulcino* – and not just tonight. The odds are stacked against a bird becoming Commander-in-Chief this side of the Millennium.'

'Oh, I'm not going to leave it to luck. I intend to make sure I merit the appointment.'

'Even so. There'll be other candidates, safer bets. You're going to be the outsider, the long shot.' It scoops up the pearls. 'You'll need these to bring you good fortune. *Le perle sono… Come si dice?* The pearls are charmed. Whoever possesses them has Fortune on her side.'

Bel-imperia is glad to hear it.

'You have been chosen. You are their rightful guardian, but there are certain conditions attached to the loan.'

'Loan?' She cannot disguise her disappointment. It hadn't occurred to her that she might have to give them back.

'You must protect them from thieves. You must never let another living soul put them on. And above all, you must never break them. Never break the thread, *capisci*? Or else... ' The creature seems troubled. Some passing thought?

'Yes?'

'Or else the charm will be broken. You'll be defeated, overthrown.'

She gazes at the string of pearls dangling from the old hag's arthritic fingers: so precious, so delicate. 'I'll never break them. Never.'

'Is that a promise, a solemn binding oath?'

'Of course.'

The prosimian holds out its hand, snatches it back. Has it had second thoughts? 'I almost forgot. There's one more condition. You can't take them to the grave. You must return them before... *Come si dice?* The final curtain.'

'You mean I have to traipse up here before I die?'

'No, *pulcino*. The pearls don't belong to me. They must be returned to their custodian.'

'Custodian?'

The specimen shambles a couple of steps closer, whispers into Belimperia's auricular feathers: 'The Lady. She's looked after them for centuries.'

Outside, the drone of an iron bird. Is that the thud of a distant explosion?

'What Lady?'

'There's no time to explain. The instructions are in the collected poems of someone-or-other. I've underlined them and hidden the book behind a radiator in *128: Humankind*.'

'In the Hunting Tower?'

'No, in the Cloisters, of course. Oh, and I left something else there too. *On the Origin of Species by Means of Natural Selection*.'

'Complete and unabridged?'

'*Si, certo*. You can keep the books until you reach the very end of your allotted span, but not the pearls. When the time comes to return them… When the time comes to prepare to meet your maker, you'll be given a sign. You'll be offered… *Fiori. Sono sempre fiori.*'

'Fiori?'

'Flowers. The sign is flowers. With the last creature to wear them it was a Tudor rose. Well, I suppose that was appropriate. I wonder what you've got… '

The aye-aye places a hand on Bel-imperia's breast and mutters some mumbo jumbo. Is that its long finger she can feel poking into her feathers? It pulls out a scrap of infantile down, drops it onto the campfire and inhales its smoke. Does the burning feather have a floral scent?

'*Mamma mia*, that's a surprise.'

'Well, what is it, then? Some rare orchid I suppose.'

'Carnations. You'll know the end is approaching when some scoundrel attempts to strike a bargain: carnations in exchange for the pearls.'

'Oh, I am sure there's no danger of that. Who would swap something so precious for a cheap bunch of carnations? Who would make such an insulting offer?'

'It shall come to pass.'

The creature drops another sprig of juniper onto the embers. The needle-like leaves catch at once, casting some much-needed light on the cathedral of stalactites and stalagmites. But there is no time to admire its splendour. Seizing the moment, little Bel-imperia Pinch scutters up to the throne and studies the thin sheet of mineral deposits. Is that the shape of the second beast's humped back? Is that a horn? Impossible to make sense of its blurred contours, but she has a hunch it might be reptilian. Is it something on loan from the Hall of Relics? Is it a dinosaur, a dragon?

'One last question, *pulcino* – and it's important.'

'Yes?' She is starting to get impatient. She hates to see her precious string of pearls dangling from the aye-aye's bony hand.

'Do you trust me? Yes or no?'

Bel-imperia appraises the nocturnal predator. Its bat-like ears and its long incisors; the terrible blaze raging in its eyes. Fire and brimstone.

She remembers listening to her father deliver one of his hellfire sermons. She remembers him turning to her: 'You must promise me, chick. You'll never trust a prosimian, will you?' She is sure she can recollect swearing on the Commandments. Dare she break such a solemn oath? Despite the glad tidings about being as great as Chartwell, she cannot dismiss the nagging thought that perhaps she might be in grave danger, that perhaps she is being lured into a trap. Yet even so, this is no false prophet – she is sure about that. Does she trust this prosimian then? Some instinct in her gut is telling her that she does. Instinct, the sign of an uncivilised animal, her father had said. Their cousins in the Serengeti that defecate on their own legs. Such nonsense. Wasn't it instinct that persuaded her to plunge her head into the man's liver? Wasn't it instinct that led her to the pearls? And there's nothing uncivilised about pure nacre. There is not. It's the height of sophistication. Her mind made up, she says, 'Yes.'

'*Allora, vieni con me.*'

Bel-imperia lets the creature lead her through a colonnade of stalagmites in the north aisle of the nave.

'Stop here.' It's still clutching the pearls in its spidery hands. 'Now, let me put them on you. Let me fasten the catch.'

Something is telling her that this is a bad idea – instinct again? 'No, it's all right; I'm quite capable of doing it.'

'It's ceremonial, *pulcino*. Think of it as a… *Come si dici?* Coronation. I am the High Priestess and you are *il Principe*. The Prince.'

She cannot refuse the crown.

'Stand over there. Just to the right a little. Now, close your eyes.'

The lemur recites some lines in Latin. *Glória in excélsis* or something. Did it just call her Imperatrix? Bel-imperia is not sure. But she's quite certain that she can detect a chill running down her spine as it loops the pearls around her neck, around her breast, around her—

'Ouch! That's rather tight.'

'You don't want to lose them.'

Yet even so, it feels as if a boa constrictor is casting its coils around her. The string of pearls is slicing through the barbs of her feathers, crushing her primaries and secondaries, digging into her sternum…

'That's quite tight enough; I said, that's quite—'

Is that something cold she can feel on her scapulars? Bel-imperia tries to turn her head, tries to see, but it's impossible to move. Never mind some sham coronation. Enough is enough. She struggles against the string of pearls. She tries to slip out of them.

'Careful! Never break the thread, *ricordi?*' The aye-aye is cackling like a hyena. 'Or else you'll be defeated, overthrown.'

It has a point. Better stop pulling on the precious stones. Better pause to take stock of the situation. Has the damned thing tied her to a stalagmite? She can tell that it has. She curses herself for not keeping the promise she made to her father.

'Untie me this instant.'

'You're in no position to give orders, *pulcino*. Not tonight – perhaps never again.' The creature scampers out of the colonnade of stalagmites, scrambles up onto its throne.

Bel-imperia's gaze settles on the great birdcage of scrap metal in the south transept. The sharp-edged sheets of corrugated steel. The blades on the gardening shears. This place is no cathedral: it's a torture chamber, a dungeon.

'Let me make it quite clear: I shall never give in to coercion.'

But the prosimian isn't listening. It casts a sprig of juniper onto its campfire, slumps back into its throne. 'I've been looking forward to this performance,' it says as it rearranges its tail, makes itself comfortable. '*Cominciamo?*'

'I have no intention of putting on a perform—'

That W**ch We Do Not Speak About glances over its shoulder at the sheet of mineral deposits and shouts, 'You can come out now, dear.'

Here she comes, then, the second beast, the intimidating presence that has been skulking in the gloom. Here she comes, then, the hideous she-monster, the old dragon, strutting out into the firelight, her big breast all plumped up in preparation for battle.

'You've got the brat tied up good an' tight I hope? She's as wick as an eel.'

'Mother?'

33

Of course, I hadn't expected him to bring up such an inappropriate subject. One's funeral arrangements? Goodness me, no. I told him I should have thought he had more pressing concerns. 'Besides,' I said, 'Ebenezer and I thrashed out the details.'

He reminded me that Ebenezer has been put out to graze.

'It doesn't matter,' I said. 'It's all been arranged.'

FitzClarence attempted to interrupt, but I had no desire to be contradicted, and so I pointed out that meticulous attention to detail is essential.

'I'm not going to tolerate East Indian spices,' I said. 'I am not. One has no intention of smelling like tandoori chicken as one is trundled into the Hall of Exhibits. I am going to be stuffed.'

'Is that so?' he said.

'Of course,' I added, 'I shall expect some rousing eulogies. Let me make it quite clear: the Order of Carnivores had better be gushing in its praises – and the Order of Herbivores too come to that – or else I shall be tempted to rise up and scare the willies out of them. Oh, and then I'm going to be hoisted onto a manure cart and draped in banners. Be under no illusions: the zoological gardens is going to come to a standstill as the grief-stricken masses prostrate themselves before one's solemn cortège. There'll be such pomp and circumstance, such spectacle.'

'There are going to be bells, right?' said FitzClarence.

'Bells?' I said.

I remember he had an insolent smirk on his snout. 'You know, ding dong.'

'I suppose a sombre funeral bell might be appropriate,' I replied. 'But do make sure it's silenced before the cortège arrives at the amphitheatre, otherwise I won't be able to hear the congregation singing 'I Vow To Thee My Gardens'. Or the choirs of ornate chorus frogs. Of course, that old amphitheatre is going to need sprucing up for the occasion. Flowers from the hothouse are essential. I shall require orchids, delphiniums, carnations. Oh, and I shall expect––'

He told me to hold it there. He muttered something about the cost being prohibitive. I seem to remember the phrase 'inappropriate in the current economic climate' or some such nonsense.

'Oh,' I said, 'I'm sure there must be something set aside to give Mummy a decent send-off.'

He handed me some scrap of paper that the Order of Herbivores had passed to him. It said: 'NO GROATS LEFT'.

I put it down on the backgammon table and glanced around the room. The grand piano I defecated on the morning I became Prize Exhibit. The gilded chair I perched on the night I decided to send a task force of alligators to reclaim Rabbit Island.

I turned to FitzClarence. He gave me one of his pompous stares. Such endangered *hauteur*. Such arrogance. I suppose that must have been the moment I realised he had no intention of offering me a position on the Board of Beasts. The moment I understood he'd invited me to dinner in order to balance the books.

'No flowers from the hothouse?' I said. 'No ornate chorus frogs?'

He droned on about the great cloud of debt louring over the zoological gardens. He used a phrase of mine. He said, 'There is no alternative.'

'There must be something that can be done,' I insisted. 'For goodness' sake, just take it out of the budget for malnutrition and mange.'

But he pretended to be committed to a Mange Service free at the point of need. 'Of course,' he added, 'I suppose there might be one solution.' I noticed his gaze had slipped down to my breast.

'I do hope your intentions are honourable, Dale,' I said.

He assured me they were.

'Well, spit it out, then.'

'That string of pearls – I bet it's worth a groat or two.'

'Oh, these aren't pearls,' I replied. 'Goodness me, no. They're just imitation.'

But he's no simpleton.

'Listen, Bel,' he said, 'I'm rolling in groats.' He mentioned something about his father and some islands in the sun. 'I'll give you a good price for them. You could put it towards the bill for all those carnations.'

'Carnations?' I gasped in horror.

He gave me an odd look. Perhaps the colour had drained out of one's lappets. Perhaps one had turned as pale as one's ceruse. I should not be surprised. You see, it was such a terrible shock. I had not expected to be offered carnations quite so soon. I mean, the zoological gardens still needs me. Doesn't it?

Nevertheless…

I suppose I shall just have to rise to the challenge. For I intend to make sure that otter never gets a chance to slip on that string of pearls.

What was that? What was that? The specimen sitting on the litterbin. The little Tasmanian devil. That's right. You.

Does Dale – what? Does Dale have a fetish for diamonds and pearls?

Oh, I doubt it, but one can never be sure. Indeed, I'm afraid it hasn't escaped one's attention that some members of the Order of Carnivores have… dear me, the most peculiar inclinations. Why, I seem to recall one specimen came to grief in an incident involving a plastic bag and an orange. That's right, dear, an orange. Of course, one is reluctant to contemplate the Rt Hon Dale FitzClarence getting up to such antics. Stockings and suspenders? Plastic bags and oranges? Goodness me, no. But even so, who would have thought he had a thing about swine? What does he call it? Chillaxing. Well, he isn't going to be chillaxing in that string of pearls. No one is. Not until the time is right. Not until the zoological gardens needs another…

Yes? The snub-nosed langur.

Oh no, dear, there's never going to be another Bel-imperia Pinch. There is not. But I suppose it's not inconceivable that in an hour of need some courageous bird might be called upon to step up and take the baton. Indeed, I am told there's an emu on the Board of Beasts that's said to be quite promising – not a true Carnivore, I regret to say: she calls us the Nasty Order. But be that as it may, she strikes me as a strong and stable specimen. Perhaps one's pearls might look becoming slung around her neck. I should hate to see them on a smooth-coated otter, though. I must return them to their custodian; she'll make sure he never gets hold of them. I must give them back to the Lady.

The instructions are here, in this book that I found hidden behind a radiator: the collected poems of someone-or-other, see? Now, which one did that creature underline? Not the one about the Northern Farmer. Goodness me, no. Not the one about the Lotus Eaters... Here it is. The one about the death of someone called Arthur. Let me read the relevant lines again:

... take Excalibur,

And fling him far into the middle mere...

Not much, is it? Just a scrap of iambic pentameter. Yet even so, I understood at once that 'Excalibur' is a reference to one's pearls. No doubt the term is some ancient name for them. I must admit the phrase 'middle mere' had me foxed for a moment. One tends to use 'mere' in the expression 'a mere trifle', doesn't one? From all accounts, though, I believe it can also mean 'a lake, a pond, a pool... ' In this instance, I'm sure the poet must be alluding to the lake in the Bog-land Enclosures – the lake that Father and I used to gaze out at during aurora matins. One cannot imagine that one is required to sling one's pearls into the penguin pool. Besides, I caught a glimpse of her once: the custodian, the Lady. Of course, I don't suppose I could have been much more than a fledgling at the time, but I've never forgotten the experience. You see, I'd just stepped out onto the boat slip to cough up a... I'd just stepped outside to dispose of some disagreeable scrap of sausage meat that I'd eaten. It must have been dusk, because I seem to recall I could almost see the landscaped gardens shedding colour. Oh, it was so magical. That place. That moment. I remember gazing at the reflection of the clouds on the surface of the lake and spotting a sudden movement in the depths. The dim shape of an arm rising out of the gloom: sinuous, graceful. I remember glimpsing a hand reaching up, as if to catch a string of pearls...

I shall take them to her this evening. I shall do it at sunset. Make no mistake: it's going to be upsetting. But it has to be done. I just hope she can forgive those dogs that turned against me for breaking them; I just hope she doesn't mind that I had to get them rethreaded...

34

```
OLD HES        OUSE x        LOGICAL GARDE
           The Escarpment

                  YE

            la Madagascariensis

      CAUTION: THIS ANIMAL        S
```

'Well, who'd ha' thought o' seeing thee?'

Here she comes, strutting up the colonnade of stalagmites: an old harridan spoiling for a fight, a monster not a mother. Is that a loose thread of spittle unfurling from the corner of her chipped beak? Is that a splattering of excrement on her legs? Bel-imperia is sure that it is. Does this mean that her mother has reverted to her natural state? Bessie Pinch (née Crust): not gone missing, just gone feral.

'Poor little stetchell. She thought she'd fligged and flown. She thought she'd shitten and gone. You should ha' listened to your mam. I told you pearls bring tears.'

Her daughter struggles against the precious stones, tries to squirm out of them, but the string of pearls is too tight. Concerned she might break the thread, she desists. 'You're quite right, Mother. Indeed, I dare say I should have heeded your advice. Now, perhaps you'd be good enough to untie me.'

'Hark at her! "Perhaps you'd be good enough... " Still talking like you cut your beak on a brocken bottle, then. Want me to unsneck 'em, do you?'

'Yes, please.'

'Well, you can kiss my cloaca.'

Bel-imperia is horrified. She has never heard such a shocking expression.

'Don't stand there gatherin' gape seed: the beezum'll think you've gone soft i' the head.'

'It's not a beezum; it's an aye-aye.'

'I call it a beezum.'

'What are you doing here, Mother?'

She turns to the prosimian. 'Shall I tell her? Shall I let the fummard out o' the bag?'

'*Si, si, vai avanti.*'

'Don't give me that cat-lap.'

'It's not cat-lap, Mother. It's similar to Latin. Our host said "go ahead".'

'Oh, the beezum an' I understand each other. We're as thick as thieving magpies, aren't we, Sibyl?'

That's its name, then. Sibyl.

'You see, I came here a fortnight since for a consultation. The beezum snorted up a load o' smoke and had one o' its turns. It said it could help me to a son. It told me to nab them letters and bring 'em up here.'

In the distance, the drone of an iron bird. The sound of an exploding bomb.

'"Is your daughter curious?" it said. She is that, I said. She wants to know the far end o' Meg's backside, she does. "Good," it said. "Then mention me in conversation. The birds of paradise sometimes perform in these parts. Tell her there's a dance. That'll bring the subject up." The beezum cooked up a plan. It reminded me what curiosity did to some cat.'

Bel-imperia glares at the aye-aye. 'Is this true?'

'For certain-sure, it's bleedin' true. Why dost thou think I were rabbitin' on about this place that night when you wouldn't eat your Mouse Tail Tangle? Who dost thou think scribbled that note for them crocs?'

'Manipulative, aren't we, Mother?'

'Like mother like daughter. We're cut from the same cloth. We got the same blood. Your eggs is the same as mine.'

'Eggs?'

'Eggs, I tell thee.' She lunges at Bel-imperia's auricular feathers, hisses into her ear: 'You're going to give me an egg, madam.'

And so that's her plan. And so she intends to use one of her daughter's eggs to beget a son.

'I'm going to do no such thing, Mother.'

Outside, the sound of another iron bird soaring over the ridge of the escarpment. And another. Has the squadron regrouped? Is it returning to base?

'You en't barren. You got a clutch o' speckled eggs a-coming. You won't miss one.'

'Don't be ridiculous. I don't have time to lay an egg. I've more important things to do. I'm going to the Cloisters; I'm going to be...'

Her mother's laughter is dismissive, scornful. 'Just hark at her. She fallen for all that cat-lap. She thinks she's goin' to become P Ex. She's forgotten she got feathers; she's forgotten she's a bod. Prize Exhibit? Prize Fool.'

Is it cat-lap? For a brief moment, Bel-imperia suspects her mother might be right. She banishes the thought. This is no time to contemplate the prospect of failure; it's time to put up a fight. 'This has gone quite far enough. I'm not prepared to tolerate—'

'Shurrup.' She is admiring the hideous structure suspended in the south transept. 'You like it, then? Your new cage? We got some rag-an'-bone baboons to build us that, didn't we, Sibyl? Did a good job, I reckon. Nice an' sturdy, no gaps. You won't wriggle out o' there afore my egg comes.'

'Let me make it quite clear: I refuse to be held hostage; I refuse to be—'

'I also got them baboons to nab me a pair o' gardening shears.'

'Decided to take up a profession, have we? Fed up with tending the nest?'

'Ay, that's right. I'm goin' to be a surgeon. I'm goin' to clip a weenun's wings. No, not clip. Beg pardon, slip o' the tongue. Clippin' en't no good. Don't last more than a month or so. You're goin' to be pinioned, madam.'

Pinioned? The permanent amputation of the alula... Bel-imperia is sure she can feel the colour draining out of her lappets. 'For goodness' sake, Mother, no one's been pinioned in these gardens since the Uprising. It's against the rules and regulations. It's barbaric.'

'Oh, it en't as bad as all that. Just a little snip. Didn't hurt me.'

'You've been pinioned?' She had assumed the old battleaxe had just been clipped.

'Me da did it when I were a weenun. Stopped me turning into a trollops.'

'Did it? I'm not so sure.'

'You'll squawk with pain o' course, but it won't damage them eggs you got a-coming. Now, where's them gardening shears, Sibyl?'

Bel-imperia glares at the prosimian as it clambers down from its throne. Is it going to put an end to this nightmare? Is it going to intercede?

It rummages around in its treasure chest, pulls out a pair of rusty pruning shears. 'You mean these?'

'Nah, not them blunt ones. I could ride to Caer Lud bare-arsed on them. I need that sharp pair.'

'*Sono nella gabbia*, Bess. Up there. In the cage.'

'Friggin' hell.' The old harridan struts across to the south transept, stops underneath the sinister-looking birdcage. Snaking her head from side to side, she studies the gardening shears. Is she attempting to calculate a safe route through the shards of scrap metal and the blades?

She leaps up onto a cast-iron bedstead. The birdcage lurches to the left, clangs against the bedrock of the cave, like a bell. Undeterred, she latches her beak onto the chassis of a broken pram, clambers up inside the structure, her gnarled talons clacking on the metal.

The rope supporting the birdcage groans.

For a specimen that has been pinioned, she is quite agile. But this is no moment to admire her mother's acrobatics. Bel-imperia must make a decision. She squints at the string of pearls stretched across her breast. Fish scales and alabaster, or pure nacre? Imitation or genuine? The stones don't appear to be luminescent, but in the dismal light it's impossible to be sure. She trusts her instincts. She tightens the muscles attached to the keel of her sternum, and spreads her splendid wings as wide as she can.

Snap.

No time to glance back at the hail of gemstones shooting across the nave. Belladonna, belladonna. She plunges her head into the pile of broken branches and snatches the dagger. She soars across to the rope anchoring the birdcage to a boulder and slices into it. One quick swipe. One clean cut.

Snap.

The severed stump of rope shoots across the cavern to the south transept. Is there a short pause before the birdcage crashes to the ground? In retrospect, Bel-imperia is sure that there must have been, because she can remember catching a brief glimpse of her horrified mother and thinking: This is the thread that needs to be broken, this is the tie that needs to be cut. She can also remember a short silence before the terrible clang of scrap metal. The clattering sheets of corrugated steel. The chiming blades.

She drops the dagger, gazes into the great cloud of dust. Is that it? Has she slain the old dragon, or is her mother going to emerge from the debris brandishing a pair of gardening shears? She trembles at the thought of the battle-scarred bird rising out of some mangled heap of scrap metal: a monster that refuses to die, a dictator that can never be defeated. But as the dust settles, she can see that the birdcage is still in one piece. Can the same thing be said about the specimen that it now contains? She isn't sure.

Cautious, circumspect, Bel-imperia creeps a little closer, peers at the lifeless mound of feathers heaped up in the middle of the cage. Is that a pair of excrement-encrusted legs she can see sticking up in the air?

From the direction of the chancel, a smell of burning juniper. She glares at the aye-aye as it gives its campfire a prod. Its rodent-like incisors. Its emaciated hands. It shambles into the south transept, slumps down beside her.

'You turned in a magnificent performance,' it says, flashing her a crooked smile. '*Bravissima.*'

The creature couldn't be less contrite. Has it forgotten that it just tied its guest to a stalagmite?

'You've got some nerve.' She rounds on the thing, gives it a piece of her mind.

'I had no choice, *pulcino*. I needed the mother to lure the daughter. You had to come to this place. You had to learn your fate.'

'But even so… You could have… ' What? What could That W**ch We Don't Speak About have done? Bel-imperia pauses to gather her thoughts.

'As great as Chartwell, remember?'

She glances over her scapulars at the colonnade of stalagmites, the balls of alabaster scattered across the ground. She hopes they're alabaster. 'You could have helped me.'

'I did.' The creature scratches its flea-bitten coat. 'I gave you a set of imitation pearls and a dagger. You rose to the challenge.'

'Thank goodness I did. She could have pinioned me. She could have amputated—'

'No, *pulcino*. There's too much at stake. I'd never let that happen.'

The specimen seems to be telling the truth. Perhaps she should let the matter drop. She hops a step closer to the great birdcage, gazes at the remains of her mother. 'She is dead, isn't she?'

'No, she's just… *Come si dice comatosa?*'

'Comatose? Unconscious.'

'She'll come round in a moment, but… '

'But?'

'She hasn't got long until she reaches the end of her allotted span. *Certo, la poverina*… She's no idea – no idea at all – but there's a reason she's barren. You see, there's something unpleasant in her ovaries, something malignant. I suspect her humours might be out of balance. If she can be persuaded to consent to leeches and bloodletting, I should be able to ease her suffering. For a time. *Comunque*… She's arrived at her last resting place.'

'You mean… You're not going to let her out of this birdcage?'

'I thought I might keep her as a pet.'

'Please do. You have her daughter's consent for the treatment. Spare no expense as far as the leeches are concerned.'

'Understood.'

Outside, the short song-phrase of a lar gibbon: the all-clear. The gibbon song should be a source of relief, but the aye-aye seems to be preoccupied about something. It springs up on all fours. '*Dobbiamo andare.* Come on, there's not much time. Let's get out of here before she regains consciousness. You don't want to be in earshot when she pronounces her curses.'

But Bel-imperia doesn't move a muscle. She is staring up at the Nile-blue envelope containing her admissions papers. It is still impaled on an old roasting spit.

'Is there a door to this cage?'

'*No, non c'è niente.* Come on.'

'There must be a gap that I can squeeze through.'

'You weren't supposed to get out, remember?'

'But Michaelmas Term starts—'

'In about an hour. Come on, it's almost morning. There's no time to lose.'

'Where are we going?'

'One last choice.'

The prosimian scampers back to its throne, scoops something up from the ground. Bel-imperia can sense that the creature is right, that it's time to go, but she's reluctant to leave her admissions papers behind.

Bessie groans.

'Never mind that bloodstained envelope. You don't need it.'

'I don't?'

'Up here. Come on.' The aye-aye is clambering up the crumpled sheet of mineral deposits.

'Laws-a-massy-me… '

'Don't just stand there. *Sbrigati.*' It leaps onto a boulder, scampers along a bedding plane in the limestone. 'There's terrible power in a mother's curse. Nothing can protect against it.'

'Well, I'll be buggered… '

'Quick! Before she gets more explicit.'

But Bel-imperia has lost sight of the creature. Has it been absorbed into the darkness of the cave? She glances around the great basilica of magnesian limestone. The gothic arches and the soaring stalagmites. The shaft of moonlight streaming in through the rent in the ceiling.

'Up here.' There it is, scrambling up a clump of stalactites.

'You little bastard… '

Ignoring her mother's foul language, she scuttles across to the north transept and beats the air into submission. She soars up to the splendid ceiling of stalactites.

'You little trollops...'

She pivots in a tight circle. From an aerial perspective, the subterranean cathedral looks different. She can see the splash cups on top of the stalagmites, the meandering curve of a dried-up riverbed.

'Over here.' The lemur is clinging to a cleft in the limestone: an opening. Is it clutching the real string of pearls in its other hand?

Bel-imperia hovers in the ceiling.

'One more choice, *pulcino*. Perhaps the hardest choice of all.' The creature steps into the moonlight and slips outside. 'Come on, it's a beautiful night. Let's get some air.'

35

Now, where was I? Let me see if I can recollect...

I seem to recall... No, I'm afraid it escapes me. Perhaps some questions, then. The specimen slumped on the paving stones. The Atlas bear.

Something about FitzClarence. Did I tell him... Did I tell him I'd decided to cast the pearls into the lake?

Goodness me, no. He's not one of us, dear. He can't be trusted. Why, he wouldn't hesitate to waterboard a cottontail rabbit if he thought the creature could lead him to that string of pearls. Indeed, I remember he looked most upset when I informed him I had no intention of selling them.

Of course, he tried to hide his disappointment. He licked that special gland of his and spread some oil onto his coat. Oh, and then he turned to me and said, 'In that case, I'm afraid an alternative solution to the problem of your funeral arrangements needs to be found.' He mentioned some enterprising jackal that has set up a small business behind the Nocturnal House. He handed me the creature's card. 'No Bird Too Tough,' it said. 'Satisfaction Guaranteed.' 'I understand his prices are quite reasonable,' he added.

Something inside me snapped. I snatched the card out of his forepaw and pecked it to shreds. 'Let me make it quite clear: I'm not going to be disposed of in some cut-price funeral parlour. I am not.'

He told me to calm down. He called me 'dear'.

'Oh, I am quite calm,' I said.

But he insisted that I seemed a little shaken. He said I looked like I'd seen a ghost.

'Ghost?' I replied. Of course, I didn't let the polecat out of the bag; I didn't tell him that he'd given me an idea. 'I am not afraid of ghosts, Dale,' I said.

'Neither am I.'

'No? Then perhaps I might share an intimate secret.' I settled down beside him on the chaise longue; I told him to dim the lights.

I must admit I suspect he might have misunderstood one's

intentions. Indeed, I seem to recall he muttered something about his she-otter being upstairs.

'I should hope she is,' I said. 'This is going to be our special secret, Dale. One P Ex and another. No peeping Tomcats.'

In retrospect, I fear that might not have cleared up the misunderstanding.

'Our special secret?' he said, sinking into the arm of the chaise. 'You mean, I can't tell Bojo de Pfeffel?'

'No, of course not. Why would you want to tell him?'

'Oh, it's rather embarrassing,' he confided. He didn't have the self-confidence to look me in the eye; he averted his gaze and stared at the folds of fat on his underparts.

'There's no need to be embarrassed, Dale,' I said. 'I'm an experienced bird – I've done it in this room before.'

'You have?'

'Yes, of course. Now, what's all this about Bojo? You can tell me.'

He glanced up and flashed me a forced smile. 'Well, when we were in the Pilkington Club at the Cloisters… '

'Yes?'

'When we went out on the razzle and had too much liquor… Well, Bojo and I used to wonder. We used to wonder what it would be like.'

'Oh, it's thrilling,' I said. 'It'll make the guard hairs on that smooth coat of yours stand on end.'

'I'm not so sure. You were in your prime back then.'

'I'm still very good at it,' I reassured him. 'You see, I keep in practice. I use a mirror.'

He darted a glance at the looking glass that hangs above the mantelpiece. 'I've never done it in front of a mirror before,' he confided.

'Oh, a reflective surface is essential,' I said.

I could tell from the smell of his secretions that the idea appealed. 'I expect it's quite a turn-on,' he purred.

'Make no mistake, Dale: it'll be an experience you'll never forget.'

He let out a little squeal.

I told him not to get overexcited. 'Of course,' I added, 'once I get going I expect you'll want to scream and shout, but you need to suppress the urge, or else you'll ruin the atmosphere.'

I remember he looked a little disappointed. 'But sometimes Snowy and I—'

I interrupted him: 'Never mind Snowy,' I said. 'I'm sure I'm much better at it than her. Just do as you're told. I expect total obedience, is that clear?'

'Ooh, I thought it would be like this,' he simpered.

I told him to dim the standard lamp and light a candle.

'Come on, then,' I said, as soon as he'd managed to get a candelabra on the pianoforte going. 'Let's make a start.'

But I seem to recall he looked a little disconcerted. He glanced down at his underparts again. 'I'm not sure I can rise to the occasion,' he confessed. 'One moment.'

He summoned an emperor penguin and instructed the creature to go and fetch some little blue pill.

While we waited for the bird to return, I persuaded him to clamber up onto the back of an armchair and gaze into the mirror. 'Don't pout at the reflection of that otter. Just focus on the flames of the candles and listen: I have a confession to make.'

Once he had settled down, I told him about a rather peculiar experience I'd had the night the boathouse burnt to the ground. 'Dear me,' I said, 'I shall never forget the sight of that magnificent bird trapped in that looking glass.' Of course, one exaggerated a little. One made one's ghost sound rather intimidating. Its tormented screams. Its penetrating stare.

'But there's no such thing as a ghost,' said FitzClarence.

'Isn't there?' I intoned a mantra that Draco taught me. 'Look into the mirror, Dale.'

He almost leapt out of his smooth coat at the sight that greeted him. Goodness me, there's an absence of courage in that otter. Oh, he might like to take irresponsible risks – ingratiating himself to the Order of Omnivores, promising them scent referendums about this, that and the other – but that's not courage. It is not. It's just the overconfidence of privilege. Make no mistake: sooner or later he'll call one referendum too many and get an unpleasant surprise. What will he do then, I wonder? Leave this Ship of Fools without a captain and ask someone else to steer it to its next destination? I shouldn't be surprised. Let me make it quite clear: there's no mettle in his spirit, no iron in his soul. Then again, I don't suppose he expected to look into the mirror and see the disembodied head of an anaconda spitting at him, do you?

36

OLD HES   OUSE ☒   LOGICAL GARDE

The Escarpment

YE

la Madagascariensis

CAUTION: THIS ANIMAL   S

Outside: a cluster of boulders, a bare juniper tree.

Some sort of outcrop?

Bel-imperia peers into the mist. Is that the moon? It is a pale imitation of the bomber's moon that looked down on her as she swooped out of the burning boathouse: a dim spotlight behind a gauze of scudding clouds. She stops beside a boulder, attends to a damaged feather in need of attention.

'*Vieni.* Over here.'

The creature has scampered onto a precarious-looking ledge. Careful not to stumble on its scarred surface, Bel-imperia hazards a couple of tentative steps, but she can sense that she is courting danger. Has the specimen led her to the edge of some terrible precipice? Is it a sheer drop? She squints into the mist clinging to the escarpment, but she can see nothing apart from the pale orb of the moon. Is she perched in the clouds?

'I'll go no further.'

'*Non avere paura.* There's nothing to fear.'

'I'm going back inside; I'm going to get—'

'Not some Nile-blue envelope steeped in pigeon blood?'

'Yes.'

'There's no need. La Scroop does all her paperwork in duplicate.'

'Edna Scroop? She'll never give me her duplicates. She despises me.'

'No, she doesn't. She admires academic achievement. She just despises the scoundrel that abandoned her, that's all.'

'But she——'

The lemur bounds back along the ledge: graceless, inelegant. Isn't it at all concerned that it might fall?

'Your mother pretended she had a sister in Le Jardin Zoologique. She offered to help La Scroop get her revenge providing she took down the notice, providing she kept the scholarship a secret. Just tell her there's no such sister.'

'I did, but... '

'*Si?*'

'I don't think she believed me.' Bel-imperia tells the prosimian about the guidebook Miss Scroop ordered during the iron bird raid.

'I expect she just needed to see it in print. No doubt she discovered there are no lappet-faced vultures in Le Jardin Zoologique.' The creature cackles. 'She must have been... *Come si dice?* Furious. She'll move heaven and earth to get her revenge on Bessie.'

Bel-imperia remembers standing on the cobblestones outside the Hunting Tower. The she-macaque scampering up to her and slipping a scrap of paper under her talons: 'That be from the bird in the specs. Edna something.' Didn't Lola say that Old Scroopers had had a change of heart?

'La Scroop is moonlighting tonight. She'll be delighted to give you the duplicates. You just need to get to the Cloisters before she clocks out, that's all.'

'And when is that?'

'Moonset, of course.' The prosimian darts a glance at the pallid moon. 'First sunrise, then moonset. Three-quarters of an hour, perhaps. No more.'

'But it's the other side of the zoological gardens. I'll never make it in time.' She can feel it rising up in her: the anger, the aggression. 'You should have told me this earlier. Why wasn't I in full possession of the facts?'

'*Stai calma.* It'll be all right. You'll get there before she clocks out.' The specimen turns its back on her, hoists its tail up into the air. 'As long as you make the right choice.'

'What choice?'

The creature disappears into the night.

'I said, what choice?'

Silence. Bel-imperia contemplates the ledge, consents to another tentative step. Is that a light in the distance? Is the mist starting to thin?

'*Occhio!* Be careful not to stumble.'

The lemur is crouched on a platform of scoured limestone: another clump of boulders, another juniper tree. Cautious of losing her talonhold, Bel-imperia creeps up to the edge of the outcrop, peers down through the parting mist. She must be at least three thousand trotters above the treetops, three thousand and more above the glassy surface of the lake. She has never looked down on the landscaped gardens from such a great height. No doubt the experience should be awe-inspiring, but she is disturbed by a curious sensation of light-headedness as she stares at – a crocodile, is it? Three miniature crocodiles gliding across the lake. She spots the smouldering boathouse: a burnt-out shell, a ruin.

'Is that Father?' He is just a smudge on the boat slip, a blemish on the slatted boards. 'It is, isn't it?'

'Did he touch the pearls?'

The question seems irrelevant, a distraction. 'No.'

'He must have touched them.'

Bel-imperia remembers instructing him to retrieve the pearls from the old lacquered tea chest. She remembers him dropping them at her feet like a dead mouse. Something about the gesture had reminded her of the disreputable specimen that had seduced Miss Scroop. 'He put them on me. He did them up.'

'Did he catch a bristle feather in the clasp?'

He said 'ouch' – she remembers that. It hadn't occurred to her that the incident might be significant. She had dismissed it as one of those things.

'Yes.'

'I thought as much. You brought that feather here, *pulcino*. You carried it in the clasp. And I touched it as I slipped into a trance. I had to stop and pluck it out, remember?'

She can recall gazing at the offending feather as it drifted to the ground. She had been concerned that she had started to sprout masculine bristles.

'*Quando l'ho toccata*... When I touched it, I glimpsed his fate.'

'You did?' She turns to the creature. 'What did you see?'

'Despair.'

Bel-imperia subjects the thing to a suspicious stare. Is it telling the truth?

'He'll roost in the ruins of the boathouse. He'll pass the last scraps of his allotted span staring out across the lake – a broken bird: abandoned, forgotten.'

'Let me make it quite clear: I shall never forget—'

'He'll pull out his feathers, like a... *Come si dice?* Like a demented parrot. He'll pull them out in order to atone for his sins. He'll just have one semiplume left come the end.'

'The end?'

'He'll sense it approaching. He'll hold on until sunrise. He'll pluck out his last plume, and climb up onto the ruins of that marble-topped contraption. He'll arrange himself into the appropriate position for a member of his species. He'll die alone.'

'Never. Not if I can help it.'

'You can't have it all, *pulcino*. You need to choose.'

This is her choice, then.

'You can go back through the cave, back through the woods. You can rinse the soot out of his feathers. You can take him to the amphitheatre to plead for Bessie's soul. You can help him patch up his broken heart.'

'Oh, I'm sure he'll soon get over—'

'You can catch mice for his supper. You can teach numbats and sloths their ABCs at Hedge School. You can set aside your groats until you've got enough to rebuild the boathouse. You can give him the strength he needs to start again. Father and daughter. *Si, certo*... It'll be a simple life, but a good one.'

'I'd end up like Miss Scroop.'

'Perhaps. But you'd have his respect and admiration. You'd have his love.'

She does not even pause to consider the option. 'You said I had a choice?'

'You do.' The old hag takes a deep breath. *'Non guardare in basso. Don't look down, look up.'*

Bel-imperia straightens her long S-shaped neck, peers out through the thinning mist, out across the lake, out across the amphitheatre, out across the landscaped gardens. She has never seen such a splendid panorama: Old Hesper House and Zoological Gardens Ltd spread out before her like a map. She can see the llama house. She can see the antelope paddocks. She can see—

'Goodness me, is that the Cages of Caer Lud?'

She is sure she can glimpse them in the distance, glittering under the barrage balloons: the bright lights of Caer Lud.

'Sì, sì.'

She gazes in astonishment at the great conurbation of cages and enclosures: a square-mile of cast-iron bars and crumbling ragstone, soaring columns and ornamental parapets. She shakes the dust out of her flight feathers; she rouses. It is so thrilling. Caer Lud: the ancient remains of Lord Hesper's old menagerie, the largest metropolis of cages outside of the United Species, the pounding heart of the zoological gardens. She stares through the last curls of mist, tries to make out the majestic promenades and the secluded rose gardens, the grand animal houses and the historic monuments.

'Is that the Reptile House I can see?'

'Credo di sì.'

'I suppose that must be Carnivorous Central Office, then – I shall have to go there. Oh, look, there's the Hall of Ex... '

She darts an urgent glance at the prosimian.

'The Hall of Exhibits is burning.'

'Not just the Hall of Exhibits. Look over there. *Mamma mia, che incendio!* And there.'

Bel-imperia gazes in horror at the diabolical pin-points of light. The creature is right: Caer Lud is burning. No doubt the squadrons of iron birds must have set it ablaze. Their incendiaries must be responsible for these bright lights. Their bombs must have turned the blackout into this glittering constellation of stars. She shudders as she takes in the scene. In the east, she can make out a blaze big enough to consume an entire terrace of cramped little cages, perhaps even annihilate a breeding population of rodents or something. And there's the most terrible conflagration raging around the Ape House. She gapes as the building's stained-glass cupola emerges out of a great pall of smoke: magnificent, defiant. She turns to the specimen standing beside her and says, 'Does it all have to burn?'

'Oh, Caer Lud has burnt before – 1666, *credo*. And it'll burn again. It's combustible; it's in its nature. But each time it burns it rises from the flames. It... *Come si dice riformarsi?* It regenerates.'

She glances over her scapulars at the ledge she crept along, the entrance to the ceiling of stalactites. 'I must go to Caer Lud; I must help rebuild it.'

'First there.' The creature is pointing in the direction of the Cloisters. Is that a bell tower she can see silhouetted against the brightening darkness? Is that a quadrangle of cages?

'The Cloisters, the Refreshment Rooms, Caer Lud. In that order, *capisci?*'

'I don't know what the Refreshment Rooms are doing on that list.'

'You'll need to earn a couple of groats to make ends meet, *pulcino*. You'll need to practise a little alchemy on some cake fillings and ice creams.'

'I hope not.'

'Come on, there's not much time. La Scroop clocks off at moonset, remember?'

'But it'll take me all morning to scuttle across the zoological gardens. It's too far.'

'Not as the lappet-faced vulture flies.'

'Not as – what?'

'You've been given a pair of wings. The time has come to use them.'

Is the old crone serious? Bel-imperia peers over the edge of the escarpment: the jagged rocks and the distant treetops, the solid ground and the lake. The slightest miscalculation in mid-air means certain death.

'Member of the Hall of Exhibits, Commander-in-Chief of the

Order of Carnivores, P Ex. All this power the Fates will give you –
and the glory of it. You just need to make a leap of faith.'

'But Father says I mustn't attempt my maiden flight until I've
completed my first post-juvenile moult.'

'*Ma che cazzate*. Your cousins in the Serengeti take to the air as soon
as they've fledged. Besides, you're not a juvenile any more, are you?
Not after tonight.'

She remembers gazing at her horrified mother as the birdcage came
crashing to the ground. 'No, I don't suppose I am.'

She turns her attention to the horizon. The darkness is beginning
to dissolve. It must be almost morning. Her mind reaches back to
another morning – no, not morning: evening, sunset. She had been
standing on the boat slip, staring up at the tempting gaps of blue
between some golden clouds. She had heard them calling to her,
urging her to come up and join them high above the zoological
gardens. Where is that instinct now? Where is the desire to unwrap
her wings and take to the air? It's not as if she is going to get
dashed against the ground. Commander-in-Chief of the Order of
Carnivores? P Ex? Her fate has been decided. She should be conscious
of an inner strength; she should have self-confidence. But she is
reticent. Is something missing? Has something been left undone?

'Don't forget these.'

The creature is clutching the pearls in its emaciated hand – precious
stones, not worthless balls of alabaster.

'Of course.'

She scutters across the outcrop. Too late. The lemur has snatched
them out of reach. It is hanging them on the branch of the juniper
tree.

'One last thing. *Solo un attimo*. I've laboured like a beast of burden
to orchestrate this evening: manipulating Bessie, supervising the
construction of that birdcage, singing the Fates. It's been exhausting.'

'Well, you can put your feet up now, can't you? And congratulate
yourself on a job well done. I'm sure the animals in these gardens will
appreciate your efforts in the years to come.'

'I was hoping for something more practical than the appreciation of
the masses.'

Bel-imperia had been expecting this. 'I didn't notice a price list hanging up at the mouth of the cave as I came in.'

'I don't have a price list.'

'Well, you should. How much do I owe you, then?' If she had a handbag, she'd be opening it and raking through her coppers; she'd be searching for the right money to make sure she didn't get short-changed.

'*Per piacere.* I don't need groats. Just a small kindness. Call it an act of compassion.'

'Compassion? Oh, I see. So I have to make some personal sacrifice, do I?'

'You have to make a promise.'

'You mean a deal.'

'Deal?' The creature spits on a clump of moss. 'The last time I cut a deal I got double-crossed. The gods spared me death, but not old age, not decrepitude.'

'Yes, I can see that.'

'Oh, *pulcino*, I'm starting to... *Come si dice?* I'm starting to shrivel up; I'm withering away. Come the Millennium, I'll be small enough to fit into an ampoule. You can't let that happen to me. Please.'

'Well, I'm afraid there's nothing I can do about that.' If she did have that handbag, this is when she would be closing it with a snap.

'Yes, there is. There are dinosaurs in the Hall of Relics – not just dinosaurs. There's a pug-nosed crocodile, an Atlas bear, a dodo. No giant aye-aye that enters those doors could ever be consigned to extinction. You must make me a Relic.'

'But only the P Ex can elevate a specimen to the Hall of...'

'*Appunto.*'

'I see.'

'I'm sure I could make a useful contribution to the Hall. I could add a little foresight to their deliberations.'

The old hag has a point. Besides, perhaps it might be expedient to have a prophet at her beck and call. 'Consider it done.'

'Is that a promise?'

'It is.' But she can tell from the creature's penetrating stare that a solemn oath is required. 'I swear on the Seven—'

'No, not on the Commandments.' It snatches the pearls out of the juniper tree. 'Swear on these.'

Bel-imperia pronounces the oath.

'*Grazie, pulcino.* Let's have a proper coronation, then.'

'Not quite so tight this time, is that clear?'

She turns around. The lemur intones some mumbo-jumbo in Latin. *Glória in excélsis.* Did it just call her Imperatrix again?

'That name you call me – what does it mean?'

'*Pulcino?* It just means chick.'

'No. The other one.'

'Gloriana Imperatrix. It's the name given to the creature that the Fates have chosen to bear the pearls.'

'One rather likes it.'

She can feel her strength returning as the specimen loops the precious stones around her breast.

'Three times. You don't want to lose them. There!' That Witch She Will Never Speak About steps back to admire its creation. '*Quindì?* The moment has come to make a choice.'

'Yes.'

She scuttles up to the edge of the outcrop and unwraps her wings. The warm air rising up the face of the escarpment caresses her flight feathers. It smells inviting, almost intoxicating. Is that the tug of instinct she can sense pulling her?

'So what's it going to be, then? Back along the ledge? Back through the cave? Back to the boathouse and—'

It requires courage, of course: the leap of faith. It requires determination. Yet even so, it is the easiest choice that little Bel-imperia Pinch has ever made. No point, then, in glancing over her scapulars. She is not for turning.

37

Oh, dear. One can sense a certain restlessness in the audience this evening. Impatience, perhaps. The beast skulking the shadows. The jaguarundi. Your question, please.

What did FitzClarence do when Draco's ghost appeared?

Oh, he hid behind the chaise longue, of course. He begged me to send the spectre back to Hades, but I pretended I couldn't hear him. 'And so, Prize Exhibit,' I said. 'Can I assume you would agree that there is such a thing as a ghost?'

I remember he just nodded.

'Then in that case,' I said, 'I suspect I might have some rather upsetting news, because make no mistake: I intend to come back as one.'

'Oh, no, Bel,' he pleaded. 'Please don't.'

I explained that I had no choice in the matter. 'Goodness me, Dale, I'm sure neither of us wants to see all the great things I've achieved come undone. I am therefore committed to haunting that little fledgling. And unless I'm afforded the honour of a decent funeral I shall have no hesitation in haunting a certain smooth-coated otter too. Is that understood?'

He promised me it all, of course: the solemn cortège; the delphiniums and the orchids and the carnations; the choirs of ornate chorus frogs. He promised to spend like a Herbivore. Oh, I've never seen an otter look so contrite. Or tremble so much. In fact, I'm afraid he lost control of his bladder, poor thing. Not that I regret conjuring up Draco's ghost, of course. I regret nothing. Besides, he had it coming. He should never have brought up such an inappropriate subject. Or touted the services of that jackal that has gone into business – where was it? Behind the Nocturnal House. Just imagine the professional standards in such an establishment. No cedar-scented embalming oil, no obsequies... What on earth would Father have said?

What was that? I didn't catch the question. The specimen sitting next to the – what is that creature? Some semi-aquatic mammal? Some seal, perhaps. I cannot see. The light has started to fail.

For goodness' sake, speak up, dear. What? What was Father's funeral like?

Oh, I am not sure I can recollect. Next question, please.

The primate loitering in the gloom. The ape?

Something about an exercise in image management. I needed a humble background and so I – what? Oh, I do wish someone would turn on the gas lamps in this cul-de-sac. And so I rebranded myself as an undertaker's daughter? And so I dusted off my dead father and put him on a pedestal?

I did no such thing. Let me make it quite clear: I shall never forget—

Yes?

Did I go back and see him after I leapt off the escarpment?

Of course I did. From time to time. But I'm afraid one had one's studies at the Cloisters to consider. Not to mention one's obligations to the League of Young Carnivores... Other demands on one's time. I remember I heard through the grapevine that he lost his licence to trade in Embalming, Obsequies and other Rites of Passage. From all accounts, the Elders turned against him. Just like those dogs on the Board of Beasts turned against me.

Poor Father.

I'm told he never got over it. Indeed, I understand he nursed a grievance until the night he died. Perhaps I should have sent him a pigeon and told him to snap out of it. There's no point in being bitter about something like that, is there? One ought to have the grace to forgive and forget. One ought to be able to get over the experience of being sacked and move on. Then again, I suppose he'd dedicated his life to serving the customers that passed through that boathouse. He didn't deserve to lose his licence like that – not a decent, upright specimen like Father. Oh, it's so upsetting. Make no mistake: it breaks my heart to picture him returning his expensive chain of office. It breaks my heart to...

Forgive me. I need a moment. Tears of compassion, see.

What was that? What was that? I'm sure I heard some specimen pass comment. Was it a marbled cat? Was it a short-tailed stoat? One cannot see.

Never mind. Now, where was I? Oh, dear, I'm afraid I seem to have lost the thread of the argument... That's right. Father.

I do miss him so.

In fact, sometimes at night... Sometimes as I sit here staring out through these bars... I am sure I can see him.

It rained last night, remember? Goodness me, such a terrible storm. The puddles on the paving stones are like mirrors: one cannot fail to notice the flames of the gas lamps reflected in them...

Oh, I dare say it must have been the figment of an old bird's imagination – just a gas lamp reflected in the stillness of a puddle, nothing more – but last night, after the rain had subsided, I could have sworn I caught a glimpse of Father's ghost. He looked just like a Michaelmas goose behind the counter in the cold store. Dear me, not a single feather. For a moment, I thought I heard him calling to me. 'Come on, chick,' he said. 'There's work to be done.'

Chick. No one else called me that.

I must admit the thought occurred to me that perhaps he'd come to collect me. I should not be surprised. One sometimes hears tales about a specimen being escorted to the other side. Besides, one can sense that the end is approaching. Just like a storm gathering on the horizon. One can feel it in one's bones.

Oh, perhaps I might be able to soldier on a little longer. No doubt there's still the odd scrap of iron coursing through this old heart. I do hope there is. You see, I should so like to set the record straight before I... before the final judgement.

Let's make a start, then, shall we? No time like the present. Next question, please.

I said, next question, please.

Come on, I am sure there must be someone out there sitting in the dark.

38

Old Hesper House and Zoological Gardens

ADMIT ONE

─── A D U L T ───

Bel-imperia slips the chains that bind her to solid ground and leaps in the air. For a moment, perhaps, she is conscious that she has passed a point of no return, but before the thought has a chance to take shape in her mind, an overpowering surge of adrenaline redirects her attention. This is no time to consider the implications of the leap of faith she has just made; it feels as if her heart has been ripped out and she is hurtling through the air in an attempt to catch it. Her concentration is intense. She inhabits this moment and no other.

Is that the tug of the ground she can sense pulling her down? Is she losing altitude? She reacts at once, beats the air beneath her wings – deep downward strokes that produce an impressive rushing sound. She increases her thrust. Perhaps one more thrash. She pauses for a fraction of a second. Incredible. She had not imagined that something as insubstantial as thin air could be so supportive. It inspires her confidence. She beats again and again: strong, purposeful strokes. She reaches and climbs. She rises.

High above the lake, she can detect a subtle difference in air temperature, a thermal current. Dare she accept the challenge? Dare she test her courage to its limits? Cautious, uncertain, she spreads her wings as wide as she can and holds them still. Can the column of rising air support her? Up, up she rises, borne in an elegant spiral. She has mastered it; she has defeated the terrible pull of the ground.

She might have been schooled in the dangers of lift-induced drag, but there's no need to recall her lessons. She relies on gut instinct to adjust her primaries, intuition to exploit the high aspect ratio of each feather. She curves to the right, circles the smouldering remains of the boathouse. The air tastes singed – a slight trace of scorched timber. Is that Father on the boat slip? Is that Silas Pinch? He is just a brown stain, a blot on the lake-shore: insignificant, irrelevant. Strange that she once thought she needed his respect and admiration, his love. She remembers standing on the marble, sobbing her heart out because she'd failed to please him. She lets the recollection go. She leaves it behind.

Pivoting, she describes a circle six thousand trotters or more above the amphitheatre. She tries to make sense of the minuscule specks in the semicircular arena: the bighorn sheep and the mountain goats, the palm civets and the collared lemmings. Is that cluster of lights bobbing up and down an armada of teacups? No doubt it must be. For on the eastern rim of the hemisphere, the sun is inching over the horizon. She lifts up her heart to Sol, the Everlasting Light.

He reaches out to her and touches her lappets, her mantle, her tail… He reminds her that there is no time to lose.

She adjusts the angle of her rectrices and beats the air. She sets her inner compass for the Cloisters.

Soaring over the antelope paddocks, she indulges an urge to inspect the herds of impala and gazelle. She searches for a specimen that is lagging behind: a mother that has just given birth, or a battle-scarred male that is limping. Does that springbok look like it could be persuaded to make itself available for breakfast? Perhaps. But she doesn't change her bearing; she doesn't alter course.

She admires the grandeur of the zoological gardens spread out for her inspection like a series of architectural blueprints: the gentle curve of the herbaceous borders, the straight lines of some provincial parade of cages. Of course, she is conscious that the ground beneath her is hard and unforgiving, but she isn't daunted at the prospect of an unforeseen fall. Failure? The possibilities do not exist. For it has been pronounced, it has been decreed. Hail Bel-imperia Pinch, Commander-in-Chief of the Order of Carnivores and Prize Exhibit. Hail Gloriana Imperatrix. She sets her sights on the quadrangle of cloistered cages in the distance: the bell tower and the colonnades, the reading room and the books. There is work to be done. Let it begin.

About the Author

Robert studied English and Drama at the University of London – an experience that led to a brief career in casting, and assistant credits on several films, including *Wonderland* (1999) and *24 Hour Party People* (2002). Come the mid-2000s, though, he realised he could no longer ignore an idea he'd been nurturing for a novel about Margaret Thatcher, and so he retreated to a small town in the foothills of the Italian Alps, took up a teaching position at a local secondary school, and put pen to paper. He still lives in Italy, where he has an Italian civil partner and a pigeon-infested restoration project. *The Iron Bird* is his first novel.

Thank You

I could never have completed this novel alone. Indeed, the not-so-simple act of composing sentence after sentence and shaping the result into something more than the sum of its parts would have been a struggle without the support and encouragement of my partner, Cristian Gelfi, and my dear friend and mentor, Lindsay Clarke. My sincere and heartfelt thanks to both of you.

Neither could I have published this novel alone. And so I'm grateful to Unbound for having the courage to take on this rather unusual tale, and in particular, to my editors, Craig Taylor and Mary Chesshyre, for their unfailing insight and precision, and to my typographer, Andrew Chapman, for going the extra mile.

I'm also indebted to the adventurous readers who supported this project when it was crowdfunding on unbound.com. It's no exaggeration to say I couldn't have done it without you. You're the best.

I'm grateful to Titch Rivett for her advice on Bessie's Lincolnshire dialect, and for introducing me to some fabulous idiomatic expressions, including the sublime: 'He couldn't stop a pig in a passage' (a term to describe a bow-legged man). Unfortunately, as there are no bow-legged men in *The Iron Bird*, I couldn't find a place for it, so it's good to be able to slip it in here.

It's also good to be able to thank all – and I do mean all – members, past and present, of Lindsay Clarke's rather special London writing group. In particular, Kathy Berriman, David Brewerton, Sue Goss, Karen Raney, Robert Stone and Philip Walford. This wouldn't have been the same book without you.

I'd also like to thank arvon.org, lamuseretreat.com, and all the writers who've offered me their generous help and advice over the years, including Melanie Cantor, Maggie Gee, Samantha Harvey and Helen Simpson.

Thank you also to Peter Roberts for *Campo delle Querce*.

Very special thanks to Jane Meenehan for her patience and her pixels, Ezio Ratti for his sound and vision, Emma Roberts for her al fresco breakfasts of figs and ricotta, Clive Russell for breathing life into these characters, and Kate Williams for smuggling a shirt onto the plane.

Finally, I'm also grateful to Martha Clifford, Caroline Pearce, Tricia Rupply, Katharine Sherwood, Sarah Shippobotham and Martin Smith.

Afterword

For more information about *The Iron Bird* and its author, please call in at robertwoodshaw.com.

Patrons

Adie Allen
Michelle Ayling
Ioana Bendixson
Stefano Benti
Monica Bianchi
Gabriella Burini-Sherwood
Maurizio Campana
Tim Cashmore
Nicola Chioda – Chiara Franchi
Mark Cobbin
Mark Cooper
Tamsin Cottis
Traci Dailey
Andy Dorgan
Jessica Duchen
Heather & Tim Farmery
Chris Golightly
Anne Goodridge
Charles Harris
Carol Hellyer
Emmet Holden
Ross Howard
Oli Jacobs
Ėlena Janavičius
Simon Jay
Jamie Johnson
Judith Jupe
Ross Kessell
James Kingston
Elizabeth Li
Miriam Lindley
Paolo Maccarini

Rob MacGrory
Jane MacKenzie
Elizabeth Malaiperuman
Amy Sophia Marashinsky
Jennifer McDowall
Catherine McIntyre
Madeleine McNeill
Sharon Mctiernan
Simon Miller
Anders Morley
Carlo Navato
Eithne Nightingale
Jeremy Orlando
Esther Paddon
Clare Pugh
Robert Rawle
Kathleen Rawlings
Tess Redgrave
Louise Reid
Marco Riglietta
Ruth Rolle
Neil Ryder
Allan Samuelson
Tamara Scepanovic
Bethany Smith
Daniel Stewart
Elizabeth Symonds
Carolyn Thompson
Richard Todd
Suzie Viazi
Philip Walford
Vivienne Westacott
Kate Williams
Phil Willmott
Jan Woolf